HE WAS ALONE WITH SAM, with his computations, his procedures arranged meticulously in his head in schemata so precise that, he was convinced, there was only one destination he could reach.

He worked slowly, painfully, the muscles in his neck and shoulders singing with fatigue.

The light came up on the Apple. Power poured into the small computer.

Piggy's whole body hummed with weariness, and he flexed his arms, shook his legs, wiggled his toes just as a terrible crash of thunder settled right over the science building, rattling the window frames. He heard it rampaging inside his own head, felt the crash and steeled himself, holding onto Sam's cold and unresisting arm.

One last time he thought, *What if it doesn't work.* . . .

FRIEND
The astonishing new novel by
DIANA HENSTELL
author of *The Other Side*

Bantam Books by Diana Henstell

FRIEND
THE OTHER SIDE

FRIEND

Diana Henstell

BANTAM BOOKS
TORONTO • NEW YORK • LONDON • SYDNEY • AUCKLAND

FRIEND

A Bantam Book / November 1985

ISBN 0-553-25315-8

Published simultaneously in the United States and Canada

Bantam Books are published by Bantam Books, Inc. Its trademark,
consisting of the words "Bantam Books" and the portrayal of a
rooster, is Registered in U.S. Patent and Trademark Office and in
other countries. Marca Registrada. Bantam Books, Inc., 666 Fifth
Avenue, New York, New York 10103.

PRINTED IN THE UNITED STATES OF AMERICA

0 0 9 8 7 6 5 4 3 2 1

Dedicated with all the love in my
heart to
Abigail Sarah Levine,
whose mother I am privileged to be.

Special thanks to Danny Goldsmith, whose technical advice was invaluable. And to Frank and Grace Wilcznski, who were both informative and kind. Also, my gratitude and appreciation to Linda Grey, whose editorial skills and insights help make me a better writer, and to Jane Rotrosen Berkey, who is not only a wonderful agent but a good, a forever friend.

1

The thick gray clouds that had followed them almost all the way down from Boston finally exploded just as they passed the Binghamton city limits, and they crossed over into Pennsylvania in a torrent of rain. The windshield flooded, the wipers inadequate, and Jeannie Conway had to bend forward over the wheel as she attempted to see through the streaming glass.

Slowing down to twenty miles an hour, she said to her son, "Paul, can you wipe the mist off? I think I put some tissues in the glove compartment."

"Huh?"

"I asked you to clean the windshield so I can see better," she said impatiently, leaning over and opening the glove compartment. "Tissues. Inside." Why, she wondered for the thousandth time, did the simplest things have to be repeated and programmed out for him?

"Oh, okay, Mom," he said, finally tearing himself away from the book he was trying to read in the waning light.

Jeannie knew without even glancing at the book, which she heard him close reluctantly, that it would be full of diagrams, complicated mathematical problems and directions that wouldn't make sense—at least not to her. All that he read might have been written in an arcane language that she would have found impossible to decipher even given a Rosetta Stone.

This aspect of her thirteen-year-old son, this scientific and mathematical brilliance that took him into realms that normal, intelligent people were unable to enter, was so out of the ordinary, so beyond anything she could comprehend that she used to imagine he was a fairy child sneaked somehow into the hospital isolette and delivered to her by mistake. That was what she used to imagine. Now, after everything, she just worried, a constant tugging at her insides that never seemed to let up even when she slept, and which caused her to wake suddenly from dreams that were clouded in fog and more than vaguely frightening.

She glanced at him quickly out of the corner of her eye and thought as she often did that he looked nothing like either her or his father, Tony, with his fair, pink complexion, round saucer-shaped face, stubby little nose and blond, almost white lank hair that lay like fine thread across his scalp no matter how she had it cut.

The rest of him followed from that chubby and innocent face. He was pudgy, a good twenty pounds overweight for his five feet, two inches, and had a soft, cushy belly and too much of a behind. It was the sum of these characteristics which had given rise to a nickname so appropriate that even though Jeannie deplored it, she couldn't at times resist it no matter how hard she tried. *Piggy*.

He cleared the mist away energetically. Then, tilting his head, he gazed up at her. His big pale blue eyes were underscored by faint purplish half-moons which—she was thankful to see—weren't as pronounced as they had been in the weeks past. When he pushed his wire-rims back into place (they constantly slid down his nose), his irises looked as large as dinner plates.

"Okay, Mom?"

"Yes, thank you," she said as he sat back, this time staring out the window at the countryside speeding by.

"It looks a little better now," he said wistfully, and she knew by "better" he meant more like the countryside surrounding Boston, more like what he had lived with all his life.

The rain began to thin and finally settled to a slow drizzle and Jeannie too was able to pay more attention to what lay on either side of Route Eighty.

He was right, it did look better. The land rolled softly away to sloping fields that ended in picturesque farms off in the distance and clumps of trees whose leaves were turning now, going red and yellow and orange.

"But it's not Boston," he said all of a sudden.

Unreasonably, she was angry. She *knew* it wasn't Boston, and just like Piggy, it wasn't her first choice of places to be either. But surely, given his intelligence, he should understand that they didn't have that many options now. In fact, this was the only one. Which is what she said.

"I know we're lucky, Mom," he replied, his soft doughy face going tight as a fist. "I know if it wasn't for me and for what happened, we'd still be in Boston." His voice rose and broke on a high note and he looked away, pressing his cheek against the chilly windowpane.

"It's not your fault," she stated as she had so many times before. "Accidents happen." The pulse in her temple throbbed alarmingly as it did whenever she remembered the last six months, whenever she thought of Tony, which was often. She couldn't help thinking of Tony, not only for what he had done to her, for how he had betrayed her, but for how that betrayal had turned their lives upside down. What had happened between her and Tony was—she was instinctively certain—an important factor in what had gone wrong with their son.

Piggy was, she thought, glancing over at him, so sensitive, so delicately balanced. And that balance had been precariously tilted by the winds of disintegration that had blown through her marriage, through their home. Winds that had turned into a raging hurricane when Tony finally walked out for that woman. And then had come the terrible, the tragic, *mistake*. Yes, she thought, as she had so many times since the dean of Height Middle School had called her in shock, barely able to articulate what had gone on in the lab, unable to believe the evidence of his own eyes. It was a nightmare with her son trapped in its center, lost and bewildered. And somehow Jeannie knew it was all Tony's fault. If Tony had behaved responsibly, if he hadn't let their marriage go right down the sewer, if he had controlled himself and not been a fool about *her*, nothing would have gone wrong with Piggy. Julia, a woman who even now was nothing more to her than a hated name, had neither a face nor credentials, which made it all worse, as if Tony had traded her, Jeannie, in, not for a newer model necessarily, but for a shadow, a ghost.

If it wasn't for Tony, Jeannie decided yet again, and what he had done to her, to them, Piggy's nerves wouldn't have been strung out like high-tension wires. And then he wouldn't have done what he did, he wouldn't have made his mistake.

"It's all over now," she said, trying to believe that was true as she reached out to pat his chubby thigh. "We're starting a whole new life."

And she thought that any day now in the mail she'd get a bulky envelope from her lawyer, Martin Chambers—the only person whom she had told where they were going—and inside the envelope would be the divorce decree. Fifteen years of marriage and all she'd have left would be an envelope. And Piggy, of course, she thought with a guilty shudder. There was always Piggy.

Jeannie glanced over at him once again. He was reading the letter which he had taken from the manila folder between them on the seat, the letter from Dr. Mellon telling them how pleased he was to have them at Mason Preparatory School, and enclosing a complete set of directions. She knew without meeting the man what he would be like. Precise and organized, prissy and well-tended like an English garden with all the flower patches neatly aligned, all the hedges clipped.

"Do you really think," Piggy asked for the tenth time since they had contacted Dr. Mellon—one of the last headmasters on the list Jeannie had gotten from Height—and applied for a place for them, for her to teach high-school English and for Piggy in the eighth grade, "that they'll really give me my own lab?"

"That's what Dr. Mellon implied—that Dr. Johanson of the science department would see to it. You'll have everything you need, right down to your own oscilloscope." She didn't really know what an oscilloscope was, but it seemed to weigh heavily on his mind that he'd have to give up the one he was using at the Height School for Gifted Children, where he had once been the star pupil, the youngest Westinghouse winner in history.

"I don't know Dr. Mellon and I don't know Dr. Johanson," Piggy said. For a moment, his face shriveled up. "But promises are meant to be broken. That's what you always say. Right, BeeBee?" he asked, looking over the back seat.

BeeBee didn't answer, though Piggy gazed at him with unblemished love before he turned around and propped his scruffy sneakers up against the dash. "I don't like the house being on three floors. It will make it awful hard for BeeBee, since he can't climb steps."

"You'll carry him," Jeannie said.

"He does weigh twenty-five kilos, Mom! He's not exactly a lightweight."

In spite of her sour thoughts Jeannie had to laugh. "So put him on a diet. I keep telling you BeeBee's getting too fat." She glanced at the back seat in the rearview mirror and called out, smiling, "Hey, Bee, you're too heavy in the aft."

"Not funny, Mom," he said, but she knew he was smiling too.

BeeBee didn't, of course, answer, just gave her his usual impenetrable stare as he sat, carefully buttressed by pillows, a blanket tucked almost up to his head, as if by some quirk of magic he could get cold. Jeannie thought: He's as real to me as he is to Pig. . . . She stopped mid-thought and said to herself: Enough of that. Among all the facets of their lives that were in the process of change, that were going to change in the future, one was that hated nickname. Even though Piggy was philosophical about it, it was going to go. He had said once when his father called him on the subject, "I don't know, I might not like it much, but it does kind of suit me."

A big black Buick came up close on their left, passing too fast in a shower of water. Jeannie shuddered and said quickly to herself like a litany: There is nothing to be frightened of now. It's all over, everything. The worst has happened and we have survived. It was behind them now, the bombed-out ruins of the past—Tony, her marriage, their family, Paul's mistake. But she felt in her bones that it was going to be a long time, if ever, before they both would recuperate.

On the dreary wet stretch of highway going south, she thought once again—as she had so endlessly in the months gone by—about what had become of her life. How it seemed to have fallen apart in her hands. She had tried so hard to be a good wife to Tony, a good mother to Paul, giving them a safe berth on turbulent seas—or at least she had thought she had. But apparently that hadn't been true at all. Little by little the ark she supposed she had constructed had begun to spring leaks. She wasn't even certain when it had all begun. Just insidiously, bit by bit, her marriage had splintered at the seams. Harsh words were spoken, doors slammed, terrible silences strangled the pleasant apartment high up on Beacon

Street. Tony, whom she had loved for so many years, to whom she had tied herself with a certainty that bordered on faith, slid away, until he became a stranger. Then, before she could reverse the tide—though Tony, by then having "discovered" Julia, wouldn't have agreed to that—Piggy . . .

A shiver ran down Jeannie's spine and she saw rising up before her on the screen of the windshield that silly little boy's face. Bertram Lennard. He was pinched and drawn and had always reminded her of a ferret the few times she had seen him at Height. Now, in the rain with his flickering image under the swishing blades of the wipers, he looked like what he was—dead.

Piggy said, just as Jeannie silently screamed, *Go away!*, "When are we going to see Daddy again?"

"What?" She turned so quickly the car swerved on the slick road before she righted it and eased up on the gas. "See your father?" Her voice rose and she repeated, "See you father?"

"I mean, Mom, it's a long way from Boston. He can't come and take me out on Sundays like other dads do. It's too far to drive to Welling just for the day. So when will I see him, Mom, huh?"

"Listen, Paul," she said emphatically, "we are starting all over again, just you and me. Remember how we said it would be better if we moved away, how we both needed a different kind of life? That there was no reason in God's green world to stay in Boston and—" She wanted to say "suffer," but suffering was too close to the surface even to use the word.

She sighed almost audibly as Piggy, not letting her finish, veered off in yet another direction, saying, "Why do you always say God's green world when God had nothing to do with anything because it's a silly idea, God, I mean."

"Paul, please, let's not have one of your religious discussions right now. I know you think you've settled the whole problem of God and whether He exists, but I don't want to talk about it!" Her voice was fluted with anger, with fear, and she took several deep breaths, leaning on the steering wheel, Bertram Lennard's mournful countenance having mercifully disappeared. I will not, she thought, argue with him about anything. So, swallowing, she simply said, "I'm sorry, I didn't mean to yell. But I can't help thinking that Welling won't be at all like Boston and Mason Prep, whatever its pluses, won't be Height. Not too many people will appreciate your feelings about God and religion. This is a small town, Paul, and, let's face it, the only gifted child at Mason will probably be you."

"I know," he said solemnly. "I'll try to be good."

"You're always good, honey." She felt the tears well up in her throat.

"Not always, Mom," he said, averting his face.

And then, because he was still only thirteen years old, no matter what happened in the last year of his life, he bounced up suddenly and cried excitedly, "Look, there's the turnoff!"

"Right you are, captain. Now settle back." She went right onto the access road and wound up a short hill. The road was narrow and pitted with potholes. The Chevy's tires whined as they reached the top and began the slow descent into Welling, just a thumbprint below them.

Welling was, she knew, from the informative letter and brochure Dr. Mellon had sent and from her phone conversations with him, a town of approximately six thousand people, including the faculty and student body of Mason. Set with rolling farmland at its back and the beginnings of the anthracite coal region at its front, it straddled the Susquehanna. Welling Proper—as the headmaster put it—was on one side of the river, and Welling East, where Mason Prep was, on the other. Normally, Dr. Mellon had written, faculty was housed near the campus, but since all the neat row bungalows were occupied for the school year, and their—hers and Paul's—situation was unexpected, they would be living in Welling Proper, in what he termed one of the river houses that the school had rented for them. Which meant, Jeannie assumed, something dark and dank and so damp that nothing would ever be completely dry. But again, beggars couldn't be choosers, and in early October she and Paul were lucky to find any school which would take them in.

She knew quite well that she owed a debt to Height, that Mason had agreed to accept Piggy on the basis of a carefully worded report. The dean, while not hiding anything, hadn't revealed much either. Piggy's genius and his obvious, overwhelming distress had encouraged Height's administration to see that he had another chance. Jeannie was also grateful to Mason not only for giving her a job at the last minute and with a minimum of experience, but in reaching out for Piggy, though she knew this new and slightly inferior—inferior to Height, that was—school couldn't resist someone like her son with his incandescent mind and ability to stack up prizes like a winner on a quiz show.

Her thoughts drifted away from the past as she listened to Piggy happily pointing out the sights to BeeBee.

"Look, Bee, there's a church, big, fat, ugly thing, and there, a school. Hey, is that—? Nope, not Mason, Welling Consolidated. A bank, a supermarket—oh, Mom, that reminds me, I'm hungry. We haven't eaten since—"

"—lunch," she interrupted, turning left onto the main street. "And we won't eat until dinner."

"Where?"

"Where what?"

"Where will we eat dinner? Can we have Chinese? Oh, Mom, please. I'm dying for egg rolls and some spareribs."

"Paul, there's not a ghost of a chance in you-know-where that there's a Chinese restaurant in Welling."

"No Chinese!" he said with shock in his voice. "That's terrible!"

"If we're lucky we might find someplace that has soggy pizza."

"Yuck!" He liked his pizza crisp and slightly scorched around the edges.

"What's the address again?" she asked him. Following the directions he read aloud, she took a left off Main Street and then a right onto a street with neat houses, shingled, squat, big and white mostly, a yellow one just at the corner listing windward. They all seemed aproned by small patches of grass, a few had ceramic figures set mid-lawn, and two or three, she noticed, had religious statues, even a crèche before one corner house. She remembered that Welling was basically a Catholic town, settled by miners.

"Seventy-two River Street. He said it was white with blue shutters and has a porch going around to the side. He also wrote that it was extremely fortuitous that it was available at this time," Piggy intoned without looking at the letter. Among his other attributes, Piggy had a near-perfect memory. "There it is!" he cried, scrambling up, leaning against her. "BeeBee, we're here! It's home, Bee," he said.

Jeannie stopped the car in front of the house and took hold of Piggy's hand. The house stared out at them with blank windows. She didn't really want to get out of the car. She wanted to keep going. Somehow she felt that as long as they were moving, nothing was truly definite. Time might reverse itself, the days and weeks and months roll backward as though life were film in a camera and she'd wake up in the warm king-size bed in their large apartment on Beacon Street, with Tony sprawled beside her, his arm trustingly around her waist. Piggy and BeeBee would be making breakfast in the sunny kitchen where the light washed across the floor and up the walls and as they sat around eating pancakes one or the other of them would flip the stereo on. Brahms for Tony or the Beatles if Piggy had his way.

And Bertram Lennard wouldn't be dead.

Sitting in the car as Piggy pulled at her to get moving, then dived right over the back seat to hug BeeBee and pat all his parts, Jeannie was reluctant to stir. As long as I stay in the car, she thought, nothing is irrevocable; once I open the door and get out, it's all going to begin. Beginnings were supposed to give you a real shot of adrenaline, but this one set loose a thin quivering of dread. As much as she tried to convince herself it was all going to work out for the best, something deep inside her whispered: It isn't.

2

Piggy wasn't convinced about the new house, even now that their own furniture had arrived, and sat around trying to look familiar in strange rooms and foreign corners. His mother's lithographs on the walls, the two sets of dishes (one with red and blue wavy lines and the good white for company) in the kitchen cupboards, sheets he had slept on all his life on the same bed—none of these accustomed trappings seemed to hide the fact that this was a house first of all, not an apartment. It jutted out in unexpected ways; went up stairs to a second floor with three bedrooms and a shabby bath with an old tub on funny feet, then down again to a dark and ominous cellar. The walls had lumps under a new coat of white paint. The floors tilted just a bit in spots, which sent BeeBee rolling frantically and then abruptly to a whining halt. It had lawns, fore and aft, but not much of either, and beyond the back patch of grass the land slid away from a wire-mesh fence right into the river, which didn't roar and didn't trickle but just sluggishly moved along, the water about two feet high.

He supposed that all in good time, as his mother would say, he'd get used to things, to the new house that even smelled differently—of dampness, of being old, of the earth outside and the river, of more than fifty years of other people. Yes, he sighed, rolling over in bed, punching his pillow and watching the way the light from the streetlamp outside dribbled in between the curtains, he'd learn to live in this house. But what about all the other changes in his life, how was he going to learn to deal with them? His father, for example.

At Height there were several kids who came from broken homes and nobody ever gave a hoot if you lived with one parent or two or a series of "steps." But that didn't make it any easier for Pig. He didn't want his parents to be apart, he wanted both of them to live with him. Of course he realized that it wouldn't be the same, not now, not after his mistake. And even if Height had allowed him to stay, he couldn't have spent one more day in the school. It was too awful, what he had done, and he pushed it away, and thought about his father.

"You see," his father had said the afternoon he had taken him out to McDonald's and tried to explain, "your mother and I don't get along anymore. We fight all the time and that's no good, not for us, and certainly not for you. Nobody wants to live in a house where everyone is yelling."

"It's an apartment, Dad," was all he could think to say. He pushed the Styrofoam box with the Big Mac inside 'round and 'round the table, unable to lift his head and meet his father's eyes.

"There's nothing to be ashamed about," Tony was saying, trying, Pig could see, to be both adult and reasonable, which was how he had noticed grown-ups usually acted when they were doing something to you that they knew was going to hurt. "And," he continued, "you have to do your part by trying to understand."

Piggy hadn't wanted to understand, he'd wanted to scream and kick at his father under the table. But, of course, that was out. He had to behave as if his partents' divorce was just a ho-hum thing, as if it wasn't tearing up his life like a road crew ripping up Boyleston Street.

Tony was asking, as he sipped at his cooling coffee, "Do you have anything to say? Any questions you want to ask?"

He thought of *that woman*, the one he had heard his mother and father fighting over, and he wanted to ask about her. Piggy longed to question his father about how he could fall in love with Julia—that was *her* name—when he was supposed to be in love with his mother. And why had he anyway? Probably his father would just get a glazed look on his face and talk about romance, about changes, about people growing in different ways—all of which Pig had heard Jeannie and Tony argue about when they thought he was sleeping. Piggy knew he was only a kid, never mind that his IQ was 194, and that kids had a lot to learn about life and sex and stuff like that. But his father was doing something wrong. He shouldn't have been loving that woman Julia and his mother shouldn't have been screaming and crying so much, which only made everything worse.

Pig's whole life was going *splat* and his father was sitting at the other side of the table surreptitiously glancing at his watch and trying not to let Piggy catch him at it. It wasn't fair. It was so unfair, as a matter of fact, that he felt himself threaten to explode, to split apart in little pieces right across the Formica tabletop. Not that he thought his father would care, or Jeannie either. They were just too far gone in their own miseries.

Now, Piggy lay in his own bed in the strange house in a town he knew nothing of but didn't want to find out about, and attempted to smooth out his feelings about his father. He imagined him somewhere else, not in their old apartment which was rented to another family now, but in Julia's house. His father hated houses, or rather anything down low, on the ground, wanting to be up high instead, as close to the sky as was possible. He should've been a pilot, Piggy had said once, but Tony, ruffling his hair, smiled in that way that Jeannie always insisted made him so handsome, and replied, "There's no money in flying."

What was Julia's house like? Like this one, ancient and smelly with the damp? Did it have bushes and trees and a big porch with a swing, that other house? The house where his father—*his father!*—walked around in chinos and bare feet, the game, whichever one it was, turned up high on the TV set.

It was no use. Piggy's feelings, no matter how hard he tried to lay them out mathematically, were all mush, just like when his mother threw vegetables in the Cuisinart. One minute he'd be so sad and unhappy that tears would flood his eyes, trickling down his cheeks before he could even get a crumpled Kleenex out of his pocket; at other times he'd be so mad at his father for deserting them that his face would go all red and scrunchy and his mother would ask if he had a stomachache.

But as bad as it was thinking about his father, as mad or as unhappy as Piggy would be at times, it was easier than thinking about the mistake. *The mistake*. That's what they all called it by an unspoken agreement. Besides, there was no other word for it. It was, after all, a mistake.

Wasn't it?

Piggy punched the pillow again and told himself to think about something else, not to think about *that*. Yet hard as he concentrated, his thoughts always curled back to that afternoon. It appeared to him in harsh black-and-white snapshots. He was there and he wasn't, sometimes half in a picture, sometimes all blurry and gray. Some parts of that time were smothered in fog, as though all of a sudden too much light had gotten into the camera and the film was overexposed. It was difficult to see those moments, and almost impossible to differentiate objects or positions, even his own. That wasn't the way he had told it, of course, not to the headmaster and the others, or his mother, or even his father, who was getting ready to move out on them. No, that wasn't the way he told it at all.

Piggy rolled over again, pulled the covers up under his arms, and stared at the ceiling. He wanted to see it perfectly clear for once, but it glided away from him in tiny cloud fragments until his head began to throb. He shut himself down like a machine ready to overload and called out to his friend standing like a centurion in a far corner of the room, "Are you awake, Bee?"

It was very silly to talk to BeeBee like he was a person, particularly when his switch wasn't on, and especially if you were smart enough to have built the robot in the first place. Anybody that smart, Piggy knew—always at ease with his own quirky intelligence—should have enough sense not to get confused. But BeeBee wasn't just a toy, nor was he simply an "achievement." He was in many ways an act of love, a giving of life. Three feet of yellow metal with complicated inner workings that Piggy was able to explain succinctly only to someone who already understood—which meant his mother and father viewed BeeBee as second cousin to a vacuum cleaner—BeeBee was voice-activated and responded only to Pig. He had a memory of two hundred and four words, could perform any number of simple and complex tasks with his movable arms and pincer hands, traveled by means of a rubberized track, and had red flashing eyes when he was activated. Unfortunately he didn't speak yet, except for the one sound—*bee bee*—which had given him his name. He was made of metal and microchips, wires and soldered parts, yet to Piggy he was as real as that sibling he'd never had. The one it now looked like he was never going to have.

Unless Mom marries again—

The thought that another man could possibly take his father's place left him with a queasy fluttering in the pit of his stomach. It wasn't going to happen, not if he, Piggy, had anything to say. And even if he didn't he would put a stop to such a betrayal on his mother's part fast.

With all his other concerns, it was, he told himself, ridiculous to think about something so remote, but still he tried to imagine some other man in his father's place, sitting in his father's chair at the kitchen table—or what would be his father's chair in this new house—reading the newspaper the way his father had always done and muttering that the world was getting crazier every day. Strolling into *their* room with his arm around his mother at night, shaving with a straight razor and a lot of foam while Pig sat on the toilet seat and watched.

"I don't care if he did fall in love with some other lady in Boston instead of coming here with us, Bee, he's still my father and I miss him," Piggy cried. "Don't you? I mean, he could be pretty funny, like when he tried to teach us to fly that kite. Remember? And he got all twisted up in the string and fell flat on his face and got so mad that he ripped the kite into pieces?" BeeBee didn't answer, not even with a beep, and Piggy, shifting his head, wiped his tears on the pillow. "Do you think," he asked, running his finger under his nose, "that he'll be the same when we see him again?"

His mother had been pretty vague about when Tony could come to visit, just as she was about Pig's going back to see him. But Piggy knew how angry she was, and how hurt. She hadn't even told Tony where they were going, just that they'd let him know when they had settled in. "He has other concerns at the moment, so let's not bother him right now," she had said. Her face had been all scrunched up and Pig knew she was about to cry. But he hadn't told Tony either, just been kind of whispery and vague. Besides, his father was pretty disappointed and more than a little upset with him. Not that he had actually said so, just, "How could you have made such a terrible mistake?" Like he didn't really believe him.

But that was another subject that gave Piggy a bellyache if he thought about it.

Which left Mason Prep, to which Piggy was going for the first time in the morning along with his mother. They had met Dr. Mellon and his wife the night before when the older couple arrived with a casserole for their supper. Mrs. Mellon wasn't much of a cook but she meant well, as he and his mother agreed after the Mellons had left. Which was a warning sign between them that signaled, *Stay away*. People who meant well either bored you or got you into trouble, like his grandmother—*may she rest in peace*, Pig intoned automatically—who made him a big birthday cake the year he was six and put the wrong something in it and he had to have his stomach pumped. Mrs. Mellon was definitely like Grandma, though he hadn't gotten sick from her casserole. Dr. Mellon was different. He sniffed a lot and because he was awfully tall kept looking down, though Pig didn't see how he could do anything else, but he didn't like all those pats on his head or on BeeBee's either, like they were dogs just slavering around waiting for love.

It made Pig very angry when people treated him as though he were insignificant, or worse, some freaky, clever child.

"I'm not a freak and neither are you, Bee," he said aloud. Sometimes he spoke aloud to BeeBee and sometimes he just talked in his head to the robot.

"It's different when you've gone to the same school all your life, except for nursery when I was three, and then suddenly to change. But you'll be there, Bee, so I'm not worried too much." Which was a lie. He was worried blue, not because he thought he'd be behind or that the classes would be too hard. In science and math he was advanced several grades, and even there his professors often had a hard time keeping up with him, but in English and history and French and Latin he would be on the normal track. In the humanities Pig was merely a straight-A student, not overly brilliant, as if only one part of his brain gave off sparks. Thank God, his mother had said, though she did have him reading Henry James. "Who is bor-*ing*, Bee! You don't know sometimes how lucky you are not being able to read."

No, it wasn't school itself which worried him. It was, as it always was, the other kids. Piggy had peer problems. Relating to other kids gave him a stiff neck and made the sweat pool under his arms and in the small of his back. He didn't know what to say or how to act, nor did he care awfully much about the kinds of things that interested them, like baseball cards and sports and television comedies. He was awkward and clumsy and terribly shy, and it was especially hard for him to talk so that other kids didn't always ask just what it was he was saying. Height had been a special place where he hadn't needed to be overly careful about the words he used, or about being interested in oddball things. Yet even there, he hadn't really gotten along.

Bertram Lennard, who had looked like a baby rat, had yellow teeth and acne rivering his chin. Piggy saw him plain as day. He heard too his whiny, insinuating taunts. And suddenly there was that blur of flames, red and yellow licking up the wall. . . .

He turned over quickly, took a deep breath, counted slowly to ten, waited until he saw spots before his eyes, and then let go.

He wouldn't think about Bertram Lennard dead and gone, he'd think about Mason and how it was going to be hell on wheels, because even though his mother assured him no one knew about that awful, cloudy afternoon, they didn't have any other geniuses, which was why they wanted him.

He settled back. Being a genius was as natural to Pig as the color of his hair. As he saw it, he could as easily have been born with crossed eyes. It was the luck of the draw and the intermingling of genes.

But if he hadn't been a genius then he wouldn't have gone to Height and wouldn't have built BeeBee. And he never would have met Bertram Lennard, who swam inexorably back into his thoughts. And there would not have been that awful, spurting jet of fire, and Bertram Lennard screaming. . . .

Thrashing about the bed, the sheet like a shroud, he fervently wished he could fall asleep, but he was so apprehensive that the moment he shut his eyes they snapped right open as if he had lost control of his lids.

Then he remembered the little girl—not that he had truly forgotten her. Instead, he had held her off like a piece of chocolate cake, waiting for the precise moment when he had earned it. He had earned the memory of the girl with her long blond hair that hung straight down her back. She was probably younger than he was, but not by all that much, and she lived in the house next door. Piggy had seen her when he looked out the window just that afternoon. She was hanging up wet clothes on a line in the backyard, an act that Piggy found fascinating in itself since he had never known anyone who didn't have a clothes dryer. Yet there she was in jeans and a sweatshirt the color of a faded grapefruit, picking wet clothes out of a wicker basket, lifting them up and shaking them in the slight breeze, and then pinning them on the line. He was so interested that he had galloped down the stairs, leaving Bee to watch by the window, and had gone out the back door to stand on the porch. If the little girl saw him, she hadn't let on, just arms going up and down much like BeeBee doing one of his exercises. Her hair waffled a bit as the breeze bit into it, and the wet clothes snapped angrily back at her. If his tongue hadn't gotten stuck to the roof of his mouth or if he was just a normal thirteen-year-old—or if elephants could fly, he thought—he would have simply opened his mouth, leaning as he should have been doing nonchalantly against the back porch railing, and said, *Hey there, hi, my name's Paul Conway and I just moved here from Boston; what's your name?* But since he might as well have been one

of the shutters on the side windows, painted blue and looking
puky, for all the attention she gave to him, Pig stood and
gaped, until his mother called him in and told him to quit
dawdling and get the rest of his clothes put away. Which was
the last Piggy saw of the girl for the rest of the day, though he
kept sneaking looks out of the windows that faced her house.
He snuggled into the blankets and the mound of pillows and
started to drift off remembering just how pretty she was and
how with a real live girl next door—and one who had blond
hair no less—maybe he'd acquire, at long last, a friend.

Morning came up with a thundering rainstorm just minutes
after, Piggy was convinced, he had fallen asleep. But there
was his mother shaking him by the shoulder and pulling him
by the arm to be sure he got out of bed. As hard as it was for
him to fall asleep, it was even harder to get up, and more
mornings than she could count, his mother would tell people,
she'd find him still asleep half in and half out of the bed. His
father would kid him that since his brain cells were over-
worked they needed extra R & R to get the juices bubbling
again. He hated to tell his father that brain cells didn't have
any juices and that all in all it was a silly idea. But he did like
to sleep once he got around to it.
Now, his mother stood right in the middle of the braided
rug his grandmother had made while they were all waiting
around for him to be born and watched him get his khaki
chinos off the hanger, his white shirt from its cellophane
wrapper in the drawer, and made him sit on the ladder-
backed chair in the corner and put on his socks before she
was satisfied that he wasn't going to drowse off on her and be
late for the first day at school. He grumbled under his breath,
but once his socks were on, he hit the power switch in the
middle of BeeBee's back and said, "Okay, Bee, com'on, let's
go wash up." Obligingly, the robot beeped and buzzed along
after him, out the door and down the hall to the bathroom. If
BeeBee hadn't Pig to follow he would have gotten lost in the
new house, going 'round and 'round in circles beeping away
as though he was having an asthma attack, Pig thought. He'd
have to reprogram the robot with new schematics of the
house, Mason, and Welling Proper.
Once washed and dressed, Piggy picked up BeeBee, whose
red eyes flashed with love, and carried him downstairs, where

the robot trailed along behind him into the kitchen. Since BeeBee was in three solid parts, disregarding his arms and pincers, he had no bend point midsection and had to stand by his side as Piggy ate. In order to conserve his batteries, Pig turned him off, though it was still like having another person at the table.

As he was forking up his scrambled eggs, his mother said, "I don't think you should take BeeBee today."

"What?" Piggy's eyes blinked behind his lenses. "Not take Bee? Why?"

"There's a lot to do the first day. You know, find your way around, get acquainted, start to fit in."

Piggy snorted. "Mom, be serious, you know I'll never fit in."

Her face went still as the black-and-white linoleum squares on the floor, but her fingers started tapping out Morse code on the tabletop, a skill she'd learned when she was a kid and had never forgotten. Pig read automatically: *Don't lose your cool*. However, all she said as the fork reentered his mouth was, "That's the wrong attitude to take."

"Sorry," he said and gulped down half a glass of milk. The Mellons, or rather Mrs. Mellon, had also thoughtfully stocked the refrigerator.

"I just think," she pushed on, her fingers silent now, "you should get adjusted before you spring BeeBee on anyone."

"No," he said with one of his flashes of obstinacy. "I won't go without BeeBee. It would be like expecting me to leave my glasses at home."

"You need your glasses."

"I *need* BeeBee."

Which was how Bee got into his usual place in the back seat, cushioned to prevent any jars to his delicate parts, and rode, tilted at an angle, looking out the far window at streets that were all liquid and runny though the rain had stopped. Piggy gave him a continuous travelogue as much to annoy his mother as for Bee's edification.

"—And here at the end of River Street we turn left and go over the bridge, Main Bridge it's called. They don't have much imagination in Welling, Bee. River Street runs along the river and Main Bridge is the main bridge. Get it? There's another bridge you could see if your head pivoted to the

right, down the river a couple of blocks. It's called South
Bridge because it's south of Main Bridge. Right, Mom?"

Jeannie clenched her teeth and drove across the two-lane
bridge to Welling East. On the other side Mason Prep
stretched out in a series of red brick buildings, except for
Administration, which was big, white, and pillared like an
old plantation. It had been the home of Joseph Welling, the
coal baron who had founded the town and then saw to it that
he was far enough removed so that a river divided him from
it.

They came off the bridge alongside a grassy verge, hemmed
by a sidewalk and stone wall that bordered the river. The
faculty cottages, all square, squat Cape Cod salt boxes, ran in
military formation at the edge of the campus, and then there
was a short incline. At the top, Jeannie parked the Chevy in
the Administration Building parking lot.

"See," she said, being spiteful, "there's a long flight of
steps to carry BeeBee up. I told you he should stay at home."

"At *home*," Piggy snapped back at her, "there are even
more steps."

Jeannie waved her hands, a signal it was all just too much
for her, and tugging at her shoulder bag went up the steps,
letting Piggy struggle with the twenty-five kilos of robot.
Inside he carefully put BeeBee down, turned him on, and
together they followed Jeannie along the narrow corridor,
where the few teachers and students passing by stopped and
stared. BeeBee was a definite event, whirring along, red eyes
dazzling, beeping now and then at a whispered command Pig
gave into the voice-receiver control he carried. It almost
seemed as if the robot was smiling from the attention; certainly Piggy's lips were twitching, because there was no de-
nying it, BeeBee was a show-stopper.

Jeannie led the parade into Dr. Mellon's suite, where his
secretary sat at a desk just outside his private office. The
woman gave a short beep herself as BeeBee came up, halting
inches from her pen tray. She was a little wispy woman with
pencils sticking out of a bun on top of her head as though it
were a pincushion, her face etched with lines that were
already filled up with powder at eight-forty-five.

"Yes?" she said, pushing her chair on its casters as far away
as she could get from BeeBee.

Jeannie, who had seen every conceivable reaction to Piggy's pride, said, "I'm Mrs. Conway and this is my son, Paul. Dr. Mellon's expecting us."

"Oh yes, Mrs. Conway. How do you do? I'm Miss Miller, Dr. Mellon's secretary. It's so nice to meet you at last. We spoke on the phone."

"Yes, of course, Miss Miller."

Piggy was ready to bend double with laughter because though the old woman spoke to Jeannie her eyes never left Bee's face, as though the robot had her hypnotized. Her lips pursed like a fish's sucking air, and she fluttered a handkerchief trying to shoo him away until she finally asked, "Just what is that?"

"A robot, Miss Miller," Jeannie said. "Just a robot."

"Oh. A robot."

They might have gone on like that for some time with Miss Miller locked into place, gulping for air and fanning herself and getting ready to faint in her chair out of pure fright, except that Dr. Mellon heard the commotion—Miss Miller's yelp, BeeBee's beep, the murmur of voices from the crowd now gathered in the doorway. He emerged smiling, his hand outstretched.

"Mrs. Conway, Paul, you've made it," he said, as though, Piggy thought, getting from Welling to Mason, a matter of a mile and a half door to door, was an accomplishment. Piggy was constantly surprised by the way grown-ups behaved and the things they sometimes said when they merely wanted to be polite. If he could redesign the world, he'd have people communicate in numbers.

"First," the headmaster was saying, "I want to take you, Mrs. Conway, down to your classroom, show you the faculty lounge, your locker—" He was ticking each item off on his fingers. "And, Paul, of course, you'll need the grand tour. Why don't I get one of the students to show you around? Miss Miller has your schedule and your locker key." Looking at the faces clustered like daisy decals in his doorway, he stabbed a hand at a small boy, shorter than Piggy, with a pinched-up face, and said, "Tommy Toomy, you're just the one. Paul, here's another day student like yourself."

The two boys stared at each other in the way of small animals, more from curiosity than belligerence. Then, as though he had scented the wind and it bore no harm, the stranger said, "Hi," and nodding to BeeBee asked, "Who's he?"

Right then Pig liked him a lot because he automatically referred to Bee as a "he" rather than an "it."

"This is BeeBee. Bee, say hi." And the robot gave his programmed beep.

"Out of sight!" Tommy cried with genuine awe in his voice. "Can I touch him?"

"Sure. Hey, Bee, shake hands." The metal right arm swung up and the pincers spread, delicately grabbing hold of the boy's proffered hand. The crowd, including Dr. Mellon, who had already seen Bee's performance the night before, was silent except for Jeannie, who was drumming out some inner thought too fast for Piggy to catch it. He knew she wasn't pleased. His mother felt, he had heard her tell his father often enough, that less attention to BeeBee and more to Paul would be *a good thing for all of us*.

"Shall we be on our way, Dr. Mellon," Jeannie said, breaking the spell.

"Right, right." He tore his glance away from the robot. "Now everyone, back about your business. You too, Miss Miller. Boys, off with you. And, Paul, you are meeting with Dr. Johanson just after lunch. Come back here and he'll take you over to your lab. Oh yes, one more thing, Mrs. Conway. I've called a quick faculty meeting at four to introduce you to the staff."

"Thank you, Dr. Mellon," Jeannie said. And then to Piggy, "Have a good day, Paul."

"Sure, Mom," he replied, looking dubious.

"Lemme see your schedule," Tommy said as they went back out into the hall, Bee behind them. Piggy handed it over and the other boy, reading it slowly, said, "Okay, you got English your first class just like me. It's that way, in the Humanities Building. Then you got French and Latin, which are in Mason Hall on the other side of Humans—that's short for Humanities Building. Get it? Then, lunch, which is here in the cafeteria, back there." He jerked a thumb over his shoulder but all Piggy could see was an endless fluorescent-lit corridor all yellow and dingy. "Then old Cantaloupe said—"

"Cantaloupe?" Pig asked.

"Yeah, for Dr. Mellon. You know, melon, cantaloupe. Got it?"

"Got it," Piggy said, though personally he didn't think it was very funny.

"Anyway, Cantaloupe said you gotta meet Waxworks, who is Dr. Johanson to you, back here after lunch."

"Why Waxworks?"

"Knew you'd ask that. 'Cause he looks like a cadaver. And he's at least a hundred and fifty on one toe."

"Hey, Slime, who's your buddy?" A group of older boys who had been coming down the hall stopped and surrounded Pig, Beebee, and Tommy.

Tommy puffed himself up, filled with importance, and said, "A new kid, Paul Conway, and this here is BeeBee."

"What's a beebee?" one of the boys asked, laughing.

"A robot," Piggy said, moving protectively closer to Bee, whose eyes were flashing.

"No kidding, a robot." One of the boys smirked and the group crowded even closer.

"Where'd he come from?"

"Is he some kind of gimmick?"

"How's he work?"

"I made him," Piggy said, and the attention swept to his short, rotund little figure.

"You made him!" A tall blond-haired boy who was Pig's image of what he wanted to be, not when he grew up, but this very minute, said with surprise, "How?"

"Well, it's a little complicated."

The boys hooted with laughter, but it wasn't a friendly sound. It had a sharp edge to it which made Piggy step back and swallow.

"What's he do?" One of them moved closer to BeeBee. He was dark, with olive skin and hair the color of coal. With his sharp nose and high cheekbones he looked like an Indian. And he wore a black leather jacket molded so tightly to his chest and arms that, Pig thought wildly, if his flesh was peeled back there would be leather encasing the bones.

"He does a lot of things," Tommy said, though Piggy noticed that he inched away, closer to Dr. Mellon's office.

The dark boy laughed. "So, show us." He moved nearer still and Piggy thought that if there had been light enough for a shadow to fall, the very weight of this tall, broad-shouldered boy would crush him right into the ground. He saw himself squashed like a bug you might step on, and BeeBee a crunched mass of wires and microchips. His flesh was weak, his heart so fragile that its thumping was about to shake it loose in his chest. And the anger that he had learned to fear like a seizure was beginning to swirl in his brain.

"It's just some faggoty toy," another of the boys sneered.

The boy in the leather jacket was just about to reach over and touch Bee when Tommy yelled, "Show them! Com'on, show 'em all the things he can do!"

Piggy pulled himself up, rapidly blinking his eyes behind the wire-rims, and muttered, "Okay."

Within a few minutes there in the hall Pig sullenly had Bee doing his repertoire of tricks. He didn't want to show the robot off because the group of boys, in a semicircle around Bee, was glancing from the robot to Pig. And that hooded, vaguely distanced look they were giving him was discomforting. They thought, he suspected, that he was strange. Nutso kid and his pet tin can.

The flash of anger jolted him again. Abruptly he switched Bee off. There was a moment of silence before Tommy babbled, "Okay, you guys, I gotta take the new kid around, so the show's over."

There was a little more pushing and shoving, though none of them got really close to BeeBee and his pincers, but then they moved off and Piggy thought, staring after them, that he hated people like those boys. Tall, straight, with broad shoulders and good looks, and the confidence to swagger around in leather jackets and appear menacing even if they weren't.

Tommy was hurrying them along, chattering like a mynah bird until Piggy, banking his anger yet again, asked, "What did they call you? Slime?"

The smaller boy stopped, sighed, and shuffled his sneakers in an elaborate two-step. "Yeah," he said, "Slime. It's kind of like a nickname, you know. Because my father's the local undertaker and everybody thinks that's funny. I don't think it's funny, being a funeral director, which is what my father calls himself. I mean, people gotta be buried when they die or they'll just lie around and stink up the place. It's an important public function, my father says."

"I guess so," Piggy agreed, and then in a burst of friendliness added, "It's okay, everybody at my old school called me Piggy."

"Piggy?"

"You know, like Piggy in *Lord of the Flies.*"

"I never saw it."

"It's not just a movie, it's a book. By William Golding. Anyway, there's this character named Piggy and he looks just like me. Only my frames are different," he said, tapping his glasses on the bridge of his nose. "I don't mind," he continued, "because it's kind of a compliment, but it drives my mom bananas."

"The same with my old lady when she hears anybody calling me Slime."

They solemnly nodded their heads in mutual recognition of the peculiarities of mothers.

The rest of the morning seemed to fly, a kaleidoscope of images and impressions and new faces that Piggy cataloged and sorted away in his filing-cabinet mind. English was so easy that it was going to be boring. The class was reading *Animal Farm*, which he had devoured years ago and remembered practically verbatim. In French (except for his accent, which made his speaking of the language sound like a rusty gate creaking back and forth), he was well ahead of the class. The same was true for Latin, and Miss Edwin immediately switched him into Latin Three, where he contentedly spent an hour deciphering Virgil. He met Slime for lunch in the cafeteria, where again BeeBee created a sensation, as he had been doing all morning. Pig's tray grasped in his pincers, BeeBee led a procession across the cavernous room, whispers of shock and surprise rolling under his tracks.

Piggy had just about decided that Mason Prep wasn't going to be all that bad, even with the older boys whom he half-resented, half-feared. It might even be better than Height because he had found a friend in Slime, who was promising to come home with him after school. He stopped for a minute in the hallway of the Administration Building after he had shown off Bee to a group of giggling girls and thought that if he had had a friend at Height—someone like Slime—maybe the mistake wouldn't have happened. Agitated, he thumped his fist against the scabrous wall and told himself: Enough of that. Several students walking by regarded him strangely, but Pig was oblivious of their stares.

Bertram Lennard go away
don't come back another day....

He was bad. Mean and cruel and bad. And he tormented me, Pig told himself.

"Paul, are you all right?" Miss Miller had stopped inches away from Pig and Bee, her hands clasped tightly in front of her stomach as though either boy or robot might decide to attack.

Guiltily Piggy swung away from the wall, almost careening into BeeBee, whose shoulder he patted for reassurance, and scowled at the woman. Around them a few stragglers rushed late to class.

"Yes, Miss Miller, everything's fine," he said, struggling to catch his breath, not to cry. And then he barged away from her, stomping along to Dr. Mellon's outer office, where Dr. Johanson was waiting for him, impatiently tapping a highly polished shoe. He wasn't tapping out a message, just signaling annoyance, which didn't diminish when he caught sight of Pig and BeeBee.

He did remind Piggy of one of the waxworks in Madame Tussaud's where his mom and dad had taken him two summers before when they went to London. Dr. Johanson was smooth and cold and shiny and just slightly human, though not quite. His skin was as yellow as old parchment and tightly stretched across a long, thin, bony nose like a chicken wing, down to narrow bloodless lips and a sharp pointed chin. His eyes were china blue and very tiny like two beads from the necklace his mother had once bought at a sidewalk sale in Cambridge. He was meticulously dressed without a speck of dust or one wrinkle. Piggy didn't like him on sight but was willing to try until he said, "So this is the toy that everyone's so excited about."

"BeeBee's not a toy!" Piggy answered angrily.

"Don't contradict me, young man," Johanson snapped. Behind his back Miss Miller typed furiously away.

Even BeeBee seemed cowed by the old man. Dr. Johanson wasn't much taller than Pig but he threw a long, angular shadow as thin as a knife blade. They left the Administration Building and went over to Science and down the stairs—Pig carrying Bee—to the basement and Pig's new lab.

And that was the biggest disappointment of all. At Height

as Piggy's genius grew, took shape, and spun off sparks, he
was encouraged to try his scientific wings. Each new experiment that danced in his brain was given the equipment to
bring it to fruition. He had had the most sophisticated computers to practice on, but here, in this long barren room,
there was only a bench, stool, a computer so primitive that
Piggy audibly sniffed at it, outlets, a tray of worn old tools
including a battered soldering iron, and a telephone hookup.

Piggy fairly bristled as he poked around, very conscious of
Dr. Johanson's cowering presence. "Where's the oscilloscope
I was promised?" he demanded. "And the logic analyzer?
There's not even a DMM."

"We went to great expense to hook up this"—he gestured
at the computer as if it was a derelict child—"thing to the
university one down in Pittsburgh. I understand it's quite
sophisticated." For the first time he seemed to thaw margin-
ally, but then, as though catching the flicker of pure rage on
Pig's face, he said, "This is the best we could do. Mason is
not IBM, young man."

"What is your specialty?" Piggy asked, sounding like someone much older than thirteen.

Johanson wilted slightly under the direct and piercing look
the boy gave him. "Biology," he said at last.

"I thought so," Pig replied with feeling, and marched out,
struggling back up the steps with Bee in his arms. He headed
back to the Administration Building for a math class that he
just knew would be for babies. It was worse than that, it was
advanced calculus that Piggy could do in his sleep.

He caught up with his mother just before his second-to-last
period of the day and wailed at her, tears springing into his
eyes, "Mom, it's plain awful. I'll never learn anything here.
Right now I know more than anybody in the whole place."

"Oh, Paul, what do you want me to do?" Jeannie asked,
shifting an armful of books. "They said you'd have your own
lab and all the equipment you need."

They were standing just outside the teachers' lounge on
the second floor of the Administration Building, where Piggy
had tracked her down. She kept glancing at her watch, late
for her second-form composition class, and said, "I can't talk
about it now. We'll discuss it tonight. Meet me in the parking
lot at five and we'll drive home."

"No," he said, gnawing at his lower lip, "I'm walking home with one of the kids."

"Hey, that's terrific." Her face went all soft and loving. "See, I told you you'd fit in just fine."

"I don't fit in at all and I'm bored stiff and everything sucks." But she wasn't listening, running off, making clicking sounds on the hardwood floor.

"Bee," he said, "I couldn't program you to spit in this lousy place. And now we have to go to gym. Ah nuts, Bee, I want to go home." He would have burst into hysterics and thrown himself on the floor, kicking and screaming as he hadn't done since he was two years old and his father had whacked his bottom, but he was already late for gym, which was his least-favorite thing in all the world.

It turned out to be even worse than Piggy had expected, worse than at Height, where it was acceptable to be condescending toward physical activities if you were smart enough in some other area. But what Mason lacked in academics and definitely in science, it made up for in sports. Three times in the last five years they had reached the state play-offs in basketball and had once gotten a high jumper into the semifinals of the Olympic tryouts. While weak in football, they had finished the season in baseball ten–two. Sports at Mason were priority business. Since Piggy didn't take gym seriously, he had no gym shorts, and his best sneakers were already on his feet. He couldn't hit a ball with a bat, soar under the basket, or make a flying tackle if his life depended on it, but he did know how to swim. Unfortunately the big Mason pool had developed a dangerous crack and was out of commission at least for the next month.

Piggy wearily trudged back into the locker room to wash the sweat off his face after a humiliating forty minutes of volleyball. He had been knocked down four times, had let the ball drop so often that the other boys, quickly taking his measure, soon simply elbowed him out of the way when the ball came anywhere near him. He had made, he realized, his usual stupid showing of himself in any sport.

He stood in the middle of a gaggle of shrieking boys, his face dripping wet, having forgotten he didn't even have a towel. His hair was all spiky but the cold water hadn't managed to dampen the red flush of his face. Finally he dried

himself with the tail of his shirt and tucked it back into his
pants, where it lay against his stomach clammy and cold.

Piggy was feeling more and more as though the end of the
world had come and stranded him alone on some rocky atoll,
as he went back over to Humans and tried to sit still for fifty
minutes of history. If there was anything that interested
Piggy almost as little as sports it was history. The past, as far
as he was concerned, was sooty, covered in ashes, and though
he had heard his mother say often enough, *We learn from
history,* he was bored by the concerns of long ago. Besides,
the teacher, Miss Markowitz, a dour young woman with her
hair pinned back in a French twist, made Piggy park BeeBee
in the coatroom, where he stood in a nest of bomber jackets
and down vests.

But at last the long awful day was over, though Piggy knew
that there was tomorrow lurking in the future and all the
tomorrows after that. It was depressing, but then he heard
his father saying: "Always stand up tall and try to be a man."
He straightened his shoulders as he went off to meet Slime.
From the minute Tommy had admitted to the nickname,
Piggy couldn't think of him as anything but Slime. It was
really so yucky that Piggy thought it wonderful. He admired
his newfound friend for being able to carry it off.

As he crossed the campus on the long, narrow walk, BeeBee
chirping at his side, he saw his mother in the parking lot,
leaning against the Chevy, talking to a man he didn't recognize. As Piggy zigzagged toward them across the grass he saw
two women stop—Miss Markowitz he noticed was one, and
his mouth went sour as though he was sucking a lemon. The
women moved on but the man stayed, his head bent. Even
so far off Piggy could see that he was watching his mother
intently. There was something frightening about the way they
stood so close, and Piggy's eyes narrowed to slits. He tried to
hurry, but it was slow going, with Bee's track moving sluggishly on the wet grass.

"Com'on, Bee, faster," Piggy said and then broke into a
trot as the man lifted his hand and touched Jeannie's arm.

"Paul," Jeannie said, looking up and seeing him at last. As
if, Piggy thought, feeling sick, she'd forgotten about me.

The man turned and smiled, holding out his hand. "Hello,
Paul, I'm Peter Bayard, assistant headmaster and dean of the
middle school."

Reluctantly Piggy gave up his hand and let it flap against the dean's. "Hello," he said. For a moment he glanced up at him, but Peter was looking at Jeannie. Pig didn't like what he saw. Which wasn't anything, not really. Just a look. Like he was a tailor measuring his mom for a suit.

Then Peter's attention came back to Pig, and he said, "Is that the famous BeeBee I've been hearing about?"

Grudgingly Piggy said, "Yeah, who else."

"Pretty impressive. What does he do?"

"Lots of things," Piggy replied.

"How about a demonstration?"

"No," Piggy snapped, biting down hard. "Bee's tired."

"Bee's tired!" Jeannie said, shocked. "Paul, what is going on? You always love to show BeeBee off." She edged closer to him but he backed away.

"Are you saying, Mom, that I'm a show-off?"

"No. I'm just saying that you're being impossible." She was working on a smile but the corners of her mouth refused to turn up properly and she simply appeared confused.

"Piggyyyyyy!"

Piggy revolved and there was Slime at the far side of the parking lot waving to him.

"Got to go, Mom," Pig said, and ran off, BeeBee rolling behind him.

"I'm sorry, Peter, I don't know what that scene meant," Jeannie apologized, clutching her books to her breasts like a schoolgirl.

"Typical," he replied sympathetically as they watched Piggy and Slime walk off toward Main Bridge. "He's bound to be upset, anxious in a new school. Don't worry about him. He'll adjust to Mason in time."

Jeannie, listening to Peter Bayard, was stung by a wild desire to blurt out the whole story of her life, her marriage, but most of all about Piggy. She longed for someone to share the heavy burden of what had gone so awfully wrong at Height and how she could see Bertram Lennard's dead face swimming in her field of vision when she least expected it. She had to clench her teeth to keep from saying, *I'm scared when there's no reason to be now*. Then, smiling at Peter Bayard until her face ached, she reassured herself insistently that everything was going to be all right.

*   *   *

"I mean," Slime said, "Mason's not Harvard, you know. And if old Bayard's such a big deal with all his books and papers and stuff, then how come he's just assistant head?"

"Don't know," Piggy howled out to the wind that was buffeting them between the guy wires as the narrow bridge quivered and rocked over the water. Cars crept carefully along and Piggy moved back so that he walked with his hand on BeeBee's shoulder.

"When he's not shuffling papers around he's being Mr. Good Guy. You know, having kids into his office and asking do they have any problems and shit like that," Slime continued. "Though I gotta tell you," he cried, shouting to be heard over the wind, "he's not as bad as some of them," as if Piggy already knew whom he meant, which Piggy did.

Dr. Johanson for one. Just the memory of that humiliating fifteen minutes in his lab . . . *Lab*! It was practically an empty barn with some rusty nuts and bolts, though Pig had to admit that he hadn't taken all that good a look at the computer. Just the memory made Piggy burn. Fat lot of any science he was going to learn. Old Waxworks probably wanted him to pore over some moldy frog that had been pickled so long it had turned into shoe leather. Miss Markowitz was another one of *them*, rattling on about the French Revolution with the same awe in her voice his grandmother had reserved for discussions of the astronauts going to the moon. *Preserve us, who'd ever think such a thing was possible!*

Still, Dr. Johanson and Miss Markowitz, as bad as they were, didn't give Pig the same shivers of apprehension that Peter Bayard did. He was someone to watch out for. He was a threat. Pig had seen the way, *the pushy way*, he had just reached out and touched his mother.

At last they reached the end of the bridge and River Street just as a long, sleek Harley Davidson varoomed right down at them, swerving to hit a large puddle in a slight depression where the street dipped. Water sprayed up in a shower, soaking the two boys and BeeBee. The black bike with its denim-jacketed rider careened away without stopping, trailed by a thin current of smoke.

"He got us all wet!" Piggy cried, his voice shredding with anger.

Slime shrugged, shaking himself like a large dog, and kept

walking, turning right onto the cracked sidewalk. Piggy helped Bee over the busted concrete, trying to wipe his face at the same time and muttering about some people, but Slime, his face impassive, simply shrugged again.

A pickup truck, its flanks tattooed with patches of rust, rumbled by close to the curb. Pig leapt back hastily, but Slime plodded ahead, saying, "Don't be so jumpy."

"You're kidding. First that bike deliberately splashed us, then that truck almost ran us down!"

Slime turned and stared at him, his face as wizened as an apple left too long on the branch. "I get a lot of that 'cause my parents make me go to Mason."

"What do you mean?" Piggy asked, stopping in surprise.

Slime danced over the cracks in the cement, regarding his sneakers. "Just that no one in Welling Proper is too hot about Mason."

Moving on after him, Piggy asked, "Why not?"

"Oh, my mom says, 'What do you expect, it's the law of the jungle.'"

"What?"

"Like being suspicious of people who are different, is what she means, I guess."

Piggy knew about being different, and he lowered his head, the muscles across his shoulders tightening. "Not that I'm the only townie, you know," Slime continued. "There's Larry Houser in the fifth form, but he's a real brain. Not like you, but smarter than most Welling kids. Everybody says he'll go to Harvard. You met him outside of Cantaloupe's office. That tall blond kid. And then there's Betts McManus, who's a year ahead of us, but her mother's a kook, makes jewelry and stuff. Nobody talks to the McManuses. Tim Jenkins, too. He's in the third form," Slime droned on with his litany. "Jenkins got a scholarship 'cause Cantaloupe thinks it will improve relations with Welling if he takes in a couple of townies. That's what my father says. He also gave one to Mary Osser, the fat girl who sits behind you in English. Know who I mean?" Piggy nodded his head but Slime wasn't looking. "So it's not just me. But nobody in Welling likes the idea of the school or that some of us kids cross the river. You'd think the damn Susquehanna was the Atlantic Ocean and we were all going off to Paris, France. It's all nonsense, my ma says, and I shouldn't pay it no mind whatsoever." He stopped finally and faced Pig, who could tell from the way his mouth pulled taut as a clothesline that Slime minded quite a bit.

"So why do you go? I mean, why not Welling Consolidated?"

Slime sighed and rolled his eyes upward toward a sky as heavy as cement. "Because that's what *they* want, you know." Almost tearfully he rolled his gaze back down to Pig and said, "My pa had an education even if it only was two years at the junior college downstate, and he wants better for me."

It was embarrassing, these confidences, Piggy thought. But he supposed it was what it meant to have a real friend. He felt a surge of warmth for the funny-looking little boy who rather resembled a drowned kitten. He would have reached out and patted the skinny arm beneath the denim sleeve, but he didn't know how. He looked away instead, across the street just diagonally from his own front door, and saw an old woman watching them from the front porch of a dingy yellow house that sat above the road as the land climbed upward toward Main. For a moment, blinking, Piggy thought she was a sack of laundry left tilting against the wall. She was a smudge of dirty white, hair and face and long dress reaching almost down to her ankles. Bony arms were crossed upon a narrow chest. Yes, she was watching them, and it gave Piggy chills that ran along his spine to the small of his back.

Just an old woman. Nobody special. Nobody to get the shivers about, he thought.

Slime noticed finally that he had lost Pig's attention and glanced over his shoulder to see what the other boy saw. "Hello, Mrs. Williams," Slime called out.

The old woman didn't answer. She shuffled off the porch and down a steep flight of steps to a mangy patch of yellowed lawn held three feet above the sidewalk by a stone wall.

"Who is she?" Piggy whispered, pinned in place by a pair of dark eyes nested in a bed of wrinkles.

But before Slime had a chance to reply, the old woman hawked, "That thing, what is it?"

"A robot, Mrs. Williams," Slime said.

"A what? Speak up, boy."

"A robot."

"A *robot*?" She leaned forward and motioned them closer with the flat of her hand. "Come here, you two."

Reluctantly the boys and BeeBee crossed the street, Pig

holding delicately on to Bee's right pincer. They drew alongside the wall and looked up at the old lady. Close up she
seemed to be made of straw and scraps of cloth, so thin Pig
was surprised she wasn't blown away by the wind. Her face
was carved with deep fissures that paralleled her mouth, and
her eyes were overly large, jutting outward as if ready to pop
from their sockets.

"Ugly thing," she said, scowling down at BeeBee.

Piggy bristled. "He is not!"

"You that smart kid people said was coming to town?" she
asked.

"If you mean am I Paul Conway who moved in with his
mother across the street, yes, ma'am, that's who I am. And if
you mean do I go to Mason, yes, ma'am, I do." He glared at
her belligerently, trying to convince himself that she didn't
scare him even though her skin hugged the bones of her face
so tightly that she appeared more like a dead person than
someone still living.

"Smart-alecky one, ain't you?"

Piggy was about to answer but Slime put his hand out like
a traffic cop and said hurriedly, "Do you want to see BeeBee
do his tricks, Mrs. Williams? He's really something."

"He? *He?*" Her reedy voice rose in a screech. "That's no
person, that's just a machine. Don't you call it a 'he,' Thomas
Toomy."

Bee beeped and the old woman drew back, shocked. Defi-
antly Piggy put the robot through his paces there on the
narrow sidewalk as Mrs. Williams hissed between clenched
teeth, crossing herself repeatedly.

"See, see," Slime kept crying excitedly, as mesmerized
with BeeBee's routine as he had been the first time he had
seen him. "Isn't he wonderful, Mrs. Williams?"

But she was drawing away, fumbling backward up the steps
to the safety of the porch, from where, when Bee grew still,
she called down, "Think you're so smart to have done that,
boy, don'cha? Well, we'll see, we'll just see."

She stomped into the house, banging the door behind her.
But immediately she was at the window, gripping the curtain
with a bony claw. Slime and Piggy backed off, buttressing
BeeBee between them as if the old woman's enmity could
reach out through the walls to strangle the robot right there
on River Street.

"She's a stupid old witch," Piggy fumed, so angry he had to push up his glasses and rub his eyes.

"Not much different from lots of people in Welling," Slime said sadly.

Piggy spun on him in a rage. "I hate this town and that school and that old bitch! I wish we had never come here. I wish it would all go up in a nuclear attack!" And he bolted, running, BeeBee furiously rolling after him to the steps. Slime, shocked, stood uncertainly for the count of ten, and then glancing back at the old woman, who was still watching, he followed. Reaching out, he lifted the beeping robot up over the steps, and opening the front door, which Piggy had slammed in both their faces, he helped BeeBee find his way into the darkened house.

3

Piggy was running, his breath tight in his lungs, tiny gusts of it puffing from his half-opened mouth. He was light-headed and his legs hurt, with streaks of pain that raced up and down the bones. He was flying, the *thud*, *thud* of his sneakers on the pavement echoing through the dark and chilly night. There was no moon, no stars, and the streetlights were mysteriously shrouded. He ran, his arms outstretched, parting the darkness. At his back, coming nearer so that he could feel its heat, was the even darker darkness of the beast.

He raced through the night, past houses with unseeing windows as vacant as empty eye sockets, the growl of the beast deafening behind him. And the street stretched endlessly away, an inky river that carried him no closer to safety until there, just ahead, it widened, spread itself into a puddle of blackness. He sprinted on then, pushing himself, hope surging in his chest.

A little further, just a block or so, and he would be lost in the darkness, out of reach of the beast. But as he entered the pool of blackness and flung himself forward, the macadam soft beneath his sneakers, the lights came on, one after the other, circling what he saw then was a parking lot just to the side of a large, spired building that hulked in the shadows. And then the beast, the Harley—*he knew it was only a bike!*—came so close that he swore the cold metal jutted into his back. And he fled even faster, right across the lot, toward the darkness, the building, the church with its cross now gleaming in the milky white light. But the bike cut him off, zooming on his left side, flanking him—*varoom, varoom*. He swerved to the right, away from the church, cut off like an errant steer.

Piggy smelled the bike's exhaust and over that a greasy, rancid stench that even the rain, suddenly starting up in thick heavy drops like glue, couldn't wash away. His legs felt as heavy as BeeBee's casing as he lifted them up and down, kept moving. His heart was ready to burst in his chest and each breath brought a painful throbbing in his lungs.

He was running in circles now, going 'round and 'round, the beast inching nearer and nearer until Piggy was certain he was going to be ground flat under its wheels. All at once the bike pulled ahead of him and he saw the rider for the first time. Until that moment he hadn't thought who it might be on the bike, who could be so determined to run him down.

The Harley flew ahead, shrieked as it spun into a narrow turn, the right leg of the rider dragging against the ground. And then it zoomed back toward him in the center of the lot where he had stopped dead, suddenly locked in place. It roared at him, growing larger and larger, filling his vision, growling so loud he thought his eardrums would crack. And atop the bike, her skirts billowing in the breeze, her hair flying in the wind, straight out behind her narrow, bony skull, was old Mrs. Williams, only she was really dead now, and there was no flesh beneath the dress or under the hair, there was only a skeleton driving the bike, naked phalanges gripping the handles, the wide, yellowing teeth gaping in death's grin.

He bolted straight up in bed, flinging the covers aside, his

heart pounding—*varoom, varoom*—and heard off in the distance, at least three streets away, the Harley growling at him.

The shadows in the room seemed to careen across the
walls, bumping into one another. In his corner, white strips
of pale moonlight crisscrossing his metal face, BeeBee stood
watching. His red eyes flashed, he clicked and hummed and
rocked as though his track had come loose, and beeped in
one long, incoherent cry as he rolled away from the wall. The
shadows and lights collided, forming patterns, then reform-
ing, and Piggy cried out, "BeeBee, what are you doing!" The
arms came up, the pincers which were sharp as fangs,
spreading.

Pig's back crashed into the brass headboard, and he held
out his hands—*Stop!*—and his mouth went all sour as if he
was going to throw up.

"Bee!" he wailed.

Suddenly the overhead snapped on and the room was
swamped in light. Jeannie was standing in the doorway,
clutching the edges of her velour bathrobe. "Paul, what's
the matter?"

Piggy looked up at her, dazed. He was lying flat on his
back, fear sliding up and down his spine. Bee was in his
corner, just where he was supposed to be, his power turned
off. And there was no *varoom, varoom* crashing through the
night out on River Street or maybe further, far away at the
top of the hill in the parking lot of St. Anthony's Church.

"I was having a nightmare," Piggy whimpered as Jeannie
came and sat on the side of his bed, smoothing the hair away
from his forehead. "I thought a big motorcycle was chasing
me, and Mrs. Williams, that mean old lady from across the
street, was driving it, only she was dead. Just a skeleton. And
I thought I got so scared I woke up and when I did I thought
that Bee was coming to get me like he wasn't BeeBee at all,
but something else, something *awful!*"

"Oh, honey, you're shaking!" Jeannie wanted to take him
in her arms, to curl him up next to her, but knew she
couldn't. He was too old for that now, and so she settled for
stroking his arms, holding his hand and saying softly, "Just a
bad dream, Paul. Everybody has them from time to time.
Especially when life's unsettled, when there are problems,
worries. This hasn't been easy for you, honey, I know that,
leaving Boston, coming to a strange place, and then that awful

woman . . ." She ran out of words and reaching down brushed his cheek with her lips. "Go back to sleep now, it will be fine."

"I know, Mom, but can you leave the hall light on and the door open just a little bit," he asked in a low, small-boy voice.

"Of course I can. And you wake me if you need me. Sleep tight."

Watching the pie-shaped wedge of light that slanted through the doorway from the hall, Piggy didn't think he'd sleep again, but he did drift off, sailing serenely through the rest of the night, and when he opened his eyes again it was morning. Saturday. The night seemed a long way off, a slice of prehistoric past that he could barely recall. He went downstairs carrying BeeBee, smiling and singing off key.

"Well, don't you sound chipper," Jeannie said as she turned from the stove, where she was stirring eggs in a frying pan. "No more bad dreams?"

"Huh?" he asked, settling himself at the table and gazing up at her.

"Forget it, champ, just drink your juice. What do you want to do today?"

"Do? I don't know. Nothing I guess. Slime's coming over later."

"Slime!" she said, raising her eyebrows.

"You know, Mom, Tommy Toomy."

"Good God, Paul, why do you call him Slime?"

" 'Cause that's his name. He doesn't mind."

"Spare me," she said, and served him a plate of scrambled eggs, saying that since he was otherwise engaged she had some chores to do. In the week they had been in Welling they had done nothing around the house. The cellar particularly needed to be cleaned and maybe later Piggy could help her take the wash to the laundromat.

After breakfast Piggy followed his mother down the creaky flight of stairs from the kitchen to the basement, where they filled up three extra-large Hefty bags with old debris, ancient newspapers, empty bottles, and a clanging symphony of rusty tin cans. Then Jeannie had him sweep the floor while she scoured the battered but functional deep freeze that sat at the far end of the long, chilly cellar just next to the boiler room.

Finally she sent him off to play when she caught him making lazy circles on the cellar windows with Fantastik.

He prowled mournfully through the house, room by room, until he reached the attic, where, he decided, he could set up the home lab he had never had the space for in the Boston apartment. That cheered him a little bit and he went back downstairs to lug up the cartons containing his equipment. When he pushed the two big boxes to one side of the attic, he thought he better go ask Jeannie if it was okay. She always got so nervous about experiments, especially now, after his *mistake*. Piggy shivered as he stomped down the stairs, forcing his thoughts away from that terrible day.

Jeannie, surprisingly, said it was okay, as long as he promised not to blow them both up, or the house either. He sighed with annoyance and reminded her that he wasn't into explosives.

Once upstairs again he changed his mind about setting up the lab just then and returned to the kitchen, where, with his small case of tools, he checked BeeBee's inner workings. Finding all the wires in place, the batteries functioning, he closed Bee's flap and the two of them went out onto the back porch.

The day had turned sunny though it was definitely cool, with winter waiting not too far off. Pig went back inside and got his down vest, then returned to sit on the porch steps and look out over the small back lawn—the grass all old and parched and dead—across the slope of the embankment and the river. Mason was on the other side, all the windows in all the buildings blinking like headlights, and he catapulted back to his dream—to Bee coming to get him, BeeBee with eyes that sparked like sizzling electrical shorts. He shivered.

There was a small wooden shed at the side of the lawn, and Pig left BeeBee on the porch and went down, pushing the door open on its creaking hinges. Inside, there was an old rake with two of the tines missing, a basket, and a shovel with its edges eaten away. He looked through the dirt-encrusted window that faced the house on the other side and saw the little girl staring in at him. For a moment they blinked at one another, her face cobwebbed in the gray light, her chin just clearing the edge of the glass. Piggy didn't know if she could see him clearly, but for once he took his courage in hand—as his father would say—and shouted hello. Then he raced outside and around to the side of the shed, leaned over the foot-high wire fence that separated the yards, and shouted hello again. She bellowed hello right back at him. Which was how Piggy finally met Samantha Pringle.

"It's Sam for short," she said, " 'cause my father wanted a boy and I wasn't no boy."

"Yeah," Piggy said, "I can see that," wondering why anybody would want someone different from Sam. She was so pretty—though she's just a kid, he thought, sniffing—even with the purplish-yellow bruise on her cheekbone just below her left eye. "What happened to your face?" he asked.

Sam, in her jeans, sweatshirt, and unzipped windbreaker, jiggled around like a puppet dancing and said, "Just fell, I guess."

"What do you mean, you guess? Don't you remember?"

Sam didn't answer, but wrinkling her pert upturned nose, she said, "You're the new kid, the one who invented the robot. Right? And that's him up there on the porch, huh?"

Piggy waved up at BeeBee and asked, "Want to meet him?"

Sam's eyes were just about the same color as the violets Pig had bought Jeannie for Mother's Day. They opened even wider, and as she swung her head the long blond hair flew around her in a silky curtain. Pig would have given anything to touch it. "Oh boy," Sam said, "sure I'd like to meet him. I've never met a robot before."

Piggy's stomach turned over and over in flip-flops, and he went after Sam on the strangest, softest cushion of air.

Jeannie came out on the back porch while Sam was throwing the big red ball to BeeBee. The robot, whirring right, then left at Pig's commands, was catching it. The girl was laughing happily and Piggy was smiling with pride. As Jeannie stood watching, smiling herself, thick gray clouds pushed against the sun and a cold wind scurried across the yard. On Sam's back porch a man appeared, big, heavy, with a flabby middle that spread in undulating jelly waves over his belt. He stood oblivious of the cold wearing an undershirt and a pair of chinos streaked with paint, and scowled at the children as BeeBee's metal arms rose and lowered, as the red ball arced through the sky. There was something ominous about the way he took up a corner of the light, like a complicated, jagged piece of a puzzle that had just been put in place.

The laughter rippled. BeeBee's beeps were as chirpy as birdsong. Then Sam looked up and saw her father. In one short second the whole tableau changed. Sam went slack, as though her bones had turned to water, her happy voice silenced. The red ball fell and rolled toward the back of the yard. Piggy, sensing something, glanced from the girl to the man, then back to Sam again. Without a word either from her or her father, she began trudging back the way she had come. Piggy and BeeBee and Jeannie on the porch saw her go, stepping over the low metal fence that jutted on the property line, right to her stoop and up, past her father, who followed her into the house. It seemed to the two people watching that his hand came down heavy on her shoulder just before the door closed, shutting them off from view. It seemed to them also that she cried out in pain, but the town fire siren went off right then, shrieking for a moment, and they might have been mistaken.

"Now what was that all about?" Jeannie asked.

"We were just playing," Piggy said, bewildered. "I don't get it."

"I don't either," Jeannie replied.

Later, over lunch, Slime tried to explain about Harry Pringle. "He's just an old drunk," the boy said, munching a peanut-butter sandwich Jeannie had made. "And mad as a wet hornet. You're always gonna see Sam walkin' around with a black eye or worse. I mean, he ties one on and then, wham, bang, starts to slug her. My ma says it's because he's upset over Sam's ma leavin' them and runnin' off."

Jeannie was horrified. "But she's only a little girl! He can't go around abusing her."

"Abusin'?" Slime said, his mouth still full. "He doesn't abuse her, just hits her every once in a while. Like my ma says, when he drinks too much. I mean, he drinks a lot too much. You can always see him when he gets off work from the factory falling down drunk outside the Five O'Clock bar. It's a shame and a scandal and something should be done about it, my ma says," he said, swallowing. "My dad says he should be locked up." Slime shrugged and asked, "Could I please have some more ginger ale?"

As they listened to this recitation, Piggy was confused but

Jeannie was angry, torn by a sense of helplessness. Having once, years before, taught school in a Boston slum, she was no stranger to the vagaries of parental behavior, and she also knew how futile it was even to attempt to intervene. But she worried now, regarding her own son. Pig's muscles had tensed and his sandwich lay half-eaten on the plate. He had his own misery and yet she could almost hear the cogs and wheels turning in that splendid mind of his as he tried to force himself to tamp down his rage. What could she possibly tell him that would help him to understand? That the human animal was a mysterious creature? That there was nothing either she or he could do about that pretty little girl until her father really hurt her, or worse? And perhaps not even then?

"He should be put away somewhere, like a dark hole in the ground with lots of snakes," Piggy said fiercely.

Slime, nodding his head, agreed. "That's what my dad says."

"Then why isn't he?" Pig asked, revolving on his chair and gazing up at his mother, his pale skin mottled with the anger he was attempting to hold in.

It was exactly what Jeannie was afraid he was going to ask. "Nobody likes to get involved in family disputes," she answered, feeling the presence of Sam, heavy as a mud slide, invade the kitchen from the house next door. "I mean," she tried to explain as Piggy's eyes held her nailed at the refrigerator, "the police and the courts have a hard time telling the difference between discipline and abuse."

"You discipline me, Mom," he shot back, "without giving me a black eye."

"That's not the point," she snapped.

"Then what is?"

They stared at one another until Slime said, "Mrs. Conway, can I have my ginger ale now, please?"

"Oh, Tommy, I'm sorry." She rushed to fill his glass from the bottle on the kitchen counter.

After lunch the two boys went up to Main Street and the five-and-dime, leaving BeeBee standing forlorn in the dining room. It's like having a dog, Jeannie said to herself for the thousandth time, as she dusted around the robot with the floor mop. She wouldn't have touched him for anything, afraid of unsettling his delicate mechanism, though Piggy had told her often enough that BeeBee was sturdy as a rock. Tony had once jokingly asked if Bee could be programmed to clean the house, and Piggy had obligingly put in another microchip, or whatever it was he did in Bee's inner cavity, and taught him how to push the vacuum cleaner. Unfortunately he couldn't get Bee to run the Hoover around the furniture, so BeeBee was only helpful in a totally empty room. Jeannie laughed remembering how the robot had knocked over an end table and made more of a mess than he had ever cleaned up. She wiped his metal face with the cloth she was using to do the windowsills.

"You're a great kid, BeeBee," she said, and began to cry. She sat down hard on one of the imitation Hepplewhite chairs and stared at Bee—who seemed through her clouded vision as runny as yellow paint—and cried and cried. "I have not cried at all, not through any of this whole awful business, Bee," she said. "Not once have I let go. I have done all the right things and been as tough and strong as you are. So what's wrong with me now?"

But BeeBee had no words of wisdom for Jeannie, and finally she went into the kitchen and brewed herself a strong cup of coffee. The tears kept sliding down her face and she wiped at her eyes, blowing her nose in a fistful of paper napkins.

She felt like a fool to be sitting at the table—her own kitchen table from the Boston apartment—crying her heart out when, she told herself, she should be concentrating on putting her life in order again. But gazing around as if charting the landscape of this new existence, she thought that all she wanted to do was to go on crying about the old one.

Before, there had always been Tony, and now there was no Tony and she was frightened. She wanted to believe that there was nothing to be scared about, that life in Welling would uncoil itself in one long seamless strip of time. She wanted to believe that Piggy was going to be just fine, that eventually all the nightmares would be blown away. But she didn't buy any of it. There was a quivering in the pit of her stomach that ran right through her flesh to her bones.

Outside, the wind came off the river, swept over the small dead lawn and rattled the windowpanes. The day had grayed again and the sky was heavy with unshed rain. In the kitchen the light was dim and the corners of the room had filled with shadows.

Jeannie was afraid to move, to speak. She simply sat and let a numbing weariness cover her as she watched the smoke from the cigarette she lit curl up in a spume. And no matter how much she tried not to think of it, the only thought reverberating in her mind was that she was alone, utterly and completely alone.

4

Woolworth's smelled, much to Piggy's amazement, exactly like the Woolworth's at home. If he closed his eyes he'd have been right back in Boston sailing down the aisles to buy his school supplies and then, as a treat, a candy apple, all sticky and crunchy and sweet.

Only he wasn't in Boston, he was in Welling, and as he and Slime prowled along the counters poking at the merchandise, he couldn't help but notice that it was a smaller store, a shabbier one too, and there were fewer items from which to choose. Also, there weren't many people. On this early Saturday afternoon Pig could hear his own footsteps echoing along the wooden floors.

They stopped by a rack of paperbacks, but except for a few romance titles Pig saw nothing except how to cook chicken or how to lose weight. He sighed and moved on, catching up with Slime in an aisle stocked with toys. Pig picked up a yo-yo and let it loop from his hand, but he couldn't get it to work and it rolled along the floor at the end of the string.

"Boys!" A fat woman with hair the color of eggplant tangled high on her head scooped down and yanked the yo-yo away. She wound it up and tucked it neatly into the symmetrical display. "Do you want something?" she asked, watching

Pig out of heavily lined small eyes in a doughy face as white as Wonder Bread.

"Just looking," he said and glanced around for Slime, who had moved across the store to the T-shirts.

Her bright red lips moved over one another as if they weren't attached. "Maybe something mechanical?" she asked. "One of the wind-ups?" She grabbed a small monkey crouched over a drum; when you turned the key, the monkey would bang rhythmically.

"What?" Pig backed away as the saleswoman thrust the toy into his face. He came up hard against the opposite counter. They were at the end of an aisle by the far wall of the store. There was nowhere to go unless he could get past her, but she stood like an overstuffed piece of furniture, and wouldn't let him by.

"You're the kid who built the robot," she said finally, inspecting him as though he were one of her toys. "The smart one," she added, bending forward slightly, hands curled on hips, as if she were searching for a flaw in him.

"Excuse me," he said politely, remembering how Jeannie always said there was never any acceptable reason to be rude, and tried to inch by her. For a moment it seemed as if she wasn't about to let him go. Piggy flushed with anger, thinking: What does she expect, that she'll wind me up and I'll play my drums?

They eyed one another and a prickle of heat flared at the back of Pig's neck. He was just about to yell and ask her what she wanted of him—if she wanted anything at all except to stare at him just as she would at the toy monkey—when Slime shouted from two aisles away, "Com'on, Pig, let's go get ice cream."

The woman dropped back and Piggy slid by her, the stale, overly sweet smell of her flowing about him in a cloud. She pivoted around on small, daintily shod feet as Pig ran to catch up with Slime.

"That saleslady is weird," he said when they were out on the sidewalk.

"Huh?" Slime peered back through the big window. "You mean Mrs. Donovan?"

"The one in toys with the funny-colored hair."

"Mrs. Donovan. She's in the sodality with my mother." He

shrugged. "The Ice Cream Hut's down this way. They have the best shakes."

The Ice Cream Hut sat in the middle of a parking lot and was trimmed up to look like a Swiss chalet. It didn't, Piggy thought, as he settled on a banana split, feeling slightly guilty over what his mother would say if she found out. She was always trying to get him to grab a piece of fruit or a carrot—a carrot!—if he wanted a snack. But as he'd once told her, ice cream wasn't a snack, it was an essential.

They were just finishing when the waitress came over to write up the check. She was a young woman with pyramids of hair, a nameplate that said "Myra," and a uniform just a shade too tight. Pig thought she was very pretty except for all the makeup she wore layered on her face.

"All right, fellas," she said, as wetting her lips she totaled the bill, "that's four-twenty-five."

"Could you please tell us what each one owes?" Slime asked.

"Two-fifty for me and a dollar-seventy-five for you," Piggy said automatically. Myra looked up surprised. "Without the tip, of course."

"Hey," she said, "how'd you do that?"

"Do what?" Pig replied, bewildered.

"The check."

"Oh, he can do lots of things like that," Slime chimed in. " 'Cause he's a genius. He's even built a robot that's just as real as a living person." He smiled, looking proudly at his friend.

Pig squirmed around. From the corner of his eye he saw Myra staring at him. Finally she said, "You must be the new kid over at the school. The one who moved into River Street. Yeah, I know who you are now. I heard a couple of guys talking about you this morning. How weird you were . . ." She stopped, embarrassed, and amended, "I mean, how different. Different from the other kids in town. Even from the ones at school. Like that kid who was written up in the paper a couple of months ago, the one who built the atom bomb."

Weird, Piggy was thinking with some pain. He wasn't weird. That Mrs. Donovan in the five-and-dime was weird. Not him. "I'm not interested in bombs," he said, getting off the stool and fishing out a fistful of money from his pants pocket. "Com'on, Slime, let's go," he said, pushing two dollars and fifty cents, and then another quarter for a tip, across the counter.

"Okay." Slime nodded, and handed Myra his share of the bill.

"Tell your mom I said hi," she told Slime automatically as she scooped the money up. "And, hey, I wouldn't mind seeing that robot sometime. I just loved *Star Wars*."

They left the Ice Cream Hut and threaded their way through the parked cars, back out onto Main Street.

Slime was chattering as they walked along, oblivious of Piggy's silence, which was as weighty as lead. Pig couldn't help thinking that everyone they passed on the street was looking at him strangely, whispering about him as they went by, as if he were an alien who had just set down in a spaceship. *Weird*. The word kept tolling in his head like the echo of a carillon, and he was conscious of his legs, his arms, his pudgy body, his pale blond hair. Nervously he pushed his glasses up the bend of his nose and jammed his hands into his jeans pockets. I'm not weird, he repeated to himself again as they trudged by the hardware store, the post office, Suzette's Beauty Parlor, where he was sure the row of women under their huge metal dryers were whispering, *weird, weird,* as they watched him through their front window. The boys walked on, by Casey's Drugs, where the white-jacketed clerk sweeping the sidewalk seemed to chart their passage. Stein's Clothing—"Garb for the Whole Family"—was next, and even the mannequins were eyeing him.

When they reached Corney's Newsstand Slime pulled him inside to riffle through the comic books.

Corney was a one-legged survivor of the Second World War—an event so far in the past for Pig that it had the patina of an old painting gathering dust. He didn't like kids much, Slime confided. Corney thumped his wooden leg—wooden right up to the knee, Slime had whispered.

"Get your hands off the merchandise if you're not going to pay for it," he snarled.

"We're trying to make up our minds, Corney," Slime called over the racks to the little man hunched on a stool behind the candy counter.

"Don't take you all day, kid. You're supposed to be one of the smarties, going to that fancy school the other side of the river."

Slime wiggled his eyebrows at Piggy and shrugged off Corney's annoyed rumbling.

Having finally agreed on one *Spiderman* and one *Amazing Horror*, they left Corney's and Piggy asked, "Doesn't it bother you?"

"What?"

"People always making cracks about you going to Mason."

Slime, shuffling along the sidewalk, trying to read one of the comics as he walked, replied, "Nah, besides, what can I do about it? As my father says, most people are just bone ignorant, so you're best off not paying them any attention."

Piggy thought that over for a moment, and seeing the wisdom of Slime's father's advice, turned away from the man in the lumber jacket who stopped to stare at them. He asked instead, "Sam doesn't go to Mason, does she? I mean, I didn't see her there."

Slime broke into a big grin and hopped around Pig, crying, "Hey, you got a crush on Samantha Pringle, don't you? *Don't you!*"

Piggy blushed deep mauve and frantically glanced right, then left, anywhere but at Slime. His heart was chugging in his chest like a faulty engine, though he wasn't sure why. "Don't be a dingbat," he said, poking out at the other boy, who danced back. "She's just a kid and . . . and skinny!" he concluded as if that settled that.

But as they walked along he couldn't stop thinking about Sam, remembering what Slime had told him her father did to her when he got drunk and mad. He couldn't imagine what it was like to get hit, and by somebody you cared about, somebody who should have cared about you, *protected* you. What did it feel like to have that much control over somebody, to be in such command as Pig was with BeeBee? To create something, somebody, just for pain?

Suddenly Slime jerked to a halt and said, "Hey, com'on, this is where I live. Let's go meet my mom and dad. Maybe you can sleep over tonight, okay?"

"Oh, sure, great." Piggy laughed, relieved that the subject of Sam was dropped.

The discreet sign on the front door of the cedar-shingled building read "Toomy's Funeral Parlor." The boys entered through a big dark door into a long hall where viewing rooms, Slime informed Piggy offhandedly, stood at either side. At the far end of the hall, stairs led up to the second floor, where the Toomys lived.

They actually lived in an undertaker's, Piggy realized for the first time with a shiver.

Behind *that* small door, Slime explained like a tour guide as they headed for the rear of the building past the third, smaller viewing room to his father's private office, the steps went down to the basement, where they did the embalming, where the dead were kept until they were ready to be shown.

Piggy felt his skin prickling, as though he had crossed a border, gone through a gate, been taken past an arbitrary line which separated the living from the dead. Though the funeral parlor was amazingly ordinary, with walls paneled halfway up and pale blue striped wallpaper above that, folding chairs, standing lamps, little barrel end tables set here and there to hold ashtrays and boxes of Kleenex, the tissues jauntily popped up, the air was stale with the lingering stench of flowers, the ghosts of floral arrangements. *Rest in peace*.

They found Mr. Toomy sitting at his big mahogany desk. He was dressed in a black suit, with a narrow black tie against a white shirt, and looked just as Piggy imagined an undertaker would, down to his gleaming polished black shoes and up to his bald head and solemn, slightly creased face. He rose from his swivel chair and limply shook hands with Piggy as though Piggy was bereaved and said to Slime, "Your mother's been wanting you. You didn't take the garbage out."

Upstairs Slime's mother bustled in the kitchen like a twitchy hen. She was almost identical to her son, only more compact, square from her shoulders straight down to the floor, geometrically precise. Also like Slime she talked nonstop, her voice running on a track that cut and sliced through his, so that the two of them were jabbering at the same time in a cacophony that left Piggy confused. It seemed, however, to make perfect sense to them, for, as they both reached the end of each long, rambling, individual paragraph at the same time, and shuddered to a dead stop, they nodded their heads.

It was decided that Pig could spend the night, though he wasn't really sure he wanted to, wasn't sure he wouldn't have bad dreams with the dead lying in wait for their graves beneath his bed. But it would have been worse to risk this new friendship by saying no.

Piggy swallowed and said, "Great, but I better go home and ask my mother."

"Okay, I'll go with you."

"No you won't. Get in your room and do that homework you were so worried about. Then when Paul comes back at suppertime you'll have it done," his mother said, flapping her hands at him.

"Ma—"

"Don't 'Ma' me! Get!" She raised the big wooden spoon she was using to stir something that smelled wonderful in a large cast-iron pot and brandished it at Slime.

"I'll come back later if it's okay," Piggy said, hurrying for the stairs.

Out on Main traffic had picked up for Saturday afternoon. Farmers were coming in from the country in their pickups and the street was crowded. Piggy saw two boys he thought he recognized from Mason and tried to say hello, but they whizzed by him and went into Corney's. He felt, all at once, bereft and alone. Everybody seemed to belong but him. Everyone had a purpose, while he was aimlessly drifting, looking in the store windows—Jackie's Gifts, the Baby Boutique, the Flower Pot. He kept walking until he reached Bridge Street, where he went down the slight slope to River and home, trying to organize his thoughts, his feelings about Welling, about this new life.

There wasn't anything wrong with Welling, he realized as he neared their house, anything any reasonable kid would want to complain about, but there was nothing to do if you couldn't ride a bike or play baseball or just hang out. It was quiet, comatose . . . it was boring. And it wasn't Boston. It wasn't home.

And he knew with a sinking feeling in the pit of his stomach that he'd always be a stranger here. Worse, he'd always be different, people would continue to watch him as though they were looking through the wrong end of a telescope and he was something unrecognizable on the other side.

Suddenly he had a fierce longing to make it all go away, the town, the river which he could hear now churning along, Mason Prep, their house and all its strangeness. He wanted to be out on the Common having his father try to teach him to fly a kite, or walking down the cool corridors of the museums looking at the paintings that his mother liked so much. He wanted his old life back without any changes, with his father coming home every night from the office and his mother all smooth and smiling without those tiny worry lines rimming her eyes.

There was a pent-up geyser in his chest just waiting to erupt. He could feel the slide and surge and the pain, the urge to strike out, break something, inflict impossible damage.

He had felt exactly the same way that afternoon in the lab at Height. The taste of bile in his mouth, the pulsing of the vein in his temple. His mind clouding up. And now if he shut his eyes he knew he would hear Bertram Lennard's voice, rising and falling, digging furrows in his brain until he, Piggy, exploded in one long, awful moment that seemed, there in the fog, to go on and on and on.

Right now he wasn't sorry about what had happened, not at all. And if Bertram Lennard had miraculously appeared before him on the front porch of the house on River Street, Piggy knew he'd do something equally terrible to the boy. It was as if he had split apart and become two people, one of whom worked the mechanism and one of whom sat captive inside, howling in an unending scream.

He opened the front door, which they never kept locked *because this wasn't Boston*, and entered the house, slamming the door forcefully behind him so that the whole structure seemed to shudder on its foundation. In midafternoon the living room was sooty without any sun coming in through the windows, the light already tilting over the far side of town as the storm changed its mind and shifted to the west. The air was heavy, tiny dust motes swimming in it.

Jeannie called out through the gloom from the kitchen. Piggy followed the sound of her voice. Passing the dining room, he automatically threw BeeBee's switch, and the robot, coming to life, rolled after his creator.

The light in the kitchen was better with the big overhead globe on. Piggy blinked in the whiteness reflected from the appliances, from the counter running along one wall, from the table at which his mother sat.

Piggy could tell she had been crying. Her eyes were swollen and red, and there was a pile of soggy napkins littered about. She was smoking too, which she never did unless she got terribly upset. And suddenly, seeing her there looking so lost, so bereaved—like one of Mr. Toomy's mourners—the cap on the geyser in his chest lifted.

"I hate it here!" he howled. The ground rumbled. Piggy could feel it in his legs, rising up, as the geyser erupted from the boiling caldron of despair, spewing out the hot, scalding anger. His vision was so blurred that his mother, the whole kitchen, went hazy. He shook his head back and forth and kept yelling, "I hate it! I hate this place!"

"Paul, what is the matter with you?" his mother cried, coming off her chair.

"It's not supposed to be this way!" he wailed.

"Paul!" she cried out again, but he was moving, lurching around BeeBee, who clicked, red eyes rolling up and down as though the rage had infected him too. And the fear.

In a moment there was the *thud, thud* of his sneakers pounding the stairs. Then the shuddering slam of his bedroom door.

Jeannie didn't stir, her hands pressed against her cheeks, until she thought to turn off BeeBee's switch, leaving him abandoned in the doorway. Gradually, as dusk fell, the house settled back on its moorings, though if Jeannie listened carefully she could hear, far off, the sound of wild and furious weeping.

5

Piggy didn't hear the boom of the heavy metal fire door slamming shut outside the lab in the Science Building basement. Nor did he hear the clack of footsteps echoing off the cement-block walls and concrete floors. All his attention was focused on a haggard-looking Dr. Johanson, who was quaking with anger. His face was on fire and the sheaf of manuals he held in his hand shook like leaves in the wind.

Having tried for twenty minutes to have a reasonable discussion with the science professor, Piggy now was electrified with rage. His voice was spiraling to the ceiling in an inarticulate shrill, his hands curled into fists on his hips.

"Hello, everybody. What's the fight about?" Jeannie asked, stepping into the lab. She caught Piggy on the high pitch of his shriek, and he turned to her helplessly, knowing he could never explain.

Dr. Johanson's mouth kept opening and closing as if he wasn't getting enough air. When he finally could speak, he rolled off a long stream of technical jargon at Piggy's mother. Her face clouded over and she got that glazed look in her eyes which Piggy knew so well. She never did understand much about science, and there were moments when Piggy suspected that she found his brilliance appalling. Many times, in fact, when she probably wished he was just like every other kid. Not stupid exactly, but not especially smart.

"Mrs. Conway," Dr. Johanson was saying, drawing himself up as he tried to reclaim his dignity, "your son is . . . your son is . . . disrespectful." He placed the manuals on the counter and smoothed his sparse hair, then shot out his cuffs from the natty blue blazer with the Mason crest on the pocket. "He presumes," the professor continued, his hands shaking so badly that he had to shove them out of sight, "that he knows more than I do. That there is nothing to learn, nothing I can teach him. He is . . ."—he paused for breath—"insulting."

"Paul!"

"Mom, I'm not," he cried, gritting his teeth. "But he doesn't know what he's talking about. He read a couple of trade magazines last night and he's trying to teach me—teach *me*!—about semiconductor processing techniques. But when I brought up alpha particles he just—"

"Enough, Paul." She held up her hand. "I for one have no idea what you're talking about and I doubt I ever will. Dr. Johanson," she said, turning away from Pig with a furious look that made him cringe, "I apologize for Paul, but sometimes he does get carried away." The professor started to say something. "No, wait, please. I know that Paul's an incredible challenge, especially in the area of computer science, but don't feel badly if he knows more than you do. He knows more than most people." Piggy could tell from the way she said it that it disconcerted her as much as it made her proud.

"That may well be," Johanson said, his eyes glittering dangerously, "but I do not like having my limitations shoved in my face."

"I'm terribly sorry. I'm sure Paul didn't mean it." She gave Pig a sour look. He had to bite down hard not to scream that he had meant every word.

"Well, I am not so sure," he said pompously. His face, a corrugated map of age, was a mottled red.

When he turned toward Piggy his teeth were bared. He really doesn't like me, Pig thought with sudden surprise. While he had always had problems with peers, he was so accustomed to grown-ups finding him intriguing that he was shocked. Even when he disagreed with adults, or proved them wrong, they never actually disliked him. But it was obvious that he set Dr. Johanson's temper very badly on edge.

"Our discussion, if you could call it that," Johanson was continuing, "was over the purposes of science, what its *raison d'être* should be. I, for one, believe that science must be concerned with the implementation of life, geared to increase our understanding." His voice skidded and broke but he swept on. "I do not, emphatically do not, think that science should replace life. What is man's is man's, but what is God's is God's!"

"Of course you're entitled to your opinion, but I—"

Interrupting, he cried furiously, "It's not merely my opinion, Mrs. Conway." For a moment it seemed as though he was going to stamp his foot. "There is right and there is wrong in this world."

"Now, really," she flared, her control beginning to ebb, "let's try to remember that Paul is a child."

"Then please have him behave in a more appropriate, childlike manner instead of performing a rather arrogant impersonation of Albert Einstein."

"Just a minute, Dr. Johanson," Jeannie cried, but he wasn't listening. He was out the door, his firm steps pounding away. Piggy, embarrassed and upset by his mother's distress, quickly began straightening an array of tools on the bench, aligning them neatly like soldiers.

"Alpha particles my foot," she said to his back. "That wasn't your fight with Dr. Johanson, was it?"

"Not exactly," he whispered without turning around, not wanting to meet her gaze.

"You were telling him that eventually science would be able to create human life—not out of a test tube, but mechanized life. Right? Sophisticated robots without all the deficits of people. That was the fight, or along those lines, with all the technical jargon thrown in. *Wasn't it?*"

"Yes, Mom." He sighed wearily, stuffing his notebooks into his book bag. He pulled on his denim jacket and slung the bag over his shoulder. "And it's true."

"Paul, everything you say might be true. I certainly don't know. But with a man like Dr. Johanson you have to learn to soft-pedal it a bit. I gather he's been teaching since the year one, and is very concerned with saving face. Which means that he might not totally appreciate the new applications of science the way you do. Do you understand what I'm getting at?"

He bobbed his head and stared straight down at the space between his splayed sneakers. He heard the rippling disapproval in Jeannie's voice and sensed that she wanted to grab him by the shoulders and shake him hard.

"Listen, you can't ride roughshod over him. He won't sit still for it. Besides, according to Mrs. Mellon, he's a very devout Catholic, so what you're saying about life and science must be anathema to him. Man, to his way of thinking and believing, must never usurp the place of God, and in many complicated ways I'm not sure he isn't right," she said with sudden intensity.

Piggy, his temper once again dangerously fraying, whipped his head up and glared at her. "There is no God, Mom. Superstitious, ridiculous nonsense. A holdover from a primitive past." He spoke quietly but with a throbbing passion, though they had had this discussion many times before. "Besides," he continued as he retrieved BeeBee from the back of the lab, "he was trying to prove to me it couldn't be done. His personal feelings are one thing, but he's a real asshole if he thinks he can explain why it's not possible."

With an uncomfortable silence hanging over their heads, the three of them left the Science Building and crossed the campus to the parking lot. Before they climbed into the car

Piggy saw with mixed feelings that one of the maintenance people had painted "Conway" on the small slab of concrete at the front.

They headed out toward the bridge and met Peter Bayard's MG at the intersection where one road climbed back along the far sweep of Mason to the field, the other over to Welling Proper. He waved at them and as Jeannie stopped, Piggy tensed. She rolled down the window and Peter came over and said, "Hi, how are you? Paul, how's it going?"

"We're both fine," Jeannie answered quickly. "You?"

"Okay. Listen, I was wondering, would you like to go up to Binghamton, the big city, for dinner a week from Saturday, and maybe take in a movie?"

Piggy, watching Jeannie's cheeks go red as she told Peter that would be very nice, went all tight and hard. Through stiff lips he just managed to ask, "What about me?"

"Sorry, fella, I'd like to take you too, but the MG is a two-passenger car," Peter said, smiling, oblivious to Pig's glare of hatred.

I knew he was going to be trouble, I just knew it, Piggy fumed as Jeannie shifted into drive and started over the bridge.

"Why do you have to go to dinner with him? We can have dinner at home like we always do."

"Because I want to, that's why. I'll fix you something and leave it in the oven. Maybe you can invite Tommy over to spend the night."

Piggy persisted, feeling a worm gnawing at his insides. "Why do you want to go?"

"Because I want to," she said in what Piggy recognized as her most reasonable tone of voice, the one that always drove him to the edge of screaming.

"Why?"

"Why what?"

"Why do you want to?"

"Because."

"Because why?"

"Paul—"

"I don't see why," he rushed on, giddy with panic, "you have to go have dinner with some dumb guy when you could stay home with BeeBee and me. We could play Scrabble. You're good at that."

"Thanks. Glad to hear I'm good at something," she said.

Piggy, ignoring her sarcasm, wouldn't let up. "Then have the Mellons over for dinner," he insisted. "We'll make our special spaghetti. And maybe you could ask Slime's mother and father."

"That's a great idea. We'll do it another time."

"What's wrong with a week from Saturday?"

"I am going out with Dr. Bayard. And that's it. Stop making such a big deal," she said as the car came off the bridge.

"Wait!" Piggy cried, his attention finally diverted. "There's Sam."

Jeannie stopped and Piggy, rolling down the window, yelled, "Hey, Sam, com'on, we'll give you a ride." Which was silly, since both their houses were only a block away, but Piggy flushed with unaccustomed pleasure at the sight of the little girl. When she hopped into the back seat with a big hello for Bee, Pig thought his heart would break.

"Did you have a nice day at school, Sam?" Jeannie asked in her best mother voice.

"Yes, ma'am."

"Come home and have some juice and cookies with me. And after, we can play Monopoly," Piggy urged, leaning over the front seat.

There was a pause before Sam replied, whispering, "Okay. But I can't stay late. I gotta get home and make dinner."

"You do the cooking?" Piggy asked, amazed.

"Uh huh. I can't make too many things, but I'm learning. Lucky my pa is a real meat-and-potato person so he doesn't get too mad if I burn something. I mean, if you throw some ketchup into a stew it's hard to tell if the meat is too well done."

She sounded like a shrunken adult sitting in the back seat. Holding on to Bee's pincer as if BeeBee were just another child, as if he wasn't exactly a machine, she smiled, and Piggy, trapped in the wide violet eyes, felt faint.

Sam was as happy as she had ever been, happier than she had been in a long time as she sat at the table in the Conways' kitchen and drank a frothy milkshake Piggy's mother made in a blender. Piggy was a funny kid, and sometimes— like the other day when he had helped her with her homework—more of an adult than the kids she was used to. He was awful smart, building BeeBee and all. Which was more akin to a miracle than anything Father Duffy spoke about during the sermon on Sunday morning, Sam thought. Bee was a big old toy and yet different because she and Piggy could talk to him and he understood. She just knew he did by looking into his flashing eyes and at his metal face that would seem to soften into expressions of a human being.

Sam would have stayed at the table, or later on the living-room floor where she sat cross-legged playing Monopoly, forever if it was possible. But *he* would be coming home from the factory soon, though maybe not. Maybe he'd stay in the Five O'Clock and get looped, which happened often enough.

With Corney that old dirty bugger—

Her mother said that clear as a bell in her head. Sam looked up expecting to see her coming in through the Conways' front door, swinging her handbag, fluffing her hair. . . .

Ma, not here, there . . . home.

She had to get home.

"I gotta go," she said, scrambling up, scattering the pieces across the board in her haste.

"Hey, not yet. It's early," Pig cried.

"No, I gotta leave right now."

"Sam?" Jeannie said in surprise as the little girl whipped by her in the kitchen, the blond hair flying. BeeBee beeped when he rolled onto the linoleum, Piggy at his side, and they watched out the window as Sam raced over the lawn, neatly jumping the fence.

"What's wrong?" Jeannie asked.

But there's nothing wrong, my mom's just coming back, Sam would have answered. She darted into her own kitchen, slamming the door, and as she had been doing for months and months now—even knowing it was hopeless—she searched every room. Up the stairs. Down again. Even in the cellar and the old coal bin. Looking, looking.

I heard you. You were talking in my head and if you were really far, far away like he says, with never a mind for me, then why, why do I hear you so plain?

But her mother wasn't there. Sam sat on the steps going up to the second floor and listened to the old clock that had been her grandfather's—*how had she left that, a real genuine heirloom?*—the tears dripping in pathways down her cheeks.

The light waned outside the front windows and Sam knew she better go put the chicken up. *He* said he wanted chicken for dinner. It was something she'd never made before, but she would put it in a pot with lots of carrots and potatoes and onions just like a stew, so it couldn't be too bad. Only the tears kept coming if she didn't keep blinking her eyes. She wanted to be back at the Conways', in a house that seemed to her to be full of life, not dark and sooty, no matter how hard she cleaned. She wanted Jeannie to be making dinner, something that smelled like it would be good to eat. She wanted another milkshake.

"I want my mother!" she wailed, putting her head on her knees, and right then she hated Jeannie Conway simply because she was not her mother who had run off—

—*the no-good ungrateful bitch,* he said.

—*your fault,* he said, as he hit her, whacking her with the folded-up *Welling Weekly Times* like she was a dog who had wet the rug.

—*dirty,* he said, *just like her.*

Sam rubbed her eyes with her fists, then wiped her face with the bottom edge of her T-shirt. Running her tongue over the teeth in her lower jaw, she felt the loose molar. The bruise from the punch he had given her right in the face had faded, but the tooth was wobbly in its socket, and just didn't set right anymore. She thought that one day it would simply fall out and then she'd have a hole in her mouth. Not that it mattered much. People could live with lots of spare places between teeth, like old Mrs. Williams across the street and down two houses who didn't have but four or five on top. It was the hole in her heart that Sam was worried about, the big fat hole that if a person looked between the bones in her chest, was as plain as could be. The hole *she* put there when she ran off and left Sam with him.

If she wanted to go so bad, why didn't she take me too?

"I wouldn'ta been any trouble," she said aloud, but nobody answered.

There was nothing left to do but get up off the stairs and make the chicken for supper, which Sam did, gathering the darkness about her and thinking: Someday things will be different.

*   *   *

Harry Pringle wasn't thinking about supper, about the chicken, but he was thinking about Sam. Or rather about Sam's mother, Grace, whose face, as he conjured it up in his mind, high-boned and slippery-skinned, shifted and slid over Sam's, locked, then broke away, drifting off again.

In his foggy state, propped up on the bar of the Five O'Clock, he blearily watched Calloway straightening bottles against the large mirror that covered one wall. In that same mirror Harry saw himself and next to him Corney, whose bullet head and ugly shriveled face looked like something a diesel rig had run over. Scowling at his own reflection, Harry tried to still the buzzing inside his ears. Around his seventh or eighth beer the buzzing had begun, a deadly singing. Once when he was a kid he had upset a hive and he knew that high-pitched shrill which he had to escape, outrun, before it drove him mad. The buzzing always started when he had too much to drink—not that he ever thought of it as too much—and when he remembered Grace and because of her, Sam. Which he did, always when he'd had a couple of Buds. Grace was his demon, sitting on his chest, weighing him down, wringing the breath out of his lungs and leaving him gasping for air. And Sam, who resembled her down to the twitching of her eyebrows, was demonic too. Something from the night, from the darkness, from bad dreams, he thought sourly, and spat on the floor.

Corney was droning on at him. Most times Harry didn't listen to the old vet, who smelled bad and was a real pain in the ass, but right now the one-legged son of a bitch was saying something about his kid. His kid and the fat little weirdo who had moved in next door. Whatever it was, Harry didn't like it, and leaning forward, nearly losing his balance, he snarled, "Shut up!"

Corney raised one scrawny shoulder in a shrug and pushed his glass along the bar to Calloway for a refill. "Have it your own way," he said. "But if it was my kid, I wouldn't have her hanging around with no fruitcake and a robot. A robot for Christ's sake!" He shook his head in disgust. "No good's gonna come of that kid, the one who made the robot. I seen 'im and your Sam the other day walkin' along River. And that piece of tin chuggin' beside 'em." He hopped off the stool and imitated BeeBee, but Harry ignored him.

Harry was concentrating on the buzzing, trying to will it into a low hum. The buzzing, along with Corney's chatter, had given him a granddaddy of a headache. Levering himself off the bar stool, he wondered if there was something wrong with his brain. Don't give a fuck if there is, he thought boozily as he stumbled out of the Five O'Clock, while Corney, left behind, yelled: Where was he going, it wasn't closing yet.

Slipping and falling, going to his knees more than once and pulling himself up each time, he managed to reach River Street. He didn't have a car anymore, Grace had taken that too when she ran off, and sometimes he resented her as much for stealing his Ford as he did for leaving. Corney had said: You can always get another wife, but cars are expensive. He thought of the Ford with longing. It had great pickup.

"She was a good car!" he yelled into the night and the empty street, tears filling his eyes. He'd never get another car like her again, and the loss was as painful as a death.

His own house was dark, cobwebbed with shadows. But the Conway house had lights on both downstairs and on the second floor. Harry stopped his weaving, lurching dance and stood still, captured by the sight of the glowing windows.

That was where she went . . . where that kid and that thing were. He tried to remember exactly what it was that Corney had been babbling, but the other man's voice echoed senselessly in Harry's head like wind in a tunnel.

Someone moved past the front windows. He could just make out the shape behind the curtains, and without thinking he ambled off the walk onto the damp grass.

"House shoulda stayed empty," he mumbled as he neared the wall. "Damn school, damn kid, damn *thing*!" And then he wrenched the word out of the fog eddying in his mind. "Robot!" he snorted.

He went rigid, thinking sourly that she had been playing with that big toy when she shoulda been home taking care of the house. If he had had his way she never woulda gotten further than the yard. But when he tried to keep her at home after Grace ran off—home taking care of her father, which was only right—the school sent around the truant officer to tell him what was what in no uncertain terms. They didn't care that she couldn't get all the chores done. The law was the law and she had to go to school. But that didn't mean that she had to go next door and play with some fat kid and a robot. A robot! He snorted again.

There was a narrow slit between the soft white curtains and Harry peeked through, his face hugging the windowpane. He caught an amputated slash of the living room, the far end musty with shadows. By squinting and hulking up against the side of the house, he could just see into the kitchen. There was a flutter of movement and Jeannie Conway came into the living room, the light from the kitchen silhouetting her body beneath a gauzy nightgown. In one hand she carried a mug of something steaming, and a book in the other.

Harry's breath caught in his throat and his head started spinning. God damn, he thought, remembering how Grace would look before she made him turn off the light. It had been so long since he had had a woman that his whole body started throbbing as Jeannie lay down on the couch, the gown falling away from her long, thin legs before she pulled it back in place. Harry clutched at the glass, rooted in place like the old tree in the side yard. He wanted to reach right through the window and cup the rounded swell of her breasts. And why not, he mumbled, woman like her, she'd probably love it.

Neither of them moved for the longest while, until Harry got a cramp in his calf and started shaking his leg, and Jeannie, finishing whatever was in the mug, rose from the couch. She turned off the light and disappeared up the steps.

Harry, drawing away from the side of the house, gazed up to the second floor and saw a light come on just above where he stood. He could imagine her up there, getting ready for bed, and he wanted to watch her so badly that his mouth went dry. But then that light went off too and he was left standing in the dark, chilled and alone.

"Damn bitch," he said aloud, and thrashed across the lawn to his own front porch. He fumbled with the door that always stuck from the dampness, pounding at the wood just above the knob. It gave way suddenly and he half-fell into the living room. Through the archway at the opposite end he could see into the kitchen. The glaring lights seared his eyes. He stood blinking as if trying to remember where he was, then stumbled ahead.

Sam was asleep at the table, her head cradled on her arms, hair falling like spider's silk over the plate, the silverware, the napkins folded a degree off-center. There was an acrid smell coming from the big pot on the front burner. Harry lifted the lid and looked inside at a scrawny chicken, the skin scorched, and sticking to the bottom a shriveled mess of carrots, onions, potatoes. It was disgusting, and his stomach was already uneasy. The beer, sloshing in a tide, lurched, bile rising to his mouth.

Grace was a good cook, he had to give her that. And now all he got to eat was crap. Not that he was hungry right then. The thought of food, never mind the garbage in the pot, made him feel like throwing up. But the idea that he was condemned to eating . . . *Shit!* Not even a good meal anymore. Another black mark against his errant wife, whom Harry suspected of being out in the world somewhere having a good time with his car, and the two hundred and thirty-seven dollars she had taken from the joint account, while he was left here in Welling with burnt chicken in a pot and the damn kid.

Sam stirred, coming awake, and lifted her head, her face creased and wrinkly from sleep. "I made dinner but you was so late it got burnt."

Harry heard in her plaintive statement, a wail of complaint, heard Grace's *you no-good bum, drinking too much, smelling like a distillery, not giving us a pot to piss in* . . .

With Grace's endless whine buzzing in his ears, his head ached even more. So did his stomach, and the small of his back from that time two winters ago when he had fallen on the ice. All of him hurt as if he were plugged into the electric socket at the base of the wall, and he struck out, at Sam, at Jeannie in the house next door, at Grace with her piercing shrill complaints that etched his failings in acid. The plates skittered along the tablecloth. Silverware clattered to the floor. A chair overturned as if by itself, as his rage surged up.

He felt the soft flesh and small bones like the chicken in the pot, and bounced and shook it, her, Sam. His fists rising and falling, swaying from side to side, metronomed to the buzzing in his head as he punched away at Sam, who wept, pleading with him. She stumbled backward, searching for a corner, a hole to crawl into away from the flailing hands. He tried to punch his way back to a clarity of vision, to a silence so deep he could go to sleep in it without fear of waking up, but all that happened was that his arms began to ache, the muscles in his shoulders and up his neck, as if someone were pinching the small bones. Even the blood on his knuckles didn't soothe him, or settle the tossing stomach, the tide that was creeping up to his throat until he could feel it reach his mouth. In a lurch he turned and threw up, spewing vomit into the sink.

He ran the cold water and stuck his head under the faucet, chill streams cascading over his hair, down his neck, soaking his collar. He threw up again, and yet a third time, his retching a hideous sound, and didn't hear from the corner of the kitchen by the refrigerator the mewing, nor the scratching as Sam on her hands and knees crawled over the linoleum, leaving in her wake tiny tracks of blood.

6

Piggy had a free period after English and he decided on this rainy, dreary Monday to use it in the library researching his paper on George Orwell. He left Humans, struggling down the steps with BeeBee in his arms, into a mist as filmy as cobwebs which left damp patches on his cheeks. He thought, as he put Bee on the sidewalk and flipped his switch, that among the many factors which made Mason more difficult than Height was how the new school sprawled across its grassy campus. At Height there was only one building for Bee to follow him through, but here there was endless, constant maneuvering, up steps and down, along tilting walks where, if Pig wasn't careful, BeeBee would just roll away. It scared him how one day, if he wasn't paying attention, Bee could just keep going, rolling right off the bank and into the Susquehanna.

The light, chilly rain slid down Piggy's collar and over Bee's casing as they went along the path to the big red building that resembled a prison block. Pig sighed and was just about ready to struggle Bee up the steep, high stairs when Larry Houser came through the wide doors. Piggy had a rush of hero worship as the older boy bounced down the steps, his blond hair flying.

"Hey," he said, landing just a few feet from where Piggy and Bee stood watching him, "need some help with your robot?"

So tongue-tied he couldn't speak, Piggy just nodded his head as Larry came toward them. In one swift, graceful motion, he hoisted Bee up and delivered him to the wide porch, as if the robot weighed no more than a paper clip.

"There he is, ready to roll," Larry said, smiling.

Piggy was trying to think how to say thank you, since simple words seemed inadequate, when Barry Rogan, his black leather jacket gleaming from the rain, came up behind them and said, "Hey, Houser, com'on, we're gonna be late for Government."

With a wave of his hand Larry raced down the steps, jumping the last five, as Piggy stared after him, his eyes shining with appreciation. And then he heard Barry say, "What were you doing with the fat kid?"

"Aw, nothing," Larry replied, "he's just so helpless I was giving him a hand."

Piggy's cheeks burned and he quickly turned his back, face to face with Bee, who stood waiting impassively to be brought back to life.

Inside the library, cold and unfriendly as a tomb, Piggy blinked back tears, his eyes moist and unfocused behind his rain-streaked glasses. Opening his jacket, he dragged a corner of his shirt out of his pants and cleaned the lenses. But when he pushed the glasses back on his nose, the room still shimmered before him. I am not helpless, he thought. I can take care of myself, Bee too. But he was fat, he acknowledged unhappily, feeling the extra weight like cement hanging on his frame.

Slowly he and Bee made their way to the desk, where Miss Howard, the librarian, watched them disapprovingly out of tiny birdlike eyes. Grayish hair as tangled as seaweed stood out from her head and sprouted several yellow pencils. "I hope," she said, "you don't think you're about to bring *that* in here." She poked a long finger with a bright red nail in Bee's direction and the robot beeped back at her. But the librarian was impassive. "I don't like it in the building." She swiveled her gaze to Piggy and added, "This is a library. It's supposed to be quiet in here."

"But I have nowhere to leave him, and I have to do some research," Piggy said, almost crying in earnest now.

She said, "I'm not running a hardware store," then, "Oh, all right, just put him over there by the umbrella stand."

"Would you watch him, please," Piggy said in his smallest voice, feeling her disapproval pound at him like a hammer.

"Have you read that sign, young man?" she asked.

Piggy raised his head and saw high up above the desk: "WE WILL NOT BE RESPONSIBLE FOR PERSONAL BELONGINGS."

Reluctantly Pig left his friend—with arms extended, pincers wide—hoping no one would go near him and tamper with his parts, and entered the main section of the high-ceilinged reading room. Off to one side was the card catalog. But when he looked for the *Or* tray he saw it was missing. He thought of Jeannie saying when everything went wrong, *It's just one of those days*, and determined to think of it as that, but his mouth was sour and he wondered if he was coming down sick with something. If unhappiness could make you ill, then he should have been flat on his back in bed, the covers to his chin, a hot water bottle on his stomach. Looking at the empty space in the big wood cabinet, he felt as though he was staring down a long chute to despair. He might as well have been an illegal alien, so bereft and lost did he consider himself.

Helpless, he heard in his head, and turning from the file, wanted to shriek, *I am not!*

Through a returning haze of gathering tears, he saw Rich Bender from his English class. The file was in front of him and he was copying down a list of titles on a long yellow pad. Dragging his feet, Piggy crossed the room, circling the table until he could peer over the other boy's shoulder. It was, he saw, the *Or* tray.

"Excuse me," he whispered, "but will you be finished soon?"

Rich's close-cropped head shot up and a splotchy red face pitted with acne came into view. "What?"

"I need to use the tray. When you're done, I mean," Piggy said politely.

"Tough shit," Rich Bender replied, scowling, and returned to his writing.

Piggy, who had so little experience with other children, didn't know if he was kidding or not. He wondered if he should ask again or come back to the library after school. Human relationships were much more bewildering than mathematics or chemistry. He shuffled from one foot to the other trying to ferret out the right response. But again he heard Larry Houser saying, *helpless,* and the word skittered in his head. Forcibly he ejected it, and biting down hard, pushed his anger away.

"Listen," he said softly, "when you're finished I need the tray."

"Get lost, fatso," the other boy said in a loud whisper that had several people at nearby tables turning their heads.

Piggy flushed deep scarlet and buried his fists in his jacket pockets. As he bent forward, wanting to bash Rich Bender's head into the table, the heavy book bag slung across his shoulders almost toppled him over. He grabbed awkwardly for the edge of the table and the boy moved quickly aside, slapping at Pig's hand. "I said for you to get lost. When I'm done, you can have the damn tray." He scowled again, staring at Pig belligerently until Piggy, getting his balance, backed off.

"Okay," Pig said between tightened lips, as Bertram Lennard's shimmering face rose in front of him. For a moment he smelled the stench of burning flesh. As the specter of Bertram levitated before him, dead Bertram with his mouth wide in an unending shrill, Piggy ran. He bolted from the reading room, switching BeeBee on as he passed him and flew out of the library, the robot beeping in his wake.

Outside, the rain had become a downpour. *I hate it here!* Piggy cried silently as he trudged across the campus, pushing Bertram Lennard into the darkness from which he had sprung. *I hate it!*

Back in Humans he saw his mother in the distance, at the end of a long hall, and went the other way, ending up eventually at a large storage closet. He didn't want to see

Jeannie right then because she'd know in an instant that something was wrong, be able to decipher from his pained and troubled face the agony he was in. And what would he say then? "Take me back to Boston"?

He wanted to explain to her that he was trying to fit in, to belong. She suspected—and he knew his father did too—that he deliberately distanced himself. But that wasn't so. He wanted nothing more than to be a part of things, to look like Larry Houser or Barry Rogan, to have a fast mouth like Rich Bender. He wanted armor on his skeleton as thick and impenetrable as BeeBee's casing, and not any longer to be such a fragile creature made of flesh and bone.

Bee was on, and his flashing eyes seemed to be regarding Piggy sadly. "Only you understand, Bee, really you do." And for a moment at the end of the dark hall, he put his arms around the robot and listened to the reassuring grinding of his parts. Then the bell rang and Pig—pulling himself up, trying to be in one single, blazing instant, tall, strong, normal— went off to his next class.

When Henry Johanson arrived at the lab they were both waiting for him. The science professor was in his customary foul mood and just the sight of Piggy made his temperature soar. As for BeeBee, Henry Johanson hated the piece of tin, itched to take a sledgehammer to it and pound all that metal into paper clips.

Snarling "Hello," he perched on a stool as far down the bench as he could get from the boy and the robot, and read over the work on the ruled paper that Paul handed him. As he slowly worked his way along the lines, he was further annoyed that the boy's handwriting was so clear and concise. The subject was covalent bonding, and he searched intently for a mistake. His finger stopped on ammonia. He read and reread the answer, going light-headed with satisfaction.

"There's an error here," he said, unable to keep the pleasure he felt from being revealed in his voice.

"An error?" Piggy inched closer and stared down at the paper which the professor was stabbing with his fingernail. "Where's there an error?" Piggy asked.

"Here, here. Don't be dense. Ammonia."

Piggy carefully read over the section and then stated emphatically, "There's no error."

"Heaven help me!" Johanson said dramatically, raising his eyes to the ceiling. "Here I have a so-called genius on my hands and he doesn't know that there are two pairs of electrons in the nitrogen atom that have not and will not form covalent bonds with the respective hydrogen atoms." He brought his gaze down and leaned across the bench. "I think you have a certain lack in chemistry, young man, that bears looking into."

The boy began to quiver—just like the fat bowl of jelly that he is, Henry Johanson thought, so delighted with himself for having caught the genius out that he was barely able to restrain a grin from curling his lips.

"There is only one pair of electrons," Piggy insisted, scrunching up his face so tightly his blue eyes almost disappeared behind the glasses. "Not two pairs. One."

"Two."

"One."

"Two."

"One!"

"Are you contradicting me?" Johanson asked, knowing that his blood pressure was soaring.

"You're wrong."

They both glared, neither willing to back down. Finally the professor sneered, "Why don't you punch up the answer on the computer? If you're so sure of yourself, that is."

He followed Piggy across the room to the Apple and stood behind him, his arms crossed. Piggy punched the question in and they both saw it come up on the screen; then, in one rapid motion, the answer followed.

Henry Johanson's vision was obscured by a glaze of red, and he thought his heart was going to detonate in his chest. He clenched his elbows and felt himself begin to shake as a triumphant Piggy turned to face him. He knew he was within a millimeter of losing control of himself, of bending over and grasping the boy by the neck and shaking him until he broke into pieces. He had never been so . . . so outraged in his entire life, and as the humiliation rose up inside him, he experienced the panic of someone drowning. I have survived worse and I will survive this too, he told himself, but still, it took every bit of strength and dignity he could muster to turn on his heel and storm out of the lab, slamming the door behind him.

7

The rain had steadied to a fine drizzle by the time Jeannie met Piggy and BeeBee in the parking lot. Jeannie could tell it hadn't been the best of days even without asking, "How did it go?" and receiving a sour grunt in reply.

Piggy tucked Bee into the back seat, mumbling in the special way he had of speaking to the robot just under his breath, as if passing secret information that only Bee could understand and decipher. Then he got into the front seat and Jeannie pulled the car out of the lot and left Mason, crossing over Main Bridge and up the hill.

On Main the town seemed underwater, sluggish. The sidewalks were almost completely deserted except for a few amorphous gray figures bent double beneath unbrellas that threatened to snap and blow away in the rising wind.

There was a space right in front of the Grand Union and Jeannie parked, putting a quarter in the meter. When she went through the pneumatic doors she glanced behind her and saw that Piggy had taken BeeBee out of the car. "Why didn't you leave him?" she asked. "We're not going to be that long."

"Because," he snapped at her, "I want him with me."

"Okay, okay," she replied, realizing that he was in one of his dark moods and it made no sense to argue.

They went around the checkout counter and Jeannie snagged an empty cart. "Here," she said, "you can push."

In the produce section she picked up a head of lettuce, a faded green beneath its cellophane, and thought with longing of the fresh-fruit-and-vegetable stalls in Boston. Tomatoes, a

bag of carrots, five pounds of onions. Turning to drop it all in
the cart, she saw that BeeBee was pushing, his pincers clasped
around the handle. "Oh, I don't know, Paul," she said, her
brow wrinkling in doubt, "maybe you should do it."

"Mom," Piggy said, "Bee's more than capable of such a
baby thing."

They went in a procession along the aisles, the white-
aproned clerks lined up, viewers at a parade. The manager
called down from his perch in the cubicle office as though
from the bridge of a ship, "What's going on?"

Jeannie's face glowed warmly and she felt herself contract-
ing, shriveling up, under her trench coat. But Piggy stared
straight ahead, as determined to ignore the clerks' gawking,
the other shoppers hastily pulling aside, the cries of disbelief,
the whispering, as though he were alone on the moon. His
lips barely moving, he spoke like a conspirator into his hand-
held control, directing BeeBee around the store.

"I said, what's going on down here?" The manager suddenly loomed large at the end of the aisle, bellowing. The
clerks scurried out of sight as he strode toward Piggy and
BeeBee and Jeannie, who was taking a can of crushed pineap-
ple down from the shelf. She ignored him until he was only a
few feet away, directly in their path, the cart almost touching
his immaculate white coat. Then she was forced to confront
him over Piggy and BeeBee's heads as a fat woman wrapped
in a shiny black raincoat called from a side aisle, "It's that
robot, Max."

"That *what*?"

"You know, the robot," she hissed, hovering over her cart
like a dark cloud.

"We're just trying to do our shopping," Jeannie said, finding her voice in a small knot in her throat. "Could we please
get by?"

Piggy was silent, but he seemed as leaden as Bee under
the manager's gaze. When the man started around the side of
the cart, Pig inched nearer to his friend, draping an arm
around him.

"I don't like this." The manager had pivoted sideways to
get by, but Pig whispered a command and immediately the
cart angled, cutting him off.

Jeannie pushed a dead smile to her face and heard a voice
that vaguely resembled her own saying, "There's nothing

wrong. We're only doing our shopping, my son and I, and BeeBee, of course. BeeBee, as you can see, is a robot. Very helpful, too, I might add. One day," she scrambled on, while the manager glowered at her, "one day, robots like Bee will be doing your unpacking, stock checking, stacking the cans . . . Oh, I don't know, lots of things. You just wait and see, robotics is the wave of the future." Her nervousness was, she knew, making her behave ridiculously.

He tried again to get by them, to reach Bee. And do what? Jeannie wondered. But again Piggy had BeeBee block him with the cart. The manager's face was fire-engine red, and his sparse brown hair was almost standing straight up on his head. In another moment Jeannie could see him lifting the cart in his big hands and upending it on all of them. A hush descended over the store.

"Get him out of here, Max," the fat lady said angrily, her watery dark eyes glistening like her slicker, "so we can do our shopping. I got dinner to put on for my old man."

"That's right," the manager repeated, as if finally realizing what he had to do, "get him . . . him! . . . I mean it, out of here. This is a supermarket, lady, and we don't have time to play games."

Jeannie could see Piggy about to erupt with a cry of fury, and grabbed his shoulder. "I'm sorry you feel that way. But if BeeBee disturbs you so much, of course we'll put him in the car. Paul," she said, digging her nails into his down vest, "take Bee outside. And you wait for me in the car too. I won't be long."

"Mommmmmmm," gushed out of his mouth, but she clamped down harder, as if by her will alone his anger could be contained.

"Now, Paul, now. Take BeeBee out to the car."

The manager stepped aside and Piggy reluctantly ordered Bee forward. At the first lateral aisle they went left and made their way like marching soldiers to the front of the store, where Jeannie took the cart from Bee and watched through the big window beyond the cashiers—all of whom had stopped checking out orders to stare—as Pig and Bee left the store and climbed into the car. When they were safe inside, she released the painful hitch of breath and realized that she was now the focus of everyone's attention. She seemed to be at one side of an invisible wall and the small crowd at the other, not one of them speaking, and she knew what Piggy must feel like, so isolated from others, so estranged by suspicion, by uneasiness. And then, as if an unspoken order had been given, the cashiers returned to their ringing up, the shoppers to collecting their groceries, the clerks to their chores. Even the manager climbed back to his aerie, his store once more secure from mechanical invasion, Jeannie thought as she pushed the cart hurriedly down the aisles. She didn't consider too carefully what she tossed inside, just wanting to get out into the air, to the street, her car, and then home to the house on River Street where she could be alone. But I won't be, she realized, there will still be the two of them.

On the short ride from the market, no one spoke. Jeannie didn't know what to say to Piggy, what could soften the harsh truth, which was that the people of Welling didn't like them—no, didn't like *him*—and resented BeeBee. Poor lovable Bee inspired some illogical fear that the townspeople could neither articulate nor let alone. They picked at their fear like a scab. But fear of what? A glimpse, perhaps, of the twenty-first century, when they might be superfluous? It was, she supposed, too much for most people to extend kindness to mechanical beings when they barely treated each other with dignity and caring.

Outside, the grizzled gloom mirrored her feelings as though a dingy shroud had been draped over the town. When they parked in front of the house and began to unload the groceries, all she was capable of saying was, "I'm sorry." But whether or not Piggy heard her, he didn't reply as he trudged up and down the front walk with the paper sacks. Elvira Williams, she saw, was peeping at them from her front window. Jeannie thought, as she followed Piggy with the last bag: I won't think about this now, I'll just let it alone for a while. It has to get better, Welling and Mason have to learn to live with him, and Piggy with them, all those fearful people who see in his brilliance a danger, a threat.

On the front porch she dug in the small black mailbox attached to the wall at the right of the door. There was a flyer from somebody named Abe selling cord wood, a copy of *The Welling Weekly Times*, and the letter. She awkwardly shifted the groceries in her arms and regarded the buff-colored envelope. Martin Chambers' name and address were imprinted in

the corner. Shoving it into the pocket of her coat, Jeannie
wished she didn't have to think about that either.

When all the groceries had been put away in the pantry,
the refrigerator, down in the cellar in the big deep freeze,
when Piggy and Bee had gone upstairs, Jeannie, having put
the kettle on, stood at the sink staring across the river at
Mason, colorless in the cinereal light.

The kettle whistled and she brewed herself a strong cup of
tea. Tea soothes away the worst aches and worries, her mother
used to say. But as Jeannie sipped at the steaming tea,
nothing inside her was soothed. She just kept turning the
letter over and over, pushing it along the table. What, she
wondered, could Martin have to say that I'm so frightened of?
That I don't already know? That the divorce is coming along,
almost final, that soon if not right this minute, Tony and I will
no longer be married to one another?

But what he had written was simply, "I assume you wanted
me to send this on. If you plan to answer indirectly—which
is, Jeannie, foolish indeed—mail your letter back to me and
I'll forward it." With Martin's note came another letter. She
recognized the handwriting before she even saw the return
address.

I can toss it into the trash without even reading it, she
thought as she was slitting the second envelope with her nail.
But that wasn't possible. Tony sat in the center of her life like
a bellyache. Sometimes she hated him so much for all the
pain that she got an actual burning in her chest like angina.
Still, at other moments she'd weep with longing, bereft without him. She didn't want him dead, she wanted him misera-
ble, aware with every fiber of his being of what he had lost,
had given up. She wished his life with Julia a horrendous
failure from which there was no possible escape, except returning to her and Piggy, who, of course, would refuse to
take him back.

It was the deception that she couldn't come to terms with,
the rupture of a trust that must never have existed in the first
place, or how could he have fallen in love with another woman?
If their marriage had been what she imagined it to be, then
they would have been able to parent their strange and difficult child with equanimity and not have flown so far apart
that Tony needed Julia. She should have been the only one
for him, like in all the soppy movies which still brought tears

to her eyes, never mind that she was thirty-four and not
sixteen. But life wasn't an hour and fifty minutes up on the
screen, no matter how hard she tried to believe that it was.
When the lights went on, the characters—she and Tony and
Piggy—didn't walk hand in hand into the sunset, happily
ever after. There was no ever after, she thought with a
shudder, except despair and death. She lit a cigarette, realizing that she was smoking more and more these days, but not
caring particularly, because this—the letter—wasn't something she could go through without a crutch.

The first letter from Tony since they had come to Welling.
The first word from him, as a matter of fact, since that
terrible phone call to Julia's house when Jeannie said: This is
what we're doing and you can't stop us. And his only answer
had been: I wouldn't think of trying. She wondered if he had
changed his mind, and a spurt of hope sputtered inside her,
but then died as she took the letter out of the envelope and
propped it against the sugar bowl, wishing with all her heart
that he hadn't written. If, she thought, he had died in a plane
crash, I'd have to cope, I'd have to mend. But there he was
still in Boston, alive and well and happy, and she was here in
Welling where she had chosen to come, being intimidated in
the supermarket.

Piggy's door slammed and his sneakers thumped along the
upstairs hall going toward the bathroom. That decided her.
The last thing she wanted was for him to find her reading a
letter from his father. So, get it over with, she said to herself,
and unfolded it. There was just one sheet of paper, with
Tony's cramped handwriting on both sides. It had always
surprised her that such a big man wrote so small.

The first part was full of inquiries about her and Paul: What
were they doing? The new school, how was it? The new house
or apartment? What was it like to live somewhere other than
Boston? He hoped that Paul wasn't having any adjustment
problems and that he had forgotten about *all that*. He especially hoped that Paul had forgotten because that was what
Jeannie had decided was the best thing to do. He went on:

> I think this is foolish, not knowing exactly where
> you and Paul are. Whatever has gone wrong be-
> tween us, Jeannie, Paul's still my son. I want to stay
> in touch with him, see him when I can. I gather

you're not near Boston, but there are school vaca-
tions and the summers. What are your plans? And
when can I talk to you? You know my phone number, and I wish you'd call. Or write me and let me
know your address. I'd like to write Paul, too. It will
be disastrous if our divorce makes a rift in his rela-
tionship with me.

Anyway, as I said before, I hope it's all working
out. I know you won't believe me, but I do miss you
as well as Paul, and want the best for both of you.
If only things . . .

It ended as abruptly as that. Jeannie read the letter over
three times, then crumpled it into a ball and shoved it to the
bottom of the garbage can beneath the breakfast coffee grounds.
She felt sick to her stomach. Still she could imagine Tony's
touch, the way he would take her in his arms, which made
everything worse. God, she thought, almost screaming, why
can't I forget about him? Find someone else and run off, or
even stay put, but just stop caring when there's no caring in
return.

Peter Bayard's face flashed into her mind. She drew back
like a camera and saw him leaning against the side of her car
and laughing about—what? She couldn't remember, but it
didn't matter, it was just the image of him she hung on to like
a talisman.

He was so kind and so pleasant, as well as being the first
person in a long, long time who made her feel good about
herself. He didn't see her as a shrew or a bitch, which was
what Tony had called her in the midst of one of their worst
fights right at the end. Peter thought she was nice, she knew
he did, and with a sizzling rage she told herself that it would
serve everyone right if she fell in love with him. But she
calmed down immediately, realizing the desperation of her
desire. She wasn't going to fall in love with Peter Bayard;
furthermore, she didn't want to. She didn't want to fall in
love with anyone, she simply needed peace, needed things to
go right with her and with Piggy.

Maybe, she thought, getting up finally and beginning dinner, I shouldn't even go out with Peter on Saturday night. It
might not be wise.

Also, she had forgotten that Saturday night was Halloween.

Mason was having a party in the gym. All those who attended were requested to come in costume. There would be music and dancing and apple dunking and a chamber of horrors that the seniors were constructing. After the judging of the costumes, Piggy and Slime planned to go trick-or-treating.

I should stay home, she thought the next day after school as she cut circles for eye holes in the sheet that Piggy would wear in his impersonation of a ghost.

"What should BeeBee be?" he asked, sliding the sheet over his head and peering out rather lopsidedly.

"BeeBee? You're not planning to take him, are you?"

"Of course I am, Mom," he said, floating to the mirror in the front hall and regarding himself with satisfaction. "I think I look pretty scary, don't you?"

"Absolutely," she replied, and then, "I'd rather you left Bee at home."

"Why?" Piggy asked, the sheet swirling about his legs as he spun around. "He's invited too, you know."

"You won't have as good a time if you have to watch out for him, that's all."

"Why would I have to watch out for him?"

She shrugged, closing the lid of her sewing box. "Oh, I don't know. Just that somebody might try to tinker with him."

Piggy giggled. "They're all too afraid of Bee, or afraid to get too close. I mean, they might come up and touch him, you know, like just to feel. But nobody would do anything with me there. Besides," he said slyly, "since you're going out, there's nobody home to babysit."

"All right, all right," she said, realizing that it was pointless to insist. "But how are you planning to get to school? It will be dark out by the time you have to leave."

"Mom!" he wailed, "this isn't Boston. We'll walk. It's safe."

"I don't like you walking over Main Bridge at night. The sidewalk is so narrow, and the way people around here drive! And on Halloween there'll be a lot of kids drinking too much. Maybe I'll drive you over before I go."

"No! That's too early," he cried, flailing his arms and puffing out the sheet. "We'll be fine all by ourselves."

"Well, go visit some of your friends in the dorm."

She couldn't see his expression, but his voice revealed just how annoyed he felt. "That's out, Mom," was all he an-

swered, and at last they left it that he and Slime and BeeBee
would walk, but would be *extra careful*.

Somehow, she thought, it was easier in Boston, but then
she'd had Tony to share the burdens. And whatever she
could say about him, whatever she now felt, she had to admit
he'd been a good father.

"You know, Mom," Piggy said, taking off his sheet, "you
have to let me grow up. You can't keep me a baby and
control me forever."

She started to say: You're not an inanimate object, not a
thing like BeeBee, whom it's easy to control just by hitting a
switch. People have wills of their own, she began to tell him,
people are responsible. But she said nothing because he
bolted at the sound of Sam's voice calling from the yard.

Jeannie took the sheet into the kitchen to iron it, thinking:
It's like hanging on to the tail of a tornado. Passing the
window, she saw the two children standing close together,
almost touching. There was something unsettling in the way
that Piggy leaned over the girl, his shadow overpowering her.
But when Jeannie stopped, blinked, and looked again, it seemed
the reverse, that Sam was backing him over the lawn, that he
was fearfully moving away from her. Then, all at once, Sam
turned and ran to her house. Piggy stood alone, his arm
extended as if he held the voice activator, as if he could speak
into the small device and move her back, reverse her flight.
She heard him call, "Sam," and then, "Sam," a second time,
but there was no reply. After a moment he dropped his arm and
wandered into the little shed.

Jeannie, setting up the board and plugging in the steam
iron, reviewed what she had just seen. Nothing, she decided.
Two children having words. Yet for no reason the little vi-
gnette was unnerving. A shiver ran through her. A goose is
walking across my grave, she said to herself, remembering a
saying of her mother's, and then, shaking her head as if she
could clear away the feeling of dread, she spat on the iron,
seeing the tiny drops of liquid sizzle, and began to flatten out
the wrinkles in the sheet. Maybe, she thought once more, I
should stay home Saturday night.

Piggy also was thinking of changing his Halloween plans.
As he poked about the small shed with its rusty cans and
broken tools, he was wondering if it might not be better just

to hang around and watch TV. Maybe make some popcorn or candy apples and, of course, invite Sam over.

He peered out the grimy window hoping to see her on the porch, hoping she had come back outside again. But she wasn't there. He could, of course, cross over to her yard, go right up the steps and pound at the door. And say: I'm sorry, Sam. Only Piggy wasn't sure what he was sorry about. All he had done was ask her what she was doing for Halloween. Was she going trick-or-treating, or to a party at Consolidated?

How could he have known that her father wouldn't let her leave the house? That he had flown into a drunken rage when she asked. Which was how Piggy translated her saying, "He got awful mad."

Piggy had scanned Sam's face carefully then, anxiety fluting in his stomach, and noticed that her lower lip was a bit too puffy. But when he had asked her in a high-pitched wail if Harry had hit her in the mouth, Sam had run off. Now Piggy was feeling like something left out in the rain. Soggy and heavy and of utterly no use. He would have kicked himself in the rear if it were anatomically possible, but had to settle for standing stupidly in the shed and chewing on his thumbnail.

Having friends was much more complicated than Piggy had ever imagined. How, he wondered, would his father make things right in the same situation? But the instant he asked himself that question he remembered that every time his father had tried to turn things around, to convert bad into better with his mother and him, he fouled up even worse.

Feeling as though someone had dropped him into the middle of the ocean from an airplane, Piggy stormed out of the shed, over the lawn, jumped the divider, and stomped up to Sam's steps. There were no maps for this kind of thing, he thought, his heart thumping, his tongue stuck to the roof of his mouth.

It was just so agonizing to see Sam upset, to think he'd been the one who had caused the tears to fill up her eyes. He had to do something to make her smile and thereby lift the lead weight off his chest. Piggy wasn't sure why an unhappy Sam affected him so much and brought on all sorts of indiscriminate pains.

"Sam!" he cried, his voice cracking. And then, "Sam!" again. But no small face peered through the window or out the glass in the back door. "Sam!" he shouted at the top of his

lungs, determined now to stand at the foot of the Pringles'
porch steps and bellow until the end of time. Once Pig's
mind was made up, he was as obstinate as a mule.

"Stop yelling, Piggy," she said, all at once appearing on the
porch. "You could wake a dead person."

"Well, you didn't answer," he said, suddenly contrite.

Tucking a strand of hair behind her ear, Sam said, "I was
scrubbing the bathroom."

"Oh," he said, "I'm sorry."

"Sorry for what?" she asked, puzzled.

He shuffled around in the dirt, scuffing his sneakers. She had
come to the edge of the porch and stood now at the top of the
steps, looming above him. She was so little and usually
looked so frail, fragile like a bird, but from this angle she
appeared large, overwhelming.

"Com'on over to my house," he said, battling a recurring
surge of anxiety, "and we'll make hot chocolate."

"I got work to do, Pig," she said in a grown-up tone of
voice.

"I'll help. That way we'll finish fast. And then we can go to
my house."

She let out a deep sigh which set her whole body shaking.
"Can't do that," she said. "He'd have a real fit if you came in
the house."

"How would he know?"

"Just the way he knows everything." She sighed again.

"How?"

"Just does."

Piggy was fidgeting, trying to find a way to bring up
Halloween and tell Sam he was sorry he upset her so much.
If she'd only come down the steps so that he didn't have to
crane his neck to see her, maybe he'd be able to blurt it out.
And maybe too, when he got that far, he might take her
hand. The idea of holding Sam's hand in his own sent shooting
pains through his chest.

"Listen, Pig, I gotta go. After I do the bathroom there's
dinner to put up." She suddenly seemed wizened and old,
not like a little girl at all. "Maybe tomorrow we can have hot
chocolate at your house. After school I mean."

"Sure. That would be great," Piggy said, feeling intolerably
sad. Then, just as Sam turned to cross the porch and reenter
the house, Piggy blurted, "I'm sorry that I upset you before.

About Halloween and . . . and . . . your lip." He swallowed hard and gazed at her faraway face earnestly. He knew things would be less painful if he could only entwine her fingers with his. Or painful in a different, more pleasant way.

For a moment she stared at him with an air of bewilderment; then slowly, almost imperceptibly, a smile tugged at the corners of her mouth. "That's okay, Pig. I didn't take it to heart, what you said," she replied softly. "But it's nice of you to apologize."

"Oh, Sam, I wouldn't hurt you for the world!" Piggy cried, impassioned. But Sam had already gone back inside.

8

Welling stirred like the waters of an untidy sea on Halloween night as ghosts and goblins surged down usually deserted streets; doorbells rang at houses where no one normally visited after seven o'clock; mothers peered anxiously out of windows; limbs of trees snapped from no natural causes; garbage cans upended one after the other; chalk drawings appeared upon the sides of cars and along the walls of Consolidated; feet scampered like nervous mice across porches; and the phone line at the north end of town went down.

A group of eleventh-grade boys decided to crash the party at Mason, but the blue-and-white police car headed them off at Main Bridge, and Charlie Volchek, the chief, sent them back up Bridge Street.

Seven-year-old Junie Bride broke her leg running from a big black dog and Doc Madison had to take her to the hospital and set it, with Junie yelling for all she was worth.

Jack Reiss decided to keep the Mobile station open late

just to be sure that nobody tampered with his pumps. Even so, practically in front of his nose, someone jimmied the soda machine and got away with a bag of change.

Elvira Williams turned off all her lights and drew the shades right down to the window ledges and sat in the living room cradling an old shotgun that had belonged to her father and hadn't been fired by him for at least five years before he died back in 1946. There had once been shells for the gun but Charlie Volchek had taken them away from her after she had blown a hole right through her front door one night when she thought she heard somebody trying to break in. Charlie had said she was more of a danger to other people with that old blunderbuss than anybody was to her.

But it was Halloween and none of the children who yearly tormented her knew she couldn't fire the shotgun as she was always threatening to. So she sat and waited for the first rock to hit the steps and hoped that it would be the boy from across the way. Oh, if she only had shells, she'd shoot apart that tin can of his. Charlie Volchek couldn't arrest her for killing something that wasn't alive.

The Five O'Clock was hosting a ghouls-and-witches party, but nobody came wearing a costume except for Doris, who waited on tables, and she wore a Frankenstein mask that everybody agreed was less scary than her own face. Corney tried to trip her with his wooden leg, but she dumped a Pabst down the back of his shirt and Calloway had to get his baseball bat from under the bar and threaten to swing it before the fight cooled down.

Harry Pringle, having gotten to the Five O'Clock early since it was a Saturday and he didn't have to work, was in his favorite seat at the far end of the bar where he could prop himself up against the wall. That meant he could drink an extra four or five beers without Calloway wanting to throw him out, since tilting back as he was doing, there was less chance of his falling off the stool. It didn't matter to Harry that it was Halloween. One night was much the same as any other except for Sunday, when the bars were closed, Pennsylvania being a blue state. But even then, if Calloway was feeling good or the register was low, he opened the back door a little after six and let everyone sit around in the dark watching a game on television as long as they kept quiet. And since this didn't happen more than once or twice a month, Charlie Volchek turned a blind eye to it

"How's the ro-but?" Corney asked, cackling.

Harry ignored him. Someone had gotten behind the juke-box and turned the sound up. Kenny Rogers' voice boomed off the walls of the Five O'Clock.

"Ro-but, Harry, ro-but!" Corney snickered again and poked Harry in the leg. "Maybe the ro-but will marry that kid of yours and old Harry Pringle will be grandfather to a can of sardines!" Corney almost fell off his stool laughing at his own wit, and then had to dodge Harry's swatting at him and yelling to shut up or he'd tromp him to death. Calloway had to break it up with the threat of the baseball bat, but still it took a couple of minutes for both men to simmer down.

Harry leaned back once again on his stool and concentrated on drowning his sorrows. He was staring out past Corney's right shoulder, but he wasn't seeing the booths arranged along the far wall, or the round tables in between, or Doris dragging herself back and forth from the bar, slapping down drinks.

Harry was seeing Jeannie in his head floating by her living-room window, the velour bathrobe she wore gaping open. He was seeing the long, trim legs.

Harry had been peeking through the windows of the Conway house just about every night except when the moon was full and he ran the risk of that old fool Elvira Williams looking out her window and seeing him. He'd sneak along the outside from room to room, feeling powerful because he could see them but they couldn't see him, didn't even know that he was looking. And yet, every time he'd stagger back to his own house, he was madder than the time before, as though the anger was accumulating.

Jeannie stirred up memories of Grace and excited a longing he hadn't had since his wife's disappearance. But it was more than that. His anger oozed like hot lava and encompassed all the Conways, including BeeBee. He didn't like the loose grace of Jeannie or the fat awkwardness of Piggy. And he certainly didn't like the goddamn robot at all. BeeBee sym-bolized for Harry all the differences between the two houses, though they were only a hairbreadth apart.

He told Sam she couldn't go over there to play, but he suspected she did anyway. Oh, if he ever caught her he'd tan

her bottom real good. Just like Grace, just like her with all
those fancy ways. For a moment he remembered Grace's
antique clock. He thought he'd smash it up and stuff the parts
in the trash when he got home. He wanted to smash something because he couldn't smash Grace.

In the back someone pushed the tables aside and two
couples started to dance though Calloway told them, "None
of that." But everybody laughed at him since it was Halloween and this was supposed to be a party even if it was only
the Five O'Clock on Saturday night and no different than it
usually was.

"Com'on, Doris, dance with me!" Corney entreated, trying
to snap the waitress's behind. But she scuttled past him in a
fast shuffle and told him that his head was as wooden as his
leg, which made Corney glower. "I got this," he yelled,
"defending democracy!" But nobody cared, nobody was even
listening, not even Harry, who had switched from draft to
straight Jim Beam and was getting madder and madder.

They came, pirates and soldiers and monsters and balleri-
nas and cowboys and at least four other ghosts that Piggy
could see. But most kids—or at least the older ones—wore
fake noses with horn-rims attached, making them look like
Groucho Marx, or fright wigs, or bushy mustaches, here and
there a full beard, an eyepatch. One third-former even came
dressed as BeeBee with legs. Piggy didn't think it was funny,
neither did Bee. Face to face with his imitator, Bee beeped
annoyance and rolled off to Piggy's command. Slime wore an
Indian headdress that was suspiciously similar to chicken
feathers, and his pointed little face was smeared down the
cheeks and over his eyebrows with his mother's rouge. If he
was supposed to look fierce, he didn't, Piggy decided, just
stupid. But the whole thing was stupid, Halloween and dress-
ing up.

Why had he wanted to put on a sheet and make a fool of
himself by coming to this dumb party where nobody even said
boo to him and he might as well have been one of the paper
skeletons thumbtacked to the wall for all the attention anybody paid? The other kids seemed to be having fun, laughing
and talking to one another. He wished he could go up to that
witch over there, who he thought was Suzy Nobel from his

English class, and say: Let's dance. Instead he leaned against the wall, Bee at his side, Slime off somewhere.

This wasn't at all like Halloween used to be in Boston when he was a kid. Back then his mother would take him from floor to floor in their building and at every apartment he'd get candy or apples or occasionally a few coins for his UNICEF canister. When they had done all the floors he and Jeannie would return to their own home and sit in the middle of the rug with his father above them in his chair and gorge themselves on treats. And even his father, who didn't usually eat candy, was tempted to snag a Butterfingers or a couple of Hershey's Kisses.

The gymnasium was dimly lit with revolving lights sheathed in cheesecloth so that purple patches, and streaks of tired blue, and soggy orange skittered over the children who rotated to the music, bobbing up and down and sideways like the apples in the metal laundry tub. Piggy was persuaded by Slime to dunk. Only he didn't get even one apple, just wet his sheet so that it clung to his face and made him look like a death's-head in the eerie light.

The sound system blared out a medley of rock songs, and that, with all the shrieking, made it difficult to hear Slime, who shouted close to his ear.

"What?"

"I said let's go into the chamber of horrors."

"Ah, that's silly. A bunch of baby tricks that wouldn't even scare Bee."

"No, it'll be fun." He tugged on Piggy, who had no choice but to go along, being pulled through the crowd, keeping one hand on BeeBee's shoulder. Maybe Mom was right, he conceded, as they had trouble shoving through the hordes of kids who all wanted to touch Bee, to make jokes, Piggy thought, at his expense. He ordered Bee to raise his arms, the pincers open, and that backed them off, particularly one persistent kid who, hidden under dark brown shoe polish and a fuzzy white wig, jumped and scuttled off as the metal fingers grasped his flannel shirt.

The chamber of horrors was in the corridor running along the north side of the gym, through the equipment room, which had two doors, out into the east corridor, up the short flight of steps to the exit doors. From there, if you wanted to get back into the party, you had to walk all around the building. Piggy had seen the seniors setting up late on Friday afternoon and thought nobody would be fooled, never mind frightened, by their childish efforts. But Slime seemed eager to try it, so they both offered up their quarters—receipts to be used for the senior trip—and ducked through the doorway into darkness so pitch black it was palpable.

BeeBee wasn't with them; Piggy had left him outside behind the card table with Miss Markowitz, who was one of the four chaperons. She looked as though she was in excruciating pain with the noise, the flickering lights. She hadn't liked the idea of keeping an eye on the robot but finally agreed when Piggy pointed out that he couldn't go into the chamber with Bee, and therefore the seniors would be one quarter short. The girl selling tickets, a plump senior with sequins stuck to her face like chicken pox, insisted that it wasn't fair, so reluctantly Miss Markowitz agreed, though she positioned Bee far back against the wall and turned away from him as if the mere sight of his metal face gave her a headache.

Piggy stumbled along, Slime panting heavily ahead of him and behind the terrified shrills of a group of girls. He slid through a spider's web which he identified at once as a curtain of gauze, and passed by two grinning skulls drawn on either side of the hallway with luminous paint. Weird laughter rumbled down the corridor, shrieks and rattling chains. Just ahead he saw a ghostly figure staring out at him and snickered—a mirror, and that's me—but as he came up on the figure he careened into the glass, bouncing off it, his feet sliding on the edge of the sheet. His head hit the jamb of the closet door and pain flashed like lightning down to his toes. His knees buckled and he flopped to the floor. It was as if someone had taken an ax to his skull. Red lights flashed erratically in the darkness and he blacked out for minutes or longer, he couldn't be sure. But then slowly he brought himself upright again, his stomach heaving into his chest. He tasted the hamburger slathered with ketchup that he had had for dinner and struggled not to be sick.

He had gotten disoriented falling, not being able to tell back from front, but turning, he faced the mirror and saw a figure swaying, arms undulating slowly. And where the face should have been was a bony protuberance, the sockets naked, the nose pitted bone, the mouth spread wide with stubs of yellowing teeth.

Closer, closer . . .

There was a putrid stench that made his mouth go dry, and a clacking as though the small bones of the figure were rubbing together, jouncing against one another as it moved. It grew larger and larger the nearer Piggy got, and though he told himself it was a trick, an optical illusion, that behind him somewhere there had to be a projector splaying out this macabre image, the hair on the back of his neck rose and a cold chill started in his stomach. He was now so near he could feel the hot breath right through the damp sheet, the warmth seeping in on him, and smell the overwhelming stink as though one of Mr. Toomy's bodies had been left too long out of the cold drawer.

"Slime," he whispered, reaching ahead of him with his hand. But no one was there. "Slime!" he called again, panicked now, and jumped: the *thing* was at his back. He peered blindly into blackness. Slime had disappeared.

Piggy whipped about, and raising his hands, felt something drift across his knuckles, something warm and wet. Blood, he imagined. A cry lodged in his throat like a fish bone and he just knew he could choke on his own fear. He closed his eyes, opened them; it didn't make any difference.

A coldness permeated his bones, rising out of the concrete floor. His legs were turning into icicles.

Blindly he pushed ahead and suddenly he saw moving down on him a speeding train, heard, the moment he saw it, the grinding wheels along the tracks, the roar. The lights were two huge all-seeing eyes and smoke belched out of the stack, clouding overhead.

The train was rushing through daylight and all around it the sky was blue. It's a movie, he thought, but then had just seconds to save himself as the grinning metal front charged with its cow-catcher teeth snapping. Piggy threw himself flat on the floor. It was as slick and freezing as the surface of an ice-skating rink; the cold burned his palms. The roaring of the train when it passed overhead shook the building, and he could feel the heat of it on his back.

Piggy got up and ran through the darkness, hands whipping out at him, trying to snare his sheet, eerie voices laughing, the cold of the floor now in the pit of his stomach and rising. He knew if he didn't outrun it, whatever it was, the dead thing glazed white, the train which now was roaring back behind him, that the cold, as searing as a flame, would flare through him, reach his throbbing head and his father wouldn't have to worry anymore about his resting his brain cells, they'd be frozen solid. He knew the cold and the train and the thing were out to get him, was as certain of that as anything, and didn't ask why, but fled, his icy legs pumping, almost too heavy to lift, tangled in his sheet that was thick as the ice itself.

He ran straight into a wall, into a ghoulish head with a wide, gaping mouth that to his horror he recognized as Bertram Lennard.

Bertram Lennard reached out with fleshless hands, dirt dribbling between his bones.

Piggy flailed, leaping away, and saw a pathway lit by luminescent white paint, into the equipment room, or where the equipment room had once been. He bolted, but something soft and gooey blocked his way, sticking to his sheet, pressing it against his mouth so that he couldn't breathe. He clawed at whatever it was, air tight in his lungs, the smell so awful it was making him gag, when an arm speared out of the blackness, reached through the nightmare with the certainty of death, and grabbed at him. He gave an unholy shriek as the naked finger dug into the soft flesh of his upper arm. Bertram Lennard was trying to pull him back, struggle him nearer the train that was whooshing behind him, draw him under the wheels and make pulp out of him.

It was now so hot in the tunnel that Piggy supposed his skin was starting to scorch, and with a strength he didn't know he possessed, he yanked away from Bertram dead and in his grave, sure that part of his flesh, a hunk of muscle dripping blood from broken veins and arteries, was left in the skeletal grasp.

Just at that second the train hit his back with a terrible thud. All his bones were shattered as he was propelled through space, sailing off the ground, his legs and lower body one gigantic icicle. He threw out his arms, palms flat, and came down on something soft and yielding. Quickly he rolled over and was up again, surprised that he was alive, that all his parts worked. And suddenly a yellowed halo of light opened before him. A door. Stumbling up the steps, he fell onto the grass, smelled the earth in his nostrils. Though the night was chilly, it was warmer outside than it had been in the chamber of horrors. Piggy gasped for air, his lungs heaving, some of the gooey stuff ingested, and before he could stop himself he vomited all over the ground.

"Gosh, Pig, are you all right?" Slime was leaning over him, looking worriedly down into his face.

His mouth tasted awful, like old socks, and he wiped his lips, his streaming eyes, with the sheet that he had fumbled off. He removed his glasses and dried his face and hair.

"What happened to me?" he asked Slime when he could speak.

"I guess you hit your head," he said, squatting Indian fashion on the dead grass. "When you didn't come out I went looking for you. You were lying right alongside the skeleton painted on the wall. I don't know why nobody saw you. Maybe they thought you were part of the horrors."

"Paul," Miss Markowitz said, rushing out of the gym. "How do you feel?" She put the cold, wet towel she held against his forehead.

"I don't know. Okay, I guess." But he really felt awful. His stomach was empty, his ribs ached. He looked at his Timex which glowed in the dark and saw that twenty minutes had gone by. It seemed impossible, too much time and too little. Where had he been? Had he simply hit his head as Slime said.

He tried to reason out what had happened in the chamber of horrors, but he was shaking too much. There was a sore place between his shoulder blades. Wincing, he reached back to rub it and felt again the punch of the train, heard the roaring which sounded like Bertram Lennard laughing long ago in the lab at Height before the flames shot out.

"No!" he cried. He bounced to his feet, staggered, and knocked aside the towel that Miss Markowitz had been holding to his forehead. Her glasses glittered in the light from the bulb over the rear door and he saw his reflection looking back.

"Paul!" she said.

"Piggy!" Slime tried to grab his arm, but he ran around the building and into the gym by the front door, his heart pounding.

Nothing had changed. "Beat It" was blaring through the sound system. The lights revolved, spots of color splattering the masked faces, sliding around the gyrating bodies.

Piggy skirted the dancers and came up at the entrance to the chamber. The chubby girl selling tickets looked at him and said accusingly, "There you are. I thought you forgot your toy."

Piggy didn't have the energy to say that Bee wasn't a toy. He just wanted to get home. A terrible tiredness had invaded his bones and he thought that if he stopped moving he'd fall asleep right where he stood.

"Thank you for watching Bee," he said automatically, and flicking BeeBee's switch, he ordered him across the room and out the door

Slime caught up with them just as they stepped outside. "Hey, what's the matter, Pig?" he asked, worried.

"What did you think of the chamber of horrors?" he wanted to know. His stomach was churning, and he was barely able to regain his breath even outside in the cold air.

Slime puffed out his cheeks, sticky with cotton candy, and said, "The scariest thing was you hitting your head and knocking yourself out. The rest was stupid, just lots of paper skeletons and flapping sheets. Jeez, you and I could have made something better than that."

Piggy nodded his head, which made it hurt worse. He was too afraid to ask about the train, about the ghoulish face, the clutching, fleshless hand which he had recognized as belonging to Bertram Lennard. He was afraid that he was the only one to see the dead boy, if he had truly seen him at all.

"I've got to go," he said, wanting to run.

"Hey, wait a minute. It's early. And what about trick-or-treating?"

"I changed my mind," Piggy replied, hurrying from the gym, from the long, dark tunnel. Bee chugged beside him.

"What do you mean? Oh, Pig! Halloween only comes once a year. We can't go trick-or-treating at Christmas, you know."

"Forget it, Slime. I want to go home. You stay or go off by yourself." He rushed down to Main Bridge, which was pale in the thin fog swirling along the roadway, through the guy wires, wafting down to the water that churned over the rocks. There wasn't any traffic on the bridge and the one globe of light at the midpoint threw a greenish glow into the night.

"Are you sure you're okay?" Slime asked, trotting behind him. Below, the rushing water made an unsettling sound, loud, insistent—*varoom, varoom*—as the two boys neared the far side of the bridge. It was almost too loud for Pig to hear what Slime was saying. BeeBee seemed to beep excitedly, and Piggy thought he could feel the robot's agitation. It had been a terrible mistake not to take Bee into the chamber with him.

He knew, hearing the roar of the train again—*varoom, varoom*—coming out of the pitch black, out of the nightmare, that something awful had happened to him.

"Jeez, Pig, you're shaking. Are you *really* sure you're all right?"

Piggy shook off the arm that Slime tried to put around him. He grimaced, his lips spread, his teeth clenched and looked, though he didn't know it, like Bertram Lennard's skull on the wall of the tunnel.

Slime drew back off the walk onto the road. The wind howled between them. BeeBee beeped shrilly, rolling along the railing. Piggy, rotating with fear, bumped into the robot, whose arms came up, the pincers against his face.

"Piggy?" Slime called, alarmed.

He sagged against Bee and realized, touching metal, how cold it was, exposed as they were out on the bridge. They stood that way for just a minute, with Slime watching, until Piggy said, "Let's go home." And then they moved off along the bridge through the mist.

Harry Pringle was staggering down the hill just as the boys and BeeBee were crossing the last ten feet of Main Bridge. Leaning against the wall hadn't stopped Calloway from seeing just how soused he had gotten, and when, spilling a brew down his pants leg and then dropping the glass, he had fallen forward as he tried to retrieve it, Calloway had thrown him out into the night. Corney had laughed and yelled he was going soft, unable to hold a few beers.

He didn't think he was drunk at all, and even if he was, the cold air was sobering him up fast, which made him even madder than he had been before. The only thing he could think of which relieved the pain stabbing at him in knifelike thrusts was getting home and smashing up Grace's clock. He imagined the relief that breaking something was going to give him, when he saw BeeBee rolling off the bridge.

"Hey, you! Kid!" he yelled, breaking into a shuffling trot.

His stomach jounced over his belt, the beer and Jim Beam sloshing around inside him. Sweat trickled down his backbone.

"Shit!" Slime said. "It's Harry Pringle and he's plastered. He's mean enough when he's only had Pepsi to drink." He watched the drunk weave toward them, but Piggy, not paying attention, kept going along the sidewalk that rounded into River Street.

"Hey, kid," Harry yelled again, "I wanna talk to you."

"Sleep it off!" Slime shouted in a burst of courage, pushing nearer to Piggy, right at his back.

"Shut up! I don't wanna talk to you!" Harry bellowed, moving faster, waving his arms. Trying to catch the boys, he tripped, fell with a crash, and rolled into the gutter amid a welter of leaves and broken branches.

They stopped and watched him scramble about in the debris until Piggy called out, "Do you need any help?" But Harry rose up with a roar. Somehow, the rock was clutched in his fist. And then it was flying through the air.

The rock hit Bee square in his central casing and he seemed to whoosh with pain.

"Run, Pig! Run!" Slime cried, galloping ahead, leaving Pig and BeeBee gaping at the raging beast, all black in his dark jacket and pants, the face suffused with blood.

Varoom, varoom. Piggy heard the train speeding toward him.

Harry was almost on top of them, brandishing a branch he had picked up off the ground, before Piggy broke, the terror too much, icing his bones, knifing through his intestines, and ran, BeeBee at his side, Slime off on somebody's lawn, yelping, "Help! Help!"

Straight off the road onto the sidewalk at full speed, Harry came down on them. All the lights exploded in Elvira Williams' house and there was the slam of the storm door. "What's going on out there?" she shouted into the night as she descended the steps to the edge of the retaining wall, cradling her shotgun.

"Shoot 'em!" Harry shouted.

"What? What? Shoot who?"

They were almost at Piggy's front walk when Harry went after the shotgun himself, staggering up the stairs and wrenching it out of the old woman's hands. "Smash it up! Smash it up!" he kept mumbling.

Slime was crying and BeeBee was rocking from side to side, whirring along at high speed. Piggy's heart was galloping somewhere in his throat. He tried to force his feet to move faster, but they wouldn't. Over his shoulder he caught a glimpse of Sam framed in an upstairs window of her house. The glow behind her gave her outstretched arms the appearance of bat wings. He wanted to scream to her but he didn't have enough breath in his lungs.

Harry, back on the sidewalk, charged, and Pig in his terror lost all sense of direction. The light dripping down in yellow streamers from the lampposts, the squares of lit windows, the beams from a pickup that gunned along River Street, and the robot and man all seemed to be running wild now in the road and over the lawns. All that light slid together, merged, split apart. In his frantic rush Piggy lost sight of Slime, whose cries bounced like little balls through the darkness. He lost BeeBee too, whose beep now seemed a terrible screech.

Harry was laughing as he roared after Piggy, circling him as though he were an animal at bay. His laughter turned into a stuttering giggle as he raised the gun to his shoulder and pulled the trigger again and again.

There was no blast. Harry lowered the gun and stared at it stupidly. A howl of rage, of pain, bubbled from his chest and out his mouth as he grabbed the gun by the barrels and began swinging, lashing back and forth.

Piggy raced on, but his house seemed to recede in the distance, as if the sidewalk was a moving track that took him nowhere, that kept him running in place

Harry came at him yet again, his howling caught up in the wind that chose that moment to race down River Street out of control, lifting up all the leaves in a swirling storm.

"I'm gonna smash you up!" Harry cried, and kept swinging.

Suddenly there was Sam, hanging on to the end of the shotgun. Her legs thrashed wildly as Harry's swing lifted her right up off the ground. "Don't do it, Pa!" she was shrieking. But the sight and sound of his daughter drove Harry Pringle even further along the runway to rage. He roared loud enough to shatter glass and his eyes bulged halfway out of his head.

"I'm gonna beat you to a pulp!" he screamed, and with a mighty thrust, shook her loose. Sam sailed far out into the night before she crashed.

The shotgun came around in a deadly arc, and this time

there was an impact, a resounding thud of wood upon metal. Piggy's heart splattered against his ribs, all his molecules alive with pain, as if the gun had cracked him. And then another slam, the crumpling of metal sliding together like an out-of-whack accordion. Space exploded with the sound and someone was screaming in a deafening wail. Someone was shrilling so loudly that the decibels detonated in Pig's skull.

"Stop! Stop! You're killing him!"

But Harry swung yet again and the thwack of the gun striking BeeBee was as ear-shattering as the locomotive going through the gymnasium wall. The gun went flying, clattering to the sidewalk, and Harry faltered, out of breath.

Then he stumbled off, muttering, trailing the old woman's cackles after him.

Piggy screamed and went to his knees, listening to the slow *beep, beep* that in one short, final second dribbled off into silence.

BeeBee was dead.

9

When Jeannie arrived home after a rather boring dinner and a movie she had seen before, Piggy and Slime were huddled on the couch. Piggy was cradling Bee's remains and Slime was as close to them both as he could get without actually touching. The two faces were ashen and glazed by bewilderment. They looked like refugees or the disaster victims who often appeared in the newspapers or in *Time*. Clutching the fragments of wreckage, they seemed to be silently imploring someone out there to explain.

Jeannie was so startled by this frightening image of the

boys that for a moment she closed her eyes. But when she
opened them Slime and Piggy were still there, rigid and
dazed like mourners at a wake. Before she could speak or
even move forward one step, Piggy, seeing her, started to
scream, a long, winding wail that streamed out of his mouth,
snagging Jeannie and almost toppling her. He sat rigidly and
howled, so loudly, so insistently, that Slime scuttled away
even as Jeannie was rushing to them from the doorway.

"My God, what happened to Bee?" she cried.

Slime tried to explain, raising his voice to be heard over
Pig's shrill that went on and on like a fire siren.

"Paul, please, stop! I can't hear." But Piggy didn't stop. He
was frozen in grief and rage, and it poured out of the gaping
hole in his face until the house rang with echoes.

Jeannie couldn't stand it. She reached across the mangled
corpse of the robot, stretching for her son, and gathered into
her arms both metal and flesh. A dangerous, jagged sliver of
Bee's casing slit through the sleeve of her jacket, her blouse,
tracing the skin, bringing up a thin line of blood that trickled
onto the couch. Not one of them noticed in the sudden
stillness that followed Jeannie's embrace.

"Hush, honey, hush." Which was anticlimactic, because he
had ceased screaming at last, gulping for air to ease his
heaving lungs.

Slime, once again moving nearer, bumped her arm with
his thigh. "Harry Pringle, Mrs. Conway," he whimpered.
"He smashed BeeBee up. He did it with Elvira Williams' old
shotgun. And she just . . . she just . . ." His voice stuck in
his throat and he sniffed back the tears that were threatening
to choke him. "She just laughed in that funny way she has.
You know."

It was at least twenty minutes before Jeannie finally got
them to explain. When she had taken them back and forth
over the story several times to be certain that she had at last
gotten it right, the three of them were exhausted. All Jeannie
could think of was that she wanted to kill Harry Pringle, beat
him senseless as he had smashed Bee. But she couldn't see
herself dashing next door and assaulting Sam's father with an
ax. Her only recourse was to phone the police and complain.
To insist that murder had taken place, though she knew the
police would at best call it vandalism.

While they waited for the chief, Charlie Volchek whose

gruff response indicated he didn't much like being dragged out of bed, Jeannie made tea. She laced the boys' with four teaspoons of sugar, as if they had sustained some bodily shock. But Piggy wouldn't let go of BeeBee to take his, and she had to hold the mug to his lips so that he could drink.

The tea didn't help at all but it gave them something to do until they heard the blue-and-white pull up in front of the house. A grim Jeannie answered the rat-ta-tat-tat of Charlie's knock and led him into the living room, then sandwiched herself between the two boys. Piggy still held on to Bee's pieces as if his own body heat as well as his agony could bring the robot back to life.

"What's all this?" Charlie Volchek asked, removing his hat and shrugging off his coat. Unconsciously he patted the revolver on his hip before he eased himself down into the big chair.

"An act of violence," Jeannie said indignantly like a character out of a Victorian novel. "Our next-door neighbor, Harry Pringle, seems to have destroyed BeeBee with Elvira Williams' shotgun."

"That old blunderbuss!" Charlie Volchek snorted, arching his brows. "Impossible. I know for a fact you can't shoot the thing."

"He beat Bee with it!" Piggy wailed, thrusting the broken casing and severed arms out for Charlie to see. The disjointed metal appeared, in the dull light, obscene.

"Oh shit," Charlie sighed, scratching the side of his stubbled jaw and turning away from Bee's remains.

"What are you doing to do about it?" Jeannie cried, her voice creeping close to hysteria.

"Do about it?"

"Yes, do about it."

"Com'on, Mrs. Conway. I can't very well arrest Harry Pringle for assault and battery. Or Elvira for being an accessory. Which is what you seem to expect."

Piggy was tensed like a wildcat ready to spring as Jeannie demanded, "If someone took a sledgehammer to my car, you'd do something, wouldn't you?"

Charlie glared at her steadily, as if trying to stare her down before he spoke. "Yeah, I'd haul him in for destruction of property. An offense that is usually settled by a fine, unless it's a *large* piece of property. Like a house or a factory."

"I want something done about Harry Pringle!" Jeannie's voice climbed an octave and she put her hand out for Piggy but her fingers slid across what had once been BeeBee's head. For the first time she noticed the rip in her jacket and she plucked at the edges nervously. "You can't allow things like this to go on, Chief Volchek. It's not right. No matter what you or the town think about us or about . . ." She stuck on BeeBee's name. "About robots."

Charlie crossed and recrossed his legs, sighing. "I don't think nothing about robots. Until very recently, I can say the subject just never came up."

"You at least have to write a summons and arrest him for vandalism," she insisted.

"You know, I'm not terribly happy about you telling me how to handle my job." Jeannie opened her mouth to protest, but Charlie didn't give her the chance. "Yeah, you only want to see justice done. I know how it is. But first of all, I haven't heard yet just what went on. Or at least not all of the details." His face was as bland as pudding. "And then, under due process of law, I gotta hear from the other side. That's the way we do things here in Welling, no matter what our feelings are."

Piggy's howl crashed through the silence, jolting everyone. "Stupid! It's stupid and you're stupid!"

Jeannie tried to hush him, but the dam had broken.

"Bee's dead and you're all sitting here debating whether it's a crime." He was rushing, words tumbling over one another. His face was crimson and a trickle of tears was curving down his cheek. "Bee's dead, don't you understand!"

It was obvious that Charlie wanted to tell Piggy to shut up but wasn't about to with Jeannie there, ready to start screaming herself.

"Okay, okay, kid, don't get excited."

Jeannie slipped her arm around Pig's shoulder and tried to clutch him to her, but he shrugged her off. She said, swallowing hard, "I think you two should tell Chief Volchek exactly what happened and after that he will decide what steps are to be taken. There's nothing to be gained from anybody losing control."

So once again they told their story, and by the time Charlie Volchek acknowledged that he thought he had it all, they were both wrung dry. Slime was almost asleep, his head nodding toward Jeannie's shoulder. Piggy was more ghostly than the specter he had impersonated at the Halloween party. His pale eyes had darkened into muddy pools and sunk behind his glasses.

"Well, there's nothing more I can do tonight. First thing in the morning though I'll talk to your neighbors. Then," he said to Jeannie, "I'll get back to you. Let you know if we can charge Pringle. If we have the evidence to charge him."

Jeannie's face went steely and she leapt off the couch. "If we can't," Charlie Volchek said slowly, deliberately, drawing on his coat and clamping the gray hat back on his tufted salt-and-pepper hair, "you can still file a complaint. Which, to be honest, is just a pain in the butt, and won't get him more than a rap on the knuckles but will take up a lot of your time."

Afraid that she herself might scream, might say something she'd be sorry for, Jeannie pressed her lips into a thin line. Her sudden silence seemed to have caught Charlie Volchek by surprise, and as she walked beside him to the door, he said in a kinder tone than he had used yet, "Don't worry. Everything will work out for the best. It's going to be all right."

Nothing was going to be all right ever, but Jeannie, fury and fear welling up in her in equal parts, couldn't tell him that. She saw herself pointing to her son, asking: Just how many shocks do you think his delicate balance can sustain? But then, Charlie Volchek didn't know about Piggy's traumas.

When the Police chief had walked out into the night, Jeannie returned to the boys. Slime's eyes had finally closed, but from Piggy's, tears continued to trickle. She got them both off the couch, asking Slime if he had ever called his mother.

"Yes, ma'am," he answered sleepily, "as soon as we got inside. I said I was staying the night, if that's all right with you."

"Of course it is, honey. I expected you to."

Piggy went up the stairs after Slime, lugging the shattered parts of Bee. Jeannie didn't know what he was going to do with them, or if it was possible even to make repairs. Somehow she suspected, as she thought he must too, that constructing a new BeeBee would be an obscenity. In Pig's room she got down the sleeping bag and an extra pillow from the closet and made up a bed for Slime on the floor. When she had both boys safely tucked in, Piggy still holding on to what had once been his friend, she went out to the hall. Below she saw the lights, a pale glow flooding the living room. But she was too tired to go down and turn them off. Let everything alone until tomorrow, she thought, aching with fatigue, as she entered her room. She stripped off her clothes and crawled between the cool, damp sheets, but it was a long, long time before she actually fell asleep.

The next day was worse, the hiatus between death and the funeral. Though there wouldn't be any official burial for Bee. His casing was irretrievably destroyed, though miraculously, his computer was unscathed.

"So why can't he just build another robot?" Charlie Volchek asked when he came to see Jeannie after lunch. Slime had gone home finally and Piggy was in the backyard. Apparently he hadn't heard the blue-and-white and Jeannie hoped that he'd stay outside until she learned just what the police chief had to say.

"Can't he make another one?" Charlie Volchek asked again when Jeannie brought coffee on a pewter tray from the kitchen.

She handed him a large yellow mug, thinking: This is ridiculous. He's not paying a social call so why am I behaving like he is? Why aren't I screaming and hollering, demanding that he do something and do it fast?

"Sure he can. He could probably build an atom bomb if he felt like it. He's a genius, not just smart. But building another robot isn't the point. He has the mental capacity, and Bee's computer is still intact, needing only a nip and tuck, or so he said. But you see," she said, sitting down and facing him, hoping he'd understand, "BeeBee was . . . well, simply BeeBee. It's as though you had a dog and he was hit by a truck. You wouldn't run out the first thing next morning and buy another, same breed, same sex, same dopey look in his eye. Would you?"

"We're talking about a machine, Mrs. Conway, not an animal." Charlie sipped his coffee daintily, surprising for such a big man.

"But BeeBee wasn't just a machine. Yes, he was metal and had a computer inside. But he was real to us. *He was part of our family!*" Tears came into her eyes and she wiped them away with a crumpled Kleenex. It wasn't the first time she had cried that day

"He wasn't a living thing, you know." He watched her impassively, though she thought he was baiting her, trying to force her to lose what was left of her control.

"You think of him as something like a Walkman. But he wasn't that to us at all. We loved Bee!" She looked down at her hands worrying the sodden Kleenex. Her coffee remained untouched on the table. "I sometimes think it doesn't matter whom you love, just that you do."

"What is it you want from me?" he asked quietly. "To arrest Harry Pringle and throw him in the can? Elvira Williams too?"

"Yes. I want justice. And I want to be able to tell my son, to have him see, that justice exists. If nothing's done, no action taken, how will he ever know that the law works for him and not against him?"

Suddenly Charlie Volchek looked angry. He put down his coffee mug with a bang and grasped his knees with thick hands. "You know, I was thinking of telling you to have him keep that thing, that robot, off the streets. That it was stopping traffic. A public nuisance. Whatever. But just locking it up at home like a washing machine. Because I knew this was going to happen—" She opened her mouth, but before she could say anything he stopped her. "No, wait. I don't mean I knew that Harry Pringle was going to get pickled to his scalp and grab Elvira's shotgun and whack the living bejesus out of it. I didn't know that. But as sure as God made chickens, I knew something was going to go wrong. No one in town liked that robot or the idea of it. And, to be blunt, nobody likes your kid much for being smart enough to build it."

"I know, I know," she screamed at him. "But does that make it right?"

The back door banged shut and Piggy came through the kitchen. When he reached the dining room arch he saw Charlie Volchek and stopped dead, bristling like an angry dog. But he spoke calmly, Jeannie was relieved to hear, asking, "Did you arrest Harry Pringle?"

"No, I didn't. He said it was an accident. That the thing was attacking him and he was only trying to get away. But it chased him. He said you"—he pointed a stubby finger at

Piggy—"told it to get him. And he grabbed Elvira's gun to save himself."

Piggy's composure shredded. He howled, waving his arms, "That's a lie! We were just coming home and *he* attacked *us*!"

"Piggy! Piggy, you home?" The back door cracked again and Sam appeared, pushing her long hair from her face. When she saw Piggy, she smiled lopsidedly. One eye was swollen almost shut and was purplish

"Sam was there, she—" But then he saw her eye and he cried out in alarm, "What happened?"

She shrugged, her slight shoulders rising like chicken wings, and peered around him into the living room. "Hi, Mrs. Conway. Hello, Chief Volchek. Did you come to arrest my father?" None of them could miss the intermingling of hope and worry in her voice.

"He says it was an accident," the police chief said, watching her. "And Elvira backs him up."

"I don't know about Mrs. Williams," Sam replied, "but you know you shouldn't believe my father. He lies."

Jeannie, unable to contain herself a moment longer, cried, "Sam! Your eye!"

She seemed to shrivel up underneath her down vest. Lowering her head, she mumbled, "Oh, I just fell."

Charlie Volchek snarled, "I bet you did."

Jeannie whipped around and pinned the chief to the back of his chair with a glare of pure rage. "Are you just going to sit there and let that man beat this child to death?"

"Samantha!" Charlie barked. "Did your old man give you that shiner?"

She moved even closer to Piggy, grabbing for one of his hands, holding on to him as though she needed him to keep herself from flying away. "No sir, I was just clumsy, that's all," she whispered.

Jeannie was sweating by the time Charlie Volchek left. She was assailed with the feeling that things were beyond salvation, that life had slipped from her control. If she had done more or done it all differently, then nothing would have gone wrong.

She put the two mugs on the tray and took them into the

kitchen. From the window she saw Piggy and Sam at the fence looking over to the river.

If only I had stayed home and driven the boys to the party, BeeBee would be out there now rolling up and down over the grass, she thought. *It* wouldn't have happened. Not then but sometime, a voice drummed inside her head, her thoughts echoing what Charlie Volchek had said. So it was Harry Pringle who was a drunk and crazy and probably out to get even because of Piggy's friendship with Sam.

Sam. . . . Jeannie got a pain far back in her head thinking about what Harry Pringle had done to the poor child. The blatant cruelty appalled her. She longed to take Sam in her arms and soothe away her pain.

Charlie Volchek wasn't going to do anything about Sam either. He was just sitting still while Harry Pringle pounded away at her like a piece of raw meat. Which made Jeannie shake with anger once again. If, she thought, there is any divine retribution, Harry Pringle would fall into the Susquehanna one night and drown. But that probably wasn't going to happen either.

Jeannie rubbed the back of her neck, feeling the stiffness in her muscles, and hoped she was getting a really bad cold. She longed to sneeze and cough, to be good and sick so that she could sleep away the next few days. Only she was the big person now, she was the one who was responsible, and if she collapsed it would be too bad because there wasn't anybody around who was about to gather her up off the floor.

This is all I need, she thought, the tears scratching behind her eyelids, to start feeling sorry for myself.

It wasn't fair! But then, nothing that had gone on in the last few years of her life had been fair, she thought.

Turning away as the children neared the porch, she went back upstairs, wanting Tony so much she felt she was going to shatter. But there was no Tony anywhere. He wasn't in the big bed they had always shared, waiting to ease her pain. He was with Julia, easing hers.

"It's all my fault," Sam said, for what was probably the hundredth time.

And Piggy said, as he had earlier, "No it isn't. If he got a gun and shot somebody, no one would try you for murder.

Besides, you came to help and you did try to stop him. That counts for an awful lot, Sam."

Sam twisted a strand of hair around her fingers, her face knotted up. "But if you weren't my friend, if BeeBee hadn't been—" She gulped, sorrow making her voice quivery.

Piggy awkwardly reached out and with one finger tentatively touched the discolored flesh beneath her right eye. "He did that, didn't he? Because of Bee and how you tried to help."

Gently she pulled away. "I told you, Pig, I fell. I'm always falling, bumping myself." She seemed heavy with sadness, weighted down.

Piggy didn't believe her. He knew that Harry Pringle had popped her really hard in the eye, and he wished he could hit Sam's father right back. A sea of churning emotions was making Pig shake, and clenching his hands tightly together, he hunched over.

"Maybe if we had a funeral," Sam was saying, "we'd feel better." She scuffed at the step with the toe of her sneaker and went on, "I always thought that if my ma had died and we had a service in the church with flowers and everything, and lots of crying and me in my Sunday dress, that I'd feel better. You know?"

Piggy was shocked. No matter how mad he got at his mother or father (with whom he felt he had very good reason to be in a rage), he couldn't conceive of wanting either of them dead.

Bertram Lennard shuffled through his thoughts, and Piggy shifted about, uncomfortable. A siren whined up on Main Street and he heard screaming. Gruffly he said, "Death is awful. You wouldn't want to be dead, would you?"

Her face paled, all the bones coming up through the skin, and she cried, "No, no! I'd hate it! I don't want to be dead in a hole in the ground."

"Then why—"

" 'Cause I hate *her*. 'Cause she left me with him like I was a dog or something. No, if I was a dog she woulda taken me. She *liked* dogs." She bent her head, the silky hair cascading over her wounded face, hiding her, but not before Piggy saw the watery glint of tears.

Unnerved, he glanced off to the right and watched the cars crossing Main Bridge. Beyond that a heavy diesel rig crept

over South Bridge, looking like a matchbox toy. Beside him
he heard Sam mewing softly like a kitten and wanted to cry
himself for BeeBee. He felt the loss, the emptiness, in the pit
of his stomach, and turning to her, saw the thin shoulders
beneath the sweatshirt and tattered down vest—little tufts of
down were coming through the quilting—and asked, "Do you
really want her dead?"

The blond head nodded vigorously.

"Why?" he asked, bending forward, trying to see her face
beneath the hair.

" 'Cause," she said.

"Because why?" he persisted.

She brought her head up, her voice raspy with pain, " 'Cause
I hate her, that's why. I told you, I hate her like poison.
More than him even. I hate her 'cause she went off and left
me and he's so mad he's gonna kill me for that."

Piggy stiffened in surprise. "Wha-at?" he stuttered. "Who's
going to kill you? Don't be silly, Sam. Your father's rotten
and no good, but he's not going to kill you! People don't do
things like that."

A haze of pure panic settled over him, almost visible in the
gloomy air. He felt it tug at him, lifting his hair up from his
scalp, and before he could even batter it off, Bertram Lennard's
scratchy voice was roaring through his head. Piggy's memory
split apart and there was Bertram rising up, cackling, as he
scampered across the lab at Height. And the lab windows,
streaked with thin rivulets of rain, were flooding with a thick
viscous substance, with *blood*! The bright red windows under
the shiny light reflected the flames that shot from the mouth
of the blowtorch like dragon's breath. Jets of fire arced across
the room, spitting at the yellow T-shirt with its faded letter-
ing, and the flames turned the shirt black, the brown pants
too, and the soft pulpy face, and the lips still peeled back in a
scathing taunt, but now in a scream. The lips, the cheeks, the
forehead, the eyes popping in their sockets were soft as Silly
Putty before they blackened.

And Piggy heard himself shrieking in an uncontrollable
fury, *He won't hurt you, Bee!* as the staggering flames soared,
shooting higher and higher. Bertram Lennard stumbled backward, bubbling his own discordant yowl like a cat whose tail
had been severed by an ax.

And he was being whipped around the lab in a tornado of

rage, his teeth clacking, his head snapping forward, then back, the blowtorch dropped from his hand. . . .

"Piggy! Piggy!"

The thin red scar just at Sam's hairline swam into view. He saw the bruised eye and the dark discoloration.

"You just went somewhere else, Piggy. And I got scared because I thought I lost you," Sam said.

He fingered the puffy skin again and said, "People do do terrible things." He knew for certain in that moment, just as he had back *then*, what Bertram Lennard would have done if he hadn't got caught by the flames. His voice stuck as he swallowed hard, a lump midway in his throat, "And they should be punished, even dead. Yes," he decided, looking thoughtfully into space, "bad people should die. Be chopped up by machetes or hung from trees until their brains turn to mush."

She vibrated with excitement, snatching his hand, squeezing it, their fingers entwined. "That's right, Piggy." Looking over her shoulder at her house next door, she whispered, "I wish he was dead too. I wish they both were and I could live with you and your mother."

The longing in her voice was so heart-shattering that Piggy was jolted yet again. He stared down at their two hands curled one into the other and a shiver of pleasure raced along his spine. He had the oddest sensation, that he was swimming in a strong tide, out of his depth. The currents were pulling, tugging at him, and if he didn't move frantically he'd be sucked under to the river bottom.

"I won't let anything happen to you," he swore, making a commitment with the intensity only a thirteen-year-old could bring to bear. "Nothing," he said, hearing BeeBee's cheery beep, seeing the robot rolling toward him, his arms spread wide. Never again, he vowed in a silent promise, would someone he cared about be hurt.

He glanced over at Sam's house, and, as if conjured up, her father appeared in an upstairs window. His bulk filled the frame, his white undershirt and hairy arms and broad, stony face. He stood watching them look up at him, and on the step below, Piggy sensed Sam's tension. He heard her breath puff in ragged gasps. Her hand squeezed his almost painfully as she held on to him.

"He's gonna kill me for being over here," she whispered, fear curling around her words. "He said for me to stay away."

She began to rise, letting go of him, as though Harry Pringle was commanding her home. Piggy clamped his hand on her shoulder, nailing her to the step. "He's not going to do anything, Sam," he said emphatically.

Shrugging away from him, she cried, "You know, Pig, you're a real baby. Don't you remember what he did to BeeBee? And nobody cared 'cept you and me and Slime and maybe your mother. That's more than would care if he bashed me in." She stood up in spite of his effort to keep her with him. "I gotta go."

Piggy was scared. "No, stay here with us." He didn't want her to leave him just then. He was seized by paroxysms of fear and grief, and something he suspected might be known as love. But he felt Sam slipping away from him. He could imagine her fading in the murky gray light, turning into particles of air. A scream was rushing through him, threatening to burst out of his mouth, and he had to bite down hard to keep it locked inside.

In that moment he ached for BeeBee, needed the reassuring presence of the robot, the same way he had needed his stuffed Teddy when he was small.

Sam looked at him with her eyes full of sadness. "Can't stay forever, you know. Besides, he's not drunk now. Won't be drunk until later and then if I'm asleep and have the chest pushed up in front of the door, he won't do nothin'."

"Sam—" But there was no stopping her flight.

"Don't worry, Piggy." Waving her hand, she ran across the lawns, appearing so little and frail that Piggy suspected he was going to cry.

10

The first schoolday without Bee, Piggy awoke sick to his stomach and threw up in the toilet before brushing his teeth. He almost said to his mother: I'm not well enough to go. I want to stay home in bed. But he knew that the next day would roll over him like a tidal wave, and the day after that, until one morning he would have to get out of bed or stay there forever. So he washed his face and combed his hair and dressed, then went downstairs to breakfast. All he could swallow was weak tea, and he alternated between chills and sweats, but he was in the car with his mother at eight-forty-five.

A boy named George from his history class was the first person Piggy saw when he left the parking lot and crossed the road to the campus. "Sorry about your robot," he called. "That was pretty a shitty thing."

Piggy bowed his head and said thank you in the age-old manner of the bereaved, and proceeded to Humans for English. He met Betts McManus on the steps and she said how awful it was about Bee. Then Larry Houser jogged by, cutting across the walk, and yelled out that he was sorry too.

The pattern of the day was set, as the kids offered their condolences whenever they saw Piggy. The tone was somewhere between losing a parent and a favorite pet. By lunchtime when Pig met Slime in the cafeteria, at least half the school had spoken to him, including Dr. Mellon, who had had both Piggy and Jeannie in his private office and raged about the "atrocity," as he called it, parenthetically referring to the downfall of Western civilization.

Piggy was even invited to sit at a table with a group of

second-form boys, and he and Slime had to repeat their story
of the vicious attack on Bee by Harry Pringle. Tears swam
in Piggy's eyes and the other boys turned their heads away in
embarrassment, but they all reiterated how rotten it was.
And then there was a moment of silence almost by mistake
before the boys launched into an argument about an upcoming basketball game.

The afternoon was a replica of the morning, and when the
last bell rang and Piggy went out to the parking lot to meet his
mother by the car, he was almost—for the first time—reluctant
to leave Mason. As he walked down the path, he felt the
emptiness beside him. He missed the comforting beep that
Bee always made. Still, for one painful second he thought:
I've never had so many people be so nice to me before.
BeeBee's death had in a strange, unsettling way brought him
more human contact than Bee alive had done. He thought: If
Harry Pringle hadn't killed him, they'd still all be ignoring me.

The guilt hit him with the impact of the train flying out of
the Halloween tunnel, and he staggered, his head swimming.
His feet seemed to have a will of their own, and they were
moving, running now, carrying him forward to the car, which
he fell against, breathing heavily. His lungs ached, and the
tears were rushing up and out of him in great hulking sobs.
He turned his back to the school and stared out over the
river, seeing his house through a blur on the other side.

Bee, he thought, won't be there when we get home. He
wasn't getting his computer reprogrammed or his casing
resoldered. He was lying in pieces, one part in a green
garbage bag at the back of the cellar, the other part tucked
under the pillow of Pig's bed.

Dr. Mellon had said: Surely you can rebuild him, or build
another robot. Piggy had simply stared. How could he explain that even if he reconstructed Bee, it wouldn't be Bee, it
would be somebody else. Robots had personalities, Piggy
thought, just like people. Quirks, eccentricities, special ways
of behaving. It didn't matter if you programmed them all the
same, stamped them out in uniform on an assembly line, or
had them perform the same simple or complex functions.
They were different. He could have picked out Bee from a
hundred robots all of whom looked alike.

No, he couldn't rebuild Bee because when he was done

that robot wouldn't be BeeBee. And he didn't want just another robot—any robot—he wanted his friend back.

Hatred for Harry Pringle rushed through his veins. He didn't hear his mother come up behind him. She put her hand on his arm and he jumped, swinging around all set to lash out.

"Hey, it's just me," she said, stepping back.

He put his hand up and let her take it, drawing him forward and giving him a quick hug. "I was just thinking about Bee and what a rotten person Sam's father is. Bee never hurt him so why did he have to do that?"

Jeannie couldn't explain, he understood that, since she had already told him that some people are crazy and some just plain mean. She suspected that Harry Pringle was both. So there was no way of unscrambling what passed through his mind.

Now she said nothing, unlocking the car and getting inside. She leaned across the front seat and lifted up the button so that he could clamber in. He pulled the door after him, locking it, as she had told him so many times, then stared over at the back seat, where Bee always sat. But BeeBee wasn't there. Not even a ghost of him remained.

When Piggy and Jeannie arrived home Sam was waiting on the back steps. She was hunched over and Piggy thought there was a strange lump beneath her sweatshirt. "Hi," he said, and sprawled down beside her.

"Was it awful?" she asked him right away. "Being in school without BeeBee?"

He reshuffled himself and replied, "Not really. People were very nice. Only—" He stopped and Sam finished the thought for him. "Only that doesn't make it better or bring him back."

"Yeah," he whispered, afraid for a minute he was going to cry. He kept his eyes straight ahead and focused on Mason in the distance.

"This won't help much either, but it's all I got, Pig. His name's Chester and I thought . . . well . . . I thought you might like to keep him for yours now."

She was holding out a stuffed animal—a dog, Piggy thought. All white and shaggy and wearing a green vest. At least it had been white once, but the fur, except for a few bald patches, was grayish. And the vest, faded, had tiny rips like moth holes in it.

"Oh Sam!" he sighed, this time only a millimeter away from weeping. He stretched out his hand and she passed Chester into his keeping. "He's your special favorite, isn't he?"

"Uh huh," she said, squirming happily at Piggy's pleasure. Her bruised face was glowing.

"I'll take good care of him," Piggy promised, pushing away the awful thought that he hadn't taken such good care of Bee.

"Not that I mean for Chester to replace *him*," she said. "Nobody could ever do that. It's just that sometimes at night when I'm especially sad, or when I can't sleep, Chester's helpful. Like a friend."

"I know what you mean," he said fervently, watching her over Chester's head. His heart was thumping in his chest and for the first time since Bee's death his emotional balance tipped from sorrow to joy. "Friends are important," he went on, feeling hot and cold at the same time. "Like you and me, Sam."

"Oh yes, Pig," she whispered, and gave him a dazzling smile.

Piggy's palms started to sweat, and staring at Sam, he was overcome by the weirdest feeling. He wanted to bridge the short distance between them and put his lips on hers. Piggy wanted to kiss Sam, he wanted to very much. So much, in fact, that he felt foolish. Sissy stuff, he tried to tell himself, but longed to kiss her anyway. Imagining himself tilting forward, leaning into her, he began to sway and saw Sam's face rush toward him. But it was only a mirage.

She had jumped down the steps and was standing on the lawn. "I guess I better be getting home, Pig," she said, her lips still upturned in a smile.

Was it even possible to kiss someone who was smiling? And where would the noses go?

He gulped and nodded his head, afraid to speak. As Sam skipped across the yards, then up to her own porch—waving at him before she disappeared inside—Piggy, clutching Chester tightly against his chest, was stricken with regret. Why, why hadn't he kissed her as he ached to do? But he had no answer to that. He sat thinking about it for a long time, until Jeannie came to the back door and called him into the house.

*   *   *

It would have been beneficial, worthwhile, if things had stayed the same for Piggy at Mason. Bee's death would have had a purpose if Pig had been brought into the community of the school, accepted as a full-fledged member, because of it. Jeannie was hopeful, but as the days passed, she saw it wasn't to be. After the first ripple of excitement, BeeBee's dying fizzled like a descending Roman candle, and Piggy was all alone again. Exactly where he had been before Halloween. The kids didn't pull away so much as they just went on with their usual concerns and didn't include him. They weren't unfriendly or even impolite, they merely forgot that he was there. And slowly BeeBee, the three-day wonder, receded into the past. Even his spectacular ending had faded from memory.

Welling too settled back with a sigh, no longer recalling that Bee had been a thorn in its side. After a few days no one even referred to the robot, or what had happened to him. It was as if no trace of him remained, as though the Susquehanna had swallowed Bee up.

Only Piggy remembered, but then Pig couldn't forget. It seemed that he was missing an integral part of himself, some essential cog or wheel, without which he wasn't really right. The only thing that saved him was friendship, with Slime but especially with Sam. He kept Chester on his bed, on top of the pillow under which Bee's computer lay at rest. And every night he forced himself to recall the good things in his life—to count his blessings as his grandmother used to say. There wasn't much, or so it seemed, but of what there was, the best was Sam.

11

There was a heavy frost the next week and the week after that. In the mornings Piggy found the ground silvery and hard, the dead grass crackling beneath his feet. They listened to the weather report and hear of storms brewing in Canada, in the Great Plains. Jack Reiss, when she took the Chevy in for antifreeze, told Jeannie that once it got going it was planning to be a bad winter. He could tell. All his joints were acting up. An early winter, too. But somehow throughout November the storms never came. On the Monday and Tuesday preceding Thanksgiving the sun shone and the air was warm, almost heavy, but then on Wednesday the clouds closed in and the temperature dropped twenty degrees. For an hour or so in the late afternoon there was a brief flurry of snow.

Piggy and Sam sat in the kitchen watching Jeannie make preparations for Thanksgiving dinner the following day.

"It's all phony baloney, being thankful," Piggy said, as he peeled carrots for the salad while Sam cracked walnuts for the cake.

"Paul!" Jeannie cried.

The knife slid down Piggy's left index finger, cutting away a flap of skin. Blood washed over the peelings. Stupidly Piggy stared at what he had done. There wasn't any pain; it might have been another person's hand.

Jeannie dragged him to the sink and stuck the finger under the cold water. "Don't move while I get some mercurochrome and a Band-Aid," she instructed. Sam came and stood beside him and together they watched the revolving, lacy patterns of blood crisscrossing the white bottom of the sink in thin streams.

Sam asked, "Does it hurt?"

"A little," Piggy replied, feeling the throbbing go right up his arm.

Jeannie came back downstairs and with a gauze pad pressed the wound until the bleeding stopped. Then she bandaged the finger and told him to sit out of the way. He hunched on his chair and held the finger straight up, pointing at the ceiling.

"I thought I heard BeeBee," he said after a while. "I mean when the knife slipped. Or really, that's why it slipped."

Sam looked wretched. "I miss him," she whispered, hiding her face. The metal crackers snapped shut. The walnut fell in pieces into the bowl.

Jeannie raised her eyebrows and said quietly, "I do too." Then, changing the subject, she asked Sam what she was doing for Thanksgiving.

"Nothing," Sam replied. "I asked him if we could have a turkey but he said it was a waste of money. Besides, we got nothing to celebrate, is what he said."

Jeannie stopped stirring the cake batter and stared at the little girl. "Do you want to come have dinner with us? We'd love to have you. Wouldn't we, Paul?"

"Oh, Sam," he cried, breaking into a rare smile, "say yes. Your coming would make it less sad. Not having Bee here, I mean."

Sam blushed and wiggled about. "Don't know if I can. Depends." She scratched her nose and sighed wistfully. "Would be nice."

Jeannie said, "I'll tell you what. We'll set a place for you and if you can come, even at the last minute, why just gallop over. Okay?"

"Thank you, Mrs. Conway," she said, "I appreciate that." But her forehead furrowed, the eyes beneath the thin blond brows were icy, as if the invitation brought pain with the pleasure.

Yet she did come, wearing a pink fuzzy sweater and a dark skirt inches too short. Her hair was neatly brushed back and held by barrettes just above her ears. Her being there made the day bearable for Piggy.

"That certainly was a good dinner your mother made," Sam

said after they had eaten what the two of them agreed was "too much." They were sitting on the floor of the living room and Piggy was teaching Sam how to play canasta. "I hope I learn to cook good like that someday."

"I bet you're a good cook right now," Piggy replied gallantly, wondering what it was like to be grown up and married.

"Not really," she said, her head lowered, concentrating intently on her cards. Her tongue flickered at the side of her mouth.

"Sam," Piggy pointed out, "you're only eleven, you know."

"Twelve next month," Sam said.

The game over, Sam sat back on her heels and whispered that she guessed she should be leaving. Her father was over at Corney's, which was why she could come in the first place, but she shouldn't push her luck. Piggy walked her to the back door, where she solemnly thanked Jeannie for a wonderful time.

A draft of cold air blew through the kitchen as Sam left, and Piggy hurriedly shut the door. He peered through the small window, trying to watch her run over the grass, but it was too dark outside. Night had blackened the landscape.

Sam, leaving Piggy and Jeannie behind, her arms goose-bumped from the cold, was happy. It was such a strange sensation that she thought maybe she had overeaten. She went into her kitchen humming. She'd be twelve soon and maybe, she thought, one day when she was grown up she'd be a teacher like Mrs. Conway. Maybe she could even marry Piggy and have a big house with lots of people to do for her, because Piggy, she just knew it, was going to be rich and famous. He was that smart.

Without turning on any lights, she went upstairs. In her small bedroom at the rear of the second floor she switched on the overhead. Taking off the angora sweater, she neatly folded it in tissue paper, just as her mother had taught her to do, and put it away in the bottom drawer. The skirt, she hung back up in the closet, wondering what she'd do when she couldn't close the waist with a safety pin anymore. *He* didn't give her any money except for food. Maybe she could get a job somewhere after school. Babysitting maybe. She thought about little babies and how nice it would be to hold one in her arms. Only she didn't know any babies or any mothers who had them. Most of the kids she knew were too big for sitters, or had older brothers and sisters themselves.

Life was just problems. The joys, like Thanksgiving dinner, were impossible to retain for long before they dissipated into mist. She pulled the flannel nightgown over her head and padded down the hall to wash her face and brush her teeth. All the food and the little bit of wine mixed with water that she and Piggy had been allowed had made her sleepy. Finally she crawled into bed, and pulling the covers up to her chin, willed herself into sleep, into pleasant dreams that were so much nicer most times than real life.

She felt herself rising, rising, arcing through the air like a paper airplane. And then the heavy thump, the pain shooting along her jaw. The hurting brought her fully awake and her eyes snapped open. The light was blinding, flooding the room, reflecting harshly against the mirror. The light was everywhere except for the patches of black that cut through the visions, the darkness of her father's arm, his jacket sleeve, his shoulder, chest, thigh, pieces of her father like invading blips on the Asteroid machine in the Ice Cream Hut.

There was a ringing in her ears and she knew she had hit her head on something. A dark, sticky fluid dribbled down her nightgown. She put her hand to her lip and it came back bloody. Her mouth was cut and her fingers all streaked with red.

"I didn't do nothing!" she screamed up at him.

He reached down and plucked her off the floor, her feet dangling in the air, his belly bumping against her. His breath was foul, as though he was putrefying inside. "I had 'nough of you, Grace! Hear me!"

"I ain't Grace. I'm Samantha!"

But he was beyond hearing, beyond reason, in some nether land where his private demons walked. His face was drenched with sweat and he shook, roaring as though the earth was falling away beneath him.

Sam went limp, hoping he'd just drop her and go away, that a different tangent of craziness would snare him down the hall, down the stairs. Let him break all the dishes or overturn the furniture; he had done both before when drink had driven him mad.

She could scream and scream but nobody would come. Piggy's house was on the other side and Mr. Mullins next

door was stone deaf. She shut her bloody lips and clenched
her teeth. He was shaking her, babbling, words spilling from
his mouth like vomit. Dropping her to the floor, he kicked at
her buttocks. She scurried away, trying to squirm under the
bed, but, for all his drunkenness, he was too quick. Catching
the edge of her nightgown, he heaved her up. She felt the
cold against her bare skin, and suddenly he had her by the
legs. She swung far out, sailing. There was the braided rug
below, the chenille spread folded primly back, the dented
pillow where minutes before her head had been. The scene
below was caught, held, like a photograph taken by a ship in
outer space. In that one brief moment before she hit the wall,
she didn't have a single thought. Fear so strong it stopped
her breath like a seizure, and then there was the wall, the
edge of the door. Pain blotted everything out except *It hurts
so much!* Blackness washed over her. Blackness shutter-stopped
the light as she bounced from the wall to the floor and lay
still, blood puddling beneath the blond hair. Above her she
didn't hear the roar. And she didn't feel the heavy booted toe
pushing at her legs. She didn't feel her arm being moved up
and down like a doll's.

She didn't . . .

She wasn't . . . not anymore.

12

Piggy slept the sleep of the dead, slept through the whine of
Charlie Volchek's patrol car coming to a grinding halt, the
slamming of doors, the arrival and departure of Mr. Toomy's
black wagon, even the howl of Harry Pringle's shrill of out-
rage. Piggy slept strangled by dreams, none of which he

remembered when he woke. He lay in bed, warm and woolly with the last vestiges of sleep, and thought of BeeBee, feeling as though a piece of his heart was missing. He reached under the pillow, and taking hold of the small computer as though it were something alive, sleepily recalled Bee's beginning roll, that initial beep, when he shook hands with Tony for the first time.

It was just after two A.M. when he tumbled out of sleep, disoriented, awake now for no reason that he could put his finger on. He thought of Bee and traced the drift of shadows on the ceiling. Then the doorbell was ringing. Short, insistent jabs of sound. Struggling up, he heard Jeannie leave her room, and the *flop, flop* of her slippers hitting the stairs.

Piggy got out of bed and crept barefoot into the hall. Leaning over the railing, he saw the pool of light below, and then Jeannie returning from the front door with Charlie Volchek. Piggy's heart accelerated and his throat started to close up. The police coming in the middle of the night, he knew, was bad. Nothing good had made Charlie Volchek ring their doorbell so late.

In slow motion he moved toward the stairs, tugging at his pajama bottoms, tightening the string at the waist. The disembodied voices floated up to him, the words like splinters.

"I heard the sirens, the cars . . ."

"Yeah . . . something's gone wrong . . ."

". . . Too tired to get up and see . . ."

". . . Something lousy . . ."

"What? . . ."

"Dead . . . the kid . . . only a little girl . . ."

Piggy was in the living room before they heard his approach. He stared across the distance at his mother's face. It was chalky, the skin stretched taut across the bones. She gaped back at him, her unfocusing eyes wide, her mouth half-open. Her hand crept up to her throat as if she were shutting off an incipient cry.

Charlie Volchek was a mountain that had just been hit by a slide, his large bulk shifting inside his rumpled uniform. "I'm sorry to have to tell you this . . ."

Piggy tried not to hear him, to close his ears to the words that were coming out of the police chief's mouth. He knew that whenever grown-ups started a sentence with "I'm sorry," something terrible had either just gone on or was about to. And he didn't want any more terrible things in his life! He had had all he could handle.

But he couldn't stop the words crawling toward him like spiders. "Sam . . . dead . . . steps . . . bedroom . . . suspicious . . . Harry Pringle."

Whoosh, all the air left Piggy's body. He was a desiccated husk as the blood turned to dust in his veins. His stomach heaved, and just barely managing to turn his head, he vomited on the rug.

Jeannie ran to him, taking him in her arms. His body heaved and tossed against hers as though he were having convulsions. Carefully she inched him to the couch and sat him down. Then she ran for paper towels and a wet washcloth.

"Anything I can do to help?" Charlie Volchek asked solicitously, his face slippery with concern.

Piggy straightened up, his head suddenly cleared, and sceamed, a bloodcurdling wail that slammed at the walls and ceiling, forced Charlie Volchek back two steps, and brought Jeannie running. The scream poured out of him as the vomit had done, so shattering that the windows rattled in their frames.

Before Jeannie could grab him, he was off the couch, flying around the room, spinning, turning like a dervish. He knocked over a standing lamp, sent throw pillows flying. Careening, he snatched books off the shelves and flung them. Spittle rolled down his chin, and the scream decelerated into a whimper, as he whirled and ran, both Jeannie and Charlie behind him now, trying to catch hold. He had gone out of control like a car that had lost its brakes.

Charlie brought him down to the couch with a flying tackle, pressing him into the cushions. Jeannie tried to wash his face with a cool cloth, but his head was flapping from side to side. "Steady, kid, steady," Charlie Volchek ordered, but Piggy didn't heed him even if his words now made any sense. There was nothing Charlie could do except keep the force of his weight bearing down on Piggy, holding him captive until he ran out of hysteria like a clock winding down. And eventually he did. His body shuddered to a slow tremor like the waves after a major quake, and then, at last, he was still.

Jeannie, only inches from hysteria herself, asked, "Should I call the doctor?"

"No, I don't think so. He should be all right now." He

watched Piggy, passive under his big hands. "You will be okay, won't you, if I let you go?"

Piggy didn't speak, his face twitching. But he nodded weakly. Slowly Charlie Volchek pulled back. Piggy coughed and his nose leaked, but he groped his way to a sitting position. Now he allowed Jeannie to pat at his face, and when she had him cleaned up, she gave him a glass of water to drink.

"I want to go to my room," he said finally. His voice was flat and he had stopped crying, but the veins in his temple were throbbing.

Jeannie glanced at Charlie Volchek, who shrugged. "Okay, honey," she replied, "I'll help you up."

"No," he said firmly, "I'm all right."

They watched him stagger across the room and pull himself up the steps like an old person. When they heard his door ease behind him, Jeannie said, "Maybe I shouldn't leave him alone."

"No," Charlie answered, "he has to work it out in his own way, whatever that's going to be."

But neither of them would have suspected what Piggy was thinking alone in the dark, alone with his agony—for hadn't he vowed he'd never let her be harmed? Alone, he cradled the computer and watched the dawn's light crawl up the shade.

The next morning Slime found him still in bed, pushed back against the headboard, the computer tucked in his arms.

"Your mom said it was okay for me to come up," he said, inching his way into the room and closing the door. Piggy didn't say anything, just sprawled in the bed like a dead person laid out for burial. "I guess you know about Sam. I do because they brought the body to us. It's terrible, my mother says, my father does too. And nobody's sure yet what really happened to her." Slime rushed on. "Harry Pringle said she fell down the steps, but I heard my father tell my mother that when they got there she was in the bedroom on the floor which is nowhere near the steps and Harry Pringle smelled like a distillery, my father said." He paused to catch his breath, then went on, "Mr. Mullins' daughter is visiting from Louisiana 'cause it's a holiday and she heard all the noise and called the cops, otherwise nobody woulda known anything about it. My mother said he probably woulda buried her in the backyard and said she ran off like Grace did. That's Sam's mother. And maybe, my mother said, they should dig up the yard anyway because who knows what happened to Grace. Any animal who coulda done what Harry Pringle did mighta killed his own wife as easy as spitting. That's what my mother told my father. They didn't know I was listening," he explained, steadier now. He stopped, the silence lapping about them, and then added as an afterthought, "They think he beat her to death but they can't prove it yet."

Piggy felt his stomach rushing up toward his throat, but he pushed the bile down resolutely and said, "Can I see her?"

"You want to *what*?"

"I want to see Sam, Slime. Where is she?"

"She's dead, Pig," he said, trying to be reasonable. "And she's in a cold drawer in our basement. There's gotta be an autopsy." Piggy winced—the first flicker of emotion he had shown—as Slime continued. "The coroner's out of town for the weekend so it can't be done until Monday morning I heard my father tell the chief."

"I want to see her," he said stubbornly. "You could fix that."

"Sure," he said. "We can always sneak downstairs when nobody's looking. But why do you want to see her? I don't."

Piggy didn't know why, didn't even care why. He just did. For one of the few times in his life, he wasn't thinking clearly. Cold fury settled inside him as he remembered how much Sam hadn't wanted to be dead, to be in a hole in the ground in the darkness. Only remembering that did him no good; it just brought more pain. There was a thick soup inside his skull: Bertram Lennard and BeeBee and Sam all mired together.

"I just do," he said lamely, adding, "Maybe it's all a mistake."

Slime said sadly, "If wishes were fishes."

"What?"

"A silly thing my ma used to say when I was a little kid. Doesn't mean anything." Absently he pulled the zipper of his down jacket up and down, up and down.

Piggy, mesmerized by the grimy knuckles and nails bitten to the quick, said again, "I just do." And all of a sudden, watching Slime's fingers, he thought of worms burrowing their way into Sam's flesh.

This time he couldn't keep the nausea from rising up to his mouth and raced for the toilet. But only a sour trickle of bile came out. He was dizzy. The toilet, sink, bathtub all spun around in his clouded vision, and he stuck his head under the cold-water faucet. The icy rivulets streamed down his neck and soaked his pajama top, but he didn't move until he felt the ground solidly under his feet once again and the churning in his stomach had settled into a steady ache.

Sam was dead.

And he had promised, *I won't let anything happen to you.*

BeeBee was dead too. He remembered the terrible crunching of metal, the shrieking . . .

And he was throwing up in the bathroom, a fact that made him sicker in a less discernible way. Throwing up isn't going to do any good, he admonished himself, turning off the water and toweling his head dry. He brushed the acrid taste out of his mouth and told his fuzzy reflection that nothing was going to do anybody any good; if he stood screaming from the top of the roof until high noon next Sunday, he couldn't bring Sam back to life.

The garage was crowded with tools, a mini snowplow under its tarp, Slime's three-speed, an old red wagon leprous with rust spots, and odds and ends of the funeral trade that Mr. Toomy hadn't the heart to throw out. A wooden coffin lid with a jagged split right down the middle leaned against one wall. The shelves were jammed with cans—paint cans, oil cans, empty cans—and all sorts of bottles. It was dusty, dirty, and had a combined smell of axle grease and something sweet. Piggy suspected it was formaldehyde.

"They're coming," Slime whispered, peering out through the crack in the door. Piggy leaned above Slime's shoulder, and looking over the hump of the hearse's hood, saw the far door open, leading up from the cellar of Toomy's Funeral Parlor—*"We bury with care!"*

Two men stepped out of the light, laughing, their voices tossed by the wind. They faded in the dusk that was quickly dissolving into darkness. The glow behind them went out and their feet pounded down the macadam drive to Main Street.

"Okay, we gotta hurry." Slime grabbed Piggy and pushed him out into the small parking lot that abutted the building. "Now that Bailey and Mort have left, my pa will be about

ten, fifteen minutes before he locks up," he whispered as
they ran across the lot, eased open the outside door that led
down, down—down to the grave, Piggy thought—and hustled inside.

They hit the switch and the lights came on, a bright glare
that illuminated the white walls, the metal tables, the sink
with its *plunk, plunk* of a slow drip. The three vaults were on
the opposite side of the room at the level of Pig's sternum.
Slime confidently led them to the middle one, flipped the
handle, and pulled at the door.

"You're nuts, Pig, you know that," he said. "Dead's dead."
He eased out the drawer on which *something* lay shrouded in
a sheet. Noiselessly Sam's body slid toward them.

They stood quietly at the side of the small hump that
seemed too little to be Sam. Sorrow scratched around inside
Piggy's head, exacerbating his fury. He heard old Waxworks
droning on about the helplessness of man before the indifference of the universe, and wanted to smash something flat.

He reached out, touching a tiny rise beneath the sheet that
had to be Sam's hand, and shook with anger as he imagined
her flesh being eaten away, going soft, flabby, a nesting place
for worms.

I don't want to be dead in a hole in the ground, she had
cried.

The awesomeness of life and death seized him and he
whimpered, "No!"

"You mean you don't want to see her now?" Slime asked in
surprise. But Piggy didn't hear him. Yanking back the cover-
ing, he was confronted with Sam's pallid face. The eyes were
closed, and the lashes, darker in death, lay against the white,
white skin as delicately as moth wings.

"Looks alive, don't she?" Slime asked. Death to him was as
ordinary as breakfast cereal. It neither threatened nor alarmed
him, he was so used to it.

Sam was still wearing the flannel nightgown, splattered
with long, jagged veins of dark dried blood. Blood was en-
crusted on the side of her face, down to her neck. On the
near side of her head Piggy saw the matted hair and the slight
indentation where the skull had been shoved in.

"Seen enough?" Slime asked, listening for his father's step
overhead.

That could easily be sawed away . . . depends which part

*of the brain is . . . Cold. How much rigor? The linkage with
the central nervous system . . .*

Piggy's face had gone as still and white and cold as Sam's, as
thoughts, ideas, flickered behind his eyes. Through smudged
lenses he stared down and saw for an instant not bones and
skin and blackened blood but a series of computations, a nest
of wires, microchips as tiny as decimal points.

"Hey, Pig, com'on." Slime jolted him in the ribs with his
elbow. "We gotta get out of here. If my old man catches us
there'll be you-know-what to pay. I mean, *whomp!* I won't sit
down for a week. Piggy, Jeezit Christmas, let's go!"

"I want her," Piggy said, turning and grabbing hold of
Slime's arm. "I want Sam's body." He was astonished at the
calmness of his voice. Even to his own ears he sounded sane.

I want an ice cream cone. I want to go to the movies.
Ordinary, everyday requests. *I want Sam's body.*

"What do you mean you want Sam's body?" Slime was
gawking at him, stupefied. "Sam's dead. What do you want
her body for?"

"Because I do."

Slime groaned, his eyeballs rotating in their sockets. "God,
Pig, you're not one of those fruitcakes, are you? You know,
one of those nuts who keeps a corpse sitting up in bed like it
was alive. Mrs. Matthews did that when her old man died.
Nobody knew about it for three months. My pa said there
was an awful stink when they finally got him out of there,
sticking to the sheets and all. Tell me you're not a loony tune
like Mrs. Matthews." He stared at Piggy. "They carted her
off to the funny farm."

"I'm not crazy," he said emphatically, thinking: Well, maybe
I am. But he wasn't feeling crazy; he wasn't feeling anything
now. His brain was working with the speed of light. He was
pushing himself, calculating, planning, taking the quantum
leap that he knew might carry him across the divide from
speculation to success. Or might destroy him. Staring into a
bottomless abyss, he didn't care, because this time *he had to
do something*.

Overhead they heard Mr. Toomy's office door slam shut.
"Jeez, let's go. My pa is gonna lock this door and then go
around and lock the outside one."

"No," Piggy said, rooting himself firmly to the concrete

floor. He grabbed hold of Slime and held on. "No, you've got to help me. I want Sam's body."

"Piggy, you're a basket case. We can't just run off, two kids, with a corpse. What would you do with it?"

Piggy tried to explain as Slime began to look like a stone effigy, bonier and more dead than Sam. *"Frankenstein,"* he croaked, breath whistling out through slack lips. "Oh, Jeez, Pig."

Thud, thud . . .

Slime's eyes rolled upward in a nervous glance at the ceiling, every part of him twitching now. He yanked loose from Piggy's grip on his upper arm. "My old man is gonna kill me!" he whispered, panicked. He shoved Piggy in the direction of the steps, but Pig clutched him again and his extra weight kept Slime from traveling more than halfway across the basement before the sharp *click* of the key in the lock. Suddenly they were plunged into near-darkness. The one window high up on the outer wall gave only the barest smudge of murky light.

"Aiiiiii!" Slime was frantic, struggling with Piggy, straining to drag him to the outside door. Both of them grunted with effort, one to leave and one to stay. But Piggy was stronger, or more determined, and he managed to force his arm around Slime's neck. He leaned in on the slighter boy, muscling him to the floor. Slime fell onto his back and his heels beat at the concrete as he fought against Piggy's weight holding him down.

Click. The key turned, the bolt shot home. The crunch of gravel. *Slam*. The office door.

Slime went slack and groaned. "Now you did it. We're locked in."

"What about the elevator?" Piggy whispered.

"What about it?" He bucked up and Piggy rolled off him. "Some friend you are," he said, drawing his knees up to his chest. They could barely see one another in the sooty light. Above them Sam lay still and dead on the steel slab beneath the white sheet.

"We can take her up in the elevator just like you told me they take the bodies to the viewing rooms," Piggy persisted.

All the fight had gone out of Slime, and there seemed nothing left but the thin membrane of the boy. "Then what do we do?" he asked.

Piggy felt a short squeeze of triumph, and running his hands nervously over his hair, he thought. "The deep freeze!" he whispered excitedly. "In my cellar. We can put her in there until I get the lab ready, get everything I need."

"What do you need?" Slime asked, jutting his head forward to see Piggy better in the dimness. "Shit," he said before Pig answered, "I'm talking like you really can bring Sam back. Nobody can do that. It's . . . it's . . . it's so many awful things, Piggy, I don't know where to begin."

Piggy sat cross-legged on the floor, the cold seeping upward, and said sadly, "You know, Harry Pringle killed BeeBee just because he wanted to. And then he killed Sam. Fractured her skull, it looks like. And nobody does anything. You wait and see, nothing will happen to him. The only thing will be that Sam's dead and in a big hole in the cemetery." *I don't want to be dead!* she had said. "We can't let that happen."

"There's nothing we can do, Pig. Jeez, if it was possible to bring someone back to life, nobody'd be dead anymore. We're born and we die, my ma says. It's as natural as the sun coming up."

"It is not!" A thin wail issued from deep inside Piggy.

The hair went straight up at the nape of Slime's neck. "Pig, don't!" He reached out and took his friend's hand, but Piggy shook him off. "Listen, okay, I mean I know you're upset. Jeez, so am I. I liked Sam even if she was a girl. And maybe you gotta try something. But when it doesn't work, promise me we'll bring her right back."

"It will work," Piggy said, jumping up. "Com'on. We've got to get her into the freezer. I'm worried about tissue damage."

"Sure, sure," Slime said, getting to his feet. "Just promise me. Promise you won't keep her like Mrs. Matthews did her husband."

"Promise," Piggy said impatiently. "Let's go."

"Hang on. We can't do nothing until my ma and pa leave for the Lions Club party. They think I'm at your house, so they should be going soon. Just sit still."

"Then we better get her back into cold storage until we're ready to go." They pushed the drawer back into the vault and quietly shut the metal door, then sat down to wait, leaning against the wall.

"We can use that wagon in the shed," Piggy said after a while. "And the tarp from the snowplow. If we take the alley behind your house, we can get all the way over to Bridge Street without anyone seeing us. Then it's just getting down to my house."

"But how do we get her into the basement?" Slime asked.

"I'll think of something," Piggy said, his brow furrowing. "The big thing is to get her there."

Slime, nervously cracking his knuckles—the small *pop, pop* exploding like caps in the quiet room—said, "Okay, I guess. But let's give it another few minutes." Then, "Pig, can you do it? I mean really bring Sam back good as new?"

Piggy stared into the night that had settled in, through time and space, seeing spread out against his inner vision a diagram, similar to the one he had used to build BeeBee, and spliced over that, his memory of the brain, the cerebral cortex, the ganglia of nerves that bunched neat as shafts of electrical wires. Beginning to dredge up all he had read on the new technology, he thought, *I'm going to try*. For an instant Sam was lost as the beauty of the experiment which men had groped toward since the beginning of time rose, shimmering before his eyes.

Feeling a thrill of invincibility, he said aloud, "I'm going to try."

After a while Slime agreed it was okay, and feeling their way through the gloom, they reached the elevator. It was really more like a dumbwaiter, though longer, with just enough room to slide a coffin in lengthwise. They slid the metal door up, felt that the lift was down, and then, crossing the room, opened the vault, pulling the drawer out. Piggy groped inward and gasped Sam by her shoulders.

"You've got to take her legs, Slime," he said, and together they heaved her off the drawer. She was heavier in death than she had ever been in life, and they staggered for a second before they got her safely stuffed into the elevator.

"There's gonna be murder when my pa finds her gone," Slime said, shutting the cold-storage vault.

"We're going to have to go up with her," Piggy said. "I just realized."

"I don't think we'll both fit. You go up in the elevator with her and unlock the door for me."

Piggy felt a twinge of fear, of being captured in the narrow compartment in which he could neither sit nor stand. He would have to lie down on top of Sam's body to ride up to the next floor. He crawled into the elevator and positioned himself upon the slight hills and valleys of Sam's corpse, colder than the concrete floor.

Slime lowered the door, plunging Piggy into darkness so thick it clotted, and with the push of the button the mechanism hummed into motion. It was the tunnel again, the chamber of horrors with the wheeze, the roar, of the train beating down on him. He closed his eyes and held on as he ascended, listening for the engine, smelling not the musty, dead smell of Sam but the hot burning of the beast. Sweat popped out along his spinal column and on his palms, his forehead—*plop, plop* onto the sheet. Hurry, hurry, he pleaded. Suddenly the elevator stopped. He awkwardly reached over. His fingers grasped the edge of the door, shoved it up. Air rushed in on him and he gratefully sucked at it in big gulps as he rolled off Sam.

Piggy hooked his hands under the already unyielding arms and heaved, dragging Sam's body off the elevator, the two of them tumbling to the floor. Then quickly Pig unlocked the door and when Slime came up, his face pasty in the pale glow from a small light in the corner like a votive lamp, they went out to the garage and got the wagon, the black, dusty tarp. Carefully they loaded Sam, her blond hair neatly tucked underneath her head, draped her with the tarp, and trudged, Piggy pulling, up the short rise to the alley.

The backs of the houses on either side of the meager dirt lane hulked at the edges of their yards, windows blazoned yellow with light. A dog barked, another ran to the ditch on the left and growled, but they didn't stop, couldn't have stopped if they wanted to, as though, Piggy realized, they were racing down the long, constricting tunnel, the train at their backs, the train that at any moment could run them over.

At Bridge Street they changed places, Slime pulling, Piggy walking behind. The wheels thumped in a low basso over the paved surface, the wagon picking up speed as the street dipped slightly. They broke into a trot until they reached Main Street.

It was brighter here, the lights closer together, a river of blurred whiteness flowing along the shuttered stores, the bars, the pizza parlor, the Ice Cream Hut. Cars crept by, two, three, four, as they waited in the shadow of Klein's Clothing Store.

"Com'on com'on," Slime pleaded, impatiently hopping from one foot to the other as a station wagon, a pickup truck, a Toyota went by. The road cleared just as Corney stumbled out of the Five' O'Clock, swaying slightly and looking greasy under the green neon. He tilted his baseball cap back on his graying crew cut and stumbled toward them. Piggy crowded closer to the wagon and felt something brush his leg. He looked down. Sam's hand dangled over the side.

"What're you two doing?" Corney muttered, his phony leg jutting before him. He burped and his bleary eyes were as red as a hound dog's in the wavering light.

"N-n-n-n-nothing," Slime stuttered, his hands behind his back clutching the handle of the wagon.

Piggy kept his leg braced against the dangling hand, and thumped his fist between Slime's shoulder blades. The other boy whinnied and jumped forward, the wagon following. They ran across the street, plunging into the gloom on the far side as it hunkered down on them, and went toward the river.

"Oh God, oh God," Slime was whispering, trotting along, the wagon jouncing behind him. Piggy, his breath coming in snorts, was unable to speak. They moved that way, as though on a conveyor belt, sneakers pounding on the road, legs automatically carrying them to Pig's house, right across the grass and to the near side. Stretching his neck, Piggy could just see into the living room. The television set flickered back at him, and on the couch, her feet curled under her, was his mother.

It was such an ordinary scene, a scene in which there wasn't even a corner for him to creep into, that Piggy's heart pumped with anger. He forgot for an instant Slime puffing beside him, the wagon, Sam dead, the grand scheme that had all his nerves jangling like exploding dynamite.

Doesn't she even know that I'm gone? Piggy wondered, closing his eyes. For a moment when he opened them, he saw Tony sprawled on the couch, Tony drinking beer, and knew if his father were really inside the house, if his father were here in Welling and still a part of their lives, he, Piggy, wouldn't be cowering in the crisp November night. His father, who could do anything, wouldn't have let BeeBee get smashed, or Sam either. A wail started up from his stomach, giving him the shakes, and he had to clamp his hand across his lips to keep all his anguish from spilling out and shattering the silence.

When he finally regained control of himself, Piggy slapped at his hair, tugged at his down jacket, and said to Slime, "You wait here." His confusion and pain having steadied into slow, throbbing anger, he entered the house through the back door.

"Where have you been?" Jeannie demanded, having heard him come into the kitchen. Her face was smooth, but he could tell she was mad at him by the tiny drumbeat just at her left eye. Piggy shrugged, and because it was what he normally did, he went to the refrigerator, opened the door, poked his head inside and surveyed the contents.

"What's for dinner?" he asked.

"Dinner was on the table over an hour ago."

"I was up at Slime's."

"Well that's funny because Tommy's mother thought you were here," she said. "Where were you?"

"Out," he replied tonelessly, and turning, gave her an even look.

"And I suppose you were doing nothing?"

He rejected her sarcasm, knowing that she was only a step away from yelling at him. He sensed her tottering on the brink, rent as she was by anxiety—which he purposely ignored—and was relieved when she began tapping furiously on the side of the refrigerator.

Snagging a handful of Oreos from the cookie jar, he went into the living room, plopping himself in front of the television set. One after another the cookies disappeared into his mouth, though he was barely able to swallow. He crunched and stared intently at the screen, though if his mother had asked him what he was watching, he wouldn't have been able to say.

She was still talking at him. He could hear her as she stood in the archway, but he tuned the words out. He concentrated on Slime waiting outside, on Sam, on a circuitry board on which ran a multiplicity of connections. Doubt skittered through his mind. *I can't do it. It isn't possible. Well . . . Maybe.*

"You going out?" Piggy asked as he finished the last Oreo. He tried to force a smile to his face, but thought if he

succeeded, the result would be a grimace so terrible his
mother would howl in earnest and rush for the castor oil. But
maybe the terror was just in his own head, maybe he hadn't
changed at all, but was still Piggy.

. . . And maybe skunks don't stink, he thought.

"Dr. Mellon is having a few of the teachers in for drinks,"
she replied. Then, suspiciously, "Why?"

He shrugged. "Just curious."

"Maybe I should stay home," she said, worrying.

Piggy willed himself to keep calm, and yawned elaborately.
"Up to you, Mom," he said nonchalantly, keeping his eyes
glued to the set. "I'm tired. After this show I think I'll go to
bed. Maybe I'll read for a while." He was electrified, his
charade of normalcy tissue-thin. If she stood there much
longer watching him, he knew he'd explode. He could already
feel the incipient scream gurgling in his chest.

And what about Slime out there in the cold, probably
ready to launch into orbit from fear?

She apparently decided that nothing was wrong, or that
nothing was more wrong than usual, because she sighed and
said, "Well, I'll go just for a little while. It will be nice to get
out."

Go, yes, that's right. Put on your coat. Kiss me on the
cheek, Mom. No, I'm okay.

Piggy was reading his mother's thoughts, following the jumbled fears, worries, love that splayed out like machine-gun
bullets.

His hands, balled into fists under his chubby thighs, had
ossified into rocks. An iron rod jutted down his back. Steel
cables kept his head secured on his neck. He held his breath
until his vision blurred with a kaleidoscope of bright red and
blue streaks.

Then she was gone. Piggy exhaled with relief. He listened
for the Chevy's engine to turn over, and when the car drove
away, he counted fast to five, then bolted for the back door.

Slime was sobbing, his cheeks slick with tears. "I thought
you'd never come back." He wiped his nose with his fist and
at Piggy's prodding pulled the wagon around to the porch.
He whimpered, "We shouldn't be doing this. It's wrong."

Piggy saw the pinched face in the spill of light from the
kitchen, the mouth working, the eyes wide, and for a moment was filled with the oddest sensation, half love, half pain.

"I'm sorry, Slime," he said, wanting to explain, but he didn't know how to begin; the tangled strands of Sam and Harry and BeeBee and even Bertram Lennard and Tony too, and his mother off having a good time, were all knotted inside him. Wearily he just reached down and grabbed hold of Sam's feet. After the slightest pause Slime followed his lead and grasped her under the arms. Together they heaved her up and carried the nonresisting *thing*—which was how Piggy tried to think of her now—into the house.

"Let's forget it, Pig, please," Slime tried one last time.

But Piggy didn't answer, wasn't even listening anymore; the sizzling was once again in his ears, anger popping his blood vessels.

Mad at what? At whom? he asked himself. But it was all just too much, like a tide coming in that he was helpless to stop. There was nothing to do but what he was doing, stumble down the steps with the body into the cellar.

Jeannie had partially stocked the freezer with frozen vegetables, a ham hard as a rock, thin packages of steaks. They pushed and shoved and rearranged, but only by taking out the ham could they get Sam, legs bent at the knees, arms wrapped around her chest, head tilted forward, into the freezer. As they finally settled her so that the lid would shut, Piggy took a handful of hair and wound it around his fingers.

"Com'on, Pig," Slime cried in agitation. "I can't take any more."

"This is just the beginning," he said, more to himself than to Slime. Leaning over, he brushed his lips to the cold, silky hair, and wordlessly promised Sam that it was going to be all right.

13

Hairline cracks were spreading through Slime's composure, widening into gaping fissures from which fear bubbled up thick as lava. Piggy, afraid of leaving him alone, convinced him to stay overnight and most of the next day until dinnertime. He didn't really want to go home anyway. Toomy's Funeral Parlor was in an uproar.

Never in my twenty years—

Slime said he could hear his father say that without hearing him say it.

Sam's body had been discovered missing.

It wasn't grave robbing to Piggy, which is what Mrs. Toomy told Slime on the phone that Charlie Volchek was calling it. They found the body gone when the coroner returned early from visiting his mother-in-law down in Wilkes-Barre.

The drawer had been pulled out and only the sheet was left.

"Your father near had a fit. I could hear him yell right up in the kitchen. You better stay at the Conways' until all the trooping back and forth is done, though why they think she might be upstairs is beyond me. They're searching everywhere, even in our hall closet."

Slime got so sick that he locked himself in the bathroom. Piggy could hear his dry retching through the door.

No, it wasn't stealing at all, and certainly not grave robbing. But Piggy was on a roller coaster, looping up and down so fast he hadn't time to think except for the logistics. What he would need. How he would get it. What procedures had to be followed. The risks. He didn't contemplate the downside, nor how he'd explain if anyone found out.

He was constantly light-headed and couldn't even eat, and kept thinking how his father used to say that sometimes you get into a situation where you've got no choice but to push forward. Just keep your eye on the ball and pray. Not that he prayed, but he did continue to forge ahead.

Early in the morning before Jeannie was even awake they went over to Mason. It was surprisingly warm for late November. Thick ominous clouds blanketed the sky, and the smell of rain was in the air. A slight breeze sang in the upper reaches of the bridges as they trudged across it. It felt like spring, which, Pig thought, would be a good sign if I believed in omens.

The campus was deserted as they let themselves into the Science Building. As a special consideration Dr. Mellon had allowed Piggy the key. It smelled lonely, and their steps rang hollowly on the stairs as they descended to the basement. Slime stayed close to Piggy, brushing his sleeve as Pig bent to unlock the door.

Opening the small black bag he carried, he sorted out the equipment he had used to build and maintain BeeBee, then prowled through the lab. Since he had upgraded the computer, it was no longer hopelessly inadequate. From Mr. Toomy's workshop he had Slime go and borrow a small saw. He swiped an armful of towels from the gym storage closet, a set of scalpels came from Waxworks' lab, and he appropriated several books on anatomy from the science library, which he pored over ardently while he had Slime scrub down the bench and return again to his house to get a box of rubber gloves from his father's storage cabinet.

He tested out BeeBee's computer, hooked up the telephone terminal to the big boy down in Pittsburgh, punched in his list of questions on the central nervous system, studied the answers, and did several sheets of mathematical computations.

He realized he'd need a large quantity of saline solution and climbed the stairs again to Dr. Johanson's lab, ominously quiet in the dead of Saturday except for the small animals— gerbils, hamsters, a warren of rabbits—scrambling in their cages.

By four o'clock he had completed all the preliminaries and

he and Slime went back to his house, made a towering pyramid of peanut-butter sandwiches and took them with a carton of milk up to Pig's room. They closed the door and had a feast on the bed, away from Jeannie's prying eyes.

"What are you two plotting?" She walked in without knocking.

They gazed up at her innocently, Slime's face going ashy white. He gulped down a glass of milk as Piggy said casually, "Nothing, Mom."

She didn't quite believe him; Piggy could tell from the way the lines of anxiety furled along her brow. But there was nothing she could do—innocent until proven guilty—and she left them alone.

"Everybody's having a shit fit at my house," Slime said when they could hear Jeannie going down the stairs.

Piggy shrugged. "So."

"If my pa ever finds out—" Slime shuddered, contemplating the possibility, and asked again as he had all the long, endless day, "Are you sure, Piggy?"

"I'm sure." He wasn't, but he had to be, he was too far along now. Still, he couldn't tell Slime that. He looked at him suspiciously as though Slime were a mathematical problem that had yet to be solved. Awkwardly he reached out and poked his upper arm. "No sweat, Slime. Honest."

Fear clouded Slime's face and he acknowledged, "I'm scared, Pig."

Piggy laughed. "Scared of what? You've been around dead people since the day you were born. What's to be scared of?"

"Don't know, except it's not that Sam's dead—"

"That's exactly what it is, Slime. That Sam's dead." Abruptly he changed the subject. "What happened to her father?"

Involuntarily Slime's gaze darted toward the window. Through it he could just see a slice of the Pringle house. "Nothing yet. I heard my dad say when I snuck home the last time that they can't do anything until they establish the cause of death. *Precisely*. Which they can't do now because we have Sam's body. Only they don't know that. I mean that we have her. Jeeze, Pig, I'll get killed if anybody ever finds out."

"Stop being such an old lady!" Piggy poked at him again, less friendly this time. Slime winced and drew back, rubbing his arm.

"I think I should go now." He put aside the empty glass and plate with several crusts of bread, and started to unfold.

Piggy jerked him back. "Please!" His voice was cold, so cold he barely recognized it. "I need you, Slime." He squeezed Slime's arm between his fingertips. "I can't get Sam over to Welling East unless you help. It's too far for me to pull the wagon by myself."

Slime yanked his arm away, gave Piggy a sour look and sat down again, moving as far back on the bed as he could get. He hugged his legs up against his chest, protecting himself, and asked, "When?"

Piggy smiled. "When my mother's asleep."

"I'll never get out of the house so late at night," he said, going 'round and 'round like a gerbil on a wheel trying to escape.

"You'll have to stay over here again."

"I can't."

"Tell them you have to study for a math exam and I'm going to help you. I'll tell my mother the same thing."

"You're not gonna give up, are you?" Slime asked, sudden anger fluting his voice. Then, "No, I'll stay home and sneak out. I've done it before. And, Pig, I'll help you get the wagon over to the Science Building, but I'm not gonna stay. The *rest*"—he thumped a closed fist on his knee—"you can do by yourself. That's the last thing I'm gonna help you with. Got it?"

Piggy drew back in surprise, but the wave of terror that had Slime near the edge of screaming was so obvious that he just nodded his head. The last thing he needed right then was for Slime to flip out. It all would come crashing down on him without the other boy. He regarded Slime resentfully but simply grabbed another peanut-butter sandwich and washed it down with the last of the milk.

Don't lose your head now . . .

"Let's play some Atari," he said, pushing the glasses back on the bridge of his nose and smiling.

"I thought it was broken."

"I fixed it."

Slime regarded him from half-shuttered eyes. "You can fix anything, can't you, Pig."

Just flat out, a statement so filled with resignation that it scared Piggy. So much so that he thought of chucking it. But

Sam's corpse was in the deep freeze; the lab was all ready; the terminal hooked up. . . . He could almost hear the buzz of the electric saw, smell the burning.

I don't have to do it.

If I do they'll think I'm nuts, maybe lock me away somewhere.

We could get Sam back to Toomy's . . .

Piggy's heart raced. His mouth went dry. He wanted to crawl under the covers and put the pillow over his head and pretend he was three. But he couldn't. Sam would still be dead as dead could be. There'd be nothing left of BeeBee but the small computer, now on the shelf in the lab.

"My mother bought me Millipede," he said, pulling himself up.

"Oh hey, great!" Slime cried, his mood brightening instantaneously as he hopped off the bed.

Reluctantly Piggy followed him, thinking: He's just a kid. But I'm a kid too. *Oh no you're not*, a voice whispered in his head. Not anymore.

By five o'clock it was already dark, and the rain which had been threatening from early morning had been falling steadily for the last thirty minutes with an occasional rumble of thunder, a flash of lightning.

Piggy, standing at the window looking out, his face illuminated by the sudden flare, thought: We're going to get soaked. Behind him Jeannie was knitting and watching a documentary on television.

The lightning slashed through the sky. The rain puddling along the sidewalk was a river of silver nitrate. Mrs. Williams' house diagonally across the street appeared suddenly out of the murkiness like a huge jack-o'-lantern with its lighted windows. Piggy shivered and went to the hall closet, pawing around for his big old waders and his rain poncho.

"What are you looking for?" Jeannie called out.

His voice was muffled. "Nothing."

"What?"

"Nothing, Mom. Just looking."

He went back through the dining room and she called again, "Are you feeling all right?"

No, he longed to say, but answered, "Yeah, I'm okay. Why?"

"Just wondering."

Piggy sat down at the kitchen table. He was sizzling with anxiety, every nerve tingling at high velocity. The waiting was going to kill him.

Jeannie came to the doorway and stared at him curiously. "Are you sure you're all right?"

Wearily he nodded his head. "Certain, Mom. Just hungry. Can we eat soon?"

The thunder rolled so close overhead that the whole house seemed to lunge and toss in its wake. The lightning filled up the windows with an eerie whiteness.

I don't want to be in the ground, Sam had said. He could see her now, sitting at the table. Her face all smudged, her hair lank and stringy and wringing wet. Piggy could hear the water trickling onto the linoleum.

"Paul!"

"Wha-at?"

The room was luminous, all the polished surfaces shining like mirrors. Jeannie was sitting where Sam had sat, the tangle of blue yarn tossed on the table, her fingers drumming away—spelling out, *What's wrong?*

"Let me feel your head." She reached forward but he jerked out of her reach.

"I'm okay!" he yelled, and whacked the chair on the floor. He went to the refrigerator and yanked the door open. The chill froze the beads of sweat along his hairline into tiny icicles. I'll never get away from her, he thought, envisioning his mother sitting by his bed all night, determined that he had a fever, was coming down with a dread disease. Or, if not, her maternal early-warning device would pick up every creak, every footstep on the stairs. Piggy, staring at a chicken carcass, felt like a prisoner.

"Let's eat," he said. "I'm just hungry."

"We only had lunch at one," she said, but got up and went to the counter.

While Jeannie put dinner together, Piggy went upstairs and inventoried the medicine chest. He knew his mother had taken something to sleep during the bad time when his father was leaving, then later after Bertram Lennard . . . died.

The lightning flashed again and the room tinted silver, the mirror on the medicine-cabinet door shimmering.

I don't want to die, Sam said, floating underwater. Her hair was matted seaweed, her face bile green.

Bottles and plastic tubes cascaded into the sink. Piggy ran the cold water and splashed his face, deep-breathing, staring down the black hole of the drain.

He wasn't being very scientific, he told himself, pressing his fingers to his eyeballs. Sam danced on the inside of his lids, turning cartwheels as she once did on the back lawn.

Seeing something that isn't something. Something that isn't there.

Sam's down in the deep freeze, doubled over like a frozen question mark.

I wish he was dead, Piggy, he heard her say, this time from somewhere deep inside his head.

He pulled out all the bottles of cough syrup, vitamin pills, nose sprays, aspirin tins, and yes, there it was, Dalmane—thirty milligrams, one capsule at bedtime. He rotated the elongated plastic vial in his hand and flipped up the lid. Tiny orange-and-yellow capsules popped out. He split one open. The powder coated his fingers.

Two should do it, he thought, feeling guilty as he dropped the capsules into his shirt pocket and tucked the vial way back on the top shelf.

In his room he kicked the door shut and retrieved the small spiral notebook from under the mattress, reading over his notes until Jeannie called him for dinner. He descended the stairs feeling infinitely better; the steady procession of equations had calmed his fears. But when he put his palm to his forehead, the skin was hot, burning.

Thunder chugged its way across the sky. A spring storm, Piggy thought. Even the weather is out of sync. It's not supposed to thunder and lightning in November—almost December. It's not normal to be so warm, close to sixty at least. A record probably. He'd have to look it up. . . .

He stopped himself and held on to the chair half pulled away from the table.

"Even your father's deserted you, Pig-head," he heard Bertram Lennard say plain as day, dancing around the table as he had been dancing about the lab, poking at BeeBee while Piggy was trying to solder his flap.

Piggy shook his head really fast, back and forth, until he thought it was going to rip off his neck, attempting to dance

Bertram right out into the night. He wondered if Slime was right, that they should forget it, leave Sam in the freezer, or maybe sneak her back into Toomy's.

There was always the river. The idea of Sam dead, Sam in the Susquehanna, made him sick.

Oppenheimer didn't lose his cool when he was building the bomb, he thought, remembering the PBS series he had watched religiously. But he'd had his doubts. Piggy sat down, gratified about the famed scientist's misgivings. He refused to look Jeannie in the eye as he forked chili into his mouth so quickly he almost choked.

I'm going to put my mom to sleep and wake Sam up . . .

He gulped down a glass of water. The chili was so hot it burned his tongue. He thought he could actually feel Sam below, frozen solid, clawing at his ankles, pulling him to her. Wait, he told her silently in his head. Jeannie was watching him suspiciously, elbows on the table, a glass of Tab lifted up to her mouth. But she didn't drink, just rubbed the rim along her bottom lip absently.

Dinner went on and on, for hours and hours it seemed to Pig. He had nothing to say, his tongue stuck fast to the roof of his mouth. He replied in grunts to Jeannie's questions. His head, rolling dangerously on the column of his neck, was as heavy as a cannonball.

Finally dinner was over, leaving him with a bellyache. They cleaned up together, Piggy feeling distinctly like Brutus, and went into the living room to watch television.

They could have been watching anything because all Pig saw on the screen were Technicolor diagrams of the brain. Finally at nine, having begun to fidget so badly that he shoved his hands into his armpits, he suggested hot chocolate.

"Good idea," Jeannie agreed, going into the kitchen to make it.

Et tu, he said to himself, feeling even more traitorous, and sidled after her.

"I'll do it, Mom." He smiled, knowing she wanted to grab him and feel his head again. There's nothing normal about me tonight, he acknowledged, wondering why she didn't yell and scream and call a doctor.

His back to her, he broke the capsules and slid the white powder through the chocolate foam, stirred and tasted just a drop with the tip of his tongue.

Piggy had seen his father only a few times after Tony had
moved out. Once, as they sat in a tiny French restaurant in
Cambridge where the food tasted strange Tony had said,
"You do what you have to do in this life, Paul. Try to
understand that." He didn't at that awful moment, staring at
the father who had left him. Maybe he was starting to now.

He stirred the hot chocolate one last time. Jeannie had
gone back into the living room and he carried out the two
mugs. She sat on the couch, knitting the endless sweater—
already one arm was far too long for him—and smiled up at
him trustingly as he handed her the floral-patterned mug.

When she started to drink it, he closed his eyes.

She was breathing slow and steady. Piggy put his hand
over her mouth and felt the warm air tickling his palm. He
wanted to cry, thinking of the nights she had stood just as
he did now beside the bed, worrying. Only she was trying to
make him better and he had put her out with two Dalmanes
like a lightbulb whose filaments go pop. It was a moment in
which Piggy was fervently glad he had decided on atheism as
a philosophic course to chart life by, because as sure as the
sun came up in the east and set in the west, if there was a
God he would have been in bad trouble over this.

There wasn't much time, however, in which to lament, so
he rushed out, firmly closing the door, and took the steps two
at a time, bouncing excitedly on the balls of his sneakers
when he reached the living room.

Slime was waiting just inside the kitchen, rain dripping off
his navy slicker, looking like a half-drowned cat Tony had once
rescued from the Charles. His teeth were chattering so badly
he couldn't speak, which Piggy thought was just as well, since
all he'd do was whine and cry.

Piggy put on his own slicker—yellow as a lemon—and
pulled on high black boots over his sneakers and the two of
them went down into the cellar. The gray light on the grimy
walls made Piggy think of a prison cell. Or a tomb.

Slime retrieved the tarp from behind the furnace and handed
it to Pig, who asked, "Did you get the wagon from the
garage?"

"Uh huh. It's by the steps. Pig—"

"Not now," he said, waving at him as if at a pesky fly.
"Let's just get going."

Piggy raised the lid of the deep freeze and peered down into the frozen depths. The cold air wafted up his nose, making him sneeze. Sam, a nest of dark shadows, was covered in a thin white rime, tiny diamonds sparkling through her hair, which was hard as a board, and on her eyebrows.

"She's going to weigh a ton now," Piggy said, reaching for the legs—they were locked together—and trying to lift her. "Here, you get her under the arms and I'll take the feet."

Slime didn't stir.

"Let's go, Slime. *Tempus fugit!*" He stamped his foot and Slime came unstuck, scurrying forward. Piggy knew he was on automatic pilot, which was better, he supposed, than having the screaming meemies.

Together the two boys, grunting with the effort, pried Sam loose. She came away from the sides of the freezer with a grating noise and they levered her up to the edge, where they paused for an instant, caught their breath—the two of them huffing—and then lifted her over the side. Carefully they lowered her to the floor, where she lay uneasily, all bent wrong, like a petrified person from Pompeii that Piggy remembered seeing in a photograph.

In starts and stops they got her the length of the cellar and up the stairs to the kitchen, where they propped her against the wall while they rested.

"We're never going to make it," Slime moaned, holding his head in his hands, refusing to look at Sam.

Piggy wanted to tell him to stuff it but didn't trust himself to speak. If he opened his mouth either a scream or a whimper was going to burst out; both were clamoring against his teeth. He just stood up, prodded Slime with the toe of his boot, and once again they lifted the body, making it all the way to the back porch this time.

The rain was coming down in thick walls of water, and the sky was black. They put Sam into the wagon, covered her with the tarp, and Piggy returned to the kitchen for the flashlight.

They took turns pulling the wagon along River Street, past sleeping houses which groaned on their foundations, slumbering beasts whose gaping faces were revealed in the not infrequent spears of lightning that turned the night white and luminescent. It was warm and wet; the muffled town shimmered in a series of streaked images as the rain rippled over the lenses of Piggy's glasses. He stopped and cleaned them with a dirty Kleenex from the slicker pocket, but they misted up and were rivered the moment he put them back on.

They slogged their way through puddles that came high as their ankles, wheels rolling through oceans of water.

Rain slicked the tarp black and shiny, the glow of the streetlamps reflecting off the glossy surface as they passed.

The night had a negative feel to it, as if everything were in reverse.

Except for the drumming of the rain as steady as hoofbeats, the rumbling of the thunder as it rose and buckled across the sky, and that crackling of lightning that flickered, tossed and splattered along the bridge wires, there was no sound. Everyone was asleep or dead as Sam, lolling on her metal bed, the warm rain beginning to defrost her frigid limbs.

Mason was too far away. They were never going to reach it, the rain having insinuated itself under their slickers, down the tops of their boots. Below, the river seemed dangerously high, turbulent; and the bridge shook, swayed as the wind and rain beat at it, the sound through the wires like harpies screaming overhead. Swirling gusts of wind and water clutched at them.

They left the sidewalk for the middle of the bridge, away from the sheer drop on either side. Halfway, with Slime pulling, the wagon jolted to a halt and Slime turned, yelling something back at Piggy, words that were torn from his lips by the wind. It wasn't possible to hear anything above that cacophony and Piggy hastily motioned him to go ahead. Again, bent almost double to the wind, they struggled forward, the wagon skidding and sliding, Sam lurching precariously.

Piggy went to pull along with Slime, to steady the wagon, but the handle was too narrow. They bumped into one another then fell away.

Varoom . . . varoom—

The storm sang at them. Piggy spun around, his bones as watery as the rain sloshing about him, and peered back through the tunnel of the bridge. The lamp at midpoint threw a gauzy halo of wet light.

Varoom . . . varoom—

The screaming, bone-crunching sound of the train along the tunnel tracks, of the train rolling toward him.

As he ran toward Welling East, Slime slogging now behind

him, the wagon moved in a crazed, gyrating dance, swinging
far to the right, then to the left. And suddenly solid ground
was under his feet, the yard pavement of the Mason drive.
Turning again, he strove to see across the bridge through the
billowing darkness. He saw instead the grinning lights of the
train, the gleam of the cowcatcher, felt beneath his feet even
here on the far bank the rumble of the locomotive, chugging,
the howl deep in the bowels of its flaming furnace.

Varoom . . . varoom—

Piggy ran up the short incline toward the Science Building,
veered off the macadam and onto the grass, a soggy swamp
that sucked at his boots. Slime, tugging the wagon, cried into
the wind that careened and buffeted its way along the stone
flanks of Science. It whirled high and squalled through the
portico of Administration, ran as fast as ground fire along the
narrow corridor between Humans and the gym, as Slime fled
after Pig.

At the two short steps that led up to the stone porch, Piggy
tripped, sprawling flat, skidding on his slicker through puddles that were as slippery as pools of axle grease, and banged
his head. Behind him Slime stopped short. In a moment,
lights detonating like hand grenades inside his cranium, Piggy
was up. He fumbled the key, almost dropping it, but finally
opened the door. Together they awkwardly carried the unresisting Sam into the main hall, along the west corridor to the
basement door.

The *slog, slog* of their waders echoed off the high ceilings,
and the wobbling beam of the flashlight cut through the
darkness that ebbed and flowed in on them. Piggy braced the
light in his armpit, and the beam jerked, spasmed as they
went down the stairs to the basement.

The building was stunningly silent after the storm outside,
dangerously so. The wheels of the wagon whined along the
corridor, and they whispered to one another reassuring, sibi-
lant sounds.

Earlier in the day Piggy had covered over the windows so
that it was safe to turn on the long fluorescent tubes overhead. The light was painful, etching into their eyeballs like
hot acid. They both lowered their heads, Piggy at the same
time slipping off his raincoat, fumbling with his boots.

"I . . . I . . . I . . ." Slime stuttered.

Piggy ignored him, whipping the tarp from Sam, whose limbs had begun to unfurl like flower petals.

"Help me get her on the bench," he said. "Please."

Slime moved reluctantly, great globs of tears welling in his eyes, mixing with the rain on his still-wet cheeks. He gasped for air, then wailed, "I want to go home!"

"You can," Piggy answered, trying to keep his temper as he tugged at the body. He felt almost as sorry for Slime just then as he did for himself. "Just help me get her up and then go."

"I . . . I . . ." he stuttered again. "I'm afraid," he cried.

Piggy looked up. "That's a waste of time."

"The bridge, the rain . . ." Slime fumbled.

Piggy jabbed at him. "Either stay or go, but you can't do both and you have to do one or the other," he said, breath whistling through his nostrils. He was jittery with impatience. "Just com'on. We haven't got all night." In truth he didn't know how long they did have, or how long *it* would take, or if *it* would take at all. He might reach the end of the long night with . . . What?

I won't think about it, he thought. I won't think about anything but trying to do what I am going to do. He burned with an emotion he was too young to recognize as passion, passion sliding unbridled into obsession where it glowed with a white heat that could not, would not, be diminished.

"Com'on, Slime." Together they lifted dead Sam and staggered to the bench. Grunting with effort, they heaved her up. She rolled slightly and then settled, arms and legs straightening out.

"Piggy—" Slime implored.

"I haven't time now. You better get back. Take the wagon with you."

Slime hesitated, shifting from one foot to the other, making tiny mewing sounds, but Piggy neither saw nor heard him, having passed into that space where he was alone with Sam, with his computations, his procedures arranged meticulously in his head in schemata so precise that, he was convinced, there was only one destination he could reach.

He turned on the computer, put the phone into the cradle and linked up with Pittsburgh, miles to the south.

Putting a towel beneath Sam's head, he began to shave away the long blond hair like seaweed floating under glass.

He tried not to think of the body as Sam. He needed to convince himself that the corpse stretched out on the bench, the skull that he was going to cut into, was simply another machine. Which it was, only not as precise as Bee's tiny computer all polished and sterilized, waiting on the side, wrapped in cotton.

At some point during the long night Slime left, but Piggy didn't hear him. He was methodically clicking off each step of his procedure.

When he had shaved a patch of hair from the shattered bone, he took a small electric drill, then a saw, and cut the skull away, neatly gouging a hole small enough for the cable in the flap he lifted out. Beneath, the whorls of gray matter, bruised and dead, came into view. Following the anatomical charts in the book he had taken from the library, he surgically excised the injured portion of Sam's brain, flushing what was left with saline solution.

He worked slowly, painfully, the muscles in his neck and shoulders singing with fatigue.

Plugging the ribbon cable, a flat strip of eight wires running together in the various shades of a rainbow, into the circuit board of the Apple, he hooked the other end into BeeBee's computer and carefully inserted the compact unit— sterilized now—into the nest he had structured in Sam's brain. It fitted snugly between gray matter and skull.

For the longest time, it seemed, the information whirled and spat along the wires, while Piggy fussed back and forth. The storm outside accelerated, pounding furiously against the walls, rolling . . .

varoom . . . varoom . . .

overhead. He tried not to listen, not to feel it whipping along him as though he was still outside. The thunder slammed, and at the edges of the dark paper fastened to the windows he saw the white, colorless lightning crackle.

Finally the light came up on the Apple. He was finished with that phase. He unplugged the ribbon cable from the larger computer and inserted that end of it into a battery recharger, neatly inserting the piece of bone so that it was flush with the rest of Sam's skull. The cable snaked out through the hole as power poured into the small computer.

Piggy, still wet from the storm, was covered in sweat. His T-shirt stuck to his back, his jeans were glued to the backs of his thighs. Even his feet were soaked, water sloshing inside his sneakers.

While he waited for the batteries to recharge, he slipped out of his sneakers and peeled off the soggy socks. His whole body hummed with weariness, and he flexed his arms, shook his legs, wiggled his toes just as a terrible crash of thunder settled right over the Science Building, rattling the window frames. He heard it rampaging inside his own head, felt the crash and steeled himself, holding on to Sam's cold and unresisting arm.

One last time he thought, *What if it doesn't work*. Then the lightning flared, reared up and split apart the sky as neatly as a piece of fruit. Screaming, Piggy lurched just as the lights in the lab flickered once, twice, dimmed, came up again. The piece of black paper on the window high up in the wall peeled back, the pane behind it furiously aglow with a nether light. Piggy rushed toward it, padding on the cold, wet floor, tripped on the ribbon cord and reached out for the wall, his hand hitting the battery recharger that was plugged into the socket. The lightning struck again, angrier this time, hitting straight at the building, and the surge went flying down through the wall, out the socket where Piggy's fingers touched metal, his arm entwined in the cord, and he took the jolt right through his body, lifted up inches off the wet, slippery floor. His back arched, his hair stood straight as needles on his head as the current traveled through him, through the ribbon cord, sparked the metal edges of the bench, and went into Sam.

Just as Sam's corpse started to levitate, arms and legs flopping like wet spaghetti, Piggy bounced on the floor. He flopped over, then went limp as a sack of feathers. Darkness rushed in on him, all consciousness shuttered in a bottomless, empty place.

14

Charlie Volchek had a terrible headache. It was so bad he was considering going up Main to see Doc Madison and ask him for something better than aspirin to take away the pain. It had been going on since Saturday, two days after that poor kid had died, from the time, in fact, when her body had disappeared out of Toomy's freezer. And it was now Tuesday.

For what seemed like the hundredth time, Charlie said to a disheveled Harry Pringle, who was sprawled half on, half off the straight-backed chair at the opposite side of the desk, "Tell me again what happened. Exactly." Not that Charlie didn't know it by heart, hadn't taken Harry through it step by step, and didn't believe one word even if Harry had sworn on his mother's grave.

"I told you and told you," Harry whined. "And what difference does it make now anyway? She's gone, just like Grace." He scowled, his dark, bleary-eyed unshaven face knotting up as if he suspected Sam of having escaped death just as her mother had run away from life with him.

"Stop your complaining, Harry, and just do what I tell you. In case you haven't got the drift yet, you're in deep shit."

"For what?" he cried, straightening up. "I didn't steal her body."

Which was probably true, Charlie thought. The throbbing in his right temple was so insistent that he closed his eyes for a second. He opened them again and stared at Harry, the sight of whom made the headache seem all the worse. "Harry," he said, and just the tone of his voice made Harry shift his eyes from side to side nervously.

"Okay," he said, "I got home from the Five O'Clock and found her at the bottom of the steps. You know them stairs, what with the carpet coming up in spots and being worn, they were a real hazard to life and limb. True, as it turned out. She musta tripped up at the top and went flying." He paused for breath, and Charlie had to give him credit, the story was the same every time he told it, right down to the stairs being dangerous and it was his fault since he never tacked the carpet down.

"My fault," Harry was continuing right on cue, " 'cause I shoulda fixed that carpet long ago. Anyway, I wasn't feeling any pain and at first I thought she was just hurt. So I picked her up and took her to the bedroom. And then that bitch, old Mullins' daughter, called you."

"So how come, Harry, when we got there she wasn't on the bed but on the floor?"

"Don't know. I went to the bathroom to pee. She must have gotten out and fell. Why'd ya keep asking me?" he whined again.

"Because I think you beat the shit out of her and then she died. And you were four sheets to the wind and never noticed until I pointed it out to you."

"That's a lie!" he yelped, coming right off the chair.

Charlie gave him a disgusted look and he sat down again almost automatically. "Harry, you wouldn't know the truth if it bit you on the ass."

"Yeah, yeah, well just go ahead and prove it, Charlie." He stuck out his chin belligerently.

Which, of course, right then Charlie couldn't, since he didn't have a body. Until the coroner told him the girl's wounds were inconsistent with a fall down the steps, were the result of a beating, Charlie had circumstantial evidence at best. Oh, it was possible to charge Harry if it was necessary, but he definitely did not have enough to hold him for long. And Charlie Volchek wanted to put Harry right in the slam, preferably for a hundred and twenty years.

"Get out of here, Pringle," he snarled, feeling so bad he thought that if he had to look at Harry's ugly face and smell the foul odor that rose off him like swamp gas he'd probably commit murder himself.

Harry didn't need to be told twice, and scooted through the

door, brushing by Emmett Sidowsky, a rangy, red-headed deputy in his late twenties.

"Guess Harry's not planning to stay for lunch," Emmett said with a grin, popping a toothpick into the corner of his mouth.

Charlie grunted and downed two aspirin with a chaser of cold coffee, thinking it was a waste of time, the headache wouldn't leave off, not one bit. He wiped his mouth and said, "It's people like Harry Pringle who make me want to throw the switch myself."

"Yeah, I know what you mean. Harry sure is a walking turd. And to think we might not be able to nail him for killing his kid. . . . Shit, Charlie, I shoulda stayed in college and become a vet. Animals don't stink as bad as people."

"Did you talk to that Toomy kid like I told you?" Charlie asked as Emmett propped himself on the side of the desk.

Taking a small notebook from his pocket, he flipped it open and answered, "Yeah, got it right here. The kid wasn't home, as we knew, and didn't see, hear, or smell anything when he got back, about an hour or so before his parents did. Went right to bed after watching television. Rerun of *M*A*S*H*, he said. And that makes it about eleven-thirty. Toomy and the missus returned around midnight." He closed the notebook. "Oh, yeah, where was he? He was down on River Street at that Conway kid's house. And *his* mother was out at a party. Though I didn't get to talk to him since he's sick in bed. So there we are." He tossed the toothpick into the ashtray and asked, "You don't think the kid snatched one of his old man's stiffs, do you, Charlie?"

"Not unless he's a fruitcake. What would he want the body for, and besides, where would he stash it?" He leaned back in the chair, which tilted under his weight with a protesting screech. He stared at the ceiling. "The Conway kid's the one with the robot that Harry Pringle smashed up for scrap. And the Conways live next door to the Pringles. And the kid went apeshit bananas when I told him."

"Nothing to put the cuffs on him for, Charlie," Emmett said.

"You're probably right. But I knew that kid was trouble right from the start."

"Who, Toomy?"

"No," Charlie sighed, deciding it wouldn't hurt to give Doc Madison a toot on the horn, "the Conway kid. He just doesn't feel right."

Charlie Volchek didn't get to talk with Doc Madison but his wife said she'd give him the message and have him call Charlie back when he got in. In fact, the doctor was just leaving the Conway house, where he had told Jeannie that with time, aspirin, bed rest, and "TLC," Piggy was going to be just fine. "Won't turn into pneumonia," the doctor said, smiling. He looked something like an aging pixie with his white hair in sprouts about his head, a button nose, and a mouth the size of a Spaghetti-O. "But I don't like this business of his not remembering. Temporary amnesia. Usually from a crack on the head. Only he doesn't have one. What he does have are burn marks on the extremities and along his back." He peered suspiciously at a haggard Jeannie, who, with her red eyes and smudges of weariness darkening her face, didn't look all that well herself. She wasn't—and hadn't been since a distraught Slime had brought Piggy home three nights before, soaking wet, feverish, shaking with chills, and looking as though he had been in a car wreck.

She had felt sick, cotton-mouthed, and groggy when Slime had finally managed to wake her up from one of the deepest sleeps she had ever experienced. Even after she had gotten a quaking and uncommunicative Piggy into bed, she still didn't understand what had happened or why. Piggy had been no help; his teeth were chattering so badly he couldn't talk. Then he had lapsed off into a troubled and restless sleep which he had been drifting in and out of for three days now.

Jeannie had interrogated Slime, who wasn't especially forthcoming, as to where they had been; what they had done; and why Piggy was soaked to the bone. But the boy seemed breathless with fear and could say nothing but "playing." Even after they had stripped Pig's clothes and had gotten him into bed—where he lay quivering beneath a mound of blankets—and were waiting for Doc Madison, all Slime could repeat was "playing."

She knew that Slime should have been home asleep himself but was reluctant to let him go. It was after midnight and still teeming. She wondered if his parents realized that he wasn't in bed.

"Tell me again," she had said, feeling so weary she thought she was going to sink to the ground.

"It was nothing, Mrs. Conway," he had managed to get out, looking, Jeannie had thought, like a drowned rat himself, his face as shriveled as a prune. But his eyes were burning and he was afraid. She was afraid too because Piggy was very sick. She had been able to tell that even if she wasn't very alert.

"I don't understand what you were playing at, outside, so late, in the rain," she had said, and went and sat on the edge of the bed. When she put her hand on Piggy's leg he moved away from her touch with a groan. Oh God, don't let there be anything really wrong with him, she prayed. Again she asked Slime, "What *were* you doing? What happened to Paul?"

Slime had looked every which way but in her direction and sputtered out finally, "We were looking for night crawlers."

"*What?*"

"Worms. You know, for fishing."

"Fishing? Paul's never gone fishing in his life. He doesn't even *eat* fish."

"We thought it would be a good idea, for tomorrow, after church. I mean, after I get home from church," he had stammered lamely. "Mrs. Conway, I gotta go. If my folks find out I'm not in bed there'll be hell to pay." He stopped. "I'm sorry, I didn't mean to curse. My father says it's not necessary if a person's educated."

"That's all right, Tommy," she had said, feeling a hysterical laugh bubble up in her throat. "*Just tell me what happened! How Paul got so wet. And where are his shoes? And his hands—look, they're all burnt.*"

"He fell in the river," Slime had said wildly.

"Maybe he did fall in the river," Doc Madison was saying just then, recapturing Jeannie's attention, "but that's not the whole of it. He did something else too, you know."

"No, I don't know," she said, shivering in the cold as she walked with him to the car. "I don't know anything, just that I'm worried sick."

"I could tell you not to worry, but you would anyway," he said with his elfish grin, getting into the Buick and rolling down the window.

Great, she thought as she returned to the house, remembering the patrician pediatrician, Dr. Hemmings of Boston, who always said worrying was a waste of time. If one didn't pay too much attention to illness it eventually went away.

She called Miss Miller and said she'd be out for another day, that Paul was still too sick to leave alone. Then she went upstairs and looked in at him, but he was sleeping soundly, his face pasty as bread dough against the pillowcase.

Back downstairs she dusted the living room, wandered into the kitchen, made herself another cup of coffee and, rolling up the sleeves of her work shirt, decided to scrub the floor. Anything to keep moving. But her thoughts were all on Piggy and she ran back up the stairs to check on him again.

He hadn't stirred, but his breathing seemed less labored—or was she just telling herself that, grasping at any little sign that he was improving? She felt his head, and the skin was clammy under her palm.

Oh Paul, she thought, what have I brought you to?

Later Piggy wouldn't remember the dreams, but tossed now in the turbulent undertow of nightmare, he groaned and heaved and listened to the pounding in his blood. He was drowning and kept fighting for air, kept pushing to the surface.

Once he recalled opening his eyes and seeing his mother, so small, way off in the distance. He cried out to her to pull him in, to get him out of the water, that Mrs. Williams was holding on to his feet, sucking him down into the depths, but before she could answer, if he had spoken at all, Piggy slipped under again. The water tasted foul, slimy, with an oily residue that coated the inside of his mouth.

Almost at once he was burning alive. He was Bertram Lennard and the flames were eating him up.

I'm sorry, I'm sorry! he cried, but no one came running.

BeeBee was beeping: Kill him, Piggy, kill him!

But how could he kill him if he, Pig, was the one on fire?

Then there was Sam . . . And he orbited off into black space.

Slime came every day after school, trudged up to Pig's bedroom, perched on the chair in the corner and asked, "How are you feeling?"

He got no answer, only Piggy's groan, until Friday, when Piggy managed to whisper, "Awful," and rolled over.

When he'd come back downstairs, Jeannie would be waiting, snaring him into the kitchen where, plying him with juice and cookies that he kept politely trying to refuse, she'd question him again. But it was all fishing and night crawlers and falling in the river. He was so tense Jeannie thought he'd snap in half as he regarded her with remorseful eyes as big as moons in a drawn, pained face. He didn't look much better than Piggy, only he was walking around.

But he repeatedly asked, "Mrs. Conway, is he going to be all right?"

By Saturday morning when he arrived only a few minutes before noon, she could say, "Yes, he's going to be fine." Because he was. The resilience of the young, Doc Madison proclaimed after he took his temperature—normal at last—thumped his chest to hear only the expected gurglings and removed the dressings on the burns that were almost healed.

Jeannie would have supposed that the burden would now lift from Slime's scrawny shoulders and he'd at least smile, but he didn't look one bit less frightened than he had the day before.

"He's going to be okay, Tommy," she repeated as he ran up the stairs, but he didn't even answer her. She heard him close the bedroom door, but just before he did she thought he had begun to cry. Standing at the bottom of the steps holding on to the newel post, she shook her head. No, she must have been mistaken.

"Oh Piggy!" Slime wailed, and threw himself across the bed, clutching the spread. "I thought you were going to die! And I didn't know what to do! And it's terrible! And I'm scared!"

Piggy forced himself to sit up and the sudden movement set his head spinning. He closed his eyes and listened to Slime weeping. "What happened?" he croaked.

"I don't know. Just, I got crazy worried about leaving you alone and went back and there you were on the floor of the lab looking dead."

"Sam?" he asked. "What did you do with Sam? Is she—?"

"Uh huh."

"Really?" He opened his eyes, excited now.

"Uh huh." Slime crawled onto the bottom of the bed and huddled there, looking seriously demented. He plucked at the blanket and gulped, "I hid her away 'cause I didn't know what else to do."

"Hid her? Where?"

"In the equipment shed on the far side of the bleachers over at the field."

"What?"

"Don't yell at me, Pig," he said, his thumb, without his being aware of it, was inching toward his mouth. "I didn't know of anything better. You were just lying there like you had died, and she was sitting up—" He stopped, his face going into spasms. He licked his cracked lips and went on. "I couldn't sleep—when I was home in bed, I mean. So I went back. And there you were. I had to do something, didn't I?"

"Sure, sure you did, Slime," he said, trying to comfort him though his head was pounding, his throat sore, and his limbs felt like overcooked pasta. "Just tell me about her. *How is she?*"

"I dunno."

"What do you mean you don't know?"

"I mean she had all these wires hanging out of her head and she looked—" Again he stopped, his voice shaking. "She . . . she looked *awful*. Like a . . . I don't know what." He gulped, an already protuberant Adam's apple rising up and down in his skinny neck. "But she walked, Pig, she walked to the shed, only very slow."

"And you just left her there?" he cried, sounding like a fingernail scratching glass. "You didn't check on her? And what about food?"

Slime's face was green. "Does she eat?"

"Of course she eats, you dope, doesn't everybody? And now she's probably starved to death if she hasn't died from the cold."

"Oh no, I found a whole bunch of old football uniforms and covered her up. I did think about that!" he defended himself shrilly.

"We've got to go see how she is, take care of her. Maybe move her somewhere else."

Slime was shaking his head back and forth like a metronome. "Oh no, I've done everything I'm gonna do with this, Pig," he said, looking, if that were possible, more frightened than ever.

"You've got to help me. I can't do it alone. Look," he said,

and attempted to stand up. His legs dropped out from under
him and he tumbled back onto the bed. "I'm too weak to do
it by myself."

"Your mother will never let you go out," he whimpered.
"And I'm too scared. No, Pig," he said, terror brimming in his
eyes. "No more. Forget I was ever involved. Besides, my
father's still screaming the place down 'cause her body's
gone."

Piggy tried to convince him every which way to Sunday,
but the more he said, the less inclined Slime was to help. He
was teetering on the very brink of hysteria. Eventually he
even stopped saying "no," but he couldn't be budged. At last
Piggy, weary, gave up, taking the key Slime pushed across
the covers.

"Okay, visiting hours are over," Jeannie said, bursting in on
them. "You have to go, Tommy, and let Paul get some
sleep."

"Yeah, Mrs. Conway, that's just what I think," he cried,
and bolted out of the room and down the stairs.

"Mom!"

"You take a nap, honey, and when you wake up I'll give
you some soup."

Sleep, he thought, was out of the question, fired up as he
was, wanting to get to Sam. But sleep he did, going out
almost at once.

When Piggy woke again it had just gone dark. The room
was meshed with shadows, and as he rubbed his eyes the
streetlight down the block came on. He lay quietly on his
back, propped at an angle by two pillows, and watched the
play of light and shadow entwining along the sheer lisle
curtains. The lassitude that had haunted him for days, trun-
dling him to the edge of a coma, had dissipated, and even his
head was clear. He tested his arms, lifting them off the
blankets and then letting them fall back with a plop. I'm
better, he decided, and only then allowed himself to think of
Sam.

He was surprised, after Slime's news, that he wasn't more
excited, that he didn't bolt right out of bed, rush past his
mother, who undoubtedly was hovering below worrying and
wondering about what was wrong with him. She always took
his illnesses—minor until now—as a personal affront, as if she

were inexplicably to blame for letting him get sick. This made him sad and he squirreled away from the thought.

He was dimly aware that during the days and nights of fever and hallucinations he'd slid backward into being a needy baby. Which wasn't good because what he had to do was take a quantum leap in growing up.

And so he came back to thinking about Sam.

He had set out to do something and had done it, and now he was itchy to see the result. Above all he had to be scientific and keep a running, detailed log because he couldn't remember all the steps of the procedure.

There was a big hole in his head—everything from the moment he had begun working on dead Sam had lifted straight out of his consciousness. The last thing he recalled was when they hoisted her up on the bench, and then there was all murk, as if the film had simply stopped. The next thing he knew he was here in bed being dreadfully sick and hurting all over. He was so angry he wanted to scream, and he frantically dug around in his memory trying to dislodge at least one little detail. But it was all pea soup.

From what Slime had said he supposed it had worked, that he had brought Sam back to life, if she was still alive. Maybe Slime had killed her by not giving her anything to eat. *The asshole*, Piggy fumed, pulling on his hair. But when he calmed down he decided that wasn't fair. All in all Slime had handled the situation pretty well. He could have left Sam where she was, left the janitor in Science or old Wax-works to find her. He could have just cowered in his bed and not gone back at all.

It was impossible to lie still like a mummy just thinking about Sam. So quietly he slipped out of bed, holding on to the headboard as he waited for the swirling in his brain to settle. When the room was reasonably in place once more he walked around until his legs stopped wobbling and then hurriedly threw on clothes and laced up his sneakers. When he was all buttoned and zipped he had to sit down again, and he wondered how he'd get to Mason without keeling over in a dead faint.

Worry about that when it happens, he told himself, biting down on his lower lip. Carefully he opened the door. From downstairs he heard the babble of the television set and leaned out over the banister to see Jeannie asleep in the big fat chair under the afghan that had been her mother's.

He took the stairs on his rump so that they wouldn't creak and got into the living room without Jeannie turning a hair.

In the kitchen he filled a shopping bag with peanut butter, bread, milk, oranges, and a rather stringy chicken leg. Then he tiptoed out to the hall closet and slipped his down jacket from a hanger. Jeannie stirred in her sleep, the afghan sliding to the floor. Piggy held his breath and sneaked back to the kitchen. Pulling the shopping bag up on his shoulder, he went out into the night.

The phone was ringing, nudging Jeannie awake like a cattle prod. She groped her way into the kitchen feeling fuzzy all over and lifted the receiver. "Hello," she said, but by the time she'd answered, the line had gone dead.

Jeannie hung up the phone and shook herself fully awake. She splashed water from the kitchen tap on her face and dried it with a dish towel.

For the first time in a week, since Slime had brought Piggy home so ill, she felt like herself. Everything's going to be fine now that he's better, she thought. The weight of Piggy's illness had pressed on her like a mountain, and it was only today when Dr. Madison said she could relax that all the tension began to slide away. It made her realize that there's nothing so awful that there isn't something worse. Just like her mother used to say.

She opened the door to the cellar and hit the switch on the wall, throwing a pale wash across the floor and up the cement walls. The house was so quiet she could hear the hissing of the gas furnace, a beast lying in wait behind the far door. Silly, she admonished herself, descending the stairs.

The inside of the old freezer looked all disarranged. Packages of frozen food were tumbled every which way and she couldn't see the ham she had bought on sale a few weeks before. Now, what is this all about? she wondered, digging around until she found a bundt cake—Piggy's favorite— wrapped in tin foil, all dented in on one side. She held it up and glanced about the basement as if the emptiness could tell her something. But there were only the heavy shadows lurking in corners. She shrugged finally, and closing the freezer, made sure that the lock caught.

The house seemed even quieter upstairs, and she put a
Bartok recording on the stereo before she went up to her
bedroom and changed into a fresh shirt and a pair of jeans. In
the bathroom she brushed her teeth, listening to the music,
which ebbed and flowed through the silence, and told herself
she should feel more at ease, that there truly wasn't anything
to worry about now. It was all passing away, Tony and Bertram Lennard, who suddenly flashed before her in the
medicine-cabinet mirror. Sweat prickled on the back of her
neck, and she ducked her head, hanging on to the washbasin.
In a minute when she raised her eyes, his squirrely little face
had metamorphosed into her own.

She appeared sick, lined and sallow, something out of
Bosch.

"This won't do at all, girl," she said to her image, and
stroked her lashes with mascara and vigorously rubbed rouge
into her cheeks. Minor improvement, she decided, adding a
pink gloss to her lips.

Outside Piggy's door she readjusted her face into a smile
before turning the knob. She got a warm feeling thinking
how good it would be to have him up and around again. She
would cook him an omelet for dinner and they'd have the
cake for dessert.

"Paul, Paul," she called softly, entering the darkened room.
Pale light stroked the curtains at the other side of the bed.
The covers were all bunched up and one pillow had slipped
to the floor. Funny, there was no hump in the middle, she
noticed as she approached the bed.

Maybe I should let him sleep.

He'll get up when the body's all ready to go again, the
doctor had said.

Only he was up already because there was no body under
the sheets and blankets, no head on the pillow. "Paul," she
said, turning on the little lamp by the bed.

It was true. He wasn't there.

"Paul," she repeated into the silence, frantically looking
around as though he was hiding from her somewhere in the
room. "Paul, where are you?" Feeling like a dope, she pawed
through the clothes in the closet and groped under the bed.
"Paul? Paul?" she kept calling, even knowing he was gone,
that he wasn't in any of the other upstairs rooms that she
checked one by one. Nor downstairs either, not even in the

smallest places, though she couldn't imagine why he'd be hiding in the hall closet or behind a chair. But by then, her heart racing, the sweat having dried up, leaving her clammy and cold, she wasn't thinking.

He's gone, gone, gone, pounded in her head. She went through the house a second time, looking everywhere she had already looked once before. But to stop looking was to give in, to say he really had disappeared, probably while she'd been napping in the living room.

Gone where? Why?

He's sick! she wailed silently, sinking to the couch; and holding herself rigid, barely able to breathe, she tried to think what to do.

15

It had gotten colder. A storm was coming out of the Midwest, a low-pressure system already building up. The smell of winter, of snow, was in the chill air. Piggy could feel the cold in his teeth. The wind slammed against him as he crossed Main Bridge, and he pulled his collar up, trying to protect his ears. With his chin lowered onto his chest, breath fogged his glasses. His head was starting to ache again. He should have worn a hat.

As he came off the bridge on the other side, the lights in Crown Hall, the boys' dorm, glowed out at him, and then, just around the bend to the left, the lights from Maddis, where the girls lived. He didn't think anyone would be out on such a wicked night, but he walked in the shadows alongside the bushes, up the short rise, the start of the row of faculty houses behind him now.

The shopping bag flopped against his ribs, the jar of peanut butter clunking around inside.

Sure she can eat, he had said to Slime. But could she? Maybe her digestive system didn't work as it once had and she needed a special diet of nutrients. Maybe . . .

There was no point in conjecturing, not until he saw how she had survived. He came around the back of Science and knew he should go in and clean up, that the lab was probably a mess. Waxworks would be wondering. *Let him wonder*. He was too stupid to figure it out. Piggy could just imagine the look on his dried-up face when he saw Sam, saw what Pig had done—the thing that no one before him had ever done, making the impossible possible. He could almost hear the awe in the science professor's voice, his stumbling apologies, and his doubt giving way to belief.

Triumph was sweet. It gave Piggy a warm feeling in the pit of his stomach.

Don't tell anyone, not yet. Don't tell; they might not understand.

Not understand! He laughed again, his guffaw carried away on the wind which tunneled and insinuated itself between the buildings as he came out at the back of the school, where the land gently slid downward to the playing fields.

In the distance he could just make out the bleachers and the gridiron, fringed along its far flank by a copse of emaciated birch trees. The equipment shed was off to the left, he thought. He couldn't see it; the night was moonless, starless, without benefit of any light whatsoever, heavy as black sludge.

The wind was at his back now, slithering down the neck of his jacket, and he shook with the cold.

Shuffling his feet over the dry grass, he groped along, stumbling, wishing he had his flashlight. It was pointless to strike a match from one of the books he had shoved into his pocket.

Bumping into one of the stanchions, he felt his way from pole to pole. The slanted seats were above him, to the right the fields. He had never watched a football game and only once had he seen the Red Sox play. His dad had taken him, but he had gotten bored. Too many hotdogs, too much sweet orange soda. He had thrown up. What was he, three, four at the most? All he remembered were the blue sky and the green diamond and the sickish taste in his mouth.

Tony had been disgusted with him for not caring about sports. But that was before he had known his son was a genius and had other talents a father could brag about.

A siren sounded from over in Welling Proper, the eerie whine drifting through the night across the river like the faint cry of someone in anguish. He stopped to catch his breath and listen. A fire? The police car chasing a speeder? Nine o'clock? No, it couldn't be that late, but he hadn't worn his Timex, which glowed in the dark, and in the blackness under the bleachers it could have been anytime. The whole night was vibrating about him.

The shed wasn't to the side—just like Slime, he thought, not to be accurate—but underneath the last section of the grandstand, built into the slope. He slammed into it, which was how he knew, fumbled around and felt the door, the padlock.

It was impossible to keep a steady flame. He had to go by feel, his fingertips tingling. He inserted the key. The shackle came loose from the case and swung free. He pulled the hasp over the staple and let the lock dangle.

Suddenly he was reluctant to open the door. He put his ear against the wood and listened, but there was no sound. A deep silence, ponderous as the night, emanated from the inside of the shed. He was stung by the quiet and in a panic flung back the door.

"Sam?" he whispered.

There was no answer.

He raised his voice, croaking, "Sam, are you in there?"

Rustling, like tissue paper being crumpled. Something was moving in the dark, moving just a little bit, scuttling around. The hair quivered on the back of his neck.

"Sam?" he called, his voice wobbling. He was trying to light a match but his hands trembled so that he broke off the head. Finally there was a spurt of light, a flame, and he thrust it out into the blackness at arm's length.

"Aaaaiiii . . . ! ! !"

He was propelled backward, out of the shed, tripping over his feet. His laces untied, he fell, coming down on his rump. There was nothing to see now; he was even blinder than before, the blackness heavier, pitch black, enveloping him. The bleachers behind him were a protective shell and he

scuttled backward until he bumped his head so hard his teeth
snapped together.

Somewhere, or at least ahead of him he thought—since
spinning around on the icy ground he had lost his bearings—
but somewhere in that direction, was . . . She had to be
there if the seats slanted to the east, and the shed was off to
the side. Yes, there. He furiously tamped down the wail that
was about to surge out of him.

With the wind whistling straight down, between the seats,
stitching itself like rain to the ground, swirling around him so
that there was no hope of escaping it, he couldn't hear. He
rubbed his eyes with clenched fists and listened to the thumping of his heart.

I won't think about it. The light . . . It was only the bad
light.

I've got to go back.

Of course, he acknowledged, clinging to reason. I have to go
back. Remembering Oppenheimer, how he forced himself to
continue.

He felt better blaming his nerves, his sickness, the pain in
his head that was scissoring his skull in half, ready to lift the
top right off.

He had dropped the matches, but there was another book
in his pocket, and he checked to make sure as he duck-
walked out from under the seats until he could stand. Approaching the shed once again, he quoted like a litany, *There
is nothing to fear but fear itself.* Only he wasn't convinced.

He thunked his head on a metal support, which made the
pain even worse. For a moment he saw red and yellow
pinwheel revolutions. A swing in the playground in Boston
had whacked him once and he had seen whirling colored
lights just like that.

He had to sit down, overcome by nausea, the puke lodged
in his esophagus. Could he choke on it? Die in his own
vomit? People did that. It went down the wrong way, into
the lungs, stopping the air. Frantic, he waved his hands,
thumping a closed fist into his chest, and his breathing—
which hadn't really ceased—started. It was just the fear and
the bile, which he swallowed, sour-tasting, licking his teeth.

After a while which seemed both a year and a second, he
got to his feet again, carefully inching back toward the shed.
He knew where it was now even if he couldn't see it. It

gaped before him like an open pit, an emptiness through which he'd be sucked, pulled down a great slide that would curve and twist its way to the bowels of the earth.

No . . . no . . . no. . . .

Nothing like that. Just Sam waiting there in the dark. Sam alive now, not dead. Sam alive because he had made her that way. Just as he had BeeBee.

He had seen her face crocheted by inky lines. He had seen her vacant eyes staring, filmy with a yellow ooze that trickled over her lashes. His stomach tilted and he backed into the door which he had left ajar.

The rustling again. It froze his blood because he knew now what it was. It was the rats, or at any rate very large mice, chewing at her, nibbling with their razor-sharp teeth at her feet.

Three tries before he got a match lit, and then it spasmed in his hand, throwing a feeble light first one way, then the other. Which didn't matter because he had his eyes closed.

He had never imagined that she'd look so awful. No wonder Slime couldn't be dragged kicking and screaming to the shed. Given his frail constitution, it was a wonder, Piggy thought, that he hadn't cracked like an egg. Just as he was ready to do himself right then.

The match burned down, snipping at his fingers, and he dropped it with a yelp. "Light another. Yes, get it down. There, that's right. Two hands now." He was whispering out loud to himself, his eyes still closed, one hand holding the match, the other grasping the hand that held the match.

With a deep, steadying breath, he tried to regulate his breathing, recalling the instructions from a book his mother had on meditation.

When he felt the tremors subside to about a three on the Richter scale, he said, "Now I will open my eyes." And he did.

He couldn't leave her in the shed, not with the cold, the rats. Not there in the dark. Somehow the dark was the worst of it.

He couldn't keep her in the lab either. Yet he had to examine her where he could see, where he had all his tools.

She walked with an awkward gait, lurching and rolling, her legs—for some reason—refusing to bend at the knees. There was a definite rigidity to her, as though a statue had gotten off its pedestal and moved. She also had a tendency to keep her arms outstretched like iron pipes, though it was possible to flex the elbows. And when she turned, she pivoted her entire body, the elasticity in her neck and shoulder muscles minimal. He had to guide her through the shadows of the campus with a hand on her upper arm, which was hard as stone. By the time he got her over to the lab he had conquered his fear if not his anxiety.

It was worse than he had even dreamed, drugged by sleep, by sickness. Still, a certain pride mixed with his revulsion when he got a good look at her under the harsh fluorescents.

He was reluctant to touch her, afraid she'd break, that any unnecessary jarring would somehow dislodge the mechanism which had brought her back to life. Gently, with the tips of his fingers, he guided her to the stool and helped her sit down. First he examined her feet. The rats had gnawed both big toes to the bone; the flesh hung in jagged shreds. He wondered if the wounds were the cause of the faint, rancid odor which seemed to hover about her in a mist.

"Sam," he said, crouching and staring into those yellow eyes like two pools of melting margarine. "Sam, can you hear me?"

If she could speak, she didn't. She looked more dead than she had on the slab at Toomy's Funeral Parlor. Her mouth hung lopsided, pulled down on the left and slightly agape. The sound of her breathing—*whoosh, wheeze, whoosh, wheeze*—was like gas escaping from a hot-air balloon. She reminded Piggy of his grandmother after she had had a stroke, and he wished he knew more about the heart to ascertain what the damage was.

He'd have to do something, that was for sure. He couldn't leave her sitting like a lump of concrete staring out of runny eyes, what remained of her golden hair all lank and dirty, the bones in her toes exposed.

As he cleaned up the lab, he watched her surreptitiously. She didn't move, just whooshed, and finally he made a peanut-butter sandwich and tried to coax her to eat. Only by pushing pieces of it into her mouth could he get her to take it. Her jaws rhythmically scissored; the muscles in her throat spasmed as the masticated sandwich went down.

While she was chewing he inspected her head. The segment of bone that he had fitted into her cranium was still in place, the ribbon connection dangling.

He plugged her up again and without thinking too clearly, pulled the switch.

Her jaw dropped open; her tongue shot out. Arms swung up as if a puppet's strings had been yanked. Legs went straight as boards. And her whole body rose up off the stool, hung in the empty air for half a second and then crashed to the floor.

Hurriedly switching off the electricity, the computer's whir, he shifted nervously about, indecisive. Remembering the jolt he had taken, or surmising that he had almost electrocuted himself before, he was afraid to touch her. As if Sam herself was charged.

He leaned over, the scream caught in his head, the panic which had been lying there just under his skin all night swirling up to ensnare him. And as he tilted toward her, almost losing his footing on the slippery floor, she began to rise, the yellow eyes rolling back with nothing but the whites showing.

Her bony little arms, scratched and dirty under the over-sized football shirt and torn frilly pink nightgown, came up to clasp him by the neck and he went down on top of her as she shrilled, "Gaaaaa, gaaaaaa, gaaaaaa. . . ."

Jeannie drove around for an hour but there was nothing to see. She went back and forth along Main, where the sidewalks were deserted, the strings of colored Christmas decorations draped across the somnolent street the only glow except for the occasional store window left lit—blinking bulbs in Woolworth's, a papier-mâché Santa in Stein's Clothing, a sparkling tree in Suzette's Beauty Salon. Up the hill and along the side streets parked cars drowsed at the curb. There was an eerie quiet that Jeannie listened to when she rolled down the window, punctuated by the distant revving of a pickup's motor being gunned, a backfire, a dog howling mournfully.

No one was out. She met only Emmett Sidowsky driving his Ford. He thumped a "shave and a hair-cut" on the horn as he passed.

She thought of stopping the deputy and asking him if he had seen Piggy, but she didn't really know him except by

sight. Still, she didn't want to call Charlie Volchek either. If
only she could convince herself that Piggy was off somewhere
on a childish expedition, or, knowing Piggy, perhaps it wasn't
so childish—which is what she really worried about.

When she had toured Welling Proper—stopping hopefully
at the Ice Cream Hut—she swung onto the bridge and crossed
to the school. There was less likelihood that Piggy had traipsed
over to Mason, but she had to be sure. She stopped at Crown
Hall and searched the common rooms, pausing for a word
here and there with the boys. But if Piggy was visiting
someone, he wasn't to be seen, and again Jeannie hated to
ask. He had made no friends among the boarders and she
couldn't just say: I've lost my son.

She had even less reason to think that Piggy was over at
Maddis, but she walked through the lobby and stuck her
head in the large rec room on the basement floor anyway.

Back in the car—her panic mounting like floodwater—she
circled as far out as the football field. She even went off on
the back road which wound its way over the mountain—no
more than a slight rolling hill—that eventually connected up
with the main highway ten miles off.

Once again on campus, she thought to stop at the library,
open until ten since midterms were starting on Wednesday.
But the reading room was deserted except for one solitary
boy, Ferris, Jeannie thought his name was, a senior cram-
ming for Brown. Even the stacks were empty. Mimi Howard,
the librarian, was doing her best to stay awake. She tucked a
paperback romance under the counter and greeted Jeannie
with a sleepy smile.

"If any of the darlings are studying, they're not doing it
here," she said, stretching out her arms as though to gather
in all the quiet. "Is there something I can do for you, Jeannie?"

"No, no," she replied quickly. "Just wandering about."

"On Saturday night?" She patted her fading hair, out of
which protruded a pencil. "You need a boyfriend, if I might
say so."

Jeannie's laugh was hollow as she waved her hand. Leaving
the tomblike room, she went outside into the cold, down the
steep flight of stone steps to the car, which she had left in the
roadway at the side of the building.

Turning the heater back on, she sat for a moment with the
engine running and tried to think of places where she hadn't

searched. The lab, of course! Where was her head! The lab
would be the first, maybe the only place he'd go.

Quickly she switched the key off and jumped out of the
car, and ran the width of the campus to Science. She came up
on its stone flank and scrutinized the windows for a shaft of
light. There was only darkness, the building silent and
unrevealing. Groping her way up the front steps, she pulled
on the big metal door, but it held firm. She backed away, the
wind whistling around her, whipping her fear into a near-
frenzy. If he's not here, then where, oh where, can he be?

She imagined him at the bench in the lab, bent over a
diagram, exploring the multicolored lines, learning, creating,
dreaming.

Circling the dark building, she ran through a plan of the
basement in her head, trying to remember, with all the twists
and turns of the corridors, which side the lab would be on.
West, she thought, but wasn't positive. She came around
after a full turn, not having detected a glimmer of light. He
wasn't inside unless he was cocooned in the blackness, which
made no sense. But what does? Certainly not his running off,
she thought, crossing the campus again to the Chevy.

Maybe he had run away, back to Boston, to Tony. But she
wasn't sure of that either. Guiding the Chevy into the night,
she crept slowly over the bridge and onto River Street,
feeling as though she were the one who was lost.

He had run, like a coward, fear pumping in his veins, run
down the basement corridor without thinking, run, the thud-
ding of his footsteps echoing like the booming of drums. He
had run away from Sam, yet not Sam, the Sam he had made,
uncertain in his terror what exactly it was he had done.
Coming to ground at last in the boiler room, he huddled
against the cold furnace, crying out his fright, his palms
pressed to his temples, pressing at the pain.

What was she?

What did he do with her now?

She wasn't like BeeBee, an invention he could show off
with pride, collect awards for, listening all the while to everyone exclaiming just how brilliant he was. There was also
nothing soft about her, soft as Bee was even though he was
constructed of metal and microchips.

What had he expected? That she'd be the same. Little by little the horror was creeping up on him, settling in.

Yet wasn't he still responsible for her?

Shouldn't he try to make her better?

How?

It was as if his brain had ceased functioning. He couldn't think anymore. The headache was so bad his skull seemed about to shatter. He wanted to climb back in bed and crawl into sleep, to wake up in the morning and find this was all a bad dream like the train and old Mrs. Williams trying to run him down on a motorcycle in St. Anthony's parking lot.

He wanted his mother!

He ached to go back to Boston, Boston before his life had crumbled into dust, Boston before Bertram Lennard had forced his own immolation. He yearned for an existence that didn't include Welling and Mason. What he decidedly didn't want was to be cramped up against a furnace afraid to move.

Yet . . . he *had* done it. He kept coming back to that.

It was inconceivable, was what everyone had said, had always said, except that he, Piggy, had pulled it off.

Only now he was cowering in terror, wishing it, her, Sam, was once again in Toomy's refrigerator under a sheet. A real scientist would have been jumping up and down, calling the New York *Times* and MIT. He blamed his illness for leaving him light in the head; he blamed the shock of Sam not looking as she had before she died. Only a fool would have thought she'd be good as new, he criticized himself with loathing. He was angry with his lapse of courage, as angry as he'd ever been at any of the others, his father, Jeannie, even Bertram Lennard. Well, he had atoned for that last, he supposed, in Waxworks' tortured mode of thinking. One killed, even if by mistake; one brought back from the dead, deliberately.

But no matter how he tried to avoid it, to circle around the question, it still remained: What did he do with her?

His left calf cramped and he shook his leg, the sneaker thunking the side of the boiler. The *boom, boom* resonated in the narrow space, intensifying his headache.

The silence was suddenly overwhelming, a coffin lid pressing on his back, his skull. He remembered the tombs in Westminster Abbey, the carved effigies on top. Swords and blank faces.

Dead means dead forever, Slime had said.

But Piggy had stood *forever* on its head. Except he hadn't planned what would come after that. He supposed in some stupid, babyish way—having forgotten momentarily that he still was a child—he had hoped to keep her, good as new, in the corner of his room, just as he had BeeBee.

Approaching the door of his lab, he slowed up. He had to move her out of Science. There were too many people around, wandering in and out of the building. Students, teachers, the cleaning crew. Sooner or later someone would see her, no matter if he kept her bolted in.

He wanted badly to take Sam and escape from the oppressive gray building, but he hesitated with his hand on the knob. As if she was inside waiting for him to return and say, *I've made us a plan.*

She was inside, or at least he half-hoped she still was, and yet half-feared it. Wouldn't it be better for everyone—who was everyone? there was just him—if she vanished like smoke in the night? As if she expected him to return and make it all right. The way his mother had expected it of his father, even that last time when he refused to make anything right anymore and just left, making everything wrong.

He twisted the knob in his sweaty palm, the metal sliding, and had to take a firmer grasp after wiping his hand on his pant leg, before he could crack the door.

Sam was no longer on the floor where he had left her, jerking out of that unbearable embrace, his head pulled down close to hers, that gargling sound in his ear like a car engine screeching when the oil had run out, the aroma of slightly off meat traveling up his nostrils. His heart careened painfully in his chest as he remembered how good it had once felt to hold her hand, and how that time on the back steps he had longed to kiss her.

She had levered herself back on the stool where she sat, legs spread apart, arms dangling. She was a study in contrasts, both monstrous and forlorn. From the rear, if you squinted, it was difficult to see that she was after-dead. Only the wires dangling out of her head, and then you had to get nearer to tell they weren't part of a barrette. But from the front . . . And then the strange affectations, the stilted way of holding herself, arms out, palms down, head tilted at a forty-five-degree angle, clicked with the gaunt face and the bones that threatened to burst through the surface. One could almost visualize those burnished bones under that parchment skin, that bruised, pulpy flesh.

The football shirt Slime had put on her gaped at the neck. The sleeves were tattered.

Beneath the shirt the pink nightgown was a rag, grimy, ripped and punctured with holes. And her feet . . . He couldn't let her walk any further on those mutilated toes.

He pulled his own socks over her torn feet, holding his breath while he tugged them up to her ankles. Then he put his sneakers back on.

Definitely, he had to make plans to move her somewhere, but the place didn't emerge clearly from his jumbled thoughts until they were outside Science in the cold, the wind snipping away at them.

The shed in the backyard. It wasn't perfect. It really wasn't even such a good idea, but it had the advantage of being easy for him to get to. There was no heat, of course, but it was fairly tight, and if he boarded up the window the draft couldn't whistle through the cracks. It would do anyway until he had a better idea. He was near the point of exhaustion and it was at least a temporary solution.

They plodded along, surging through molasses, frozen stiff, or at least Pig was, pushing at her with his fingertips. We'll never make it, he thought, yanking her against a tree on the main campus as a car veered off the bridge and climbed up the slope to Crown Hall. No, they wouldn't reach Welling Proper without someone seeing them. Once on the bridge, they'd be totally exposed. No place to hide. And there was something terribly wrong with Sam, something so awfully wrong that a driver might speed right off the bridge in fright.

Besides, he wasn't sure he could walk the mile, shaking with the cold, his heart pounding like a kettledrum. He was stalked by fear, by an illness he was only managing to hold at bay with a concentration of will. The fever burned behind his eyeballs with a hot flame.

Bertram Lennard going up in smoke.

The streetlight at the edge of the main drive threw a perfect circle of whiteness on the black grass. Bertram Lennard was standing in the middle wearing his yellow T-shirt, his lips pulled back, ferret teeth gleaming. He was a piranha about to sink into flesh.

"Shut up and leave me alone! You're dead."

Piggy clenched his fists, shaking them at dead Bertram Lennard, who was dancing between him and Sam, protecting her as Bertram tried to thwack at her chest, to prod with pushy fingers into her cavities, upset the delicate balance of her perfectly engineered parts, as he tried to hurt her . . . him . . . BeeBee. The thin jet of flame from the blowtorch swung around suddenly, sending bright streamers of red and orange flying.

"Don't touch him! He's not yours, he's mine. Mine . . . mine . . . mine . . . mineminemineminemine. . . ."

Only this time Bertram Lennard didn't spin and twirl like a gaily painted top, all the colors merging into flames, into charred strips of T-shirt and jeans and stinking muscles, tendons pulling away from joints, screaming in an unending squeal so that sound and color and flame all convulsed and danced before Pig's eyes like a total work of art.

Bertram Lennard now, here, on the Mason campus in the chilled circle of light, went white, faded into the already-whiteness, paled, then glowed, and blew away. Only his laugh remained. It melted into a shriek that sailed on the gusting wind up into the denuded treetops and finally merged with the fire siren of Welling, pealing out over and over again until suddenly it too stopped and there was silence.

16

He had to get home. Each moment he spent standing in the middle of the Mason campus with Sam at his side like a faithful dog, he ran the risk of being discovered. Of *their* being discovered.

His breathing had finally slowed, and peering through the quaking gloom, he searched for the revolving flames, the fading image of Bertram Lennard going up in smoke. But there was nothing to torment him, and for that, anyway, he was grateful.

His feet wouldn't carry him much further. And what about Sam's? He looked down at the bulky white socks and thought his heart would break.

A car was the only way. He glanced to his right at the parking lot by Admin and saw several cars angled into the curb. They must belong to the teachers who lived in Welling East, in the small houses on the other side of the road. He prodded Sam in the back, pointing her in the proper direction, and they made their way to the lot.

There were only five cars and he moved stealthily from one to the other, trying the doors. Only one was unlocked, a Ford Fairlane. He wasn't sure he would be able to drive it, but when he thought of the long, grueling walk back to River Street, he gritted his teeth with determination. Carefully levering Sam into the back seat, he positioned her much as he once had BeeBee—which gave him a pang—and then slipped behind the wheel.

The seat was too far back and he fumbled around until he found the right handle and yanked himself forward so that his feet could reach the pedals. Still, he would have been better with a cushion under him; the steering wheel was impossibly high, so that he had to strain his neck in order to see over it. Which gave him a shooting pain across the shoulders to add to all his other aches.

Getting the Ford started was the easy part. He had read enough to know how to hot-wire it under the dash. But when the motor sputtered and coughed, eventually settling into a low growl, he wiped his sweaty palms on his damp jacket and wondered if he could do it. It was different driving a car than being a passenger. And he doubted it mattered that he probably could have taken the engine apart in his sleep. Or at any rate understood perfectly how it ran and why.

Luckily the car was an automatic, and he shifted into reverse, gently easing on the gas, and backed the Ford out of its parking space. Once he was clear of the cars on either side, he lifted the shift down to drive and cautiously turned the wheel. Suddenly he shot forward and smacked the bumper of a Pinto to his right. He gulped, and went once again into reverse, hoping that no one had heard the metallic *thwack*. This time when he shifted to drive, he fed in the gas slowly until he—inch by inch—paralleled the back of the other car. Then, in short, chugging motions which kept throwing his stomach against the bottom of the wheel, he maneuvered the Ford out of the lot and onto the road which led down to Main Bridge.

Once he began the decline, he let the car roll of its own accord, his foot poised nervously over the brake, ready to stamp hard at the slightest increase in speed.

This isn't so bad, he thought, his spirits lightening—though he worried about Sam being jounced around on the back seat. He glanced in the rearview mirror to see if she was all right, and the car left the road, rolling up on the grass, plowing furrows in the wet earth, as it angled toward a tree. His foot hit the brake with a slam of panic, and he was almost flung over the steering wheel. But at least the car had halted its inexorable run for the tree, and turning to the right, Piggy got them back on the road. He shuddered to think what he had done to the grass, but realized that on his list of problems, of concerns, that came last.

"Sam, are you okay?" he called as they bumped along for a few feet on the asphalt.

She didn't answer, not even with the strange, unhuman noise she made. Though she was acquiescent, he worried that she couldn't function on her own, except for the most basic movements. He got a chill thinking of her as a trained dog. Tell her to leap and she leapt, tell her to sit and she sat. Or rather yank her up and she came. He wasn't sure she responded to spoken commands as BeeBee had. Still, he had thought she was more alert than when he had found her in the equipment shed.

He shuffled around, all his nerve ends singing. There was so much to do with her, so many tests he should be performing, procedures that ought to be followed. He wished he had help, a group of scientists he could work with. But that was out of the question. He knew what people would say if it ever came out, *this* on top of his mistake. They'd think he had done something wrong, that he was crazy, and Sam would be spirited away. He could see her locked up in some government installation, treated like a wind-up toy, or worse, a monster.

But *what* was he going to do with her?

It wouldn't be so bad if she at least approached a level of normalcy, functioned, if slowly, more like a person did. There was something about her that unnerved him. And if he was nervous, how would others react?

He was just overtired. Sick too. In the morning, though it was close to morning now, he'd have the energy to start researching. There was so much to learn if he was going to help her . . . himself. . . .

His thoughts returned to the car. Which was just as well, since there was another car already at the Mason side of the bridge coming up the hill toward him. Piggy froze. What did he do now?

His eyes went wide in the glare of the approaching lights, which seemed to be about to meet him head-on. Pulling the wheel sharply to the right, he came down hard on the brake, fishtailing slightly. The engine stalled, though he pounded on the gas. His foot off the brake, the car resumed its rolling.

The lights were almost upon him now, and all at once he realized that he would be recognized in the glare. Or at least the other driver would see that it was a kid behind the wheel of the Ford. Ducking his head, though now he couldn't see the road, he tried to keep a shaky foot steady on the brake. Just let them think we're only going slow, he thought, gripping the steering wheel like a lifeline. He heard the car move along on his left, and waited for the screech of brakes and a voice shouting: Hey, what's going on? But to his amazement, it simply passed him by, and when he lifted his head again he saw he was at the bottom of the short hill. With a sigh of relief he wired the Ford a second time and headed for the bridge.

His sense of coordination and of distance were no better in a car than on a volleyball or basketball court and he misjudged the moment when he should have turned, swerving just a second too soon. The right-front fender crumpled against the side of the bridge in an ear-splitting shriek. *Somebody will hear that!* Piggy thought in fright, not thinking to back off, straighten out, and then go right. He pushed down on the accelerator and felt the whole side of the car shudder, but in an instant he was on the platform of the bridge. Carefully now he pulled the wheel until the Ford had a direct shot to the far side. Slowly he started out, but what he hadn't counted on was the wind, which hurled itself at him, making him once again lose control of the car. He jerked rapidly to the left, careening from the railing with one swift tug of the wheel. He tapped the other side of the bridge and bounced into the middle of the swaying span again. Flattening himself right against the steering wheel, his leg outstretched for the gas, he tried to pilot the car in a straight line.

Main Bridge stretched out through endless space, the darkness in the distance like a black hole. For a moment he thought of abandoning the car right there and walking the rest of the way with Sam, but he couldn't do that either. His foot fumbled off the gas, searching for the brake, which had disappeared under the dash, and he just kept moving. *I'll never get home!* he wailed in his head at the exact moment he felt the wheels hit the tarmac of River Street.

He missed the culvert on the left by inches, swung far to the right, and there was his house in the middle of the block. It was the only house with harsh yellow light pouring out of all the downstairs windows. His stomach knotted. He knew his mother must have awakened and found him missing. What would he say to her; how would he explain?

"Sam, Sam," he whispered, "what have I done?" But he didn't know if he meant the experiment or hurting his mother.

He glided past the house, driving smoothly at last, and through the front window thought he saw his mother pacing the living room. He thought, too, that her face was ravaged by worry.

Then he was past the house and at the end of the block. He put on the brake and came to a dead stop. As he tugged the wires, the engine died, and quickly he doused the lights. He couldn't go any further; he hadn't the energy. As it was, he had to walk Sam back and hide her in the shed. And then . . . and then . . . he'd have to face his mother, he thought, breaking into a cold sweat.

Jeannie stood in the kitchen, her hand on the wall phone. She wore the afghan wrapped around her shoulders and upper arms. The house had gotten cold, tiny puffs of air filtering in along the windowsills, beneath the back door, which, warped, didn't fit tightly. She had gone down to the basement to see if more heat could be coaxed out of the furnace. She had first thought of calling the police around midnight. Now, at two o'clock, she was thinking again of calling them. One part of her was screaming for help while the more cautious Jeannie was saying: Wait, don't get them involved. Her feelings about the police had been ambiguous since Bertram Lennard's death. They had treated Piggy suspiciously, not saying he was guilty by intent, but not saying he was totally innocent either.

She could just envision Charlie Volchek—whom she remembered sitting in the green velvet chair by the window listening to Piggy describe how Harry Pringle beat BeeBee to death—saying, "What do you mean he disappeared while you were sleeping?" As though she shouldn't have let down her guard for an instant, with a child like Pig. Well, maybe she was remiss. But then again, Piggy wasn't an infant. And he was better. That's what the doctor had said: that there was no reason to worry anymore.

No, Charlie Volchek, who vaguely reminded her of the actor Rod Steiger, mightn't believe her either. He hadn't really believed Piggy about Halloween. Or was it just that they were outsiders, not to be trusted? Or not trusted more than someone from Welling, even if that someone was a liar and a drunk? The chief should feel really proud of himself now, after what had happened to Sam.

Her nerves were fraying, and she felt sore, raw, She jumped when the furnace rumbled down below, dropping her hand from the phone. In the living room she curled in the corner of the couch and sipped at a mug of tepid coffee. She should warm it up, but this was her fourth or maybe fifth cup already.

She didn't want to move, afraid of the scream all the way down in her belly that was waiting to break out. Shivering, she pulled the afghan tighter.

What was she going to do? Whom could she call? She didn't really want anyone aware that Piggy was gone, that he had wandered out into the night. Though they'd all know soon enough. Tony. She suffered with the thought of calling him. She was half-desirous, half-afraid. Should she phone him now and say Piggy was missing? And what would he answer to that? Would he upbraid her for running from Boston? And what was he able to do, anyway, hundreds of

miles from here, that she hadn't already done? Nothing. But
her aloneness appalled her and tears started in her eyes, and
once she began sobbing, she couldn't seem to stop.

Bertram Lennard rose up before her out of the brown rug
in the middle of the living room, as if he was rising from the
earth itself, from the grave. His hands were extended, his
fingers twitching like worms, and she shrieked at him in her
head, *Go away!* A mistake, it was all a mistake! She held on to
that word, which she had repeated for months like a trained
seal. *Mistake* was the towline that would keep her from
drowning. But Bertram Lennard was not to be pacified. He
thumped toward her on leaden feet, even after she cried
silently: The dead don't rise, they stay buried until the end of
time.

She could smell the fetid odor of his decaying flesh, and
pushed herself away, back against the cushions, bunching the
afghan at her chest as if that flimsy material could protect
her. But nothing could stop the dead boy's advance, his eyes
bright like glittering fireballs.

The scream that had been waiting all night in Jeannie's
insides exploded as she closed her eyes. And in the darkness
she thought she could feel Bertram Lennard's hands reach
out and touch her face.

She must have passed out or perhaps just fallen asleep.
Bertram Lennard might have been an episode in the endless
dream. Shaking, she came suddenly awake and rubbed at her
eyes. When she could see, she saw him standing just inside
the kitchen, a dark silhouette, the white glare at his back.
For a moment she was disoriented; then the curtains of
fogginess shifted, and almost without thinking it, she swore to
herself: I never thought it was anything but a mistake!

Swinging her legs off the couch, she rose shakily to her
feet, screaming at him before she could restrain the words,
"Where have you been? I've been worried sick!"

Stumbling out of the living room, she launched herself
toward the brightly lit kitchen, the glare painful. Piggy backed
away, and she thought: He knows I want to slap him, that I'm
so angry I want to turn him over my knee. She shoved her
unsteady hands down into the pockets of her jeans and scrutinized him.

He looked terrible; his clothes were rumpled and streaked
with dirt. His face was reddened, blotchy, from the cold. In

spite of her anger, Jeannie forced herself to be calm, and asked softly, "Are you all right?"

"I'm fine, Mom. Sorry I got you so worried."

"Where were you?" she demanded, her voice fractured with fear.

"Out," he said, after a long pause.

"I know that. But you've been sick and it's"—she glanced up at the wall clock over the refrigerator—"four in the morning."

He was so cold, distant, like a stranger who had wandered into the wrong house. This time she did reach out with trembling fingers and felt his head. He slipped away from her and went to the sink. Filling a glass with water, he drank it down while she stood and watched him uncertainly. Jeannie didn't know how she restrained herself from hollering her head off, from demanding to know where he'd been, what he'd been doing, and who did he think he was, for he was only thirteen and sick, and he had made her sick with fright. Anger danced behind her eyelids, but still she didn't let go. There was something about the way he refused to defend himself, to explain. He was so obviously at the edge of collapse right there on the kitchen floor that she held the anger in check, though just barely.

"I'm tired," he said, walking around her through the living room to the stairs. "I want to go to sleep." And with that he started up the steps.

"No, Paul, this won't do, won't do at all. I want to know where you've been and why you sneaked out without telling me."

"You were asleep," he said, three steps up, much taller than she was now. She came to the railing and had to tilt her head back to see him properly. "And I didn't want to wake you," he added.

"That means you know I wouldn't have let you go."

"Mom," he said, "I'm sorry! But I had something to do." Jeannie waited. "An experiment," he confessed reluctantly.

"What experiment?" Jeannie wanted to know.

"Just an experiment. It didn't work out, so it doesn't matter. Now, can I go to sleep?" And wearily he climbed up the stairs without waiting for an answer.

It was dawn, and early light was creeping in a mist over the sleeping town before Jeannie got into bed. She sat in the kitchen, guarding the doors, though she didn't suspect he'd go out again that night. She was just so wide-awake, strung out, as though high on some foreign substance.

Finally, however, she did go upstairs, telling herself that it was another day, that her fears would vanish when the sun came up. And if they didn't? She had no idea what she would do then. She had come so close to calling out to Tony for help, and maybe, just maybe . . . But she was suddenly too tired to think of that possibility either.

The worst of this long and awful night for Piggy was, strangely enough, facing down his mother. He hadn't, until he opened the back door, considered what he would say, how he'd explain his absence. Once he had sneaked out, he had no thought but Sam, and it was only when he saw the lights that he realized there was no chance Jeannie would have slept straight through, or gone up to bed without checking on him. The fact that she didn't throw a first-rate scene he attributed to her being afraid. Perversely, he resented that. But it was a worry Piggy had to put aside. The priority was Sam, locked up in the shed, or rather in the shed with the door closed, because the shed didn't have a lock. And there was no way he could attach one to the door without his mother noticing. The last thing he wanted was for her attention to be drawn to the little lean-to in the backyard. In the morning he would have to board up the window, not only to keep out the draft but on the odd chance someone—meaning Jeannie— might look in. Which wasn't likely since the window faced the Pringle yard and to get a good peek meant stepping over the low metal fence and going around to the side. He didn't think his mother would do that. He couldn't see Harry Pringle getting curious enough to stick his nose to the glass either. But then Pig expected that Harry would either stay dead drunk or end up in jail. At least he hoped he'd get arrested. Though could they take him away and charge him for murder without a body? That was something he hadn't thought of, that Harry Pringle might go free because he and Slime had stolen Sam's body. It didn't matter that Sam wasn't dead; her father still had killed her.

So many worries, so many fears. They fluttered in his mind like a flock of birds. He thought he was going to cry seeing his mother's face creased like an unironed sheet, deep craters

under her eyes. And finally tears did come, leaking over his
lashes, rivering down his cheeks. He wept silently with his
face in the pillow. His nose filled up and he gasped for air,
but still, for all that, the pressure in his chest melted away
like a block of ice. Eventually, with some misgivings, frightened of possible bad dreams, he slept.

Both Jeannie and Piggy slept through most of Sunday,
waking in the overcast, drizzly afternoon, when the light was
already beginning to fade.

When Piggy went downstairs, feeling better than he knew
he had any right to feel, feeling fine as a matter of fact, his
sickness barely lingering and then only in a slightly stuffed
nose, he found Jeannie whipping up pancakes in the kitchen.

"I thought you'd probably be starving to death," she said
with a faint smile that didn't reach her eyes. Purplish shadows underscored them.

"Swell, Mom," he said, pouring himself a tall glass of
orange juice. "I think I could eat a brontosaurus, but pancakes will be much better for my stomach," he joked, and
went over and planted a kiss on her cheek.

"Now, what's that all about?" she asked, cocking an eye-
brow at him. He didn't kiss her so willingly these days,
kissing one's mother being a sissy thing to do, as he had so
often told her.

All the demons had vanished in the long sleep and his
courage had come back in waves. There was nothing he
couldn't do now, he had decided on awakening, his fears
silent, muffled by pride. He had done it! He had . . . He
had!

"Just that I'm sorry I gave you so much trouble last night,"
he said, ducking his head. Upsetting his mother was the last
thing he wanted to do.

"Care to tell me now what you were up to, Einstein?" she
asked, nervously tapping her fingers on the edge of the
kitchen sink. Piggy tried to read it but she stopped mid-word
to flip the pancakes and he lost it.

He drained the last of the juice and shrugged. "It wasn't
anything."

"It must have been something to make you leave the house
when you were sick and to keep you out most of the night."
She had her back to him, so she didn't see the sudden

shadow darken his face. Why can't she leave me alone? he brooded, his good mood starting to ebb away. "You're only thirteen, you know—"

"But this isn't Boston," he interrupted, trying to make her laugh, trying not to tumble downward into the awful terror which was still there—out of sight, but no further than the shed in the backyard.

"Okay, peace," she agreed reluctantly, handing over a plate of pancakes, "but there are rules, and one of them is that you don't go wandering around without letting me know. And your curfew, if I remember correctly, is nine o'clock."

"I said I was sorry!" he exploded, and almost grabbed the plate out of her hand. "It was just an experiment," he repeated when he had his control back. He forked a mound of pancakes into his mouth and chewed. "I didn't know it would take so long."

"Can't you tell me about it? I'm not the KGB, you know."

"Oh Mom," he mumbled with his mouth full, trying frantically to think of some scientific jargon he could throw at her. Then he half-remembered an experiment that Bertram Lennard had been working on that day in the lab at Height.

"Something to do with the properties of phosphorus," he told her, then proceeded to unreel a list of chemical formulae. He complicated the explanation as much as possible until her eyes glazed and she came and sat beside him, helping herself to a fresh batch of pancakes. "Now," he said at last, when he knew he had totally bamboozled her, "do you understand?"

"No," she admitted, "you're talking Greek. But I didn't know you were doing any chemistry experiments."

"It's not chemistry exactly," he said in mock exasperation. "It has to do with—" And then he ran on for another five minutes, knowing she was fogging out.

"All right. I give up. But don't do it again. This might not be Boston but—"

"I know, I'm only thirteen and you worry," he interposed, and like an aged uncle, patted her hand.

"Okay, peace, I mean it," she sighed, and got up to clear the table.

The itchiness began creeping up his spine. Sam was in the shed and needed food, water, a blanket too.

"Is it cold outside?" he asked innocently, starting for the back door and the thermometer on the porch.

"Hold it, champ. You're not going out minus your jacket. And maybe you shouldn't go out at all. It's drizzling, and another day in the house won't kill you. Especially after last night."

"Mom!" he wailed. "I'm fine! Look at me, the picture of health!" He couldn't stay in and stare at the shed through the window without going bananas. He'd be worrying and wondering himself sick. *Just like Mom last night*, he realized, amazed, and sat down again, saying softly, "Really, I feel fine. And it's not raining out. Just yucky, that's all."

Jeannie insisted. "You're still white as a ghost and I distinctly heard you coughing up phlegm." But he looked at her so earnestly she finally relented. "Only if you bundle up and don't stay out too long. And be sure to come in at the first sign of rain."

"Thanks, Mom. I'll be careful. Promise."

"Where are you going anyway?" she called after him as he bolted for the hall closet and his down jacket.

"Nowhere," he called back. And nowhere is where he went after reading the thermometer. The temperature hovered at thirty-eight degrees Fahrenheit. She was watching him, standing at the kitchen window and peering out. He went back into the house and hung his jacket over a chair. "See," he kidded, "I didn't die on that trek to Antarctica."

"Funneee," she drawled, but seemed satisfied and went upstairs to make the beds.

Galvanized, he hustled around, filling a big empty Cranapple jar with water, stuffing a bag full of Wonder Bread and Velveeta slices and marshmallows and chocolate chip cookies, then running down to the basement and returning with a hammer and nails. He could hear her in the bathroom when he tugged on his jacket and left the house, galloping across the back lawn to the shed.

Sam was sitting in the corner where he had left her, her legs straight as pokers, her arms limply by her sides. Maybe he was getting used to her, but he told himself she didn't look so bad now. She could use a bath and her hair washed and definitely a change of clothes. Ragged, dirty, unkempt. And she still faintly smelled.

"Hi, Sam," he said in that phony voice he'd always em-

ployed with the retarded son of a friend of his mother's back
in Boston.

She didn't answer, but then he didn't think she would.
Something had definitely happened either to her vocal cords
or the speech center in her brain. He thought the latter,
suspecting irrevocable damage either from the long period of
time she'd been deprived of oxygen, or from the shock of the
electricity, or simply from the trauma of the experiment.

Dumping the bag of food in her lap, he uncapped the
Cranapple bottle and tilted it to her lips. Most of the water
dribbled over her chin, but she did managed to swallow
some. Joy bubbled up once again in his chest and he sang to
himself, *She's alive, she's alive!*

When he had coaxed her to eat, pushing the bread and
cheese into her mouth as he had had to do the night before,
he turned his attention to the window. Yes, it had to be
boarded up, but the only thing that he saw which would do
were the shelves attached to the wall. While he was struggling to pry them loose, he glanced down and saw that she
was feeding herself marshmallows, picking them up almost
daintily one by one and inserting them between her lips. He
surged with excitement. She was learning, no question of
that, and for half a minute he had a vision of Sam the way she
had been, the Sam of before, laughing and skipping around
the backyard. But he pushed that dream away. It wasn't to
be. *That* would certainly take one of the miracles old Waxworks was always yammering about.

The bottom shelf finally broke free with a crash, and Piggy
nervously peeked out the door to see if his mother had heard,
though he didn't think she could with the house shut securely
against the cold. There was no face anxiously pressed to the
glass and he breathed a sigh of relief before he pried the
other two shelves loose.

He hammered the first one into place and, without even
being aware that he was doing it, began to talk to Sam, just as
he once had talked to BeeBee.

"I know this has been a shock for you, like it's been for me.
Being dead one minute and alive the next. A medical marvel,
that's what it is. I just wish you could tell me what it was like.
I mean, there's nothing better than firsthand knowledge.
People all over the world have been hooting and howling for
years about afterlife experiences, but you're the only real,

bona-fide case that I know of. Or trust. People can be awful liars, Sam, when you come right down to it. They'll say anything if there's someone to listen. Flying and looking down on their past life. Going through tunnels—" Which made him stop, remembering the train. For a moment he could hear it again, see the gleam of the polished brass lamps, the shiny black skin. He shivered and hammered harder, getting the second board up alongside the first. Piggy was very good with his hands; his father had often teased that if he ever got tired of being a genius he could always take up carpentry as a profession.

When the second board was in tight, he paused for breath, wiping the film of sweat off his forehead. "One more to go," he said, and turned to see her legs and arms jerking, flapping like ungainly wings. Fascinated, he watched her mouth flop open, slam closed, flop agape again. One partly masticated marshmallow fell out and he realized with a shock that she was trying to speak.

"Gaaaaa," came out weakly in a croak. Piggy shook to his marrow. She was trying to tell him something!

"Sam, what is it?" He bent closer and got a whiff of her stale breath. Hastily he drew back and wondering if it would be possible to brush her teeth, asked again, "What do you want?"

Her legs drummed on the floor and she scratched at the dirt, trying to push herself erect.

"Up, Sam? Up? You want to stand?"

Of course she wants to stand, you dodo bird, he said to himself. She must be stiff as iron sitting in the same position all night. If she could feel, that was. If her nerves were working. Another question to add to the long list he could see filling his notebook.

"Here," he said, and reached down, lugging her to her feet. She was heavier than stone, not light as the other Sam had been. Deadweight? he wondered, and that too went into the list of questions.

Once upright, she stood without moving, seeming satisfied just to be on her feet. For one wild moment he saw her as embodying the whole anthropological history of mankind and imagined her evolving as the days and weeks and months went by into Sam of before. . . .

No, no, let go of that idea! Whatever she's going to be, it's never that. And yet . . .

"Okay now?" he asked, but she simply stared at his face as she would have stared at the wall or the door, except that his face was in front of her and her eyeballs seemed to be stationary.

It was much gloomier in the shed now with three-quarters of the window boarded shut. When the last shelf went up, they'd be plunged into darkness. Piggy didn't like that, being closed up with Sam when he couldn't see. Since the tunnel, the dark had given him the willies, and he wondered if he had enough money in his private stash, an old ceramic Smokey the Bear, to buy a kerosene heater at the hardware store. Or at least a kerosene lamp. Tomorrow first thing after school he'd check it out.

He returned to the window and felt her at his back, the *whoosh, wheeze* of her breath whispering by his left ear. Then suddenly, "Gaaaa . . . gaaaa. . . ." More urgent now.

"What?" he cried, pivoting. She was looking out the window and he thought it was simply because the window was there . . . until he saw Harry Pringle standing on his back porch. Piggy jumped as though Harry had put his beefy hand on him.

He can't see in here! No, the light would refract against the sooty pane.

"Gaaaa . . . ga . . ."

She recognizes him!

Piggy's head whipped back and forth between Harry Pringle standing there and Sam in her jiggly agitation. For the first time a flicker of emotion skittered across her ruined face.

What was going on inside her head?

She floundered nearer, the scraping of her feet in Pig's torn socks dragging through the quiet. Out the truncated slice of window she stared at her father, glued to his presence. The scratchy syllables came more rapidly now, puffing out with each breath.

Harry Pringle lumbered from one side of the rickety porch to the other, glared at the Mullins house and its curtained windows, then came back and continued his mute inspection of the yard, the shed, Pig's house, before—perhaps feeling the cold through his dirty undershirt—he abruptly yanked the door open and went inside.

His disappearance did nothing to diminish Sam's jitters, and Pig—twitching with excitement himself—had to tug her back to her corner and sit her down, bending the knees like pipe joints, before he could nail the last board up.

Suddenly the shed went as black as the inside of a closed fist, split only by the white lines of light where the boards didn't quite join together. He hammered quickly, leaving the last nails sticking halfway out. The shed was oppressive now with Sam wheezing, shuffling in the dirt. Breath bunched in his lungs, and he sneezed three times in rapid succession.

"Got to go," he said, pushing open the door without even looking out first to see if his mother was anywhere in sight, "but I'll be back. I'll bring you some warm clothes and a flashlight too. Yeah, don't worry, Sam," he babbled, and raced for the house.

In the kitchen he drank two whole glasses of water, wiped the back of his neck with a paper towel, and ran a series of algebraic equations through his head before he could go into the dining room, where Jeannie was sitting at the table correcting English themes. She had a pencil behind each ear and one in her hand and wore the pink frame glasses she occasionally used for close work.

"Where were you, Paul?" she asked without looking up.

"Nowhere special," he said, and before her attention could be diverted from the papers, he escaped and ran up the stairs, plunging into his closet for something that might be small enough for Sam to wear. Warm enough too. Colder than a witch's tit out there at night, he thought, echoing one of Slime's silly expressions. He wondered why she hadn't died—*could she die?*—from exposure. Her body temperature had been lowered dramatically, that was for sure, and she seemed impervious to discomfort or even pain: he remembered how he had pulled her across the campus, buffeted by the wind, on toes that had been gnawed to the bone as though they were lamb chops. And she hadn't seemed to notice.

He found an orange sweatshirt from the seventh grade that should have been given to Good Will, not packed up for the move. Pants were harder. He only had three pairs of jeans and two of chinos and his corduroys, plus his good suit for dress. Maybe he could borrow a pair of his mother's sweatpants. He hadn't seen her wear the purple ones in a long time.

He sneaked down the hall to his mother's room and carefully eased out the drawers of her dresser one by one until he found the pants balled at the bottom. He grabbed them and hurried back to his room for a clean pair of heavy socks. Then he thought for a moment. He really had to clean her up. It couldn't be good for her, all that dirt. And he did want to make her look nice, or at least nicer than she did now, because, really, he cared about Sam.

Gathering up a towel, washcloth, his hairbrush, he rolled everything into a bundle, and tucking the flashlight in his pocket, went back down the stairs.

Jeannie was still lost in the mysteries of the second-form themes and didn't hear him as he took down the silver candlesticks and a box of candles from the shelf and left by the kitchen door.

Harry Pringle was nowhere in sight, not on the back porch or spying out of one of the upstairs windows, Piggy noticed with relief. It had frightened him, the way Sam had reacted. Not that she could be expected to feel affection or even indifference for her father after he had slammed her head in.

"It's me," he said, groping his way into the darkened shed. Setting the candles into the holders, he lit the wicks with a match. Light spurted up to the ceiling, then fanned out in soft circles. The shadows deepened into crevices on her face. If anything, Sam looked worse by candlelight.

He switched on the flashlight and positioned it in the corner so that the glow spread across the floor and along her legs.

Piggy took a deep breath and said, "Before I put some clothes on you, Sam, I've got to wash you up. Understand?" But she just gave him that same blank stare out of her pus-filled eyes. Maybe he should try treating her with the ointment his mother had used on him when he had had pinkeye.

There was enough water left from what he had brought her to drink and he wet the washcloth, working up a mild lather with the soap. Then, shimmying closer to her on his knees, he scrubbed away at her face. Dirt came off in streaks, leaving tracks to her chin. Pig washed and wiped and dried, even remembering behind her ears, and when he was finished, except for the bruises on her white, white skin, and the filmy eyes, she didn't look half bad. If you didn't notice the lack of animation or that her lower lip sagged as though her mouth had come unhinged. But it could be that he was growing accustomed to her. After all, he reasoned, it wasn't Sam's fault she wasn't as pretty as she used to be. If there was any blame, it was all his, but he pushed that notion aside and started on her hair. That was more difficult because the strands were tangled into knots, and even if she felt no pain, he didn't have the heart to pull and tug too hard. Anyway, with one side shaved to the bone, and the wires dangling, no matter if he got the rest of it silky, she would still look weird.

Once he had gotten her as clean as he could with cold water and a washcloth, he rested, sitting cross-legged on the floor in front of her.

"Have you had enough to eat, Sam?" he asked, digging into the bag. There were still the chocolate-chips, and he handed her one, but he couldn't get her fingers to take it, so he ate it instead. "Good, Sam. See, good. One of your favorites, remember?" Apparently she didn't. But they were Piggy's favorite, too, so he ate another one. After the fourth cookie he gave up trying to get her to take a bite, and just forced one between her lips. Once it was in her mouth, she chewed it, and then was more willing to take another one as he stuffed it inside.

When the cookies were gone, Piggy having eaten more than Sam, he dusted his hands off on his jeans and began to change her clothes. It gave him a funny feeling to strip her down to the skin. He was both embarrassed and interested, though he tried not to look. As a scientist he knew he shouldn't get personally involved, but still it made him fidgety to touch her naked stomach even if it was as cold as stone.

He worked quickly so that she wouldn't get too chilled, and yanked the sweatpants over her unresisting lower limbs. Then the sweatshirt went on, Pig being extra careful as it cleared her head and wires. When he pulled it down, it bloomed out over her like a maternity top. After the fresh socks were slipped on her feet, she was as good as he could get her. Only she still smelled. Not quite as badly, it was true, but maybe he should spray her with his mother's cologne.

Satisfied, he sat back on his heels, saying, "Do you feel better now? I mean I really should get you into the tub, but I don't see how. Maybe later, when things quiet down and I work out how to tell people. Soon I might have to tell, but only when I get you more into shape. Right, Sam?" He was whistling in the dark and knew it, chattering on to her as he

had in the past when she was Sam-before. Pretending that
nothing had changed, like some stupid two-year-old, he
thought. He knew he couldn't tell, that he had violated every
rule of science, performed an unauthorized experiment because of his grief, and not even kept meticulous notes. Besides, he had stolen her body from Toomy's deep freeze, and
there was probably some godawful law that covered that.
Maybe they could send him away to prison. He got queasy
just thinking about it. He didn't want to be locked up, and
besides, his mother would be awfully upset.

It was getting colder in the shed. The temperature was
dropping. Snow was a possibility and he hated thinking of
Sam out here. He'd rather have her inside in bed, no matter
that she apparently didn't feel the cold as he did. It was the
idea that counted.

"I've got to go now, Sam," he said, suddenly bone weary.
As his mother would say, he had overdone. "But don't worry,
I'll come back later and bring you something more to eat."

He thought about leaving the candles lit, but she didn't
seem to care particularly whether it was dark or not. She
didn't, if it came to that, seem to care about anything.

Except Harry Pringle. She cared about him, or at least she
showed some emotion—if it could be called emotion—when
he had come out onto the porch. But Pig was too tired right
then to figure out what it might mean.

"I really do have to go," he repeated, as if she had objected
to his leaving. He got to his feet after tucking the blanket
about her, just as he once had bundled up BeeBee when they
rode in the car.

He was struck with such longing for Bee, who, he supposed, had come back to life too, since his computer was now
in Sam's head. Only it hadn't exactly worked out like he had
figured.

Don't be silly, he thought, you didn't plan anything, just
went ahead and fudged around, and this is what happened. If
you really had anticipated at all . . .

He cracked the door and a thin breeze crept in and doused
the candle flames. He picked up the flashlight and flicked the
switch.

"See you later, alligator," Pig whispered into the dark.

But no one answered, "After a while, crocodile."

17

School was torture. Pins and needles were being stuck in Piggy's flesh, making him so agitated that he couldn't sit still. All he could think about was holding on until the last bell.

The day was made of molasses. Piggy kept sneaking surreptitious glances at his Timex, but the hands stayed resolutely in place. He thought he'd scream when lunchtime finally came around and he caught up with Slime in the cafeteria. Though they'd had English together first period, Slime had crept in just after the last bell and scuttled out before Pig could grab him. As if he's trying to avoid me, Piggy thought at first, and then decided he was being paranoid from the strain.

Slime was getting into line when Pig squeezed in behind him, thumping his back. Jumping as though goosed, he spun around too fast and clipped Pig's stomach with his tray. "Watch out, Slime, will you!" Piggy yelped and moved away. But Slime had already stepped back. "What's wrong?" he asked, surprised.

"Nothing," Slime said, and held out his tray to the pump boys and dinettes, as the cafeteria staff were called by one sophisticated upperclassman from New York. The name had caught on and now all the students used it without really knowing what it meant.

"Why didn't you wait for me after English?" Piggy asked, not looking to see what it was that one of the dinettes slapped down on his plate.

"Didn't know you wanted to see me," Slime said, threading his way to a table crowded with a group of second-formers.

"No," Pig said, giving him a nudge with his shoulder, "let's go to the back, where we can get a table alone and talk."

"Pig—"

But Piggy was moving ahead, zeroing in on a distant table which was largely ignored by the students in the winter since it was under a window with bad molding so that a draft punished anyone who sat there.

Piggy unloaded his tray and took the inside chair. When Slime was seated across from him he said, "Why didn't you come over yesterday? Or even call?" Until that moment he hadn't thought to wonder why he hadn't heard from his friend. He hadn't, with all he'd had to do, even missed him until now. But suddenly he realized that here was the one person he could talk to, share his doubts and fears with, and try to ferret out some course of action that made sense. He beamed at Slime happily and, for the first time in days, the tension melted away. He wasn't in this alone! Or not totally anyway.

Slime dug into his food with the avidity of a famine victim. His right hand gripping the fork went up and down from plate to mouth as mechanically as one of BeeBee's pincers. His head hovered an inch and a half over his plate and he didn't raise his eyes as Piggy, uncharacteristically ignoring lunch, told him about Sam.

"But I can't go on keeping her in the shed," he was saying as Slime, working in a clockwise pattern, reached the last quadrant of his plate and dessert. "Do you have any good ideas about where we can move her?"

"No, Pig," he said, lifting his head finally and staring across the table, not into Piggy's eyes, but lower down, to the left of his chin. "I told you, I can't. No more. It's . . ."

He was acting strange, Piggy noticed finally, his eyes focusing on Slime for the first time. His features had flattened out into the pale white matte of his skin. He looked dim-witted, unaware of the huge tear that was sluggishly creeping from the corner of each eye. Piggy sat back shocked and asked, "What's the matter?"

"Nothing." Slime swiped at his bottom lip with his tiny pointed tongue. "I just told you," he croaked, "that I won't do anything more with *her*!"

"You're crazy, Slime, you know that. This is the experience of a lifetime. I mean, it only happens once, you know, and you're part of it. Like my assistant. What do you mean you don't want anything to do with it?"

"With *her*, Pig," he emphasized, his voice quavering like wind chimes. "She's scary, and . . . I can't sleep! I got these awful nightmares and I can't sleep. No, no, no." His skin had gone even whiter and was washed suddenly with sweat, Piggy saw with dismay.

"Slime, listen—"

But Slime was up and away, hurrying across the cafeteria, the dishes and milk carton jiggling wildly on his tray.

The momentary joy dried up and Piggy felt decidedly queasy, as if he had eaten something not quite right. All around the large room, chattering, laughing students clustered at every table except this one where Piggy was marooned wringing his hands. The noise ballooned up to the ceiling and echoed back. The noise pounded against Pig's eardrums and he wondered if he was going to be sick, was still sick, should be home in bed under the covers. Only he couldn't do that anymore, pamper himself like a baby.

The south doors swung apart and he saw his mother step inside, do a quarter-turn until she saw him, and start weaving among the tables to the other side of the room. The sight of her coming toward him with purpose and a smile on her face made him unreasonably angry, so that when she was no more than ten feet away and already beginning to ask how he felt, he was almost convulsing with fury.

"Leave me alone!" he cried when she went to touch his forehead, and bolted from the table, leaving her looking hurt. Only he wasn't going to think about that, even if he could. What took precedence, he kept telling himself out in the hall, was Sam. But the rage churning like lava in his skull made it hard even to remember her.

He was supposed to go to gym, but his mother had given him a written excuse because of his illness. It was funny because today was the one time when he thought he could appreciate physical activity, when he wanted to pound around the gym floor, thumping out his anger, his pain. He wanted to throw something really hard.

But the excuse did mean fifty minutes in the library with every book he could find on the brain. Only there wasn't one which gave any more information than he had already. Why would there be? he thought with disgust as he closed the last one of a tottering stack. The book I want hasn't been written yet. Maybe I'll have to write it.

But his notes were a mess. There were just too many blanks where he couldn't remember what he had done.

I should be shot, he seethed, thinking how he had lurched from step to step like a boozy old drunk. Procedures muddled, steps skipped, details ignored. And nothing written down until yesterday, when his memory was already blurred by the horror of the last few days. So much for my total recall, he chided himself, and dragged his resisting body back to Humans and history, the last class of the day.

At least I can sleep through *this*.

But Miss Markowitz seemed out to get him and wouldn't let the hour go by without an attack. They were midway into the Franco-Prussian War, which Pig, having missed a week of school, hadn't read about. He supposed it was fought over Alsace-Lorraine, as so many wars were, but he was wrong. It was more complicated than that and he flubbed answer after answer. Miss Markowitz, smelling blood, didn't leave him alone and the other students were gawking at him enthralled. It was so unusual to see him flounder that they were intrigued. By the time class ended Piggy's head was ready to burst.

Jeannie was waiting for him in the parking lot, standing by the Chevy. She was bundled to the chin in her pale mauve down coat. A light snow had begun to fall, dusting the fuzzy purple hat that she wore pulled over her ears. When she saw him come down the steps of Humans she waved and he plodded on heavy feet to the lot.

"Hi, honey," she called cheerily, but her eyes scrunched up with worry. "Ready to go home?"

Piggy regretted yelling at her. He wanted to say that he was sorry, that he hadn't meant it at all, even if the whole thing was her fault for treating him like a baby and not leaving him alone. And worse than that, she was to blame for Sam and the trouble he was in, because she was the one who had had the bright idea of moving them from Boston to Welling. But then, it was Dr. Mellon's fault too, since he had given her the job and him a place at Mason, and rented the house for them on River Street next door to the Pringles. All of which meant that by the time he actually reached the parking lot, imprinting faint tracks in the gathering snow, he was angrier than before.

He stomped past her and crawled into the car. The snow was coming down quickly now, puffing across the windshield.

How could he leave Sam outside in the cold?

"Looks like we're about to get our first snowstorm of the year," Jeannie said, as determinedly cheery as a department-store Santa as she slipped into the driver's seat and turned the key in the ignition. Piggy grunted, hugging himself, his hands in his armpits for warmth. It was freezing in the car and Jeannie flipped on the heater, though they'd be home before the Chevy warmed up.

Where could he put her? He couldn't leave her in the shed if a storm hit.

"So, how was your first day back?"

"Okay."

"What happened?"

"Nothing."

"Get all the assignments you missed?"

"Yes, Mom," he said in a tone of voice that made her glance anxiously over at him. He could see her from the corner of his eye, and slunk further down in his seat.

Body temperature, he thought. *That's what I have to find out about. Something's happened to her body temperature.*

"How's Tommy?" she asked, carefully driving onto the bridge. The surface was slick with a fine weave of snow, and the cars moved like slugs, going no more than ten miles an hour.

"Okay I guess," he muttered in reply, still stung to the quick as he was by the rejection. *He's not being a friend,* he thought, though he realized sadly that he didn't know too much about the intricacies of friendship.

Pig wiped a portion of the window clear and stared out. Off in the distance he could just make out the back of their house, the tiny shed like a coffin upended in the yard. Sam was alone there in the dark and the cold, and he felt the weight of knowing that he was her only link with the world, with survival.

"Didn't you see Tommy?" Jeannie asked, not letting go.

Piggy almost screamed at her, *Stop!* But he gritted his teeth and replied, "Yes, Mom, I saw him, and he's fine. In

good health and all that. Just singing his way through life
happy as a fat clam."

"That bad, huh?" She laughed, trying to jolly him out of his
bad humor, but just then the Chevy went into a short skid.

"Way to go, Mom," he snapped as she righted the car,
"run us into the river."

"Okay, smartie, I know, I've got to get the snow tires put
on." Her voice quivered but she got them to the house
without further skidding. "There, we made it, didn't we?"

"I guess so," he said, and mournfully stared at their front
door. His anger had mysteriously abated and he was just
weary. All of a sudden it seemed too much for a kid.

"What's the matter?" she asked when he sat without stirring. She sounded distant but her eyes had that film of terror
they often did when she looked at him.

He couldn't tell her that Sam, whom he had brought back
from the dead, was waiting in the backyard shed propped up
in the corner like a rusty rake. Sam, who wasn't Sam; who
wasn't anything that anybody had ever seen before. No, he
couldn't tell her about the experiment that worked, though
he didn't know why, and, in fact, sometimes thought he
might have dreamed the whole episode.

Piggy didn't tell his mother any of that, just sighed and got
out of the car. It was, when you came down to it, like having
a pet. The responsibility was his. Only Sam wasn't a dog and
nobody else could walk or feed her even some of the time.
He had to keep her secret because if he told, they'd lock him
up for any number of crimes. Or for being batty, he worried
as he trudged to the front door. Jeannie was ahead of him,
saying something about the snow, the path, the sidewalk—

"What?" he yelped, her chatter suddenly filtering in.

"I just said," she repeated, walking right through the living
room and into the kitchen, heading for the back door, "we
better see if there's a snow shovel because by tonight or
tomorrow at the latest, we're going to have to clear off the
walks. Maybe there's one in the shed in the back. There isn't
one in the cellar and if we don't have a shovel I better go up
to the hardware store before the hill is a sheet of ice."

She was going to go into the shed! The hair on Pig's neck
went rigid, and he almost couldn't speak he was quaking so
badly, but he did manage to croak out, "I'll go, Mom. You
need a rest."

"No big deal, Paul," she said, surprised. But he was already gone, shouldering past her, jumping the steps and hustling to the shed.

He burst inside, whispering warily, "Sam, Sam?"

The silence was palpable. It oozed around him like Krazy Glue.

"Sam?" he called again, wanting to cry. He just knew she wasn't in the shed. He could feel her not being there. The emptiness was like a black hole in space. Lost, alone in the dark, he fumbled with a pack of matches as he imagined his mother waiting in the kitchen, watching out the window. In a minute, if he didn't do something, she'd come after him. Wait, that's okay, he said to himself, there's nothing to panic about. Sam's not here. But then he realized that her not being there was worse than if she was because *he didn't know where she had gone.*

18

Harry Pringle woke up too hung-over to go to work. Which was just as well, since everybody on his shift at the shoe factory was treating him like Typhoid Mary since Sam died. Even in his own head Harry described Sam's demise as Sam having *died,* not as his having beaten her to death. Maybe it was that he didn't really remember Thanksgiving night all too well, and maybe he honestly believed, since he had told the story so many times, in her falling down the stairs. Or—though this was dubious—maybe he was sorry. He wanted to think that he regretted killing her, but that meant admitting to himself that he had, and what that did was get him rattled and afraid he'd forget, would blurt it out in one awful moment when Charlie Volchek just might press him too hard.

What Harry was really pissed about was not Sam's death, but her missing body. At least sometimes he was pissed about it; other times he wondered if it was all a nightmare, the kind of bad dream he'd had for months after Grace left.

Ran away, just like her mother did. Bad . . . bad. . . . No good to begin with.

He imagined her off in that mythical place where Grace was, having a good time, eating well instead of that crap she would cook up for him, riding around in his Ford, spending money that Grace had stolen from his bank account, and laughing. He could see mother and daughter laughing at him. Talking about how they had put one over on the old man. It made him so mad that he sat up in bed with a jerk and the hangover attacked the top of his skull like a rabid dog.

"Son of a bitch," he slurred, and climbed from the tangle of blankets, holding the side of his head with his hand, afraid his skull would topple off his neck and roll across the floor like a bowling ball.

What would anybody want a dead body for? he asked himself again as he stood under the shower and turned the cold water on. Icy needles assaulted him and he leapt back in the tub, almost sliding on his ass. He grabbed hold of the curtain rod and kept himself erect as he groped for the hot-water faucet. When the spray was lukewarm he ventured back under and soaped up his sparse hair.

He wouldn't want a dead body, no way, he swore, letting the water ease the pain out of his sagging fish-belly flesh. No matter what that asshole Charlie Volchek thought. What would he want the kid's corpse for? He shuddered. Even the idea was sickening. Charlie must think he was a ghoul.

He never particularly wanted the kid alive, so why should he want her dead?

It was, he decided, probably some stupid mistake. Toomy could have misplaced her, shoved her in the wrong box and into a hole in the ground. Harry wouldn't have put it past the undertaker, dumb as one of his stiffs.

Getting out of the shower, he toweled himself dry with a damp rag he found on the floor. The house was really going to rack and ruin. One thing, he had to admit, the kid had been good for, was keeping the place from walking away.

Even better than Grace, who was a filthy slut, more interested in watching her soaps all day than cleaning up.

Who was going to take care of all that shit now? Washing his clothes and ironing his shirts and cooking something passable to eat? Who was going to do that? he wanted to know. Not him. Nobody in their right mind could expect him to do it. He worked hard at the factory all day. There was no time to take care of things, and besides, the house was a woman's job.

The bitches, walking off on him, he grumbled, for a moment really forgetting that Sam was dead, that in his rage he had bashed her against the doorjamb.

In the middle of the hall he stopped and went back to the end and Sam's room. It was much the same as it had been the night she died. The bed was still mussed. And on the floor was the chalk outline of her sprawled body. There were smudges everywhere, brown spots on the wood and the rag rug that didn't look like blood anymore. He glanced at the jamb and smiled. He wasn't so gassed that he hadn't thought to wipe all the blood off with some toilet paper, then flush it down. Chortling, he ran his finger along the wood. Nope, say what he would, Charlie Volchek wasn't about to catch Harry sleeping at the wheel.

The hangover was sliding away and he would be able to finish it off with a strong cup of black coffee and a hefty shot. Trying to remember where he had stashed the bottle of Dewar's that he had lifted from the Five O'Clock one night when Calloway was breaking up a fight and not keeping an eye on the bar, he fumbled his way barefoot downstairs, after pulling on a soiled T-shirt and the same black chinos he had fallen asleep in.

There was a peculiar smell on the lower floor and Harry wrinkled his nose in disgust. The place really was a pigsty, with garbage piling up. Nothing for it but to empty the kitchen can and at least put all the dishes and pots in the sink and let them soak. He didn't have to wash them. With enough soap powder they'd probably get clean by themselves. If not, who gave a fuck? One day he'd do just like Grace and the kid had done and leave. Walk out and lock the door and let the whole place rot.

Why not? There was nothing in Welling for him. No family, his mother dead almost thirty years, his father in the ground for twenty. His brothers—there had been two of them—were long gone, and Harry had never heard where. Dead too, he supposed. No one would know or care if he just pulled up stakes. Why should he stay in this shitty town?

He felt a little better drinking off a can of cold beer he found in the refrigerator. Turning on the gas under a sauce-pan of water for instant coffee, he rummaged through the cabinets looking for the Dewar's.

Jesus, the place really did smell bad. If he didn't put the garbage outside, he was going to puke.

But when he came back inside from tossing the trash in the plastic can at the rear of the porch, the kitchen still stank, even with the door ajar. Phew! He wrinkled his nose. Maybe a small animal, a mouse or a squirrel, probably a river rat, had gotten caught between the walls and died there. It was that kind of smell.

He closed the door because he was freezing to death, the temperature well into the twenties, and just hoped the stink would eventually go away. Or maybe, when he felt more like himself—which meant after a couple of shots—he'd see if he could find the cause. Meanwhile, what was important was the bottle of Scotch, which he finally tracked down in the small cupboard over the sink.

The bottle was still three-fourths full, and he poured him-self half a glass to sip at while he was waiting for the water to boil. It went down like velvet and his head felt suddenly light, his sinus passages clearing with a pop.

He decided that he didn't need the coffee, the Dewar's having done the trick all by itself. He would have really been tip-top, he thought as he drained off the Scotch and refilled the glass, this time almost to the rim, if the place didn't stink so. His stomach lurched from the stench, and lifting himself off the kitchen chair with a grunt, he went looking.

It was definitely worse on the first floor than upstairs in the bedrooms, but rooting around, all the time sipping away automatically at the Scotch, he couldn't seem to unearth the source.

The cellar! Shit, why hadn't he thought of that before? There were enough cracks in the foundation for a battalion of small animals to have slipped through and died.

He opened the door just outside the kitchen and stared

down into blackness. Yeah, that was it, all right. He stepped back and wiped his mouth on the back of his hand.

Muttering, he shook himself like a large wet dog and plodded down the steps, fumbling for the light switch.

The twenty-five-watt bulb in the middle of the ceiling did little to dissipate the gloom, a thick, powdery grayness that cobwebbed the cellar. It clung to the sink and gave Harry's normally ruddy face a ghostly pallor.

At the foot of the steps Harry stopped. The concrete basement floor was like ice under his bare feet. Years of having lived in the house, and his family having lived there too, had filled the cellar with an accumulation of junk. Boxes, piles of old newspapers yellowed and moldy, a stuffed chair minus its seat cushion, the spring stabbing through the material like barbed wire, an antique washing machine . . . junk, all of it junk. The damn dead *thing*, squirrel or mouse or river rat, could be anywhere. He might search for years. But it was definitely here; Harry could smell that. He took a deep breath and made his way to the far end, where the furnace belched and groaned, the empty coal bin behind it. The furnace had been, by necessity, converted to gas, which had taken him years to pay off and he still resented it. He gave it a thump with his fist as he passed, circling around it to peer into the bin, all black and sooty, culm dust still clinging to the wood.

It was even darker in the bin, shadowless, and strangely enough, freezing cold, though it was so near the furnace. Harry hesitated about stepping inside the small square box, not quite a room, with an oblong-shaped window in the far wall, the coal chute still attached. The window should have given some light, but it was so grimy with gray sludge that it was barely discernible in the wall.

For some reason he couldn't put his finger on, he flashed back to the summer he was eleven, when he and Willie Novick went out to Stone Face, the clutch of rocks that jutted off a small mountain three miles along the Susquehanna. They had gone to shoot birds, appropriating Willie's brother's brand-new bee-bee gun because the brother was sick in bed and had been a real pain about letting Willie even try it out in the backyard.

He hadn't thought of that in years, of going to Stone Face and finding the cave, Willie tumbling inside before they even

knew it was there. Harry had fallen in right behind him,
yelling his head off because as a kid he hadn't liked small
dark places—still didn't, if it came to it. Maybe because when
the old man got pissed he always locked him or one of his
brothers in the hall closet and more times than not forgot
about them. And the cave was like that closet, only dank and
smelly with bat dung, just like the coal bin. He was suddenly
afraid to put another foot into it, and cursed himself because
he wasn't an eleven-year-old snot-nose anymore, afraid of the
dark. Except he was. Afraid of the dark. Or this dark anyway,
that seemed charged with electricity, making the hair on his
arms stand up. He tried to tell himself it was the cold. He
might as well have been outside.

The furnace rumbled, the gas coming on or going off, or
doing whatever it did in its innards, and then settled like a
cat into a low purr.

The kid had always liked the furnace, he recalled with a
jolt. It was funny, the way she got a kick out of trying to put
her little arms around it—she must have been three or four
when they converted—and listening to it hum. Never afraid
to come down to the cellar, that one. They had laughed about
it, him and Grace. When they didn't know where she was,
they'd find her in the basement hugging the big metal furnace. It might have been a stuffed dog the way she'd croon to
it and listen to it hum right back.

Thinking of Sam spooked him even more than the dark, or
the stench which had crawled up his nose and insinuated
itself in his skull where the headache began again, pounding
all at once, a sledgehammer whacking at the bone. He started
to pad backward out of the bin. *Screw finding the smell.* . . .
He'd go up to Main Street and hang around the Five O'Clock
until Calloway opened at noon. Then maybe when he came
back it would have faded away. Maybe it was just part of his
hangover. Migraines did that, he'd heard somewhere. Got
you smelling noxious odors that didn't exist. Why shouldn't
hangovers?

One foot went behind the other and he was shifting his
weight, when he heard the shuffling. Something dragging
along the floor of the bin, there in the corner, in the dark
where no light penetrated, where he couldn't see. He was
thrown off balance, pushing himself away, knowing he should
turn and run, but he wouldn't put his back to *that*. To what?

Nothing, he tried to tell himself, but a river rat or a squirrel. Only it didn't sound like an animal. It didn't sound like anything he had ever heard before, and goose bumps that weren't from the cold, though it was cold enough, rose on his arms. Suddenly he could imagine Sam in his hands as he swung her around the room. So light. Like a chicken.

The shuffling grew louder. Whatever it was was coming closer, would soon creep out of the blackness, take shape. Bigger than an animal. He *heard* that. And he tried to move away from it, thinking of the steps at the other end of the cellar, wanting to run up them and shriek. Lock the door at the top. Put a chair under the knob. Let whatever it was stay down here and stink until the smell permeated to the very bones of the house and the only way to get rid of it was to blow the whole place up.

But he couldn't move. His feet were stuck to the floor. They had grown numb from the cold, two blocks of ice.

"God damn!" he cried. And then, just where the light shaded into gray, he saw it.

Somebody was playing a joke on him, and it wasn't funny. But he couldn't laugh. The air locked in his lungs, making it difficult to breathe. His heart clamored in his chest like the old coal furnace.

It wasn't true but it was. *Sam*. Advancing across the floor of the coal bin, her arms outstretched, her hands curled.

Harry threw up all over himself, vomit spewing out of his mouth and dribbling down his T-shirt, splashing on the concrete, coming in waves from his heaving stomach.

"Oh God, no!" he moaned as she neared him, and he finally stepped back in a fast two-step, bumping into the wood side of the bin. For a moment he couldn't find the opening to scramble out to the main room of the cellar. Then he was through and pushing away. But nothing worked anymore. He was a machine in overdrive, and he stalled, stuck in the middle of the room, the old chair just to his left, the wall of cartons blocking him off on the right. Where were the stairs? He had forgotten how to get out of the cellar of the house that he had lived in all his life.

Suddenly he felt so sorry for himself that tears sprang to his eyes. He was going to die—he knew that instinctively. They all must have made a terrible mistake, because she wasn't dead after all. She was alive, shuffling toward him with a

ravaged face that looked like a train had run over it, only
worse. But she was dead too, because he had killed her. He
couldn't lie to himself anymore.

No, no, he wailed silently, I'm not going to take this lying
down. Who does she think she is, threatening her old man? If
I did that to mine, he'd take the broom to me like he used to
when I sassed him back. Once broke it over my head, Harry
remembered.

"Hey, where've you been hiding all this time? Huh? Half
the town's been going crazy trying to find you. You got some
nerve, miss, don't you just. I'm gonna beat your ass. Just you
wait." But it was all hot air and he was whimpering. He *knew*
he had killed her, could still hear the thunk her head had
made when he smashed it against the doorjamb like a melon.
She couldn't have survived that.

He saw the wires dangling out of the side of her head, the
stiff way she held herself like a block of stone.

"What's wrong with you anyway?" he shouted.

But nothing could stop her, and as she neared him he saw
her yellow runny eyes and the smell hit him with the force of
Calloway's baseball bat. He gagged on the smell and put up
his hands as if he could ward it, her, off. But she came closer,
moving in between his arms like a lover seeking an embrace.
Harry tried to shove her away, but she wasn't a soft little girl
anymore. Her flesh didn't give. And he thought her bones
must be made of steel. With loathing he remembered the
robot, all metal and shiny.

She hit his hands aside and the pain shot right up his arms
and along his shoulders. He was blubbering now, tears leaking down his stubbled cheeks, mixing with the vomit.

"Stay away from me, you!" he cried. "I'm your father." But
father or daughter or *anything* didn't have meaning for her.
He could tell that. And he shrieked at last, the terror too
much, digging into him like an ice pick. It was the terror
which forced him to move, stumbling, his feet sliding on the
freezing floor so that he fell backward.

She soared after him, falling like deadweight, lying across
his outstretched body as he shrilled, panic running up his
throat and emerging in tiny squeaks. She was so heavy on top
of him that the air gushed out of his lungs. And then her
hands found his throat. Circling his flesh, they were as steely
as the robot's pincers. He tore at her, gagging on the smell,

pumping his legs against the floor, his face pushed up into hers, right into hers. And then when he didn't think he could stand to look at that horror another moment, he realized that he couldn't breathe, that her hands were slowly, inexorably squeezing the life out of him, stopping the air, and one last time he heaved upward, attempting to buck her off. But she was too heavy to dislodge, as though the whole house had fallen on him, flattening him into the ground with the weight of wood, of cement, of years and tortured memories.

His throat narrowed, closing down until there was no room any longer for even a breath to slither through, and the pale, vapid light from the bulb in the ceiling flickered, dimmed, grew faint like the last gasp of a winter's day. Darkness slid up from his toes, traveled along his belly, into his heart, until it finally whispered across his face and he couldn't see anything, thinking at the end that at last she was gone for good.

Where was she?
Somewhere . . . anywhere. . . . Her disappearance made him hope for an instant that she had been a figment of his imagination. But Piggy knew it wasn't true, no matter how much he might want it. After all, Slime had seen her too. Slime had taken her to the shed under the bleachers.

Slime. He focused on his anger momentarily, the edges melting into pain, but it slipped away. Piggy was more scared than anything. Awful things could happen to her out there. People wouldn't understand. And he had learned that everyone in Welling was gun happy, good hunting country just at the town limits. Somebody might shoot it. *It!* He had called Sam an *it.* Which wasn't fair, not even in his mind. She was a person, a living being. He had to hold on to that.

If only she didn't look so bad. And smell like a dead person starting to decay.

But no matter what, he had to find her. It was snowing, even though it really didn't look like it would stick. And it was bitter cold. Not that she seemed to feel it.

Where did she go? Back to Mason? Why would she go there? Why not? Piggy didn't understand how Sam's mind worked; the synapses of her brain must be all out of whack. She wasn't BeeBee, no matter that she had his computer in her head. He couldn't turn her on and off; she didn't react in established patterns. Obviously she could veer and thrust and her program was erratic.

Just thinking about Sam made him so nervous he shook.

Be scientific, he told himself, and taking a small notebook out of his knapsack, he started to make a list.

The equipment shed . . .

Her own house next door . . .

Piggy remembered how she had gawked at her father through the window, and got queasy. He became even queasier at the thought of Harry finding her back in her own room. He'd hurt her, Piggy was certain, before or after he called the cops. And once Chief Volchek saw the wires dangling from her skull, he'd know. Or if he didn't, someone else would point it out to him.

Yes, her own house. He'd have to hurry and search it before Harry Pringle got home from the shoe factory. Piggy prayed that today would be one of those when he'd get fuddled by drink at the Five O'Clock.

She'd get in easily enough, because the back door was always unlocked, just as theirs was—

Theirs. Back door. She could be here, in this house, right now.

Suddenly he heard Jeannie coming up the steps and he froze.

In this house!

His mother could find her. He imagined his mother's screams and grew faint.

He'd never be able to convince her it was a mistake, not after Bertram Lennard. And even though this time he had brought someone back, he knew that to Jeannie it would be just as bad.

If she were in the house, he had to find her. Now. He couldn't wait until Jeannie went out to look around.

Obviously Sam wasn't on the first floor unless she was hiding in one of the closets. But after pawing through the coats, he found she wasn't there. Nor was she lurking in the pantry by the shelves of canned goods.

The basement was the most obvious place, yet she wasn't there either.

It was only when he was back upstairs, panting out of breath, hearing his mother splashing and singing off-key in the tub, getting ready for dinner at the Mellons', that he felt she wasn't in the house. Still he went through the bedrooms meticulously, looking under each bed, in every closet. And then he toured the attic with its bare beams and dusty relics from other people's pasts, and the unopened cartons with the equipment for his home lab. Still no Sam. His stomach was settling to a quiet ache when he returned to his room, to sit cross-legged on the bed and try to add to his list.

Back to Toomy's Funeral Parlor? Yes, that had to be added.

The cemetery at the top of the hill? Could she want to be dead? For the first time he thought about Sam thinking she might be in the wrong place.

I don't want to be dead, Pig, in a hole in the ground.

No, the cemetery wasn't likely. But she had to be somewhere. She couldn't just vanish like mist.

"Are you sure you'll be all right while I'm at the Mellons'?" Jeannie asked, appearing suddenly in the doorway. She was wearing her terry bathrobe and a towel wrapped around her hair. Her face was shiny with cream.

"I asked you, Mom, to please knock before you enter my room. It's only polite, you know," he said, scowling.

She tapped furiously on the door. "You're right. Sorry about that. Now, what would you like me to make you for dinner?"

"I'll just stick a TV dinner in the oven if it's okay with you."

"It's fine with me, honey. Whatever you want. But I won't be going until seven, in case you change your mind."

"Seven!" He couldn't wait that long to go looking for Sam. And there was no way he'd be able to wander off, not now while his mother was keeping such a sharp eye on him. He did a slow burn and felt like a little kid, somebody who couldn't be trusted, never mind that he really couldn't and knew it.

"What's the matter with seven?" Jeannie was asking. Every word he spoke these days seemed to ignite her suspicion into a raging bonfire.

"Nothing, Mom. But aren't you hungry? You haven't eaten since lunch."

"I don't usually eat between lunch and dinner, you know. And we almost always have dinner at seven," she said, her face twitching.

"Sure, Mom," he said, and sighed when she closed the door. Maybe he'd have time to search the Pringle house while she had the hair dryer on. With all that whirring, she wouldn't hear anything.

He ran out of the house, not even taking his coat, across the back lawn and up onto the Pringles' porch, leaving footprints in the faint dusting of snow. Once inside, he knew she was there.

Leaning against the kitchen door, he listened and watched the dust motes swimming in the narrow shaft of soiled light cutting through the window above the sink. The house groaned like an octogenarian, just as his house did. Now that he had found her, even if he hadn't discovered the precise cranny she had secreted herself in, he was giddy with relief. If he didn't have to hustle her out of there and back into the shed, he would have slumped on one of the chairs at an angle to the kitchen table and let his head sag on his arms. He could even have fallen asleep. His eyelids fluttered behind his glasses, blurring his vision. But he had to get home before his mother finished drying her hair and found him gone.

"Sam," he called quietly, "where are you?"

But there was no answering *gaaa*, or shuffling as she made her way toward him. He'd have to unearth her. Reluctantly he left the door and went upstairs, charging from room to room until he came to hers in the back.

There was a sudden sputter of light, like a flashbulb popping, as he saw the stains of blood, the chalk on the floor, and in a circumrotation of time Harry Pringle was swinging Sam off into space as though it was a game they were playing. The smell of Sam, Sam dead, disappeared, replaced by the odor of alcohol which seeped out of Harry Pringle's pores. It was more disgusting than the other stink and Piggy gagged as round and round Sam went, her nightgown ruffling, bare legs white as pearl. Blond hair swirled around her head, billowed out in a golden cloud. Piggy thought how pretty she looked, like an acrobat just getting ready to fly, when all at once Harry Pringle let go and Sam's body smashed into the doorjamb. Piggy jumped aside at the terrible thud of bone striking wood, the static electricity humming around the room, dancing like fireballs, Harry's greasy hair standing straight as porcupine quills, the sweat on his brow glowing psychedelically.

Piggy heard the tinkling of the music box on the dresser though the lid was closed, and saw Sam settle into the outline the police had drawn.

It was as if the whole house was alive with the memory of what had gone on here, and the groaning gave way to a high-pitched screech. For a moment the floor seemed to tilt as Sam lay at his feet and Harry Pringle gazed stupidly down at her, spittle running over his bristly chin.

The scene dimmed as Piggy watched it, fluttered and died, and he was once again in the cold, empty room. Only Harry Pringle's angry roar throbbed against his eardrums, grew faint, and then that too passed away.

He didn't stop to consider what he had seen, or if he had seen it at all, like the train in the tunnel. Only then he had deduced he had conked his head on the wall and gone out, and this time he was standing upright on his own two feet, hadn't fallen, hadn't put himself under. It had just happened, like a movie flashing on the screen in an empty theater. One minute there was nothing, the next you were watching people move about as though you were present, part of the action but outside the camera's range.

He thundered down the steps, sensing there was no reason to be quiet. Nobody was in the house except him and Sam, Sam somewhere, waiting for him to come to her as she had waited for him to wake her up from death. Like Sleeping Beauty, he thought, and felt silly, like a two-year-old, for imagining himself as Prince Charming. Besides, the waking up had taken more than a kiss.

He came to a sudden halt on the bottom step, realizing that he had never kissed Sam, had always suspected kissing was a baby thing, or maybe a grown-up thing that he wasn't ready for, all tongues and sloppiness. But he had wanted to kiss her, and his face went red as he remembered. Only now he never would. He was horribly aware that nobody sane would kiss the Sam he had saved.

Better to have left her dead, a voice whispered.

"No," he said aloud, surprised by the word popping out of his mouth like a marble and bouncing along the bald patches on the cheap floral rug.

Thumping the wall with his hand, he muttered, "Got to find her, get her back in the shed."

After five minutes of searching there was nowhere else to look but the cellar. He knew she had to be down there, but he had perversely left it for last. Maybe it was just that a part of him wanted never to find her.

Somehow he had sat down at the kitchen table after all, as though he had all the time in the world, and eyed the cellar door. Waiting for it to open all by itself. Waiting for Sam to thump her way up the stairs with that terrifying grimace on her ravaged face. He could, when he looked at her and wasn't trying to be kind, see the skull under the skin just waiting to burgeon.

But Sam wasn't coming to him, and Piggy, forced into motion, turned the knob, opening the door, and came not into the darkness he expected but to a dull glow. He really didn't want to go down. The basement seemed to be lying in wait for him there like a pool of quicksand. He'd be sucked in and have to struggle to extricate himself, and then it wasn't certain that he wouldn't drown, if one drowned in quicksand and didn't suffocate. But he had to descend anyway. In this strange new country where he had taken up residence all by himself—if he didn't count Sam—there was nobody else to do the job for him. No, Piggy had crossed a border and right then he desperately wanted to be somewhere else, to get back into the land of *before*, with no Bertram Lennard and certainly no Sam. But it had been like going down the chute in the playground when he had been a kid. Once you started the long slide, there was no way to climb back to the top. It was an impossibly endless ride and you couldn't even close your eyes because then the ground would come up like a bump and hurt your butt. You had to keep going and keep your eyes open too, which was how he descended the stairs, the stinking air of the cellar rising up his legs, thighs, stomach, chest, swirling into his lungs, choking him at the neck like a too-tight collar, into his mouth, bringing with it the taste of metal. And then he was in it over his head.

19

Thunk, thunk, thunk. . . . The basketball bounced off the gym floor, directed by Ronnie Brooks, a second-former with, as Coach Harding said, potential. The blues were under their own hoop, the reds elbowing them furiously right and left, trying not to get caught by the coach, but Neil Hammon took one in the ribs and let out an unholy shriek that forced the coach to blow his whistle. The reds had the ball now, taking it in from the corner and moving it down the floor to center court with a steady *thunk, thunk, thunk,* like the sound of Harry Pringle's head bumping the side of the coal bin.

Piggy, sitting on the bench, heard the *thunk* reverberating in his head long after the coach had called another foul. He hadn't actually seen Harry's skull striking the wood because he was dragging him by the feet, but he had heard it and winced.

Not that Harry could feel the whack, dead as he was already. Pig had put his hand over Harry's mouth to feel for air, but no breath was escaping. When Piggy could look at him, could open his eyes long enough to look at him seriously, he saw the band of inflammation girding his neck. He realized, as the bottom of his stomach dropped out, that Sam had strangled her father.

The coach was rotating the teams, taking the boys one after another off the bench and sending them in for a few minutes of play. Piggy would be the last one called and he knew it, but today it didn't bother him; today he didn't wish he were somewhere else doing something that wasn't childish and silly like basketball. Today he didn't mind being embarrassed, falling all over his feet. He didn't even bother to see if his laces were drooping. The part of him that had worried about gym and resented being as awkward as an octopus was entombed. They might as well have used him for a basketball, and he would have only been dimly aware of the fact, back as he was in the Pringle cellar staring helplessly at Harry dead on the floor and Sam huddled by the furnace with her arms around it.

He had hidden Harry's body way back in the coal bin, piling papers over it, surrounding it with boxes. It didn't make too much sense secreting him away like that because if anybody was determined to look for Harry really hard, they were bound to find him. But the need to get him out of sight was overpowering, to hide him somewhere at least for a little while until Piggy could think what to do. He would rather have dragged Harry's corpse across the back lawn and flung it into the churning river beyond the embankment, letting the waters carry it away. But Harry Pringle had been a big man in life, and though, lying dead in the middle of his own cellar with terror plastered over his unshaven face, with his bulging eyes fat as grapes about to burst and the tongue protruding from his mouth like a piece of meat at the frozen-food counter, he had shrunk, he was still too heavy to move. Pig couldn't have gotten him up the steps, not by himself, and Sam wouldn't . . . or couldn't . . . help. And there was no one else. Not Slime certainly, who would, Pig knew, go bananas over Sam killing her dad.

Piggy was ready to go to pieces himself, but it was useless. There was no one to patch him up if he cracked. Jeannie couldn't help him this time, and Chief Volchek or Dr. Mellon would never believe it a mistake. It was like having a dog who bit someone; you were to blame.

"Conway, get in there and replace Wicker," the coach shouted at him.

Piggy was a blue and he trotted to the far court, where the reds were at their basket, Jerry Meadows taking a foul shot. He missed the first and the coach came roaring off the sidelines to tell him about bending his knees, about allowing the ball to lift up and off his hands.

"For Christ sake, Meadows, if you give it a push you'll sink it." But the ball fell short of the hoop again and the blues took it out. Ronnie Brooks looked at Piggy for a second as he stood in the clear to the side. No one bothered to guard Piggy because none of the other boys would throw him the ball if they could help it. Piggy always dropped it. This time, however, whether out of perversity or because there was a furious shuffle in front of him, Ronnie did throw the ball to Pig, and surprisingly, since he was paying even less attention then he normally did, Piggy caught it. But Jerry Meadows knocked it loose before Piggy could even dribble once, and then one of the bigger boys, whose name Pig always forgot, clipped him going down the court and Piggy fell flat. The coach blew his whistle and play stopped, but Pig was on his hands and knees staring at the floor. Under his chin he could see Harry Pringle's swollen tongue.

"Get off the floor, Conway. You're not hurt," the coach yelled. Normally Coach Harding didn't take the second-formers in gym, but his assistant was out sick. And he always liked the chance, as he'd tell them, to get to know the junior talent. In truth, however, he had little tolerance for the younger boys.

Piggy didn't have to be told twice. Bile rose to his mouth, Harry's stink and Sam's smell mingling in his nostrils. "I think I twisted my ankle," he said, getting to his feet and hobbling a few steps to show the coach he wasn't kidding. The coach gave him a mean look but sent him back to the bench and another boy took his place.

Piggy sat the rest of the period out and when the bell rang started to run to the locker room. Harding grabbed him by the arm and snarled, "Thought you hurt your ankle, Conway."

"It's better now," he said, ducking his head.

"Don't shirk, Conway, or you'll never be a man."

Piggy wanted to scream in his face, but the coach stalked off. He hustled on into the locker room and hurriedly changed his clothes, wishing that it had been Coach Harding dead on the floor. *No!* He shook his head, almost sending his glasses flying. *No!*

Harry Pringle was *really* dead and Sam had killed him and Piggy had stuffed the body into the coal bin and left Sam in one of the unused upstairs bedrooms of her own house because he didn't know what else to do with her and he wanted to cry. He wanted to do more than cry, he wanted to howl until he had worked all the terror out of his pores.

He was afraid to put her back in the shed because she had

escaped so easily. Not that he had taken any precautions to
keep her in as he did this time, locking both of the doors with
keys that he had found on a hook by the refrigerator. He
hadn't thought she would wander. Wander! She hadn't wandered like a stray cat, she had gone deliberately into her own
house and strangled her father. The fact that she could do
that, put all the anger and hate she must have felt together
with a physical action—going to her house, killing Harry,
having the strength to choke the air out of his body—terrified
Piggy to his toes. Not only for being an accessory after the
fact—before it too—but because Sam wasn't who or what he
had supposed. She obviously could think in some meandering
fashion and, by some quirk that he couldn't even begin to
explain, had grown strong.

What will they do if they find her? he asked himself as he
walked to his history class. Can you execute somebody who's
already dead?

And what am I going to do with her?

Peter Bayard was coming out of the Science Building as Pig
came around the back from the gym. "Hey, Paul, wait up,"
he called, and moved in beside him. "How are you?" he
asked, looking down. Piggy didn't really like big men much
because he was afraid he was always going to be short.

"Okay," he muttered, walking faster, but Peter Bayard just
walked faster too.

He was smiling, which made Pig even angrier, made him
want to kick him in the knee. Peter Bayard trying to be nice
to him he didn't like one bit. He still suspected the assistant
dean of being sweet on his mother, though Jeannie didn't
seem particularly interested in him.

Switching tracks abruptly, Peter asked, "What class do you
have now?"

"History."

The wind was raw, sweeping between the buildings, and
Pig lowered his head. Peter didn't wear a coat over his suit,
and as he sauntered along, he didn't seem to feel the cold at
all. They approached Humans, and together, moving in tan-
dem between the groups of students, went up the steps, with
Peter making what Jeannie would have called polite conversation. Piggy was glowering, wasn't replying, was being snitty,
in fact, but Peter Bayard didn't appear to notice, and when
they parted before Dr. Mellon's office, he poked him affection-

ately on the arm the way men and boys often did to one another.

Piggy stood in the doorway for a moment after the assistant head disappeared into Cantaloupe's private office. He rubbed his arm and seethed, the anger dripping into the caldron of rage already boiling inside his skull.

"Looking forward to Christmas, Paul?" Miss Miller chirped from behind her desk.

Piggy had forgotten about her there, alert as a bird. He started at the sound of her voice but answered politely, "Yes, ma'am."

"I bet"—she smiled at him, pecking away at the typewriter without losing a beat—"that Santa's going to bring you another big toy just like that one you lost."

For a second he couldn't think what she meant. Then he realized she was talking about BeeBee and got so enraged he wanted to pound her sparrow head into the keys of her IMB Selectric. He bit down on his bottom lip and twitched his nose. There was definitely a conspiracy of adults all determined to set him off, force him to lose what little control he had left. Yes, positively, they were out to get him—Coach Harding, Peter Bayard, and now Miss Miller.

Keeping his cool, though the anger was just below skin level ready to pop, he stomped off to history and bumped into Slime, who was trying to scuttle through the doorway of Miss Markowitz's room without Pig's seeing him. Piggy knew that Slime had planned to slip by him unobserved, and stalked after him into the coatroom, where he grabbed him by the tail of his shirt.

"Where're you going?"

"What do you mean where am I going? I'm going to hang up my jacket."

"How come you're avoiding me, Slime?" Piggy demanded, though he knew quite well why the other boy was afraid to speak to him even now. Slime hoped if he kept his head lowered it would all blow away. "I thought we were friends," he said, suddenly overcome by an unsettling wave of emotion. He bumped his glasses back on his nose and glared at Slime. "Huh?"

"I'm sorry, Pig," Slime mumbled, breaking away as two of the girls hung up their jackets and lingered in the coatroom for a moment to pat down their hair.

Before Piggy could say another word, Slime was gone, sliding into his seat in the second row, opening his book and bending his head over the page as though the Franco-Prussian War was the most interesting phenomenon since the breakup of the Beatles.

Abruptly all the anger and pain and fear ran over and Piggy began to cry, thin trickles of tears leaking under his eyelids. He took off his glasses and wiped his face on his sleeve, and then, because he thought he would suffocate there on the heights of Spicheren Plateau, he yanked his jacket off the hook and bolted from the coatroom. He grazed Miss Markowitz as he went through the classroom door into the hall, but he didn't even wait to see if she had heard him mumble about feeling sick. Piggy didn't care. All she could do to him was something silly, like detention, or an extra chapter or two. School, classes, history, learning, were as meaningless as the battles of Colombey-Borny or Orléans.

As he ran across the quiet campus, the last bell having rung, puffs of breath clouding about his head, ran down the short incline to the bridge, the urgency to get back to Sam overtook him, and he pounded along thinking, feeling, that she was all he had left.

Piggy was panting when he reached his house, but he didn't slow down. In the living room he dropped his book bag onto a chair and went straight through to the kitchen and the back door. He didn't even stop, as he usually did, at the refrigerator for an after-school snack.

When Piggy leapt the steps of the porch and stomped across the back lawns, he didn't see the car in front of the Pringle house. The first time he realized that someone was at the front door, he was halfway through the kitchen.

Piggy froze, and then in his panic flailed, knocking over a chair. Quickly he set it back on its legs and tried to think. Was there time to escape to his house? Or should he hide here, upstairs with Sam?

Maybe whoever it was would just go away.

But before he could make up his mind he saw, through the window behind the kitchen table, a figure sneaking around the side of the house. There wasn't time now to get home.

Piggy bolted into the living room and crawled behind the couch, pressing himself against the wall. The dust was heavier than the silt in an Egyptian tomb and Pig held his breath, hoping he wouldn't sneeze as he heard the man on the rear porch.

He'll go away when he realizes that nobody's home, Pig hoped, and then was shocked as the door opened, squeaking on the hinges, and the man walked inside.

He can't do that, it's breaking and entering!

But he had, and was suddenly in the living room. Pig, peering around the corner of the couch, caught a glimpse of his legs. He knew who he was now because he recognized the uniform.

The house was ice cold but Pig was sweating, droplets of water dripping off his brow. His shirt was sticking to his back, and under his skin he could feel the blood pounding. In just a few minutes, the deputy, Emmett Sidowsky, was going to find Sam, and after that . . .

The after was like dropping off a high cliff. Piggy felt sicker than he had ever been in his life, listening to the deputy poke around the first floor, in and out of the pantry, the closets. Suddenly there was the sound of wood creaking and Pig understood that the policeman was climbing the stairs. As he carefully lifted his head, he saw that Emmett, looking upward, had drawn his gun.

I have to stop him before he hurts Sam!

Aching with urgency to protect her, not to let her be harmed, Piggy was out from behind the couch and at the opposite end of the room when Emmett disappeared down the second-floor hall.

Piggy crept up the stairs on his hands and knees, hugging the wall, being extra careful to keep the steps from creaking, from alerting Emmett that he was there. Not that Emmett wouldn't discover that for himself in just a few minutes, right after he found Sam. There was no way that Pig could run now and leave Sam to her fate at the hands of the police.

Up, up he went, more frightened with each step. Parts of him were peeling away, and he was afraid that when he reached the landing he'd be a skeleton inside his down jacket and corduroys. Who'd save her then? Who'd go to her rescue? He could almost hear the click as Emmett would release the safety on the gun, and then, in the next moment, the thunder of the shot. In his heart Pig could feel the slow trickle of Sam's dying.

Had he brought her back to life for this?

Emmett was moving from room to room, his footsteps quicker, louder in the thickening silence. As if he felt safer, more assured.

Piggy hurried faster too, determined to throw himself between Sam and the deputy, to shield her with his body. Emmett wouldn't shoot him, or at least he didn't think so. But he wasn't sure of anything, except wanting to keep Sam safe here with him and not locked up somewhere. He didn't suppose there was any chance they'd let her be now, not after she had choked Harry to death. Murder, after all, took precedence over resurrection.

Just when he could see along the hall, he saw Emmett hesitate for a second outside the bedroom where Piggy had stashed Sam, as if listening, and then, with a shrug, push open the door. Pig's heart flip-flopped in his chest, and bounding up the last few steps, he ran.

The gun, when it went off, was more deafening than he had imagined. Rapid, booming shots, one after the other. The whole house seemed to shudder.

Piggy flung himself into the room, hearing someone screaming, not worrying at all about being shot. *Sam, Sam, Sam*, echoed with each heartbeat. Tears had streaked his glasses, and his vision was smudged as he threw his weight against Emmett, crying, "Don't hurt her!"

He should have hit Emmett square, midsection, except that he tripped on his trailing laces just as Emmett, his face scrunched up like a baby's about to bawl, jumped back.

Piggy was flat on his stomach, having cracked his nose on the bare floor. A thin ripple of blood dripped from his nostrils and dribbled over his upper lip. His tongue snaked out, catching the drops. The blood tasted salty. He spat it out and groped to his knees, forgetting in his daze about Emmett standing in the middle of the floor waving his gun.

The room orbited for a minute before it anchored itself, and Piggy wobbled to his feet just as Sam retreated to the hall. Whatever the deputy had shot, he apparently hadn't hit Sam, because she moved in the same chunky way as she had before, like a large block, a square traveling on its edges. Piggy couldn't see Emmett, but he heard him, his feet scuffling along the runner, his little yips of terror. And over all that the repeated *bang, bang* of the gun until it clicked into silence.

By the time Piggy had staggered into the doorway, gripping the jamb, his legs unsteady, they were at the end of the hallway. Emmett was fumbling in a clumsy dance to the stairs, and Sam, relentless in her rolling approach, was stalking after him. Pig didn't know what she intended to do, if she actually intended to do anything except reach the deputy and put her hands on him. There was no way of deciphering what thoughts bounced about her brain cells, or between Bee's computer and her brain. Maybe she was merely curious as a child was, wanting to touch, to feel, to smell, to taste the world, envelop it in the infantile senses and that way make it—whatever *it* was—known. The *it* at this moment was obviously Emmett, blanched white as whalebone. He couldn't retreat fast enough to outdistance Sam, her arms straight out like a blind person's—though Pig knew she could see, if only dimly—her legs scissoring without bending at the knees, giving her the lurching gait of a drunk. She should have been funny-looking and they, both he and Emmett, should have been laughing. Only Sam wasn't silly at all. She was something dark, out of dreaming, from the pitch and toss of sleep.

Terror was reflected in the deputy's eyes, wide as was anatomically possible, rolling in panic from side to side.

"Stop Sam!" Pig screamed. They had reached the top of the stairs. Emmett was groping backward with one foot, trying to begin a descent that would lead to safety. Only in his fright he missed the first step, stumbling. He just barely kept himself from falling as his hand shot out grasping the railing.

Sam was closer now, and even though Emmett was a step down the stairs, his large frame bent and twisted with fear, he seemed to loom like a dark cloud above Sam. Piggy wanted to cry to her to be careful, to watch out for the deputy, to move back to him so that he could protect her. But his mouth was so dry that the words would not come.

Desperate to save her from Emmett who, like a dog gone suddenly mad, might lurch in panic and attack, Pig wobbled forward. He imagined the deputy falling over Sam so frail looking there in the distance. He saw Emmett crushing her flat, grinding the delicate mechanism which was keeping her alive into shattered pieces of metal, bits of plastic ribbon.

Maybe it was a trick of the light that sloped into the hall from the opened doorways of the bedrooms and elongated the shadows but Sam seemed to shrink and Emmett to loom larger. He reared up in his frenzy just as Sam's little hand, which Pig at times would hold in his own with such an ache in his chest he thought he'd implode, went out. Her small, puffy fingers waggled as she reached up to Emmett's face. What was it she was seeing? Did she think she could soothe away the fright and terror that had made him go pale and contorted his mouth into a horrible grimace?

"No, Sam!" he cried, forcing himself down the long hall, bumping against the walls, determined to pull her out of harm's way.

But it was the deputy who leapt just as the cold fingers grazed his cheek. For a moment Piggy was grateful that Emmett catapulted backward instead of over onto Sam. But his relief shattered as he realized that Emmett was sailing away into space, gliding so easily he might have been free-falling. For one long unbearable instant, as his feet left the secure anchorage of the steps, he appeared to fly. But the stairs rose up to meet him. His head cracked along the wood. Pig thought again of the basketball thunking down the court, of Harry's head bouncing on the cellar floor, and he screamed a shrill of sound but not of words. Sam turned then and gazed at him through the curtaining shadows, through the gloom, and he saw the glint of surprise in her pus-filled eyes.

"Gaaaaa," she said, and "gaaaa," again, questioning. As if he could explain to her what had gone wrong, why down below there was an awful gurgling in a weak trail from the deputy that much too soon faded away and died.

20

Jeannie was late getting home. It was past dark—though the light began to fade by four, four-thirty this far into the year—when she parked the car and hurried along the walk. Lena Markowitz had caught up with her just at the start of the monthly teachers' meeting, saying Piggy had cut history, saying he was sick she supposed, saying with a glint in her luminous dark eyes that he should have asked permission to leave campus and go home. But then she said she thought he must have checked with Jeannie.

He hadn't, and, in fact, the only time she had even seen him was at lunch, when she caught a glimpse of him pushing through the far door of the cafeteria as she had walked in. Jeannie would have fled right then, slipped her papers and notebooks off the scarred conference table where she had just put them down, and bolted for home. But Dr. Mellon was settling in, already clearing his throat and reminding them that this was the last meeting before exams began, the last meeting until the end of term, and that there was a great deal of business to get through. He wanted them to remember that and move it along. Jeannie, half out of her chair, sank back. She couldn't leave. She had an obligation to Mason, to her job, to the other students.

But she had been agitated throughout the endless, waning afternoon, as the light beat against the high windows of the conference room, growing fainter, dying finally into darkness. She had had to force herself to pay attention to what the others were saying around the long, narrow table. Her concentration, when she spoke herself—about the two students

who were in danger of failing, whose records she had spread
out before her and was quoting from—her concentration even
then was splintered and pitted with worrisome, nagging
thoughts of Piggy.

When the interminable meeting had ended at last, Dr.
Mellon walked with her down to the teachers' lounge on the
second floor to get her coat. She tried to pace her steps to
his, to hear whatever it was he was telling her, but the words
slipped away, as though they were in a foreign language and
she no longer had the energy to understand. And when he
looked at her quizzically and asked what was it that was
bothering her so, she kept thinking: *It's nothing, he's got a
headache, or a stomachache, or something else that's minor*.

Inexplicably, now that she stood on the porch, lifting the
lid of the mailbox and extracting the sheaf of letters, she was
calm. Her jitters had settled, and she convinced herself before even entering the house that Piggy was safe inside, that
whatever it was that had upset him was insignificant and
would pass.

She walked into the living room and switched on the lights,
but he wasn't there. He wasn't in the kitchen either. She
went up the stairs, along the unlit chilly corridor. The house
wasn't weather-tight, and the cold found its way through the
cracks in the wood.

He had been sleeping. She saw that as soon as she hit the
switch and the overhead globe threw a flat, dull glow around
his room. His head lifted up off the pillow and then fell back.
He was lying fully dressed across the spread, and hadn't even
bothered to take off his down jacket or his sneakers.

"Are you all right?" she asked, not leaving the doorway.
His face was red, creased like a baby's, and his hair was
matted with sweat.

"What do you want?" he slurred, nestling back down into
sleep.

"Are you all right?" she asked again. "Lena Markowitz said
you cut history."

"Leave me alone," he growled into the pillow.

"Do you feel sick?" She inched closer until her legs hit the
side of the bed and she was bending over him.

He shifted away, his face sullen, and turned to the far wall.

"Take off your things. Get under the covers," she said.

"Go away!" He shrugged off her hand when she touched

him. "I've got a headache. I want to sleep," he grumbled as she hurriedly stepped back.

He seemed so big sprawled on the bed, like a man almost. For the first time she recognized something of Tony in him and that frightened her, even as she said to herself: Don't be silly. She saw Piggy in a brief flash framed beside his father and knew in her bones that there was more to the headache that had made him leave school. That there was more to his sudden shifts in behavior than adolescent upheaval.

Fear roared inside her and she backed out of Piggy's room, switching off the light, and stumbled down to the kitchen without being conscious of what she was doing. Once there, standing by the sink, she realized she was still wearing her coat. She retraced her steps to the hall and hung the coat in the closet, her movements slow, sluggish. There was dinner to be made, the last two essay questions to be designed for the final exam, a skirt she had promised herself she would hem. But she had so little energy that even the thought of doing anything concrete exhausted her.

She returned to the kitchen and sat down at the table. She rubbed her hands together and tried to remember what it had been like to live without anxiety, without a nameless fear. She smoked one cigarette and then another, feeling sorry for herself, feeling old, until she was choked with disgust at her self-pity. *Enough!* she cried silently, and jumping up, gathered together the fixings for a salad from the vegetable drawer of the refrigerator.

Taking a collander from the cabinet beside the sink, she shredded a head of lettuce, tearing at it. She sprayed the brimming collander with water, shook the basket and let the lettuce drip while she cut up tomatoes, cucumbers, some slivers of cheese and ham.

When she glanced up at last, she saw a palid version of her face thrown against the pane of glass. Her mouth pulled to the side, her eyes squeezed with anxiety.

She couldn't bear to see her image, and filled with self-loathing, moved quietly through the downstairs. She switched off all the lights and groped her way to the front windows. River Street was a sleepy current of dim yellow under the lamps, her car a bulky shadow at the end of the walk. There was another car, one she didn't recognize, in front of the Pringle house, and she felt ill remembering that poor child, dead now, and her body missing. It was a horror she shied from contemplating, not only for her sake but for Piggy's. There is always something worse, and then there is the worst, and Sam's death was that, she thought, and averted her eyes from the house next door, returning to the kitchen.

She opened the back door and stepped out, the cold air whipping through her. She shivered, anticipating snow at last. The storm that had been threatening for days, then drifting away, over the mountains, now, she felt, was almost upon them. The snow would be a relief, blanketing the town, which she finally recognized was ugly, even Mason, a blister on the opposite bank of the river. The snow would close them in and Piggy would be here, safe with her.

Safe from what?

Confused, she went back inside and bolted the door, once again switching all the lights on. Almost immediately the phone rang, setting off an inexplicable alarm in Jeannie's head. She fantasized something awful being told her over the phone, and her hand was shaking as she lifted the receiver on the third ring.

"Jeannie, it's me. I finally got your phone number out of Chambers and I thought I should call," he said quickly before she could hang up.

She didn't want this, and strove to shift her mind into neutral, to shut off her hearing. But still Tony's voice snaked through, telling her that he was worried about them, was concerned that she hadn't answered his letter, that he missed his son.

"Look, as long as Welling is the place you've decided to live, I'd like things to work out for you there. For Paul too, obviously. And after everything . . . Christ, I don't know. I just got the feeling that something might be wrong. Are you okay? Are you happy?"

"Happy!" She started to giggle and slapped her hand over the mouthpiece. The silence at the other end grew heavy, then heavier. When she finally penetrated it, her voice was as even as she could manage. "Of course we're happy, Tony. Why shouldn't we be?"

Go away, goddammit. Go away! No, don't go away!

She had never wanted him to go away and that was the problem. It was an impossibility for her, so that even now— long after his leaving had become a fact of life—when she understood that Tony was gone, a pain as searing as an electrical shock traveled through her. Never, she had never believed that he'd leave her, them, any more than she presumed that one day she'd awake and find the sun had disappeared from the sky. Some things were, had always been, inconceivable. Some things were beyond her. And she almost screamed at Tony again, screamed at him as she had done when he did finally go.

"I want to talk to Paul, Jeannie. Find out how he is for myself."

"No!" she cried down the wires to Boston.

"Jeannie, I don't want him thinking that I don't care. That I've just disappeared into the sunset on him."

"Well, haven't you, walking out at the worst moment in his life?"

"I didn't abandon Paul," he said, and she could hear the steeliness, the cutting edge that was in Tony.

Panic rose up her throat in a wave of nausea. Was she right or wrong not to let him speak to his son, their son? Would it help Piggy more or hurt him irrevocably to hear his father so far away, so lost to them both? She had supposed that if Piggy had time to adjust, to Welling and Mason, to the divorce, to the devastating aftermath of his mistake, he'd learn to do without a father there in the house every morning when he woke up and every night as he put his head on the pillow, and eventually he'd go into dreaming more easily. And it would happen one day, would finally come about, that he would be her little boy again, that he wouldn't be different.

Only Piggy was spinning away from her, flying out of reach, and she was afraid. Yet how could she tell Tony that? How could she say she was losing control?

"I don't want to continue this conversation," is what she at last spoke into the phone, riding right over what he was saying. And hanging up, she went into the living room, as if distancing herself even further from Tony. She slipped a cartridge of *The Four Seasons* into the stereo and sat for a moment in the big chair, hugging herself, hoping the music would wash her clean, roll the terror away, stop it at the other side of the silence.

Elvira Williams came home from the novena at St. Anthony's and noticed Emmett Sidowsky's Ford sitting in front of the Pringle house. She knew it was the deputy's car because she made it her business to know as much as she could about Welling and the people who lived there. Never mind that some called her a gossip; she considered herself the compiler of living history. Besides, she had an insatiable curiosity and the only way she had ever learned in her long life to quiet the beast was to feed it morsels about her neighbors.

Elvira let herself into her house through the back door, where a light was left burning over the sink, and padded her way to the front and stared at Emmett's car, wondering. The Pringle house was dark, its windows as unrevealing as closed eyes. What could Emmett be doing in there? Where was Harry? Had the car been there when she had left right after lunch, taking in the sale at the Flowered Bee Fabric Shop, then going on to her monthly appointment with Dr. Madison, and from there to Cynthia Billings' for dinner before the novena? It wasn't like Elvira to be out for such a long time, and her various commitments had taken planning, occupying her attention, so that she just might not have noticed Emmett's car before. But she didn't think so. Elvira was vigilant, and nothing worth seeing ever escaped her eye.

Maybe Emmett had gone to question Harry about the child's death, and then his car wouldn't start and Jack Reiss would be coming out soon with the truck to tow it into the garage. *Maybe*.

Elvira made herself a nice, soothing cup of Earl Grey and brought it back into the living room and sat in her rocker by the front window in the darkness, sipping her tea and keeping an eye on Emmett's car.

"If Emmett's in there talking to Harry, why aren't there any lights on?" she asked aloud.

When she had drained the last mouthful from the cup, she levered herself out of the old rocker. It creaked, then settled into silence.

She was going to call Charlie Volchek, that's what she was going to do, call him down at the station and ask him if he knew that Emmett's car was parked on River Street in front of the Pringle house and that there were no lights on inside, and ask him where he supposed the deputy was and what he was doing. Elvira didn't think much of the boy, but then she didn't have a high opinion of Charlie either, and it would please her mightily to catch one or both of them out.

Milly on the switchboard answered finally at the fifth ring. Charlie wasn't in. Milly said he had gone down to Scranton to get a part for his boiler and he should have returned by now. She'd tell Charlie to call if she, Milly, couldn't handle Mrs. Williams' problem for her. But Elvira didn't trust Milly an inch.

"You tell Charlie to call me *right away*, the minute he comes in, where he should be and not down in Scranton. Do you hear me, Milly?"

"Yes, ma'am," Milly replied, and Elvira was certain she heard the disgusting pop of chewing gum.

But Charlie Volchek didn't call back, and Jack Reiss's tow truck didn't come for Emmett's Ford, so after a while Elvira Williams pulled on her galoshes and her coat and hat and scarf and gloves and muffler, and went out into the night. She angled across the street and peered into the car, but there was nothing to see. Then she rang the doorbell of the darkened house. When nobody answered, she tried to peer through the windows, but it was like looking into a bowl of chocolate pudding.

She had thought they might be in the kitchen, though what Emmett Sidowsky and Harry Pringle could have been doing there all this time, even she, with her wondrous imagination for improprieties, couldn't fathom. Besides, if they were in the kitchen, the light would have filtered into the living room, and she'd have seen something, if only shadows.

Still, because she was determined, she stomped around to the back and drew herself up the sharp little rise of steps to the porch and banged on the door. "Is anybody home?" she called, not thinking for a moment what she'd do if the door suddenly swung open and she was confronted with the large disgusting bulk of Harry Pringle.

But there was no answer, only the silence, so oppressive in its thickness that it seemed to siphon the air out of Elvira's lungs, making her short of breath. There was something about all that quiet, so weighty that it alarmed her. She was ready to back away from it right off the porch, but before she did she decided to peer into the gloom of the Pringle house one last time.

There was no more to see from the small rear window than there had been from the front, but just as she was about to step away, to scurry home and call Charlie Volchek a second time, she caught a faint blur of movement. It was like the lazy shift of a cloud in a dark, moonless sky. She didn't quite trust her eyes and pushed right up against the glass, her nose flattened, her mouth actually kissing the pane.

"Who's in there?" she breathed in a mist and tried to catch another flutter of gray motion. For just one instant she thought she saw a blurred cameo, a face, and gasped in disbelief, jumping back from the door. Nonsense, Elvira! she admonished herself, and thrust up against the window for another look. But there was nothing to see now, only the nighttime murk of the Pringle kitchen. Still, she didn't like the way her heart was fluttering, and moving faster than she normally did, she made a hasty retreat to River Street.

Safe on the sidewalk she looked squarely at the rotting old house coated with a greenish cast of light from the street lamp, its tortured, ridged shadows that were simply the arms and fingers of the towering chestnut, and had the weirdest sensation that it was threatening to fall on her. She saw it wrenched loose from the foundation, lumbering toward her, as though it was about to suck her right off the sidewalk, swallow her up and grind her between its walls.

"You're a foolish old woman, Elvira," she stormed, biting down hard on her false teeth. But she fled anyway, scuttling with a crablike quickness, and crossed the street, her blood pressure up.

In her kitchen she warmed her hands over the stove as she boiled up water for another cup of Earl Grey. And right then, just when she had convinced herself she was seeing boogeys like a child, and just when her heart had finally settled down, she had the strangest thought. *I shouldn't have lied to Charlie Volchek about what Harry Pringle did to that piece of tin.*

"Stop it, Elvira," she said aloud, "you never lie!" and turned off the kettle as it began to whistle.

Charlie Volchek still hadn't called back by the time Elvira finished her second cup of Earl Grey, and she contemplated phoning him again, but then decided to take her bath first. No matter how she refused to admit it, there was something about that house, about that momentary vision she had had of its crushing her, about the bottomless silence, about Emmett's car looking so abandoned, which frightened her. A hot bath would quiet the willies. If Charlie Volchek hadn't gotten back to her by then, she'd call him at home, no matter what time it was, and give him what for.

She carefully washed out the cup and saucer and put them in the dish drainer to dry. She systematically switched off all the lights downstairs and moved in the darkness up the steep staircase, firmly gripping the rail, pulling herself forward step by step, the dampness in her bones and in her joints sending pain up and down her legs.

In the homey little bathroom, its one window discreetly shuttered by a thick shade, Elvira ran water into the big cast-iron tub which stood opposite the door on lion paws. Slowly she undressed, taking care not to touch herself more than was necessary. The water now at a proper level, she closed the faucets and lowered herself, wincing slightly, into the steaming tub.

Oh, she sighed, refusing to take too much pleasure in the warmth penetrating her gnarled joints, easing the muscles along her back and upper arms. She sank lower, until the water was level with her chin, and stretched out her legs, her feet bouncing against the far end of the tub.

Taking a washcloth and a bar of Ivory from the little wire dish hanging off the side of the bath, she lathered up and began the slow, laborious process of cleaning herself. Midway up the cadaverous body she heard a noise. Her hand stopped its rhythmic circling around her stomach and she raised her head like a suspicious dog sniffing the wind.

The faucet dripped, drops plunking into the silence when she lay still and didn't make a sound. Elvira maneuvered around and glared at the toilet, the sink, at the medicine cabinet with its foggy mirror that should have reflected the wall opposite, and at the towel rack with its threadbare towels, as if she suspected all of these inanimate objects of making the creaking, wheezy sound she had heard.

The wind, she decided, and returned to soaping the breasts and along the shoulders. Her head bent, she worked assiduously up each arm; then, rinsing the washcloth, she put it to her face.

Her eyes closed, she did her ears, inside and behind, under the chin, and the long, hawkish nose.

Gaaaaa . . .

That wasn't the wind.

Eeeekkkk . . .

That wasn't the wind either. Elvira recognized *that* noise. It was the bathroom door turning inward on its squeaky hinges.

Her heart beat faster and faster, frantically, like the wings of a trapped bird. The saliva in her mouth dried up and she pressed the wet washcloth against her lips.

You really are foolish, Elvira Williams, hearing things that go bump in the night. But still, she didn't open her eyes. *There is nothing, nobody,* she admonished herself, *out there in the upstairs hall.*

Just when she had almost convinced herself that no one was waiting in the darkness, the door creaked again, the sound nearer. She *knew* the door had swung further into the room, that it was gaping wide now, revealing the blackness at the top of the stairs.

The wind, she prayed, knowing that the wind couldn't get inside the house. She tried to pitch her mind outside, into the night, where she hoped the storm was rising feverishly, and the wind was tossing the house, riding in stampeding gusts along its flanks, causing the sounds she had heard. But there was no storm and no wind worth sneezing at, and the snow, if it came at all, was hours away from falling.

Her hands were shaking so that she dropped the wash-cloth, and scrambling for it to press it against her withered breasts, she opened her eyes and saw the water rippling along her skinny thighs. Far away, under the surface, her cracked toenails twinkled at her like ancient jewels.

The sight of her body was reassuring and she said loudly, "You're being stupid," as she turned her head.

She couldn't help but see that the door was opened all the way, the inside knob touching the wall. But instead of darkness filling the frame, there was something else. She peered nearsightedly, trying to make the lines and angles coalesce into a recognizable form. But it was all murky gray and indistinct, and she thought it was simply a trick of the light, that there was nothing there after all but steam dissipating in the colder air. Only then *it* began to surge in slow, ponderous steps toward her. Her heart seemed to crack apart like an egg, because all at once she realized it was a child, only it wasn't a child, it was the dead girl from across the street.

Wildly, Elvira tried to remember her name, but terror careened in her skull, clattering like a rack of billiard balls suddenly set spinning. Her breath puffed in short little squeals, and she flapped at the water, trying to push herself up and out of it, to flee, to fly by that dread thing which was so relentlessly pursuing her, or would be if she were running from it. She couldn't run. She couldn't get out of the tub, sliding along its slippery sides and bottom, water splashing.

The floor will be a sea. I'll have to mop up, she thought inconsequentially as a scream battered against her teeth.

And Sam moved closer still, until she was so close she blocked the doorway and hung over Elvira with her out-stretched hands, hands that could have touched the opposite wall if she leaned forward. Only she didn't, she leaned down. Down, down, descending on Elvira Williams like a crashing tide, until those hands, so cold that they sent a shiver of pain rippling through her cooling body, touched her head. Slowly, inexorably, Elvira felt her head jammed into her neck, felt her body shoved forward along the tub as the water rose up to meet her, impossibly high now, running over her chin, along her lips, and then, her arms waving, her feet beating against the porcelain, up and into her nose. She sputtered, coughing, and the water poured into her mouth, and then she was under it, her eyes wide open, looking upward into the grayness that gradually, imperceptibly shaded into death.

21

It was Henry Johanson's turn to take the main table at Crown. There was always a teacher at dinner each night in both dormitories, and the rotation schedule was a weekly one. None of the teachers particularly enjoyed this Mason custom, which meant being seated at a big round table surrounded by dorm personnel and a changing roster of students. Conversation was intended to flow, with ideas exchanged, the young encouraged to speak their minds in a social situation. Sometimes this actually happened when one of the more popular teachers ate with the students. In Henry Johanson's case, however, it was, as the boys said, "all doom and gloom." Table manners were scrutinized and invariably found wanting, syntax criticized, and any divergent views considered suspiciously.

If his having to eat with the boys was a drain on them, dinner was also aggravating to Dr. Johanson. It increased his awareness of how times had changed, and solidified his feelings that things weren't as they once were, were, in fact, in a very bad way. His mood, therefore, was sour by the time he left Crown. He sucked at his bottom lip and made a mental list of the many problems he discerned in the boys he'd just dined with, a list he meant to go over at the first opportunity with the headmaster. He thought, as he got into his cold car and turned over the engine, waiting for the heater's blast, that Thaddeus Kroll was a little snit, and that Roger Forrest had dangerous ideas, and that Herbert Rector didn't bathe enough. Sometimes he wondered, sitting muffled in the dark, the lights of the dormitory behind him, Welling Proper a smudge across the river, if he actually liked children.

It was quite late, much later, in fact, than he usually stayed at Crown, but he had taken the opportunity, after dinner, of having conferences with three of his students who were doing badly, one in biology and two in chemistry. The conferences were held in the prefect's small office off the main hall and were quite painful to all concerned. Henry Johanson thought the boys dunces who didn't work nearly hard enough and whose study habits were obviously in shambles; the boys just wished him stricken with the plague, preferably before marking time.

He shifted into drive and carefully inched his old Dodge out of the parking lot by Humans. Starting down the hill, he couldn't for a moment locate Main Bridge and then realized it was sheathed in a rolling blanket of fog. A white, cottony fog puffed out over the Susquehanna, licking at the banks of Welling, curling along the bridges, and dancing like wisps of smoke up into the guy wires.

How odd! he thought. How really peculiar. It was, he

would have sworn, much too cold for fog, and, what was stranger, much too dry. But there was fog nonetheless, so much, in fact, that the bridge was all but obscured, and the access road leading into it swallowed.

He crawled along and almost at once was engulfed in the cloud bank, so thick it was like mashed potatoes. Dimly he could make out the railings as he felt the wheels of the Dodge hit the bridge. Proceeding cautiously, he hoped that no cars were coming the other way. Visibility, even with the yellow, almost incandescent glow from the light high up in the bridge, was almost zero. He never, in all his years, remembered a fog this time of year, nor, if it came to it, one this thick. It wasn't at all like moving through particles of water, but more like milk, he thought, suppressing a giggle. Henry Johanson didn't normally giggle; most people would say he didn't even know how to laugh; but there was something frightening about such a thick *slab* of whiteness pushing ahead just in front of his car that gave him a tickly feeling in the back of his throat.

He was down to barely ten miles an hour and moving largely by instinct as he crept past the middle of the bridge, the Susquehanna roaring below, Welling invisible ahead. For a moment he stopped altogether and glanced behind him at Mason, which he had just left. There was nothing to see, not even barely discernible shapes with faint glows where the windows would be. The rear of the car was bandaged in white.

Henry Johanson broke out into a cold sweat and for one brief flicker realized that he wasn't very young now, that he was not merely getting older, but old already, that he wasn't up to a rogue fog springing suddenly for no reason out of a winter's night like a visitation. He knew that he wanted to be home in his warm and cozy house at the very top of Welling, drinking a glass of port and reading *Scientific American*.

The car was so stuffy that he sneezed from the tickle of musty air in his nostrils, and reaching down, he switched off the heater. The instantaneous silence was as thick as the fog outside.

He was never going to get home, he chastised himself, if he sat with an idling engine in the middle of Main Bridge. Fog or no fog, he had to keep moving. Once in Welling Proper, if it was this dense he could park on River Street and walk, even if it was mostly uphill and he was, all of a sudden, dreadfully tired.

He nudged ahead a few feet. The fog plastered against his windshield. He turned on the wipers, even though he knew there was nothing they could push aside, that the fog wasn't solid.

He had a vision of having sunk into a drift of snow. There was nothing but whiteness about him, a world of white, the glare so lucent it hurt his eyes. Which was foolish, because in the middle of a snowdrift there was darkness, not light. Suddenly he remembered the Billy Sunday storm when he was a very small boy. It was called that because the famed evangelist was supposed to have preached, if not in Welling— Henry Johanson wasn't sure exactly where—then down the line, possibly in Scranton. And, of course, just like everybody else, the minister was stranded. Whether he ever did appear, Henry had been too young to remember, but the storm had passed into history with its famous name.

What was remarkable about the Billy Sunday storm was that it was the worst ever. In living memory there had never been a storm like that one. Snow fell relentlessly, as if it meant to bury the world forever and after. It fell for days and days, and when it finally did stop, Welling was completely buried. There was snow up to the second floor of the buildings along Main Street, and there was no question about shoveling out. It was impossible, in those days anyway, to move that mountain of snow off the town, and people finally got about by tunneling through the drifts. Which turned out not to be the best idea, because the moment the thaw began, the tunnels collapsed. Two people had been caught inside and died.

The young Henry had had nightmares for a long time, wondering what it must have been like to be trapped under all that snow, to have that whiteness press down on him, crushing out all his life.

At last, without being truly aware of how he had done it, he reached the end of the bridge, and just then, the light went out. The fog was transformed into a dinginess like an unwashed bedsheet, illuminated in his headlights, which didn't penetrate it, but hurled themselves upon it, and then fell back, reflecting in Henry's eyes.

He slammed on the brakes, though he was barely moving, and the old Dodge stopped with a painful jerk.

The fog swirled like a curtain of ghosts, shifting and seeming now to blow in gusts about the car. He strained forward, attempting to see River Street, and across it the hill and the start of the bridge. It was then that he saw her. Good heavens! he thought. There's a child lost out in this soup. He got a terrible turn thinking he could have run right into her and not known it except for a small bump. But he hadn't and he was grateful, crossing himself and mumbling a short prayer of thanks.

It was impossible to see who she was, or even to make her out completely. There was just a form, a bulky shape, long hair, and flapping hands at the right fender.

He couldn't just leave her here, wandering about. Leaning across the seat, he rolled down the window on the passenger side and called out to the dim form cocooned in the fog. "Little girl, get in. I'll drive you home." He opened the door and gave it a slight shove, beckoning toward her with his other hand. But she didn't come nearer, rather receded into the fog. Henry squinted, but all he could see was shifting fog and gray shadows fluttering. He didn't think she was wearing a coat, one of those ubiquitous down jackets, but decided that was nonsense. She couldn't be here in the cold without warm clothing. Also, he had the vague impression that she had ribbons trailing from her hair.

With a blink she disappeared out there, smothered in the whiteness that hadn't diminished at all. He glanced around and wondered if he should get out of the car and look for her, but knew once he stepped into that cloying mass he'd be swallowed whole, just as though he had actually leapt out his bedroom window into one of the Billy Sunday drifts.

Truly, there was nothing to do but drive on. Children had the homing instinct of pigeons, particularly in a town as small as Welling. Besides, she wasn't a little child, and if she had gotten this far, she could, undoubtedly, find her way back, Henry argued with himself, not liking to admit that he was afraid to leave the warm car and plunge into the fog.

Just as he decided there was nothing else to do but to drive ahead, inch by inch, he heard a noise. The left-rear door of the Dodge was opening.

"Well, there you are," he said, relieved, and shuffled around.

She wasn't wearing a coat, only a sweatshirt, he saw to his
amazement as she clumsily climbed into the car, bent over so
that he couldn't see anything of her but the back. "What are
you doing out here, so late, and why aren't you warmly
dressed?" he asked in his most officious manner, thinking:
Really, children, they're a breed apart.

He was annoyed and said, more sharply than he intended,
"Who are you? What's your name?"

She didn't speak, didn't then even straighten up, and the
fog glided after her, through the gaping door, mushroomed
out inside the Dodge, so that when she shifted and came
around, full face, he imagined that the dense, almost liquid
whiteness was wreaking havoc with the faint light, the shadows, the lines and hills, planes of her cheekbones, chin, nose.

"Gaaaa . . . gaaaa . . ." she said.

"What? What did you say? Speak up, child!"

And then the fog, slipping and sliding in the car, slithered
aside, like a curtain parting, and Henry Johanson began to
scream, the terrible cry ripping up his throat like a flume of
vomit, choking between his teeth and exploding in the en-
closed space. He jumped back so fast the steering wheel
rammed into his side. And he scrambled for the door handle,
ducking his head and knocking his brimmed hat to the floor,
trying to escape that awful, unmoving vision which sat immobile on the back seat of his car.

By some miracle (or so he would think later when all his
spasms passed and he tried to clear not only the fog outside
but also the fog from his mind), by God's good graces, he
found the door handle, and the door swung out and he went
with it. He tumbled to the pavement, striking his shoulder,
but was oblivious of the pain. Almost at once he was up on
his feet, which was a miracle in itself, given his age and the
perilous condition of his bones, and running. Henry Johanson
ran right across River Street, leaving his old brown Dodge
half on and half off Main Bridge, and raced up the hill
without knowing where he was going, his heart chugging
furiously in his chest. He sped up and out of the fog, which
stopped absolutely and completely twenty feet from Main,
and he fell into the light, grasping at the pole of a stop sign,
hanging on to it like Corney or Harry Pringle in the midst of
one of their worst drunks. He hung on to that pole as though
it was the last thing in the world, as if it was the only

substantial element which tethered him to the ground, keeping him out of the fog and away from the grasp of that . . . that *awfulness* in the back seat of the Dodge.

Piggy woke up long after his mother had gone to bed. Lying still, he listened to the house sleeping. He hurt all over and was as tired as when he had lain down hours before. Nothing had changed. Fear still gripped his insides in a terrible spasm, and he was as queasy as though he had the flu.

But, astonishingly, he hadn't dreamed. He supposed in that sleep he would have seen the deputy, seen him crumpled at the foot of the steps like a rag doll, his arms and legs at peculiar angles. But Emmett, his mouth still agape with the scream that had torn through him, had left Piggy alone.

Hugging Chester in his arms, he stared at the window, remembering how Bee used to drowse in the corner, and how, coming awake in the dark, he would talk to the robot, soothed by his presence. There was no one to talk to now, except Chester, who was only rags and stuffing, no one who would listen once he started to speak. The minute he said anything, he'd be doomed. And Sam . . .

He had run past her, clattering down the stairs to gape stupidly at Emmett, not believing what he saw. The crumpled dead body of the deputy.

It was an accident, he wanted to say to Emmett, not that it mattered to the dead man. You shouldn't have panicked, he wished he could tell him.

All Sam had wanted to do was, for whatever strange reason, touch him, to run her fingers along his face. She hadn't wanted him dead like her father. Pig was certain of that. And if Emmett had stayed still he'd be alive right now. But that didn't make any difference either because Emmett was stone dead and no one was going to believe that he had died in his sleep from some unspecified disease.

He ruthlessly stomped on the niggling little thought: if Emmett hadn't fallen they both would have been found out. He gnawed at his thumbnail and knew he should do something. Lots of things. Get rid of Emmett's body. But where? In the cellar with Harry Pringle? He could possibly manage that, dragging the deputy's corpse through the living room, into the kitchen, then rolling him down the cellar steps, and then maneuvering all that dead flesh into the back of the coal bin. Yes, it was possible. But he'd still have to get rid of the Ford. And that he couldn't hide, or at least not well enough so that Charlie Volchek wouldn't eventually find it. If Harry Pringle vanished, no one would give a hoot in hell, but the deputy was an officer of the law and belonged to Charlie Volchek. He'd never rest, Piggy realized, until Emmett was unearthed.

So, trying to think it all through clearly, trying to part the terror which wouldn't go away, he concluded that hiding Emmett's body was just a waste of time. He couldn't hide both the corpse and the car so that they'd never be found.

But he had to get Sam out of her house. He had left her standing at the top of the stairs staring down at Emmett, dead below. Her face was a wound. She looked worse every day, like someone terminally ill. Only she wasn't dying—if the dead *could* die! If anything, she was growing stronger. An anomaly, she was beyond Pig's understanding now. To do justice to her would mean a lab, doctors, and skills that he had merely read about. He knew he owed it to science to give her up, but even if he did, the law wouldn't allow it.

Pig shuddered, sitting up suddenly, dizziness assailing him. He lowered his head and tugged at his hair angrily, wanting in some way to hurt himself as Sam had been so gravely injured. But he couldn't. He was scared. *For shit's sake,* he cried furiously, *I'm only a kid! Why aren't I like Slime, playing Atari and reading comic books?*

He was still fully dressed right to his down jacket. He had a vague memory of fleeing Sam's house as though it were riddled with smallpox, of flying into sleep like Daedalus with his wax wings. And he thought that sometime while he lay in a stupor his mother had come in and told him to take his clothes off. But he obviously hadn't, and he guessed she just left him alone.

Learn by yourself, his grandmother had always said. And *Look before you leap* was another one of hers. Well, maybe he was learning, but he just wished he had known before what he knew after he had leapt. Thinking back to the experiment, he saw that he had been wild with rage, with grief, striking out in the only way he had ever understood, with his intelligence.

There's too smart, he remembered hearing that same grandmother telling his mother after they had found out about

him, about his IQ and the kind of mind he had. Not that
Piggy had ever suspected as a very young child the difference
between him and the other kids. He thought they all could
think as he did.

None of this rambling was solving his problem. But he was
so reluctant to move, to leave his bedroom and secure house,
going out into the cold across the yard to get Sam. No matter
how he looked at it, he couldn't see any solution but to hide
her again; and because Welling was pretty much a mystery to
him, all he could think of was to secrete her in this house.

He didn't want to do that. Have her here. And where,
anyway? Not in the cellar. Pig didn't think he'd ever go
below ground again. And certainly not in his room, stationed
like BeeBee in the corner. It had to be someplace where his
mother wouldn't go, as she had almost gone out to the shed.

He thumped his forehead with the palm of his hand, making the incipient headache grow worse, which served him
right, until he thought of the attic. She had only climbed up
there once, a day or so after they had arrived. And most
likely she wouldn't go up there again, supposing he had set
up a mini lab under the rafters. He had planned to, after all,
but events had simply overtaken him.

It was just an attic, like every attic he had ever seen in the
movies. The rafters jutted out naked from the sloping ceiling,
insulation pocketed in between. There was one window, in
the back wall, through which you could see over the river,
see Mason, and, if you craned your neck, all the way down to
South Bridge.

There wasn't much in the attic. A few rickety pieces of
furniture, a cardboard closet with hangers swinging faintly
inside. An old trunk which turned out disappointingly to be
empty, and a few boxes that were sealed with tape and had
belonged to one of the families who had lived here before.
Yes, he could leave her in the attic, at least for a little while,
until he thought of somewhere better. Piggy had a vision of
himself going through life pushing her in front of him like a
lawn mower. Maybe by the time they both grew up . . . No,
that wasn't possible, that she would grow, mature, evolve
into something other than she was. At least he didn't think it
was possible. *But maybe it was*. Right then he hated himself
for not knowing more, for information outside his ken.

What would he do with her when he went to college in two

or, at the most, three years? He couldn't take her along, like Chester, whom he hugged again extra tight. And he certainly couldn't leave her behind to starve to death in the attic or wherever.

Stupid! Why are you worrying about what's going to happen in a couple of years? he castigated himself, leaving his room at last, and the house, sliding out in the night, his feet moving in spite of his head, which said: *Don't.*

The deputy, still contorted in death, hadn't gone anywhere. Maybe, Pig thought hopefully, they'll think he fell down the stairs. If it wasn't for that awful look on his face.

Girding himself, Piggy leaned over and tried to smooth out the cheeks, push the lips closer together, take out all the twists in the dead deputy's face, which looked even more horrific in the pale light that filtered in through the window. But rigor had set in and there was no erasing that grimace of terror.

Piggy recalled reading in a book that the last thing a dying person saw was imprinted on his eyeballs—particularly if he had died traumatically, which Emmett Sidowsky surely had done. An old wives' tale, but Pig, curious, stared into the deputy's eyes anyway, searching for some vague image of Sam. But there was nothing there, only a bottomless blackness.

He straightened and glanced up the stairs for Sam, but she wasn't in sight. He guessed she had wandered back down the hall and was in one of the bedrooms. Stepping gingerly around Emmett's corpse, he went searching for her.

She wasn't in the bedroom where he had secreted her before, nor in her own room with its reminders of death. But Piggy wasn't worried until he realized that she was nowhere on the second floor. She wasn't in the Pringle attic either, because the door to that was stuck and wouldn't give.

Running down the stairs, he almost fell on the deputy, righting himself just in time by a good grip on the banister. Carefully he went through each of the few rooms, trying not to succumb to panic, holding in his galloping imagination with a tight rein.

"Sam," he kept calling, but she failed to answer with that funny sound she made, and he didn't hear the muffled dragging of her feet. She could be in the cellar with her father, dead and hidden away, only Piggy had locked the door to *that*, and the little bolt was still thrown.

He was wild now in the dark house with the dead. It was worse than being in Toomy's, and fear prickled his skin like a rash. He ran back and forth, bumping into the furniture, slamming into the walls, tears washing down his face and dribbling onto his jacket. His nose was clogged with so much silent weeping, but he didn't stop to blow it.

Where had she gone? What was she doing?

Why was he always misplacing her?

He knew now what his mother had been through the night he was missing. Terrible visions flung themselves up on the screen of his imagination. Piggy saw Sam falling over the enbankment and into the river, saw her smashed by a car and thrown into a ditch, saw the dogs of the neighborhood which sometimes ran in packs grabbing hold of her leg or arm and ripping her flesh into jagged strips. He saw all the horrors from the six-o'clock news. And even if none of those was true, he fantasized that somebody had found her and *knew*.

Fear was tugging at him with frantic hands as he ran around the house looking for her in places he had already searched. In Harry Pringle's room with its piles of dirty clothes and the smelly unmade bed he glanced out the window at the empty street, half expecting to see Sam stomping along right up to the front walk. But she wasn't there. His gaze traveled across the road and slid up the façade of Elvira Williams' house to a yellow square of light on the second floor. Oh no! Piggy thought, feeling sick along with being frightened witless. She'd never hide there. The possibility of the old woman meeting Sam made the blood drain right out of Piggy's head. Before he fainted dead away, he ran out to the upstairs hall, trying urgently to convince himself that Sam was some place safe. Like the shed, he thought, with a surge of hope. Yeah, that was it, the shed. She probably thought of it as home now, that dinky little lean-to.

She was probably too upset to remain here with her father dead in the cellar and Emmett lying broken at the bottom of the stairs. That made good sense because he knew absolutely that buried somewhere inside the awful thing he had so clumsily turned her into, she did have feelings.

He hurried to the back door and was leaping the porch steps when Sam thumped her way around the side of the house. He was so relieved to see her that he cried out,

"Where have you been?" as if she could answer him and explain.

There was no time to examine her, to see if she was injured, harmed in any way. Piggy didn't allow himself to think of the alternate possibility: that she had by mistake done something wrong again and that maybe out there were more bruised or dead bodies. He had had more to do with death in the last few days than in his entire life, and he fervently wanted all the dying to stop. Not that he really blamed Sam.

Except for Harry. . . .

He deserved what had happened to him, but Piggy refused to dwell on that, just telling Sam to com'on, which she did, obedient as a dog.

He turned once, as they reached the short fence, to see if she was following him. She was. Just like Bee. "Step over it, Sam," he ordered, and she did that too. On his own back porch he told her to be quiet when they got inside, not to make a peep, that they were going up to the attic, "which will be," he said, "your new home."

Once in the kitchen he entwined her fingers with his. It pained him that her skin was icy, chapped and cracked. Maybe he could rub her hands with some of his mother's lotion. Her face too. His mother had some really expensive stuff in squat milky bottles that might take away that leathery look and return Sam's skin to the satiny smoothness which he remembered with longing.

Piggy sniffed, trying to tell himself that he wasn't getting stuffy with tears at the memory of Sam-before, and caught a whiff of her smell. Maybe it was his imagination but it seemed that she was worsening, and he worried about the pungent odor permeating the house, seeping down from the attic until they choked with it. His mother couldn't help but notice. If he kept spraying the attic with Lysol, if he burned those two incense candles he had bought Jeannie for Christmas two years before and which she had never gotten around to using because, as she said, they were so pretty she hated to see them melt, maybe then no one would be able to smell Sam.

The crash came unexpectedly, catching Pig with one foot off the ground. He almost cried aloud, and just managed to shut his mouth in time. Going past the counter by the doorway to the dining room, Sam had somehow knocked over the canning jar in which Jeannie kept tea bags.

It sounded in the silence like a bomb exploding.

Pig frantically snatched up the jar, which miraculously hadn't broken, and put it back on the counter just as he heard his mother's door open and her calling groggily, "Who's there?"

"Just me, Mom," he yelled back, trying to keep the quiver in his voice to a minimum. "I dropped something," he babbled on, "getting a snack because I'm hungry since I didn't eat dinner."

Please don't come down! he was begging her silently. *Stay upstairs!*

He had to put Sam somewhere fast, he thought, yanking off his jacket and throwing it into the darkened pantry. That was where he'd shove Sam. But she had wandered off, right into the dining room.

"Do you feel all right?" Jeannie was asking, coming down the stairs. Pig heard her getting closer and screamed soundlessly, *Stop!* as he ran after Sam, and jerking her by the arm, pushed her behind the floor-length draperies.

"You stay right there," he insisted furiously.

"What did you say, Paul?" Jeannie asked, approaching.

"Fine, Mom. I feel fine now. Just hungry. Go back to bed, Mom. I'll just make a sandwich," he cried, running out to the living room to meet her in the muddy light.

"What's that funny smell?" she asked, automatically feeling his head, then walking by him, though he grabbed for her arm.

"What smell?" he asked, fear expanding like mustard gas within his rib cage as they went through the dining room, and he saw the socks poking out under the bottom of the draperies. They were ripped and Sam's toes poked through. He thought he was going to be sick. But Jeannie continued into the kitchen, and taking a deep breath, he followed, saying, "I don't smell anything."

"Well, I do. And it's not roses."

"It's your imagination, Mom." He stationed himself in the doorway and tried to keep calm. "Or maybe you were dreaming. There's this strange phenomenon, you know, of smells in dreams."

"No, I didn't know," she said, furrowing her brow. "And

I'm not dreaming." She wandered around the kitchen seeking to identify where the smell was coming from, stopping finally at the sink.

"That's it," Pig said wildly, "the drain. I remember now, Slime telling me that lots of people in Welling have this problem. Of the drains backing up. When it rains heavily."

"It's not raining, Paul," she pointed out, but leaned over the sink and stared wonderingly into the drain.

"Then it's the river. He also told me about the river. That it does something to the drains down here that it doesn't do in the rest of town." Pig just hoped the remnants of sleep were still clouding her brain, because he was making no sense. There was, however, one good thing about being super smart: people tended to believe anything you said, as his mother apparently did, nodding her head.

"That could be it," she agreed, "but I wonder what we should do."

"Nothing, Mom." He sagged with relief. "Just leave it alone. Sooner or later the smell will go away. I just bet it will."

"You're probably right, as you usually are." She smiled at him. He saw the love in her eyes and it scalded him like acid, igniting his anger. *Stop loving me so much!* he wanted to shrill at her. *You don't know who I am at all. What I've done.* And there, suddenly, standing right in the middle of the kitchen floor, feet firmly planted on the geometrically patterned linoleum, was Bertram Lennard burning up. And he, Piggy, was grasping the blowtorch. He glanced down at his hand with the blowtorch in it, clutching the handle so firmly that his skin was dead white from the strain. He was pressing down on it, exerting all his strength, forcing Bertram back against the lab bench, stroking his face with the fire as his screams pitched so high they splintered the glass beakers on the shelves.

He had no other thought except to convert Bertram Lennard into ash, making him dead again just as he had in the lab . . . only, he *was* in the lab, not in the kitchen of the house in Welling, as though he had catapulted back through time, been transported molecule by molecule.

This time, watching it all once again as he relentlessly pursued the boy, saw him blacken, seething with smoke, it was no accident. Piggy was grimly satisfied. But running side by side with the sense of gratification, of having gotten his own back at last on his tormentor, of wiping out the awful threat to Bee, was a vast, throbbing horror at himself. *What had he done?* And in a moment he wished it all away, Bertram Lennard alive again even if he persisted in his taunting, Bertram with his weasel's face and bad breath. He'd have given anything to put new flesh on Bertram's bones.

Jeannie was saying something to him from the other end of a long corridor, but he couldn't distinguish the words, the letters all messed up like in Boggle. Even as the vivid image of Bertram Lennard writhing in his fiery dance began to fade, went from Technicolor to sepia, to black and white, until, overexposed, Bertram blended right into the kitchen cabinets, he couldn't hear her.

"Paul," she was saying, "Paul! What's the matter with you?"

His ears came unclogged with a roar and he gaped at her, at her hand shaking his arm as though it were the limb of a tree. "What?" he rasped, his voice creaking in his larynx.

"Are you sure you're all right? You went so goofy just now you scared me." Her eyes were glassy with fright.

"Daydreaming, Mom. Nothing to get hyperactive about." He jerked away from her and opened the refrigerator, the cool draft drying the sweat on his brow.

"Well, I'm going to make you a nice bowl of soup, and what about a toasted cheese sandwich with tomato? Then, it's up to bed with you."

"I'm not hungry, Mom," he said, slamming the door, wishing with all his soul that she'd go upstairs and climb into bed and fall asleep. He was so tired all at once that he wanted to sink to the linoleum. But he had to get Sam up to the attic, and he wasn't sure she just wouldn't slip out from behind the draperies and come thumping into the kitchen. She wasn't Bee, who stayed where you left him when you threw the switch.

"What do you mean you're not hungry?" she asked, her eyes going wider yet. "A few minutes ago you were starving to death."

"Well, I'm not anymore," he gulped, hoping that he looked innocent. "Let's go to sleep."

Piggy could tell that she was worrying, but he couldn't help that. It made him feel bad that he was such a burden to

her, that he had to lie so much now that he doubted he'd
know the truth anymore if it came and stood beside him. She
deserves better, he thought with anguish, noticing for the
first time the puffiness under her eyes and the paleness of her
skin. Just like she gets when she's been crying, he realized,
and his stomach dropped, wondering what it was she had
been crying about. *Not me*, he pleaded silently; *don't let her
be crying about me*. It made him feel impossibly guilty to
have his mother up in her room alone crying about him.

"Okay," she said wearily, "if you don't want to eat, then
get yourself to bed. It's late, after one."

"You too, Mom. You need your sleep just as much as I do."

"In a few minutes. I want to toss some Drāno down that
sink." She was starting toward the pantry.

"You don't need Drāno. The sink isn't clogged, it just
smells!" he cried, and darted after her.

"It can't hurt," she insisted.

He pushed past her and plunged into the small, dark
pantry, groping around with his foot for his jacket, which lay
on the floor. He kicked it into the far corner, calling out, "I'll
get it, Mom. You go to sleep!"

"Are you sure you're not sick?" she asked.

"I'm not sick!" He was frantic, searching the shelves in the
dim light. If she found his jacket she'd know he'd been up to
no good, and while he had managed to stonewall about the
night he had stayed out so late, and about the night he had
done the experiment on Sam, he didn't think he could do it
again.

"I just start worrying," she said with a nervous laugh,
"when you want to be helpful."

"Don't be such a cynic, Mom," he said, his hand grasping
the can of Drāno. Gratefully, he ran back into the kitchen,
where he flung the contents down the sink. "I'm growing up,
you know."

He threw the empty can in the trash, thinking he had
passed growing up and was simply now growing old, his
whole life accelerated. "Let it sit for tonight, Mom," he said,
turning around to face her as she leaned over and kissed his
cheek.

Through the doorway he saw Sam standing by the table in
the dining room. She was watching them like a spectator in
the third row at the theater. Pig's knees almost gave way, and

he had to grab at his mother, giving her a fierce hug, holding on to her.

"Hey, that's an unexpected treat, Paul," she sighed, rumpling his hair. "You're not much for sissy stuff these days, like hugging, are you?"

"Oh, Mom," he whispered, and hugged her again, glaring at Sam, waggling his fingers at her, trying to tell her to go away. But she simply watched, forlorn, out of her runny eyes. When Jeannie turned, she was sure to see her. "Better check the Drāno." He pulled her to the sink.

Obediently she bent over and he darted around her, into the shadowy dining room.

"Are we supposed to run some water?" she asked.

"Yes!" he cried. He pushed Sam back behind the draperies, hissing furiously, "Don't you move!"

By the time Jeannie had finished at the sink, he was back in the doorway. He was so agitated that he clenched his teeth, and curled his hands into fists in his pockets.

"I guess that's it, though it's still smelly in here. You know"—she looked thoughtful—"it really doesn't seem to be coming from the drain."

"Leave it, Mom, and let's go to bed. Please!"

"Okay, honey," she agreed. She turned off the lights and they went together through the darkened house, Pig holding his breath, listening for Sam following, but she wasn't. Once upstairs, he let Jeannie kiss him good night, and counted to ten, leaning against the door of his room before he stepped back out into the hallway. He could hear the squeak her bed made as she got into it, and in a moment he saw the sliver of light beneath her door vanish.

Slipping off his sneakers, he tiptoed down the stairs and retrieved Sam from the dining room. He knew he should give her something to eat, that she probably was hungry, but, once in the attic, he didn't have the energy to creep back down to the kitchen. And he still had to find the incense candles. He thought they were in a box in the spare room. If he didn't do something about the aroma, his mother wouldn't rest until she tracked it down.

Finally he had Sam in a far corner of the attic, plopped on an extra blanket from the linen closet, and the candles burning as far away from her as he could put them. He didn't want her to tip them over and set the house on fire—which is what he thought she had done when he awoke later in his own bed with a jolt, thinking he smelled smoke. But then he realized he had been dreaming. It was Bertram Lennard still burning somewhere, forever on fire in the coils of Piggy's brain. But he was so tired, his arms and legs aching in pain as though a ton of earth had settled on him, that Bertram Lennard was just then one more bad dream in a night hideously full of nightmares, and Pig rolled over and, almost at once, fell asleep again.

Father Duffy, the Catholic priest, noticed that Elvira Williams didn't turn up for early Mass. As he looked out over the church, where only a pitifully few communicants were scattered about the pews, Elvira's black winter hat and its speckled pom-pom didn't bob up at him. He supposed that she had slept in, that her arthritis was giving her misery, and decided he better call her later to see how she was.

He was also missing Henry Johanson this morning, which wasn't surprising since he'd been up with his old friend for what seemed like half the night. The professor had come banging on the door of the rectory very late, banging and babbling incoherently, even after Father Duffy had pulled him inside, relieved him of his overcoat, and shoved him gently into a chair. After a stiff brandy Henry had begun to calm down, but he still didn't make much sense. He had gone on and on about a monster who had come out of the fog into the back seat of his car. A monster who looked like a little girl with the face of a squashed prune.

Father Duffy, who might have laughed, thinking Henry was joking, kept silent, because his friend's eyes were black with terror. He did try, however, to settle Henry, but the more he soothed, the more agitated Henry became.

"She was a terror!" he screamed. "Like a dead person. Like she had come right up out of the grave and walked!"

"Henry, Henry," he calmed, but Henry wasn't listening.

"And the fog!" He reeled. "That fog could strangle a person!"

Finally Father Duffy shouted, which seemed to be the only way he was going to be heard, "Henry, what fog? There was no fog tonight. I was out on the porch no more than a half-hour ago, three-quarters, if that, and *there was no fog*. I could see right down the hill and there wasn't even a wisp, all up and down the Susquehanna!"

*   *   *

"You better call Elvira Williams first thing," Milly told Charlie when he arrived at the station the next morning. "She was calling half the night."

Screw Elvira, Charlie Volchek wanted to say, but after brewing up a pot of tea and settling himself behind the desk, he reached for the phone anyway. If he didn't call her, she'd only phone again and start screaming at him.

The old woman didn't answer, and Charlie put down the receiver with a sigh of relief. But almost immediately it rang, and Milly yelled out that it was Father Duffy.

Elvira Williams hadn't turned up for Mass, and when he, Father Duffy, called her, there was no answer. What, the priest asked, did Charlie think?

Charlie thought she was probably down at the grocery store, but he reluctantly agreed to run by her house later on when he was making his rounds.

It wasn't until after ten when he had pushed around a pile of paperwork to his satisfaction that he noticed Emmett hadn't showed up. He walked out to the outer office and asked Milly if she had heard from him.

Milly gazed out at Charlie from heavily mascaraed eyes that gave her an uncanny resemblance to a raccoon and said there hadn't been a peep.

"Did he say anything yesterday when he left for the night?" She shook her head. "Call his house and tell him to get his ass in here on the double," he ordered as Milly lifted the receiver.

They stared at one another as the phone rang and continued to ring. Finally Charlie motioned for Milly to hang up. "We seem to have a missing deputy," he said, going for his coat.

"You don't think anything's happened to him, do you, Charlie?" Milly asked, her voice see-sawing with concern.

"Of course not," Charlie boomed as he slammed out of the station. But once behind the wheel of the blue-and-white, doing an even twenty miles along the quiet, unruffled Welling streets, a cold chill began to creep up his spine. He tried to shake off the increasingly strong premonition, but when he hit the bottom of the hill and went left onto River Street he saw Emmett's Ford parked before the Pringle house half a block away and his stomach sank. He felt a painful bubble of gas rise up into his chest and thought, as he speeded up, *oh shit.*

22

Anybody else would have stayed home in bed, would have called in sick for the day or even the whole week, but Henry Johanson was not just anybody. Not only did he see teaching as a higher calling, but he wasn't accustomed to coddling himself. So, quavery as an aspen in high wind, and his color the same hue as a ghost, he staggered into Mason the day after his experience on Main Bridge in the fog.

Henry didn't want to think about what had happened to him, didn't even want to admit that anything had. But his sleep had been punctuated by nightmares, by monsters with ribbons in their hair, and even in the gray light of a new day he couldn't shake his feeling of dread. Something had been determined to get him there on the bridge, something that had come out of the night.

Every time he closed his eyes he saw her sitting on the back seat, incongruously prim and proper, and he began to tremble. His forehead was constantly damp, and he kept dabbing at it with a handkerchief that was soon wringing wet. By the time his first class ended he was a nervous wreck and his students were too. The word immediately went out that old Waxworks must have sat on a tack because he was meaner and surlier than usual.

Even Peter Bayard caught the broadside of Henry's temper when he saw him in the hall between classes and asked if he was feeling well. Henry snapped he was just fine, thank you, and why didn't Peter pay attention to his own affairs and stop annoying him.

About the only person who didn't realize that the science

professor was feeling drastically out of sorts, and to be avoided or not riled at all costs, was Piggy, who had concerns of his own. And when they met up in the lab after lunch, Piggy wasn't paying strict attention. He dropped his book bag on the bench and didn't notice that the thud made Henry Johanson wince. Then he settled down to read over a mini test he had taken on electromagnetic energy on which he'd received the humiliating grade of B-plus.

"I don't accept this mark at all," he snapped, flaming with annoyance. "You made a mistake."

"I made a mistake!" the professor cried, rising up off the stool, stung. "How dare you, you little whelp! You're the one who was wrong, not I. Your answers were sloppy and not to the point."

Something in Piggy went pop, and with a savage sweep of his hand he cleared the bench, books and papers flying. "That's stupid, really stupid!" he yelled. "You're wrong and you know it, and you're just trying to blame everything on me!"

In a moment they were screaming at one another, both in high pitch, stalking around the bench, arms waving, their faces flushed. Henry Johanson swiped furiously at his forehead, trying to keep the sweat from dripping over his eyebrows. His heart pounded painfully and he thought he understood right then what it meant to have one's blood boil. A red haze rose, clouding his vision, and—his control in shreds—he would have strangled Piggy. He would have lunged out and grabbed him by the neck, jiggling him up and down until he had wrung all the life from his body, just as he once killed chickens for his mother when he was a boy. He could even see it, see the way his hands bit into Piggy's flesh, see his face blacken as the white fog swirled up and. . . . Suddenly he was back in the Dodge on Main Bridge, imagining the *thing*—for truly once settled, she hadn't moved—struggling toward him over the seat. His breath caught in his throat like a fishbone and he couldn't breathe. Fear swam up his legs and into the pit of his stomach as Pig's voice shrilled on and on, the words a blur. And now it was Piggy—only it wasn't— coming for him, wanting his life like a frantic shark in a bloody sea. Terror made Henry Johanson's bowels go loose, and he frantically backed up, away from the nightmare which was folding in on him. A stool crashed, and he almost tripped on the book bag in his retreat to the door. But he kept to his feet until he came bang up against the knob, which hit him just above the right kidney. He fumbled behind his back and when he grasped it he stepped aside, yanking the door open, flying away from the horror, though even in his flight he knew the horror was as much in his mind as outside.

The last bell rang, ending the day, and Jeannie gathered together her books and papers as the class shuffled noisily out of the room. She had the beginning of a headache and was feverish to get home and lie down.

Out in the hall she saw Slime leaving the nurse's office and stopped him. "Tommy, are you all right?"

"Not really, Mrs. Conway," the small boy, appearing even smaller, answered seriously. He held a bloodstained handkerchief to his face.

"What's the matter?" she asked, concerned.

"I had a nosebleed and I was resting. Miss Cooper put an ice pack on my face."

"Did you fall or get hit?"

"No, ma'am, nothing like that. Just a nosebleed. I get them sometimes. My ma says when I'm tense and upset."

Jeannie, the pulse beating in her temple, narrowed her eyes and carefully scrutinized him. His skin was gray, his large brown eyes sunk like withered walnuts into his skull. "Worried about exams?" she probed.

He shrugged his small frame without answering and avoided looking directly at her.

They were walking down the hall toward the front door when Jeannie blurted out, "Is it something to do with Paul?"

Slime skidded to a stop on the scuffed floor. A wash of sweat broke out on his brow and he blinked nervously. "What?" he whispered.

"I just asked if there's something wrong between you and Paul?"

"No, Mrs. Conway. Honest!" he bleated. "There's nothing special about me and Pig at all. I try to be helpful 'cause he's new and everything. You know? But I got lots of friends, really I do." He was pleading with her, inching away, almost ready to break into a run.

Fear was rising off the boy. Jeannie could smell it and her own terrors accelerated. "I just thought," she said carefully, not wanting to infect the boy with the panic just there quivering beneath her skin, "that you and Paul were special friends, best friends, in fact. But maybe I'm wrong."

"Yes, ma'am, you're wrong. I don't know nothing about Pig or what he does or anything like that. No, not me!" His voice pitched, spiraling to the gloom overhead, and he shook himself so vehemently that Jeannie worried his nose would start bleeding again. "Me and Pig are just in some of the same classes, that's all!" He was begging her to believe him, the smell of his fear rank now, almost overpowering.

"Tommy, it's okay," she consoled him, rubbing his shoulder, feeling him shrink away from under her fingertips.

They were stopped outside Dr. Mellon's office. Miss Miller called out from her desk just inside the door, "Oh, Mrs. Conway, did you hear the news?"

"What news?" Jeannie asked distractedly, not taking her eyes off Slime.

"A triple murder!" Miss Miller gushed with whispery satisfaction.

"What?" Jeannie spun around to gape at her. "What are you talking about?"

"Three people done in in Welling Proper!" Her voice was lush with excitement. "My sister heard the news from Charlie Volchek's wife and called to tell me. Three people! Can you imagine! Harry Pringle, Emmett Sidowsky—Charlie's deputy— and old Elvira Williams. There must be a madman loose. Why, I'll be afraid to sleep in my own bed," she said with relish, not sounding frightened at all.

Jeannie heard a strangling noise, and pulling her startled gaze away from Miss Miller, was just in time to see Slime slide to the floor. Blood spurted from his nose in an arc. Jeannie tried to catch him but wasn't fast enough. The boy's body, loose as a sack of feathers, slumped at her feet in a dead faint.

A chilly winter world waited for Jeannie at the foot of the Administration Building steps. The river was a gray banner of sludge, and the town, which climbed up the other embankment, looked soiled, like a photograph someone had stepped on with dirty shoes. The headache had settled into a throbbing pain at the base of her skull, and she felt sorry for herself, thinking how nothing awaited her in the house on River Street but the faint smell of sewage.

All she had was a pudgy, genius son whom she could just discern slouching against the side of the Chevy in the parking lot, his lank blond hair ruffling in the rising wind, and an emptiness in her heart where love had once been safely stored. And she had terror. Fear was now a component of her being, as steady and certain as the blood in her arteries and veins.

Stranded on the steps, immobilized as though her joints had ossified and to move would mean irrevocable damage, she rolled the day backward through her mind and shuddered.

Piggy raised his head and with his habitual gesture poked the bridge of his glasses, pushing them nearer his myopic eyes. He saw her and stared—dejectedly, she thought—and she plodded unwillingly toward him, only the fear alive inside her, eating at the lining of her stomach.

Piggy was still agitated from his fight with old Waxworks, still aghast at how he had given way, when they came up on the scene surrounding their house. One ambulance was just pulling away from the curb while another, its doors agape, was waiting to receive the shrouded remains being transported on a stretcher by two troopers down Elvira Williams' steep front steps.

Piggy felt his stomach climb all the way up to his mouth and wanted to crawl under the dash and hide. He had avoided thinking about that moment when someone would stumble over the bodies, but now that he came up broadside against the hard surface of discovery, he didn't know what to do. He closed his eyes and tried to pretend that it wasn't old Mrs. Williams whose corpse was being trundled away. But he knew it had to be and wailed, in his head, *Oh Sam! Why did you?* That had obviously been where she had gone the previous night when she disappeared. To Elvira Williams' to kill her.

He remembered his nightmare of the old woman without any flesh on her silvery bones chasing him down on a motorcycle in St. Anthony's parking lot. But had he ever told Sam, and in her befogged condition, would she remember?

It was, however, Elvira Williams who had backed up Harry Pringle's story that he hadn't meant to whack BeeBee to

death. For one fleeting moment, forgetting how she had
gotten that way, Piggy was deliriously happy that Elvira
Williams was dead.

He opened his eyes finally and saw that in addition to the
ambulance and Charlie Volchek's blue-and-white, there were
several state-police vehicles filling up River Street. The pho-
tographer from *The Welling Weekly Times* was out snapping
pictures with his big Graflex, and there was a scattering of
housewives, children, and a few men clustered curiously
along the sidewalks.

They had to park three houses away from their own, and
when they got out of the car, Piggy saw Charlie Volchek
watching them predatorily, like a hawk. Piggy tucked his chin
into his down jacket and lowered his eyes, wishing he were
invisible or could flap his arms and float up to the sky. But
the chief, from where he was standing on the old woman's
front steps, called out that he wanted to speak with them. In
a loping trot he crossed the street and arrived just as they did
at the walk.

"Let's go inside," the police chief suggested in a tone that
gave them no choice.

Once in the house, Piggy made a break for the stairs, but
Charlie Volchek snagged him back, saying, "I want to talk to
you too, son."

"There's no need for this. We don't know anything and
have nothing to say," Jeannie said, her voice escalating an
octave. Piggy sensed she was remembering the police in
Boston when they had asked all those awful questions about
Bertram Lennard's death. He remembered them too and
anxiety prickled the base of his spine.

Piggy crept across the room, staying out of Jeannie's reach,
and threw himself into a chair by the television set.

Charlie Volchek was glowering with anger, his face as
terrible, as stony as an Aztec mask. "There's been a fucking
massacre on River Street," he yelled, "if you'll excuse my
French. A fucking massacre. Three people dead and one of
them my deputy." Jeannie was stricken and backed up into
the couch. "I don't know who knows what right now," Charlie Volchek continued, "except for me, and I don't know a
goddamn thing!"

And then Charlie Volchek proceeded to describe with Technicolor details exactly what had happened on River Street.

Piggy was so jumpy that he sat on his hands. But in spite of his anxiety he noticed that his mother was badly shaken, the corners of her mouth puckering as if she was going to cry. Even sitting down, Piggy saw that her knees were quaking, and the color in her face had gone from white to a fungous shade of green. Along with everything else, he was killing his mother, he just knew it, and that added to the rising mountain of guilt.

"Do you want some water, Mom?" he asked when he got his tongue unstuck from the roof of his mouth. She nodded and Piggy, jumping up, ran to the kitchen. He filled a tumbler to the brim, and neither he nor Charlie Volchek said a word until she had drunk nearly half the glass. When a pale, almost imperceptible tinge of pink began to creep back into her cheeks, and her eyes seemed to focus, the chief sighed and sat down. He unbuttoned his jacket and eased his big belly over the strangling clasp of his belt, saying he'd have to ask them some questions.

"Elvira was killed last night, Emmett sometime yesterday, and Harry Pringle before that. Which means that over a long period of time some loony was running amok around here."

"Who would do such awful things?" Jeannie whispered, and Piggy had to concentrate on algebraic formulae to keep from screaming.

"If I knew that, my name'd be Houdini," Charlie Volchek was saying nastily. "Now," he went on, "did you people see anything strange the last few days? Anybody wandering around who didn't belong here? Any funny noises from the Pringle house? Anything, no matter how small?"

In a trance Piggy swung his head from side to side. Involuntarily his fingers danced up and down along the arms of the chair.

"What time did you get home yesterday?" Charlie Volchek asked him, leaning forward, his arms propped on his knees. His hands were big, like two slabs of beef. Piggy was mesmerized by the sprouts of hair growing on the backs of his fingers.

"Early," Piggy said, his eyes shifting to the chief's face. Charlie Volchek was a wall about to descend on Piggy's bones and the only thought in his head was that he wanted his father. He needed the bigness of Tony to stand between him and Charlie Volchek, and, horrified, he suspected he might faint.

"What time?"

"About three or a quarter to, I guess," Piggy heard himself replying from far away.

"Did you see anyone?"

"No sir, but I wasn't paying much attention. I felt sick, which is how come I came home so early."

Like a wandering dog Charlie Volchek suddenly changed direction, stating, "You and the Pringle kid were good friends as I recall."

Piggy, feeling that he had just been attacked on his flank, sank lower into the chair and pulled up his knees. "Kind of," he whispered.

"You were pretty upset when she died," the chief reminded him.

"Of course he was," Jeannie interrupted.

Piggy couldn't look at his mother right then, certain she would read all sorts of lies on his face. Resolutely he stared at the chief and said, "I mean, she was only a kid. Kids aren't supposed to die!" He was electric with fervor, which discomfited the chief.

Charlie grunted and conceded, "That's true."

There was a pause and Jeannie rushed to fill it. "All these killings . . . it's terrible," she said. "But what can we do?"

"I don't know, Mrs. Conway, but nothing like this has happened in all my years on the force. And I plan to find out who's responsible," he said grimly, pulling himself to his feet.

"I'm sorry," Jeannie said, rising off the couch. She's being silly, Piggy thought; the murders aren't her fault.

Charlie Volchek left at last and a wave of despair lapped over Pig. Watching his mother place one foot in front of the other on the return trip from the front door, Piggy thought: There must be some kind of normal conversation to have at a time like this. Some social amenity—as his grandmother would say—required for the occasion. But he had swum so far out from normalcy that he couldn't even think how to begin. Besides, he had to get to Sam.

Before Jeannie could hold him back, he leapt out of the chair and was at the stairs. Though tottering with dizziness, he took them two at a time. Sam, Sam, Sam. . . . Worry throbbed in his brain. What if she had gotten loose again?

Jeannie called something from behind him, and he yelled down on her head, "Homework, Mom." And then he was up in the attic, snagging the dangling string of the light.

What if . . . what if . . . what if . . . ? reverberated with his heartbeat.

The big room with its sloping ceiling finally coalesced into all of its hard edges, but for an instant he didn't see Sam. The breath whooshed out of his lungs in terror and he swung around in a full circle.

There, there she was, trapped by the shadows in a corner of the attic. "Sam, Sam," he whispered, relieved, and walked toward her.

From the back she looked so exactly like Sam-before, that for an unrealistic moment Piggy fantasized it was all a bad dream. That there was no Sam-dead and therefore no Sam-come-back-to-life. No computer in Sam's head. And, of course, no dead bodies along River Street.

"Sam," he said, and crept behind her. She was facing the wall and one hand rose up to touch her hair. She pulled the knotted tangles awkwardly through her fingers, then pushed at the wires.

All at once Piggy saw the mirror, a jagged piece of glass hanging on a nail from one of the exposed studs. There was a wavery crack right down the middle, and Piggy, looking past Sam to her reflection saw her splintered in half. If anything, she appeared more deformed in the mirror, and the memory of that other Sam shimmering in his mind's eye filled him with sadness.

"Sam," he crooned as her fingers passed across her face, touching, feeling. He thought he saw shock and surprise, but knew he was imagining. One finger probed at the nose, then trailed down and crawled between swollen, purplish lips.

Piggy, awash with pain, could stand it no longer and gently tugged her around. "Gaaa, gaaa," she said happily when she saw him. Piggy wished he were dead, not dead like Sam, but truly buried underground, as a hand crept toward him and took his arm. But he knew he couldn't hurtle his body through the window to an instant death below. The responsibility of Sam kept him firmly nailed to life.

"Listen, Sam," he said softly, leading her away from the awful image in the shattered glass. And then slowly, without recriminations, he began to tell her what she had done wrong and why.

23

The ripples etched into the placidity of Welling by the murders were wide and deep, extending the length and breadth of the town, from the top of the hill to the other side of Mason. In the more than eighty years that the town had been in existence, nothing had occurred that had such an impact, or was as terrifying, as *wrong* as the wholesale slaughter on River Street. Everyone was screamingly unsettled, and in each household, each store and market, at Consolidated, St. Anthony's—Mason too—no one could talk of anything else. Or if they did, eventually the subject veered sharply back to the killings. It was as though a jackhammer had been taken to the town, and the jarring reverberations had people shaking.

Almost at once the word went out that a stranger had trespassed the boundaries of Welling, had worked out a mysterious and perverted blood lust on three innocent people and then disappeared in the dead of night. This was the initial, and for most, the only acceptable explanation. The *Weekly Times* propounded the theory, quoting "official sources." But the reasoning was scanty, and the details to sustain such an idea were invisible. Yet even Charlie Volchek cleaved to the possibility that someone from somewhere else, just passing through, had taken it into his or her head, or better still, *their* heads, to behave like lunatics. He thought of the Manson murders and didn't doubt for a moment that such atrocities were rife across America. Killings without cause. Insanity that sprang from the blackness of the psyche, that cut and slashed—or, in these cases, pushed, shoved, and choked—

simply *because*. And no one would ever know the why of it, even if they did eventually find the who.

The troopers, and Captain Suswicki, who was in charge of them, were less inclined to support the theory that some mysterious stranger had strangled Harry Pringle, drowned Elvira Williams in her own tub, and pushed Emmett Sidowsky down the steps. But then, not one of them came from Welling Proper and they were more able to accept the grotesque, that the killer was known. That the killer lived next door, went off to work in the morning, to church on Sunday, had been to Consolidated—or at a long shot, Mason—and was a neighbor who planted his garden, raked his leaves, and shoveled his snow. If a townsperson was arrested and found guilty, no trooper would ever lie awake at night and wonder how he hadn't realized that his familiar neighbor harbored such madness.

As Captain Suswicki said to Charlie Volchek, these were all such clean killings that it stood to reason there was some motive involved, however implausible. After all, nothing was stolen or even damaged. There were no graffiti painted on the refrigerators or walls. In fact, no one had broken into the houses to commit the crimes. But, of course, Charlie Volchek pointed out that in Welling few people locked their doors. So it was a simple matter of just turning the knob and walking inside. Suswicki said that was foolishness, and he hoped, if nothing else, everyone had learned a valuable lesson.

"If we're not dealing with a stranger, what difference would it have made if both Harry Pringle and Elvira had chained and bolted up?" Charlie asked sarcastically. The captain was comfortably ensconced in Charlie's swivel behind Charlie's desk. Forced to sit on one of the straight-backed chairs or to stand, Charlie was steaming. Since the troopers had jurisdiction, and because Charlie Volchek had sense enough to know he wasn't equipped to handle crimes of such magnitude, they had taken over his office. Like the Allies at Normandy, they had swept in.

Captain Suswicki sipped at his coffee out of a Styrofoam cup and chewed on a ham-and-cheese, both of which had been brought in by one of his men from the Five O'Clock. His fleshy, dark-shadowed face beneath a jagged thatch of salt-and-pepper hair tightened in a scowl, as if he didn't like what he was consuming, or didn't like his surroundings, or the job which he had come up from the barracks down the line to handle, or maybe Suswicki simply didn't like Charlie.

Charlie didn't give a rat's ass about what was annoying the captain, he just wanted him out of his chair, his office, his town. With the killer in handcuffs, of course. Murder wasn't to Charlie Volchek's liking, though he had never actually come up against it before. Or at least not murders like the ones he was now so plainly confronted with. Of course in his twenty years on the force, he had handled a lot of killings. Hunting accidents, for example, some of which he had wondered about more than once. And the usual family stuff. The kind of business where it didn't take much mental energy to figure out who had committed the crime. Usually, in those cases, the poor slob was still standing around holding the shotgun, or he'd confess before Charlie was halfway through the door.

"Chief, you're gonna have to face the inevitable, you know," Captain Suswicki said condescendingly, tossing the crusts of his sandwich into the trash. "There's a psycho in your town. Some nut who looks as normal as you and me. A guy you've probably downed a few beers with over the years."

"Yeah, well then, how come, if we've had this unknown fruitcake running around Welling for God knows how long, it's only now that he blows his gourd? Answer me that, will you?" The chair, which was not designed for comfort, was giving Charlie Volchek a pain in his tailbone, so he stood and paced back and forth. From the outer office the steady buzz of the troopers filtered under the door. The only one, he thought sourly, who didn't mind the commotion was Milly, who was painting and preening herself for all the young men around. She'd probably get a boyfriend out of the deal with the way she was tossing herself about, fluffing her hair, and jutting forward her small, pointy breasts.

Captain Suswicki sucked at his teeth, probing between two molars with his tongue for a stringy remnant of ham. "Motive, Volchek. It all comes down to motive. Even a crazy person has a reason in his head somewhere. Not a reason to you and me, you understand, but still some explanation that makes sense to him."

"I know all that shit," Charlie snarled at the captain, who was talking to him—or so he felt—as though he were the rawest rookie. "But there's no motive that covers killing both

Harry Pringle and Elvira Williams, never mind Emmett. And even if you eliminate the boy, because he probably just walked in unannounced, that still leaves two people who had nothing in common besides the fact that they were both members of the human race. And in Pringle's case, just barely. That son of a bitch was an animal who most likely killed his own kid."

"If he didn't, you got another homicide on your hands."

Charlie thought: You asshole, it's *your* hands, because I forked over the whole mess to you. But he didn't say it since he knew he had to cooperate with the troopers if anything was going to get done.

"Elvira and Harry," he muttered, trying not to look at the captain, who, with his two-hundred-pounds-plus, was most likely wrecking his chair. It tilted forward, then back, squealing in protest. "Elvira and Harry," Charlie repeated, "never got along. Hated one another's guts as far as I know. And couldn't of agreed on the time of day if you held a gun to their heads. If one said black, the other just out of meanness would say—" Suddenly he stopped, his mouth half-opened, and thought: Wait a minute, just wait one minute. That robot. They saw eyeball to eyeball on that. *That* they probably even lied themselves blue in the face on. The two of them. Harry Pringle insisting the damn piece of tin attacked him, and Elvira backing him up. The robot, he thought again, the muscles in his face twitching.

"You look like a man who's just sat bare-ass on a hot slab of concrete," the captain said, drinking the dregs of the now-cold coffee and crumbling the Styrofoam cup in his paw.

"It's nothing, nothing at all," Charlie Volchek lied. He'd be goddamned if he'd share the first good idea, the only idea as a matter of fact, that he had had since he discovered Emmett dead at the foot of Harry Pringle's stairs. Besides, the connection between the old woman and the town drunk was tenuous as tissue paper. But even if he did blurt out the weird supposition to Suswicki, the trooper would most likely say: So what? The robot was on the scrap heap, and if it wasn't, tin-can toys don't go around killing people.

One of the younger troopers had knocked and walked in. He and Suswicki were engaged in a chin wag that Charlie Volchek paid no attention to, listening as he was to his own voice and that of the captain inside his head. *The robot*,

Charlie postulated. *What about it?* he heard the trooper say. *And the kid. . . . What kid?* . . . *The kid that built the robot. . . . Ah, com'on, Charlie, you're dreaming. A thirteen-year-old kid, for Christ's sake! . . . But he was pretty pissed off about what Harry Pringle did to his invention. And how Elvira lied to back Harry up. . . .* Besides, Charlie thought suddenly, the dialogue sputtering into silence, there was the little girl. And he recalled again the night at the Conway house when he had told the boy and his mother what had happened to Samantha Pringle. How the boy went bonkers, absolutely freaking out and flying around the living room like a tornado through the state of Kansas.

He found himself at the window looking out at nothing and thinking seriously of Paul—a.k.a. Piggy—Conway, and wondering how many ways to Sunday he, Charlie, could be an idiot. And whether the strain had coddled his brains or if he was just reaching way, way out into the stratosphere. But once the idea of Piggy had settled in, he couldn't dislodge it no matter how hard he tried. Because, when he came right down to it, Piggy was the only person who had a reason to want both Harry and Elvira six feet under ground.

"Listen," the captain was saying, "there's a hit-and-run over the mountain on Route Six. I gotta take a look-see. But I'll be back later this afternoon. The autopsy reports should be in by then."

"Yeah, sure thing," Charlie replied without turning around, the idea of a thirteen-year-old kid being a killer clinging to the inside of his skull. He was working up a case of hives just from contemplating the possibility, and he wanted to sit in his chair, put his feet up, and consider whether or not he was being a horse's ass. "See you later," he added as he listened to the heavy tread of the captain's feet across the floorboards.

When the door slammed shut, he looked around as if seeing his own office for the first time. Slowly he edged toward his chair, and sitting down, thought: Okay, let's take it from the top. Suppose the kid had a motive, where did he go from there?

24

In the week following the murders, Piggy maundered about in shock. Even quiescent, Bee had had more life, more animation than he did. He picked up his feet and put them down, spoke when queried by Jeannie or one of his teachers, ate whatever was served to him at meals, and went to bed at the prescribed time. Only he didn't sleep. He'd lie awake staring sightlessly into the night, trying to click off his mind, to sweep up the thoughts marching relentlessly through his head and lock them in darkness at least until dawn. But it was hopeless. If he slipped for a few seconds into unconsciousness, the thoughts, fears, worries, transposed themselves into bad dreams that haunted his sleep.

He knew he had his mother on the thin edge, that she watched him as though he were a volatile experiment and she was waiting for the miscalculation that would engender an explosion. The half-moons beneath her eyes darkened and her flesh clung against the bone, sharpening the lines and angles of her face. She appeared much as she had done during the worst of those times with his father and after his mistake, and Piggy was anguished. He wanted not to give her pain, to make up somehow for all the unhappiness she had suffered in Boston. But what could he say? Nothing that wouldn't wound her more. There were no explanations any longer that would put it all right. There was no way out of the hole he had tumbled into, no way to grapple back up and eventually be free.

At Mason he slipped from class to class like a phantom, the tentative acceptance he had won from the other kids with

262

BeeBee's death having eroded away. He hadn't taken advantage of their sympathy and insinuated himself into a group. And now it was meaningless to seek a place for himself and try to belong, even if he had been able. He was standing at the other side of a pane of glass, and if he had reached out—if he had had the resources to do so—he could only have come up against an invisible wall.

He was so isolated and alone that he sometimes thought he could have been abandoned on the moon and wouldn't have felt any less bereft. Even Slime, the few days he actually attended school, was a stranger. He shied like a skittish horse from any encounter with Pig.

A longing for his father rippled under Piggy's skin, though he knew that was ridiculous. Tony had been even less forgiving than his mother about Piggy's mistake. What, therefore, would he think of Sam? Still, he found himself late one night, after Jeannie had gone up to bed, at the phone in the kitchen. His heart pounding painfully, he told himself that there was no way Tony would be in the office so late. That he was at Julia's, and Piggy didn't know where that was. And even if by some miracle he got Tony on the phone, his father wouldn't listen. Or if he did, not believe him one bit.

Supposing, Piggy thought, tightly gripping the receiver in his sweaty hand, he does take it all in. What could his father do? There was no saving him or Sam. Not even if Tony came to the rescue and spirited them away to South America.

But in spite of common sense, Piggy had an aching need to hear his father's voice, to bridge the distance. So with a shaky hand he dialed the number and chewed on his lower lip while it rang and rang. There, he thought, as the phone shrilled three, four, five times, leaving him feeling more adrift and alone.

And then he heard his father's voice, painfully clear on the other end. Piggy was so shattered he almost dropped the receiver. *Daddy!* he shrieked inside his skull. *Daddy!* But his lips wouldn't move. The words were glued to his tongue.

"Hello, hello," Tony said in Boston. But still Piggy couldn't speak. Leaning against the wall, he held on, almost not breathing, until Tony hung up. Maybe, he thought, listening now to emptiness, I could write him a letter. Yes, maybe I could do that.

He replaced the receiver and wearily went up to bed. He didn't have the energy to think about a letter at that moment. But the next day when he thought it over, he decided he was dumb. He imagined his father in Boston living a normal life and reading a letter that arrived one day in the mail saying everything was just fine. The only letter he could write to his father would be a fairy tale. As he said to Sam, "I don't know what would be worse, if he'd believe me or if he wouldn't." The lie that life was going swimmingly, he meant. He realized there wasn't the smallest chance of telling his father the truth. Or telling anybody. Yet, how could he continue to keep people from finding out?

If he worried about what would happen to him, how he'd explain this new mistake when he already had the terrible dark stain of Bertram Lennard in his past, he worried much more about Sam. It wasn't, he told himself when he'd feed her, trying to entice her to eat with any delicacy he could think of, like pizza or Cheez Whiz, or when he'd carefully, gently, draw the hairbrush through the long hair, her fault for not being dead and buried. She was the innocent victim of his unhappiness just as she had been of Harry Pringle's drunken rage. Poor Sam, he'd think, time and again squinting his eyes so that the mushed lifelessness of her ruined face fuzzed and took on the shape, the contours, the loveliness of that face he achingly remembered from before.

You're looney tunes, Pig, he'd say to himself after he'd wretchedly trudge down from the attic late at night, having spent an hour or so in semi-gloom, the only illumination the hazy glow from the candles, talking to Sam. Talking nonstop. Telling her about Boston, about Tony, about baby things, like the time he was six or so and had gotten separated from Jeannie and Tony in Cambridge. He'd stood right in front of The Coop, tears leaking from his eyes, feeling lost and abandoned until both his parents swooped down on him out of nowhere, yelling with worry and relief. He'd even remembered how the towering frozen yogurt—the treat they'd given him because he had finally been found—tasted that day.

It was love he was attempting in his fumbling, thirteen-year-old fashion to explain to Sam. He could roll back his formidable memory and hear again with chilling exactness the anguish when she mentioned her mother, and her terror of the drunken, abusive, and finally murderous Harry. He didn't know it was love, however. He just couldn't stand her hurting so much, *then* as much as *now* when he wasn't even certain she felt anything at all.

Whatever else Sam had become, she was, he told himself repeatedly, mumbling the fact over and over in a litany, one of the greatest scientific achievements ever. In his constant muddle of confusion, Piggy tried to hold on to that. But when he did think of Sam as an experiment, he simply felt more guilt gnawing at the lining of his stomach. *She's Sam!* he'd cry out silently, not a gerbil in a lab.

"What are you mumbling about?" Jeannie'd ask when Piggy's conversation with himself spilled from the privacy of his head into his mouth and almost into words.

"Nothing! Nothing!" he'd yelp, drawn up short, his redrimmed eyes wide with fright. He worried incessantly that he would babble out the whole business in his sleep one night, that Jeannie standing by his bed in her usual fret of motherhood, would hear each and every detail.

He agonized and stung with pain at the notion of hurting his mother any more than he had already done. In anguish one Saturday morning at the imagined horror his mother would display if she ever found out, he flung himself into her arms almost toppling her and wailed, "Oh Mom, I love you!"

"Whoa, Paul, what have I done to get all this affection?" she asked. But her arms tightened around his back, and her face when he peered up at her was flushed with tenderness and pleasure.

But the sight of Jeannie smiling, which she so seldom did since they'd come to Welling, made the churning in his belly worse. "I'll do the errands, Mom. All that Saturday stuff you hate so," he cried, back-pedaling out of her embrace. Her arms dropped to her sides.

"Do you feel all right?"

"Of course I do," he snapped. "I just want to be helpful."

"Mine not to reason why," she laughed, though her eyes were glazed with a film of apprehension. "But if you're sure. . . ." And she sent Pig up to Main Street and the hardware store where he didn't really want to go at all. But then about the only thing he would have relished doing was to crawl into bed and sleep a good part of the future away.

Maybe, he reasoned, when he had climbed the hill, a chill north wind stirring his hair and insinuating itself under the

collar of his jacket, I'll see Slime and we can look at the
comics in Corney's or get a Coke at The Ice Cream Hut.
Maybe I'll bump into Slime and we can get my kite and fly it
on the little hill just past the garbage dump. Sure, stupid, he
said to himself, see if Slime doesn't break into a gallop and
run the other way. Just as Pig wanted Sam-before, a Sam
magically restored, he wanted Slime, his friend, returned
intact. Slime being funny with his lightbulb jokes, Slime
energetic and talkative instead of the pale, silent Slime who
avoided Piggy.

Going left on Main Piggy saw the hardware sign in the next
block and lowered his head, keeping his gaze locked on his
sneakers as he plodded along the sidewalk. He could sense
Welling throbbing with anxiety, suspecting—as almost everyone did—that a psychopath was on the loose. From the
corner of his eye Piggy saw one black state trooper car and
then another cruising by. He almost bumped full tilt into a
gray-uniformed figure coming out of Toomy's.

Bolting, he scuttled half a block and threw himself against
the plate glass of Woolworth's. When he had caught his
breath, and stilled the *thump, thump* in his chest, he glanced
down at a rainbow display of ribbons and barrettes, a flowing,
colorful stream of silky scarves.

He was jolted with a vision of Sam's hair pulled back in a
pony tail and tied with one of the wide red ribbons or maybe
a flowered yellow and green scarf. He saw her broad smile of
delight; heard her soft coo of pleasure. You really are a
dunce, he immediately thought, but found himself pushing
through the door anyway. The desire to do something nice
for Sam, to at least try and make her happy, overrode his
intelligence. One part of him could bellow loud and long,
nothing's going to make her happy anymore, while the other
Piggy would only snap, *who says so!*

Piggy glided from the counter with ribbons and scarves to
the one with hair ornaments, glancing about now and then to
be sure that fat, powdery Mrs. Donovan wasn't about to
materialize and attack him. He finally narrowed his choice to
the red ribbon or a dazzling pair of butterfly barrettes.

His hand was actually reaching for the butterflies when the
shimmering memory of Sam-now drifted before his eyes. He
had been so overcome by wanting to please her, that he'd
forgotten the ravaged side of her head. Computer ribbons

dripped from her skull, not ribbons of silk. Even with brushing her hair forward, with draping it over her ear, he wasn't able to hide the damage. Where would the butterflies go? Swallowing, he swept around to the other counter and scooped up a cellophane packet of pre-cut red ribbon. He'd tie her still long and golden hair back with it in a floppy bow, and then maybe, just maybe, if she stood at an angle, if the light was faded, she'd be Sam-before.

Back out on Main Street, the small paper bag tucked into his jacket pocket, he continued on his way to Sullivan's hardware. Lulled into an uneasy calm, he was suddenly shaking at the sight of Charlie Volchek's blue-and-white sliding by the cars parked along the curb. When Piggy arrived at the corner and had to wait for the light, he sneaked a quick look sideways and caught the chief owlishly scrutinizing him. They locked onto one another until the signal went to green and the blue-and-white pulled away.

Everywhere that he turned, Piggy thought, there was Charlie Volchek in his car. The police chief seemed to patrol River Street as though it were the demarcation line of a war zone. Whenever Piggy glanced out one of the front windows, there would be the police car like a ghost ship gliding along, Charlie Volchek's quizzical face turned toward him.

He'd come across him also in Welling East when school was out, at the bottom of the short hill, or in the blue-and-white crawling slowly over Main Bridge. And sometimes the police car would be idling in one of the drives when Piggy cut across the campus between classes, the chief crouched behind the windshield, as stoic as a large stone Buddha.

The afternoon that Piggy dragged the shopping cart up to the laundromat to do the wash, he saw Charlie Volchek following him and park at the meter. Through three wash cycles and four dries, the chief never stirred. Piggy sat frozen with his back to the plate glass and attempted to read *War and Peace*, but the letters made no sense. They scrambled themselves on the pages like a search-and-find puzzle, and worry fogged his vision. He knew that Charlie Volchek was staring straight across the sidewalk, through Piggy's sweatshirt, piercing flesh and bones, right into his heart. He fantasized that even from so far away, the chief could smell his fear, hear it bubbling in his lungs like a severe case of pneumonia; that he *knew*.

Knew what? he asked himself, bending his head over the book, trying to trudge a path through the mire of Napoleon's battlefields.

There wasn't a possibility that Charlie Volchek could know anything, Piggy reasoned, but that didn't lessen his fright. He clung to the idea that since he had done the unbelievable, no one would believe he had, even if they ran smack into Sam. She wasn't the sort of phenomenon a person might even begin to suspect. Still his stomach performed somersaults, and when he yanked the cart behind him out of the laundromat and Charlie Volchek beckoned him over to the blue-and-white with a jerk of his grizzled head, Piggy grew faint with dizziness. Colored spots danced before his eyes and he saw himself collapsing on the sidewalk, the clean laundry spilling all over the street.

"Hey, kid, how you doing?" Charlie Volchek asked with a rubbery smile below dark, suspicious eyes.

"Okay," Piggy mumbled, panic goading him to run. But he and the chief were eyeballing one another so intently it was as though a steel cable stretched taut between them.

"Build a new robot yet?"

"No, sir."

"Then what've you been doing with your time?" Charlie Volchek inquired.

He's only being friendly . . . or maybe pretending to be. Piggy couldn't tell which. He tried not to imagine Charlie Volchek saying things he didn't mean, and kept his answers monosyllabic. He was twitchy to escape, to fly down Main Street, the shopping cart rattling behind him, to the hill, then River Street and home, where he'd hide in bed—or better yet, under it—until so much time had passed that the police chief would have forgotten his name.

They both shortly ran out of things to say—or rather questions to be asked and answers grudgingly given—but remained linked to each other, for a few minutes longer, as if Charlie Volchek was reluctant to give him up, and Piggy, for his part, hadn't the energy, the strength to break loose. Then, at last, just at the instant when it seemed they'd be joined forever in the gathering dusk, the chief sighed, saying he'd see him around. And rolling up the window, Charlie Volchek drove off, leaving Piggy, alone on the sidewalk, half-crazed with fright.

Now, hurtling himself into the temporary sanctuary of the hardware store, he wanted to believe that the blue-and-white hadn't turned at the end of Main and wasn't rolling back up the street, that Charlie Volchek wasn't in the driver's seat. He longed to think that moments from now when he was forced once again onto the sidewalk the chief wouldn't be there waiting, that the police car wouldn't slowly, but oh so definitely, follow him all the way home.

25

For at least an hour that Saturday afternoon Piggy hid behind the curtain of his bedroom window and watched as Charlie Volchek prowled by. The blue-and-white slowly went from one end of River Street to the other and then back. Minutes passed when Piggy, relieved, thought the chief had finally gone off to ticket somebody for double parking. But then, just like a bad penny—as his grandmother used to say—the police car would turn up. It had Piggy's nerves singing operatic arias. He felt as trapped as a polar bear in a cage with bars and precious little room to maneuver.

Got to move her somewhere, he kept thinking. The idea that he had to find another place for Sam, a place safe from Charlie Volchek who might decide to get a search warrant and come investigating, gave Pig a headache. Which only intensified the dull ache he already had, the spasm that came from worrying why the police chief was watching him all the time. Paranoia, nothing more, he tried to believe, but that explanation wasn't convincing. Charlie Volchek really was stuck to him like a second skin.

There's nothing he can prove, Piggy whispered, the curtain

clutched tightly in his fist. But everything hung by a hair. If Slime flipped out and began telling. . . . Piggy shuddered and in his convulsion almost yanked the curtain right off the rod. Or if he got into the house and stumbled over Sam. . . . This time there was a definite tear in the fabric, and guiltily he dropped the curtain and wrung his hands.

"What do you want for dinner?" he heard his mother call from below.

Food! Yuck! He felt anything but hungry.

Don't care, he was about to shout back, but an indefinite reply might bring his mother right up into his room. A glance in the mirror revealed a face the color of pea soup and daubed with sweat.

He yanked the door open and shouted, "Spaghetti!"

"Okay," she yelled back.

He closed the door and slumping against it, let himself drop to the floor. He sat with a thud and drew his legs up against his chest.

Tonight, he decided, thinking furiously, after Mom's asleep, I'll get Sam out of here. But to where?

There had to be a vacant house where he could secret her. A shed maybe. An old, unused garage. The geography of Welling swam in his memory, the streets muddy as if washed by rain. He rolled the blocks up in his mind one by one, rolled them across the screen of his total recall and stopped at the sight of a boarded-up house near the top of the town, not far from the big Catholic church.

Maybe he could make a home for Sam with blankets and candles between those four walls. He could buy some posters and tack them in her room. That way she'd even have something nice to look at. And every night when Welling was shrouded in blankets of sleep, he'd climb the hill to see her. To take care of her. He'd bring her food and something to drink. They could talk quietly without fear of discovery—or rather he could talk and she could listen.

Getting Sam out of the attic, away from his mother, to a new place where Charlie Volchek would never think of looking, was a really smart idea. Piggy felt his fear diminishing, his energy returning in waves as the plan formed, grew more distinct. A home for Sam . . . for us, he couldn't help thinking. And he fantasized making it liveable, pretty, like a colored picture in one of Jeannie's magazines. Instantaneously he created a whole new life for Sam, for himself too, and in that fiction she began with his care and concern, with his increased knowledge of how to make her better, to meta-morphose into Sam-before.

No, no! he tried to tell himself, but the illusion was much too tempting. His intelligence was elbowed aside by what he longed to be true, by what he needed, by the image of poor Sam, ravaged and unhappy, as against the Sam who had gracefully floated across the back yard during their games.

I'll wash her up, make her pretty, then tie back her hair with the new ribbon, he thought. That way she'll be all nice and clean when we move.

He was already at the attic door, the key in the lock, when Jeannie called, "We're out of grated cheese. Do you abso-lutely have to have it?"

"Oh Mom," he wailed, going to the banister and leaning over, "you know I like spaghetti on my cheese!"

"Okay," she conceded, "I'll drive up to the A&P and get some. As long as I'm going, what about some garlic bread?"

"Terrific! I love garlic bread!"

"Anything for you, my friend."

"Let's have some salad too, Mom. We can't forget our greens. And maybe something special for dessert." If she stayed away long enough he could give Sam a real bath. Bring her downstairs and put her in the tub. Throw in Jeannie's bubble stuff and all that sweet-smelling bath oil. Finally he'd be able to scrub all the crud off her, to perhaps even get rid of her rancid odor.

The second he heard Jeannie go out the door, Piggy was in the bathroom running the water. He got the temperature just right, hurled a whole jar of bubble bath granules under the gushing stream, and then hurried upstairs for Sam.

"Listen," he said, bursting in on her, "I've made us all sorts of plans. Lots of nice things, Sam," he said, hustling her to her feet and out of the attic. Impatiently he escorted her down the steps babbling about her bath, about the new home he was planning. And then shyly, he added, "And I got you a surprise, Sam. But that will have to wait until you're all cleaned up."

The taut face that was growing more leathery with time, the skin which was beginning to have the same texture as one of Jeannie's pocketbooks, rippled and twitched. Staring at her mesmerized, Pig's heart leapt. She was smiling! She was definitely smiling!

He was so soggy with emotion, tears prickled his eyes. He was afraid he was going to break right down in the upstairs hall and burst into sobs. But he chastized himself for being unscientific, for being a sentimental baby and only grimaced at her in return.

"Com'on," he said sternly, "we don't have all day." He felt strangely like he thought his father must have when he'd mobilize them for an outing. Very firm and definite. The connection was reassuring as he took Sam into the bathroom.

The water was curtained by white puff clouds of foam. "Doesn't that look nice, Sam?" he asked, carefully tugging the sweatshirt over her head. She stood rigid as a lamppost while Pig, embarrassed, pulled down the pants. He averted his eyes, but then he couldn't get them over the ratty sneakers. He had to sit her on the toilet seat. Kneeling, he removed the sneakers, the socks, and yanked the sweatpants free. It would really be something if he could dress her up in new clothes, in good jeans and maybe a heavy pull-over. He had, however, nothing to fit her, and he didn't want to take anything else of Jeannie's. Not only was borrowing his mother's belongings without asking her wrong, she might miss a sweater.

"Okay, into the bath, Sam," he instructed, his gaze directed to the left of her right ear. It made him uncomfortable to have Sam in front of him without any clothes, and he sighed with relief when he had struggled her over the side of the tub. She sank beneath the suds until only her head was visible.

"I bet that feels real good. And warm. My grandma used to say that there's nothing like a hot bath to work out all the kinks. Right, Sam?" he said as he pushed up his sleeves.

Softly, gently, as though her parts were as fragile as papier mâché, he bathed her with a wash cloth and Ivory soap. He tried to persuade her to lift her legs, but either she didn't understand him or the impulse stubbornly refused to travel from her brain, from Bee's computer, to her hips. He had to plunge into the water and raise one leg at a time.

He was especially solicitous of the mashed toes where the newly formed scar tissue was tender and frail. Still, flesh and skin were growing over the exposed bones, which meant that her body had the ability to heal itself. And if her toes could do that, maybe her brain could also. No, he reminded himself emphatically, destroyed brain cells never rejuvenate. He'd discovered that fact from all his reading. But he was too happy right then in the steamy bathroom with a contented Sam muffled in suds to dwell on what was or wasn't going on in her cranium. At that moment it was enough to have Sam as she was, alive even if not perfect.

He swabbed at her face, her neck, and under her chin. "Do you think you can do the rest?" he asked, not wanting to paw around on the hidden Sam which was under the bubbles. She gazed at him dully. No *gaaaa*, no anything. He drew a deep breath and said, "Please try, Sam." But she didn't reply. Piggy wasn't sure—he never really was—if she heard him; or if she was just being stubborn. The old Sam was most often agreeable, but along with all her physical changes there were definite alterations in her personality. "Well . . . if you don't want to be absolutely spic and span," he said, hoping the stern tone would galvanize her into motion.

When it was obvious that Sam was going to sit as immobile as a piece of furniture, Pig sighed and bent her forward as he scrubbed her back. Leaning her again against the porcelain, he swabbed awkwardly at her chest, but that made him so nervous that he dropped the washcloth, letting it sink to the vicinity of her lap, and said, "I think that's enough, Sam." What he hadn't thought of, however, was how to get the soap off her. Lacy sleeves of foam dripped from her arms when he raised them. If he didn't rinse her, she'd be as sticky as chewing gum.

Piggy sat back on his haunches, thinking. If he didn't hurry and get her out of the tub, dried and powdered, reclothed and into the attic, his mother would be home. She just might stay downstairs cooking up spaghetti sauce or chopping vegetables for salad. But then again, she suspected him of all sorts of stuff, and she did worry, so she might come upstairs simply to check on him. He had locked the door, but she was capable of waiting out in the hall until he emerged. He shuddered, and more loudly than he'd intended snapped, "Let's move it, Sam." Only it wasn't Sam's fault that she didn't splash about freeing herself from the suds.

He groaned and thought suddenly of the shower. All he had to do was close the curtains, pull the plug, and let the water cascade over her. He was ready to throw the lever which would send the water out of the shower head when he remembered her wires. Aaah! I could have ruined her! He hadn't the faintest idea what would happen if her wires got soaked, but it couldn't be good. Hastily he snagged Jeannie's shower cap and yanked it over Sam's head. The cap was too big and a splash of roses slid down to her eyebrows.

By the time he heard the front door slam Sam was out of the tub standing on the mat and wrapped in a large, fuzzy pink towel. Jeannie yelled up something and Piggy fled to the top of the stairs. "Back so soon, Mom?" he called down.

"Soon? I've been gone ages," she said. "What have you been up to?" she asked, her voice edged with suspicion.

"Nothing, Mom."

"Well, com'on down and help me make dinner."

"I have to work on an experiment," he improvised, watching her hang up her coat and retrieve the sack of groceries from the hall table. She stared up at him and he presented her with an expression he hoped looked innocent. "It's a new idea I have, Mom. But I promise to stop for dinner. Okay?"

"I guess so," she replied. "But you have to quit the minute I call you."

"Promise. Besides, by that time I'll be starving. Mmmmm, spaghetti, I can't wait," he said, feeling idiotic. Deliberately he was making himself into a real kid, a little kid, for Jeannie's benefit. She fretted less about him when he appeared babyish. Piggy hated that, disliked acting like an infant, but consoled himself that it was as much for his mother's peace of mind as for his own purposes.

When she drifted off to the kitchen he gathered up Sam, her clothes, Jeannie's box of Chanel dusting powder, the hair dryer, a brush, and the new ribbon and retreated to the attic.

It really was a new Sam he dried and powdered and dressed under the pallid glow of the hanging bulb. He convinced himself that she smelled if not sweetly at least not like something left to rot in the sun. And if her skin wasn't as smooth as the silk of Jeannie's favorite shirt, nor pink and shiny, at least she was clean.

There was an outlet by the attic door and after he had dressed her, he plugged in the dryer and directed a warm gust of air at the wet ends of her hair.

"Now," he said, finished at last, "for your present." He

pulled the ribbon loose from the cellophane and draped it over her fingers. "Isn't it a pretty color, Sam? You always loved red."

"Gaaaaa," she said finally, and then "gaaaaa," again.

Piggy smiled broadly and hopped about on one foot. He knew he was blushing. "It's something," he said, and then quickly, "let me tie it in your hair."

He brushed the long strands to the back of her head and lifting her hair onto the ribbon, made a large bow.

"Oh Sam," he said, stepping away and squinting, "you look great." Which she did if he remained at a distance, if he didn't look too closely, if he took his glasses off. And if she stayed in the shadows, out of the light. There were so many "ifs" necessary to sustain the illusion, but Piggy didn't care. All-in-all the last hour had been wonderful. For a short while there had been a hiatus in the nightmare which was Pig's life—Sam's too. One hour, during which he had not thought about the deaths or of Charlie Volchek, and he held on to the memory. He was even near to being happy when he went downstairs for dinner.

Piggy's euphoria lasted through most of Saturday evening. If his high spirits made his mother arch her brows, he didn't notice. For the first time since he had brought Sam back from the grave—or rather out of Toomy's deep freeze and up and walking—he had a glimmer of hope. That his optimism wasn't triggered by anything substantial didn't deter him from dreaming. He knew that all great scientific breakthroughs were based on the three "D"s: the dream, the desire, and gritty determination. So until "News At Eleven," he was content. The future shimmered in mist, but still seemed less of a miasma than it had appeared earlier in the day when his only thoughts had been hinged to Charlie Volchek and discovery. Silly, he thought, there's no reason the chief ever had to find out. Certainly not once he resettled Sam in the old untenanted house on Delaney Street. But it was just the idea of moving Sam which nudged him off his cloud, and started Pig down the long drop into fear and despair.

Once Jeannie was asleep he'd have to get Sam through the chilly streets to the far end of Welling and into her new home. The hours—filled with unknown terrors and confusion—waited ahead in the night. What if. . . . But his mother was

already kissing his cheek and suggesting it was time for bed.
He tried to convince her that his very life depended on
seeing the upcoming "Creature-Feature."

"Oh, Paul, I wish you wouldn't," she said, and reached out
to ruffle his hair. But his good mood was rapidly disintegrating and he jerked away. "You'll have bad dreams," she added,
shoving her hands into the pockets of her dress.

"Won't," he snapped.

"Paul. . . ."

He wailed, "Mom, please! I won't have a nightmare, and if
I do I'll handle it."

"Oh God, do what you want!" she cried. But moments
later, she called out, her voice neutral and low-key, "Wake
me if you need me."

Itchy with anxiety, Piggy sat biting his nails until trucks
piled high with pods were driving into San Francisco and
Kevin McCarthy was powerless to stop them. His mother
most certainly was sleeping, and when he crept past her
room there was nothing but darkness showing beneath the
door. Still he went clumsily on tiptoes up to the attic and
down again with Sam and a large brown shopping bag. He
had her blanket, the candles, a hairbrush, a packet of Oreos,
three cans of ravioli, a can opener and a spoon. At the last
minute he remembered to take a large box of kitchen matches
and a roll of paper towels.

The night was heavy with frost and when Piggy exhaled he
could see icy aureoles of breath. She'll freeze, he thought,
thinking of Sam in her sweatshirt and sweatpants, socks and
sneakers. Pulling her back into the front hall, he burrowed
through the closest, desperate for something to cover her
with. All the way to one side he found a pea coat which
Jeannie seldom wore. He buttoned Sam into it, yanking the
collar high about her neck. "There now," he whispered, as
they sneaked outside, "isn't that better."

Welling was drowsing in silence, buried in darkness except
for isolated puddles of streetlamp light and the occasional
bleary glow of a lit window.

Sam lurched like a tank off its track, but by tugging and
cajoling Piggy got her up the hill to Main Street. From one
end to the other there was empty space, the only vague sign
of life the traffic signal in the next block clicking red then
green. A piece of cake, Piggy thought, wiping his sweaty

brow. He hustled Sam across the river of brightness and into
the comforting dark alongside Klein's Clothing. He suddenly
remembered that this was the path he and Slime had traveled
with her from Toomy's, with Sam dead then, an unresisting
passenger on the wagon. That was only weeks before, but
Pig's world had changed as radically as though Welling had
been hit in a nuclear attack.

They continued their climb up the flank of Welling, Piggy
puffing, but Sam oblivious to the steep hills, to the wind
which made Pig's ears sting. He thought it was wonderful
that she had so much endurance, that the once delicate little
girl was now as flinty and strong as Bee had been. But he
fretted at the same time, because people, living people,
should have to stop and catch their breaths, should feel
twitches in their leg muscles and an occasional stitch in their
sides. Well, maybe she does, only she can't say, he thought
as he gripped her arm tightly and guided her to Delaney
Street.

Halfway down on the left was the stony bulk of St. Anthony's.

They slipped down a black corridor beneath the naked
elms and though a trembling Piggy whispered over and
over—to himself as much as to Sam—that things were going
to be fine, he heard the roar of the train. It was the tunnel
again and at his back he felt the heat like fiery dragon's
breath. Any moment now he expected to be struck and
imagined the sickening pain of the impact.

"Hurry, Sam, hurry!" he cried, louder than he intended,
breaking into a trot. He pulled her at his side but she was as
awkward as a leash-shy puppy. The shopping bag banged
against his leg, and he stumbled, but he didn't stop. Fear was
unfurling in his insides. He wanted to believe he was halluci-
nating, but couldn't. *All life is a dream*, he had once read
somewhere. But even if it was a dream, or more precisely a
nightmare, he still hurt like blazes.

With a sigh of relief Piggy saw the deserted house on their
left. It was almost at the end of the street, just two houses
away from the corner where Delaney curved. Way in the
distance Pig could just make out the stone arches of the big
Catholic cemetery. Oh Sam! he wailed inside his head, and
knew no matter what, there would be nothing worse than her
in one of those small cramped graves. Six feet down and
rotting. He shuddered and would have stopped right then

and hugged her protectively if he didn't think the train was rushing behind them somewhere.

He scrambled with her up a short flight of crumbling stone steps and stood in the narrow yard in the bleak angular shadow of the house. The front door was boarded closed, so were the two front windows.

Pig left Sam in a dark corner of the porch and circled the house. It wasn't as large as it appeared from the street, and though definitely creaky, not as derelict either. Sturdy, as a matter of fact, and sealed up tight. All the windows were hidden behind wide planks of wood, the back door too.

Dunce! he swore as he circled the house a second time, you should have found a way inside before you dragged Sam up here. He fumbled for some bright idea, but this wasn't a matter of intelligence. What was needed was brawn rather than brains—brawn and a crowbar. It seemed unlikely that he could pry one of the boards loose with his bare hands, and certainly not without a splintering noise which would rupture the night. In a snap of the fingers Charlie Volchek's blue-and-white would be out front and Pig would be trapped in the glare of the car's all-seeing spotlight.

The small window to the cellar was also covered with a thick plank; but if he sat on the ground and braced his feet against the shingles, and yanked. . . . Maybe. He looked over his shoulder at the next house, only twenty feet away. It was dark and with luck, everyone inside was sleeping.

Piggy dropped down and wiggled his fingers between the board and the window frame. He tugged, but the wood wasn't giving.

It took six Herculean struggles with the board before the nails began to loosen. The gap widened.

When his heart stopped galloping, he braced his feet again and muttered, "Heave!" In one savage tug that had the muscles in his arms and shoulders shrieking, the wood popped free. But the ripping sound slashed through the stillness just as he had feared. Piggy, seriously frightened, scrambled around the back and hurled himself into the protective darkness near the porch.

No one heard! They're all sleeping. But a light came on in a second floor window of the neighboring house. The shade rolled up, and then the window opened. A thick, woolly head thrust out over the sill. A quiver of panic shot through Pig's stomach when a loud masculine voice growled, "Who's out there? That you kids?"

Piggy crept around the other side of the porch as the voice continued to promise painful punishments. He wanted to reach Sam, to huddle beside her until the window slammed shut and the irate neighbor returned to dreaming.

When he finally crawled up onto the porch, he hissed, "Sam! Sam, it's okay!" She wasn't moving. He had told her to stay, not to stir so much as an inch, and that was what she was obediently doing.

He padded to the corner and hissed "Sam!" again, but even in the darkness he could see she wasn't there. She hadn't really disappeared! She wouldn't! But he tiptoed around the entire porch and all that was there was the shopping bag. She was gone again.

The whole of Welling spread out before him like a dark sea, and Sam, a small cork, was bobbing in it somewhere. He was terrified that unless she returned of her own free will—as she had before—he wouldn't find her. But where would she go, to the house on River Street? He wanted to weep with rage and unhappiness and that awful fear which nibbled away at his insides.

The growler from next door had stopped sending out threats into the dark, and Piggy stood in silence, shaking. He had to do something, only he didn't know what.

After wasted minutes spent in indecision, he jumped the steps and fled to the sidewalk. Frantically he rushed up and down Delaney Street, peering sightlessly into the darkness. He searched under the trees and scoured the yards. He even went flying through the cemetery, running around the gravestones. An owl hooted from the top of one of the trees and he almost fell dead in his tracks. But he thought of Sam, lost and bewildered, and he found the courage to go on. An hour might have passed, or even an hour after that. Time was as runny as rain water.

When he was drenched with sweat right through to his down jacket, when he was so weary he wanted to throw himself into a level-filled gutter and dream away all his aches, when he saw a horrible future that starred Sam in a laboratory cage like a white rat and himself in a padded cell, he decided to go home. To climb into his own bed and just hope she'd find her way back. Like a stray dog or a prowling cat.

He couldn't help crying as he dragged himself along Delaney Street. He rubbed his eyes with his fists, and stopped before the church to clean his smeared lenses.

The church! Oh no, Sam, you wouldn't go in there!

But he had to look anyway. Reluctantly he climbed the stairs. The door was slightly ajar and Piggy slid inside. He was assailed by the faint odor of incense as he squinted, trying to pick out a small, lurching little girl in all the gloomy obscurity. But nothing wandered in the vast emptiness.

At the far end, just to the sides of the altar were two faint lights; another was behind it. But the pallid yellow faded into gray at the middle of the church and the rear pews were all but invisible in the dark. Slowly Pig crept along the side aisle and searched for Sam. He crawled over the pews and finally, by a circuitous route reached the altar.

There were few places, no place really, where Sam would have hidden herself, and he was wasting precious time. Time to do what, he wondered, but fear rushed him back down the aisle. It was just when he reached the font that he saw the high wooden booth. He knew it was the confessional and that you crept inside one half to reveal your sins to the hidden priest in the other part. It was too late for anyone to be in there, but he could have sworn he saw the drapery that covered the openings sway. All at once the empty church seemed sinister. A cold chill lodged in his spine and he wanted to bolt out the doors, to run along the Welling streets until he was exhausted. What he didn't want to do was inch nearer the confessional where the curtain was now wafting agitatedly from an invisible breeze. But that's what he was doing, his sneakers whispering along the stone floor. His throat was closing up on him. An iron band was cincturing his windpipe. He was going to suffocate with fear as his hand stretched out and his fingertips caressed the rough, heavy material.

In one jerk he yanked aside the curtain, and a terrible screech filled his mouth, boiled through his head, and burst out in a silent scream as Bertram Lennard, his eyes blazing, his hair tendrils of orangy fire, his arms and hands burnt into blackened crisps, threw himself out of the booth and fell into Piggy's arms.

The crack of his skull against the stone brought on an avalanche of darkness, and Piggy slid into it effortlessly and

not entirely against his will. Enough! he thought with the last
tattered edge of consciousness, and wasn't even aware of his
arms and legs going loose as he gave himself up to oblivion.

Something cold was fluttering about his face, slapping softly
against his cheek. He tried to shrug it away, to drop back
down into the deep pit of sleep. But his back hurt, and there
was a definite stabbing pain in his left hip. He was chilled to
the marrow and he shifted about, searching for the quilt to
pull over him. His hands flapped in the air and came down
on something hard and even colder than he was. Stone. Flat,
hard stone, not the soft warmth of his bed.

The lights blinked on in Piggy's consciousness and he groaned.
He opened his eyes.

"Gaaaaa," Sam said, her face inches from his. He caught
the sour aroma of her breath, but didn't even turn his head.
He was so happy to see her! She patted at him with her hand,
from his hair to his shoulder. "Gaaaaa," she crooned again.

It was Sam, he realized even in the lingering fog, who had
been inside the confessional and not a dead Bertram still on
fire. Sam who had hurled herself into his embrace.

"Oh Sam," he said, tearfully, "I'm so sorry!"

Clumsily her hand continued to pat him, and when it
crossed his mouth involuntarily his lips pursed and he kissed
her palm. He felt foolish and sad and so embarrassed he
blustered, "Help me up."

He took her hand and awkwardly scrambled to his feet.
The church tilted around him, and he swayed in dizziness.
But Sam kept him erect, and when he could focus, he said,
"Let's go home."

Together they went out into the quiet street, to a slumbering Welling. And together they made a return trek, this time
down the hills. Home, Pig had said, and that was where they
were heading. It wasn't possible to stash her in some strange
place, nor would it have been even if he had gotten inside. At
the last moment, he realized now, he would have gotten cold
feet. Because she'd be too far away, like a kid sent off to
school in California. And he really didn't want that. He
needed her nearby. As irrational as it was, Piggy—the child
of reason—preferred Sam in the attic. She was, after all, his
friend, as well as his responsibility.

"We'll work it out, Sam," he promised as they descended

to River Street, hand in hand. Just on the horizon dawn was preparing to break.

With a deep sigh right from his belly, Piggy brought Sam back into the house. Again he locked her in the attic, and wearily went to his room. His bones had been ground to dust, and he felt achy, sick. Only a few hours, he knew, lying still dressed across the bedspread, until he once more had to be up and moving.

He was half asleep when he remembered the shopping bag. Oh no! he wailed. He had left it on the porch, or in the church, or maybe dropped it somewhere on Delaney Street. But he couldn't go back for it. There were limits to his strength. In a second, no more, he had lumbered into sleep, taking with him the memory of Sam-before rather than Sam as she was now.

26

Jeannie stayed later and later at Mason these days, not wanting to return to the house on River Street. It was home because she and Piggy lived here, but it wasn't really home at all. It smelled worse and worse as time passed, as though something disgusting was rotting in the walls. Then there were the deaths, next door and across the street. The house seemed to Jeannie to be in the middle of a battleground. Given a choice, she would have fled it and moved into another place. But the house was rented for the year, and to give it up would mean paying out the lease, which she couldn't afford.

Most afternoons Piggy left school long before she did, walking home alone. She sensed that his friendship with

Slime was faltering, but when she asked what the problem was, he shut her out. That blank look which always made her swallow hard would slip over his face, and she backed off the question at once.

It was nearing six and dark as midnight when she hefted the bag of groceries and the flowers on her hip and unlocked the door. The house was quiet, but the lights were on, so Piggy was inside somewhere. Probably in the attic, she thought, walking through the kitchen and dropping the bags on the table before she went to hang up her coat. In the attic cooking up some ghastly concoction, she shuddered. Maybe it was one of his brews which made the house smell so foul.

She yelled out, "Paul! I'm home." But there was no response. She considered going to look for him, then decided not to. He's doing something perfectly ordinary, maybe even taking a nap, she forced herself to believe. With stern resolve she returned to the kitchen and put the groceries away. Then she arranged the white carnations, which had tempted her from the window of the Flower Pot, into a vase and put them in the living room on the coffee table.

Jeannie was just about to start dinner when the phone rang.

"Christ," Tony said at the other end, "you'd think Welling was in Saudi Arabia, I had such a hard time getting through."

Jeannie's knees buckled and she had to lean against the wall. "Why are you calling now?" she accused him, her heart hammering against her breastbone.

"I told you I would, that I intended to call and keep calling. To see how you are and to talk to Paul."

His voice rushing down the phone lines was reassuring, yet she hated how it made her feel. All jelly and quivering. She thought, as she had when he called before, of hanging up on him, telling him to go to hell and leave them alone. But just hearing him made her realize once again how isolated she was in Welling. No family except Piggy and only a few distant friends.

Then there was fear. Fear was almost a constant companion, but she was never certain of what she was afraid. Nothing and everything, she thought, and then, before she could censor her tongue, she told Tony about Sam, and in a torrent, of the other deaths. She was urgent, insistent, and though horrified at her weakness, for an hour following the

telephone call she was weightless, calm. He had taken the
terror with him back to Boston, drawn it from her through
the phone. She couldn't, however, if she had been forced to
do so, remember what he had said. Sitting in the kitchen at
the table as night swelled over the house, Welling, the accu-
mulated tension eased out through Jeannie's pores, and right
then, in that peaceful hiatus, she refused to even think at all.

The drift she languished in like a warm bath was almost
sensual. Then, out of a quiet as soothing as a Bach cantata,
came the *thump, thump* of Piggy's footsteps on the attic
steps. All at once like a treacherous tide rushing over the
sand, fear flooded back in, obliterating her calm.

A door slammed and she stiffened, sitting upright in the
chair, pained and aching as, for a reason she couldn't put her
finger on, the awful terror roared back, rampaging through
her with a demented howl.

After a dinner heavily embroidered with silence, and after
the cleaning up, Jeannie settled in a corner of the couch to
read a magazine. It was, however, difficult to concentrate.
The conversation with Tony intruded into her thoughts, Piggy's shuffling back and forth distracted her, and something
else. . . . Something out of place that she was having difficulty putting her finger on. She was bothered, nagged, but
she didn't know by what. Finally she tossed the magazine on
the coffee table in disgust and started to sit up. That was
when she saw it. The cut-glass vase. It was standing just
beside the ceramic candlesticks . . . empty. No carnations.

"Paul," she called, catching him midstream of what must
have been at least his tenth trip to the kitchen since dinner.

"What?"

"Did you move the flowers?"

"Flowers?" he said, sailing back through the dining-room
arch. "What flowers?"

"The carnations, white ones, that I bought this afternoon.
And that I put in the vase on this coffee table."

"Huh?" he said, his face wrinkling in confusion.

"Listen, I know your mind is on something important, like
the 'big-bang' theory," she said sarcastically, wanting to shake
him for not being in the same world with ordinary, everyday
concerns, "but there were flowers in this vase before dinner
and now they're gone."

His lips pursed in and out like a fish sucking air. "I never saw them," he said.

"Well they didn't just get up and walk back to the Flower Pot."

"Don't ask me, Mom." He shrugged and gave her one of his most mulish looks. Then, before she could get out another word, he was up the steps.

In the darkness, reaching for the light string, Piggy didn't see her. He expected her to be bedded down in the corner where he had settled her after a tuna-fish sandwich, three Mallomars, and half a glass of Tang. His hand waving in the air, he danced around a small circle, groping upward. His fingers caught the string at the exact moment he thumped into Sam. A scream gurgled up in his throat and spurted out in a small, mouselike squeak as he fell forward.

"Ssssammmm?" he stuttered as he teetered off balance, someone . . . something . . . holding him up.

Right then he found the string again and gave it a savage jerk. The room sprang into light. He looked down at Sam's hand grasping his arm. In the other, she held a mangled bunch of white carnations.

"Gaaaa!" she said, and Piggy would have sworn she was smiling, the puffy lips drawn back over tiny teeth. The flowers were thrust out at him, flapping against his chest. "Gaaaa," she trilled again, and pushed the carnations until he was forced to take them from her.

"Ah, thank you, Sam, that was very nice of you—"

He went suddenly cold, freezing, as though he had been hit by an avalanche. She had been down in the living room! He stared at the flowers . . . his mother's carnations . . . and had a stomach-churning vision of Sam wandering through the house while he and Jeannie sat in the kitchen and ate. His bowels rumbled as the now familiar nightmare of his mother walking right into Sam blossomed in his head.

"No, no," he crooned, leading her to the other side of the attic and tugging her down. With her purulent eyes she was staring at the carnations, and again he said, "They're really beautiful, Sam, and, well, it was very thoughtful of you. But Sam"—he hunkered down on his heels and admonished her in his most serious voice—"you can't wander around alone. You can't go anywhere unless I'm with you. Okay?"

One of her bent clawlike hands snaked out and the yellow fingers tugged at a fat flower, crushing the petals.

"No, Sam!" he cried. "You're ruining them!" And as he pulled away, he thought: I must be crazy. What difference does it make? She could eat them if she wanted to, and he realized he'd have to wrap them in newspaper, stuff them in the very bottom of the big garbage can. If his mother ever found them. . . . He felt sick at the thought.

Her fingers were still waving about the flowers, and Piggy, selecting the fattest bloom, said, "This is one you can keep, Sam. Here." He broke off the long stem and carefully tucked the carnation beneath the red ribbon that held her hair back. "Oh, that looks really pretty," he sighed, wanting to believe—if only for a moment—that she looked an awful lot like Sam-before.

Piggy started to climb to his feet, but she made her high-pitched squealing noise like a small animal caught in one of the pipes. "I really gotta go, Sam. I mean, if I stay up here too long, my mother might get curious and come looking for me." She squeaked at him again and tried to capture his hand. "Sam," he sighed, standing up, "I know it's lonely here for you and that's why you went downstairs. And it's all my fault. I mean, because you're, well, you know, like you are. And then I musta been careless and left the door unlocked. But still, Sam, you really can't just walk around the house. My mother would be awfully upset if she bumped into you." He was at his most earnest trying to make her understand.

Though it really was better having her here instead of in the house on Delaney Street—no matter what the problems—he was raked by sadness, thinking of her so alone. If only she had company . . .

"Wait!" he cried. "Don't you move an inch. And here, hold my flowers for me. I'll be right back, Sam."

Piggy hurried down the steps, and carefully opening the door, slipped out into the hall and raced for his bedroom. Chester was propped up in the chair by the window. Piggy snatched him and rushed back up to the attic.

"Here," he said, smiling himself now. "Look who I have for you. Chester, Sam. It's Chester. Remember?"

"Gaaaa, gaaaa, gaaaa," she shrilled as he took the carnations from her lap and handed her the stuffed dog. She put one nearly hairless ear in her mouth and started to suck it.

Piggy's heart turned over and he almost wept at how pleased she was. Happy, he would have said.

"See, now you have a friend." And with Chester in her arms, he tucked her in for the night.

27

It was much too late for Slime to be calling. He knew that. He didn't need to have Jeannie tell him even after he apologized. It made him snarly, the mild reprimand, and immediately that made him feel guilty. He *liked* Pig's mother. For a grown-up he thought she was just fine, and he would have felt sorry for her if he wasn't so terrified that he could barely think without getting nauseated.

At least Piggy hadn't been asleep. Slime could tell that when he finally came to the phone. Talking to Pig when he had just woken up was a real pain, as though he had a wall in his head made of cinder blocks. Still, when Pig did say hello, Slime had a hard time trying to speak. The words froze in his mouth like ice cubes even though he had rehearsed what he'd planned to say.

"Are you practicing to be a heavy breather?" Pig asked testily when Slime didn't respond.

"I'm here," he said finally.

"Glad to hear it. What do you want?"

Piggy was mad at him because he'd been unfriendly in school. And because Slime ran off every time he saw him coming. But Pig should have understood that anybody would have freaked out by now. Besides, he, Slime, was a coward. Not that he wanted to be. He had heard his father, who was a great reader of war stories, say often enough that courage was important. Not shirking your duty. Not being weak-livered under fire. Only it was one thing to read about battles in a book, to imagine the artillery fire overhead and to think what the tracer bullets would look like streaking across a dark, moonless sky, and quite another to be involved with Piggy and Sam. Or whatever Sam was now. Slime hoped that if he ever had to go fight the Russians his bowels wouldn't turn to rice-pudding as they had the night he had found Sam and hidden her away in the equipment shed. He had had bad dreams ever since, in which he saw her face over and over in a pattern that wallpapered his sleep. And that wasn't the worst of it.

Miss Cooper, the nurse, had suspected he was coming down with the flu when he fainted in the hall of the Administration Building. But he wasn't feverish, he was simply petrified. People were dying like bubonic-plague victims ever since Piggy had brought Sam back. Slime just *knew* she was killing them, only he didn't have the courage to ask. What if Piggy said yes? What would he do then? He had this image stuck in his mind of an enraged Elvira Williams rising up from her watery grave to choke him.

It took Slime a lot of time, most of which he spent in bed, reasoning it out. Pretending to be sick, only he wasn't really pretending all that much. Except that he couldn't explain to his mother if the pain was in his head or his stomach or his left big toe. He was cocooned in pain like a caterpillar before it emerges into the light. They had learned that in science back in the fifth grade, how a butterfly evolves out of the larva stage. And he hoped, in a flight of imagination that was totally unlike him, that he'd swoop in a beautiful, dizzying arc when he unburdened his conscience. That's what he had decided, or yearned for, when he was burrowed in his bed almost ill.

"Pig," he whispered at last into the phone, the receiver pressed against his teeth even if his parents were both downstairs at a wake that was running long. "I gotta tell."

"What?"

"About Sam I mean."

"I know what you mean."

"It's making me sick," he said, and then again, "I gotta tell somebody, like my father, even if he gets crazy with me. You know?"

"Slime—" It wasn't quite a wail, but it made Slime leap away from the phone. He imagined that Piggy had reached through the wires and was shaking him hard. It must be awful for Pig because Slime didn't think that he knew how to be scared, not really down-to-the-bone scared. Or maybe it was just that he was so smart his thoughts outran his feelings. For the first time Slime was grateful that he wasn't especially bright.

"I'm sorry, Pig," he said, "but it wasn't right. Stealing her and all. Doing what we did."

"Slime," Piggy breathed again, almost weeping, "please don't do this to me."

"I'm not doing anything to you, I'm doing something for me," he said, proud that he could make the distinction.

Piggy cried, "If they get her they'll hurt her!"

It was on the tip of Slime's tongue to ask: But what about all the people she's hurt so far?—but he shut his mouth tight. He couldn't chance hearing Pig say something terrible, like: She didn't mean to; or: She's sorry. The only refuge was in not knowing absolutely for sure.

"Slime, let's talk about it."

"I got nothing to say."

"Please!"

"Pig, what difference would it make? You can't keep her forever, you know, like she's BeeBee. The dead gotta be buried, my father says, not walking around missing. And you'll feel better once I tell. I know you will!" Would he? And what would Charlie Volchek and the troopers do to Pig when they found out? That was the one sore spot he shied away from probing too much. "And don't forget," he stampeded on, "how excited all the scientists will be because you did something none of them could do before. I bet you'll get famous and have your picture on the cover of *Newsweek* or something like that. You might even be on television. Won't that be swell?" He thought he sounded like his mother before she made him take a dose of medicine that was going to taste really bad.

"Slime, you're an idiot!" Piggy hissed in his ear.

He knew that, but he was just hoping to make Pig feel better. "Don't be mad at me."

There was silence while they both held their breath. Then Pig said sadly, as if he weren't even talking to him, as if he was telling himself something and Slime just happened to overhear: "You're my only friend, the only one I ever had except for Sam and BeeBee." Slime could hear him crying and he began to give way. You weren't supposed to cry if you were a boy and thirteen. Slime's knees went wobbly and he slid down the wall to the floor of the upstairs hall, where the telephone was on a little table.

"Don't, Pig," he said softly, immeasurably sad. He had never had all that many friends either, and never a best friend like Pig. No matter what he had said to Mrs. Conway because he was a coward and afraid, Pig *was* his best friend and the impending loss cut through him with a keen edge, like the carving knife his mother used on a turkey or ham.

"Can't we discuss it a little bit?" Pig asked through his sobs.

Slime had a hard time focusing on anything except spilling out all the terror that had collected in his stomach like hot vomit. He thought if he didn't tell he might truly get sick. Until he met Piggy he hadn't really had any secrets, or not such an awful one. Still, Piggy was his friend. "Okay," he said at last because maybe it wasn't so awfully much to ask, maybe it was what friendship meant.

Before Slime had a chance to change his mind, Piggy was saying, "We both have exams tomorrow in the morning. Let's come over here after. It'll be the two of us, just like before. And we can talk, okay? Please?"

"Yeah, I guess so," Slime replied, full of doubts.

"Promise?"

"Promise, Pig." Slime sighed and hung up the receiver.

It was a good thing that Jeannie was preoccupied, though Piggy was afraid to know by what. After calling him to the phone, she had returned to the living room to stare glassy-eyed at television. From the way she curled in the corner of the couch covered by her afghan, he knew she wasn't really seeing anything that was flickering on the screen. She was just as intent through the commercials, he saw from the kitchen doorway, as she was through the program. Which meant she hadn't heard anything he said, nor how he had burst uncontrollably into tears.

He splashed his face with cold water and dried it on paper towels. Then he cleaned off his glasses, which were all streaked with tears, wondering what he would do if Slime was determined to tell. If he couldn't convince him not to. He groped for an idea, or at least a fragment of one, but his head might as well have been an old Coke can sitting on top of his neck, it was that empty.

Trudging across the kitchen in slow motion to the refrigerator, Piggy opened the door, forgetting almost at once what he had come for. He didn't see the shelves with bottles, covered dishes, a translucent green bowl filled with shiny red apples, mysterious packages wrapped in tin foil. He only saw Sam's face with its stringy skin and pus-filled eyes. She was purply and soft and looked like a bloated fish that had swollen with gas. Sam, who had been so beautiful.

Jeannie had finally moved, because suddenly she was standing behind him. "Don't leave the door open like that. I've told you a thousand times to get what you want and shut it. The food spoils. Besides, it costs money." Her voice was squeaky with annoyance. He turned in surprise as she reached around him for a half-full bottle of Chablis.

"You never drink wine at night by yourself," he said accusingly, shutting the door.

"Never is a big word," she replied, and poured herself a glass. She pushed the hair back off her forehead and stood sipping the wine, looking out the kitchen window, though there wasn't anything to see except her own faint reflection, and beyond that the even dimmer image of him.

Piggy wasn't particularly astonished that his mother was acting weird. Not when he was behaving so strangely himself. She had to be worrying about him.

Then there were the times when Sam walked around the attic. Piggy had told her not to, told her she had to sit still and not move. But she didn't listen and he could hear her padding across the floor overhead if he was in his bedroom. Jeannie could hear too, only she couldn't identify the creaky noise which grated on her nerves.

Piggy worked on convincing his mother that the shifting sounds were made by the wind, by the old house with all its cracks and weathered joints. Old houses, like old people, often made raspy noises, he informed her. But this morning she had been in the upstairs hall staring suspiciously at the attic door when he emerged from his room. His heart had done a double flip-flop and he barely suppressed a screech.

"I keep hearing noises," she had said, her brow wrinkling.

He immediately started in about the wind again, but she wasn't so easily deterred. She thought she should go up and take a look, that maybe there were mice running around, nesting in the rafters. Piggy insisted that the attic was absolutely rodent-free, that there was nothing up above but his small lab. If she trespassed, he'd be pretty mad. Along with his bedroom the attic was, he snarled with mock ferocity, his private space. He didn't tell her that he had the sole key to the rusty lock, and the only way she was going to get up the attic steps was by breaking the door down.

They had glared at one another, but then his mother had backed off as he knew she would. His experiments made her more nervous than the wind or the possibility of mice. Only she held on to the tail end of her anger and didn't call him "honey" or tousle his hair. And only grudgingly did she wish him good luck in his math exam, though they both knew he'd finish in no more than half the allotted time, getting all the answers right. Which was what he did.

"Do you know this house stinks," she said, still sipping at the wine. "Like some animal got trapped between the walls."

"I told you, Mom," he said, finally remembering he wanted orange juice and opening the refrigerator once again to take out the carton, "it's the drain. The backup from the river."

"No," she said, shaking her head, "that's not it. It smells just as bad upstairs as down here. Worse in fact."

Piggy gripped the Tropicana to his chest. He had done everything he could think of to make the smell go away, or at least to mask it. The two new incense candles burned for hours. He sprayed with Lysol whenever possible. And he had rushed out to the hardware store and bought those little deodorizers that stood propped up by themselves. There was lemon and pine scent and even lilac. But the attic still stank because Sam did. Though he had bathed her and every other night sponged her off, gently running the washcloth up and down her arms, her legs, being especially careful with her face, that didn't help either. He had tried spraying her with his mother's Chanel and for a few minutes she was cloying and sweet. But then the cologne dissolved too, or was overcome by her fetid odor. It worried him a lot why she was smelling worse.

"Oh that," he said, shrugging. "I'm running some experiments with sulfur. It must be the hydrogen sulfide you smell.

It stinks pretty awful." Drinking the orange juice straight
from the carton, he emptied it. He crumpled the container
between his hands and threw the twisted remains in the
trash.

"Well, I wish you'd go back to computers and stop all this
fussing with chemistry," she said. She had finished off the
wine and rinsed out the glass, putting it into the dish drainer
to dry. When he turned around, she saw the clock above the
refrigerator. "It's late," she said, pointing to the round face.
"You should be in bed."

"Right, Mom," he agreed, and headed for the stairs.

"What did Tommy want?" she asked, following him out of
the kitchen, turning off the light.

"Just a couple of questions about history. For tomorrow.
The exam. It's not his best subject and he's kind of worried,
you know," he said, running on, wanting her asleep so that
he could get to Sam. Should he consider moving her again,
he wondered, and did it matter? If Slime told, they'd find her
no matter what he did. Besides, once they knew, he'd have
to tell them where she was anyway. He couldn't pretend with
Charlie Volchek, nor clench his teeth and just shake his head
no, no, no, over and over again. Somehow or other Charlie
Volchek would worm it all out of him. Which made him so
mad that he wanted to flail his arms and stamp his feet.

Upstairs she managed to rouse herself to smile rather lopsidedly at him and kiss him on the cheek good night, but she
wasn't being totally Mom. Her head was somewhere else and
she wasn't paying strict attention to him, which she usually
did. The deaths, he supposed, were keeping her preoccupied. Only she didn't seem like other people in Welling,
whom he saw along Main Street, in the five-and-dime, the
hardware store, in Casey's, where she had sent him for
toothpaste. They were all scared and shaking their heads, and
being apprehensive, as though sensing a storm just back of
the mountains. But also, everyone whom he had seen was
wiggly with excitement. He overheard some dumb clerk in
Casey's exclaiming, "Nothing like this has ever happened in
Welling before!" As if Welling had been nominated for a
Nobel Prize.

He couldn't sleep. His mind from being blank had filled up
with voices. He was stuffed, as if he had a head cold, and
wished he could blow his nose, clearing them away. But they

buzzed frantically like bees in an upended hive. All those
voices! Not only his mother's and father's—now very faint—
but Slime's too, saying, *I've got to tell*, and old Waxworks
screaming at him. The girl in Casey's with her nasal shrill was
there also, and Jack Reiss, whom he heard repeating just as
he did when his mother stopped for gas, "What's the world
coming to?"

Charlie Volchek barked loudly, "Gotcha!"

He was going to drown in words.

It was impossible to close his eyes, to be in the dark for
long with Emmett Sidowsky's broken body and Harry Pringle's
contorted face, like Silly Putty pushed all out of shape.

He had to talk to somebody and there was only Sam.
Throwing back the covers, he tiptoed up to the attic. Wanting to run, he forced himself to be cautious. It wouldn't do
now for his mother to find him sneaking up the stairs. No,
not now, when all his lies had ganged up on him. He didn't
think if she came out of her room and caught him halfway up
he'd be able to tell her anything except that he was on his
way to see Sam.

And maybe she couldn't believe him! She might just feel
his head and order him back into bed if he said that Sam was
alive and well and living in the attic.

He didn't, however, think it was safe to try out his theory.
She was acting so funny that who could tell which way she'd
jump? She just might say: I want to see for myself, and troop
right up after him. And then wouldn't she be surprised?

He groped around in the darkness playing a one-person
version of blindman's buff until he found the cord dangling
from the middle of the rafters. When the light came on it was
thin as watered-down lemonade, but bright enough to see
Sam standing by the window. His heart gave a lurch. What
could she see from so high up and facing the river? Maybe
him and BeeBee, and her too, in the backyard playing ball
not so long ago. Did she have memories like cut-up pieces of
film? Could she see ghosts?

Sitting down in the old rocker, he kept it steady so it
wouldn't squeak. "Come away from the window," he said.
"It's cold. There's a draft." He sounded like his mother and
wondered if someday he'd be a father, torn apart by some
crazy kid of his own. Not that he thought he could ever get
married, not after Sam. Which was silly. Even if she hadn't

been bashed to death by Harry Pringle and resurrected into some terrible mistake—because he, Piggy, had got so mad at the world—probably nothing would have happened. He would have gone off to MIT when all the experts decided he was old enough to cope, and become a scientist living in a lab day and night. And Sam? He guessed she would have stayed in Welling and gotten a job in the five-and-dime, or maybe checking at the supermarket.

It was all so sad, and not only because he suspected he'd never get to MIT now.

"Slime's going to tell," he said. "I'll try to make him change his mind, try to make him understand, but I don't think I can. He's too chicken, what with everything. I mean, he guesses that you hurt those people and he's scared." *Me too*, he wanted to add, but didn't.

In the dim light, with her turned just a certain way so that all he could see was her back and the long blond hair which he had finally by washing and brushing, tugging and pulling with a comb, made to look as it once had, he could fantasize that she was Sam-before. If he took off his glasses and scrunched his eyes half shut, he could swear almost certainly that it was she. And then he could pretend that none of this was true, none of what had come about like a tidal wave. That Harry hadn't killed her; that she hadn't died. That he didn't, some-how or other—he still wasn't sure what he had done, though he was groping around with his notes, his computations, his faulty memory—bring her back from the dead.

It was really nice in the attic, just the two of them late at night. He knew he should get to bed and sleep because of exams tomorrow. Especially history, which he had neither read nor paid much attention to in class. He might not even do well, which would be strange. He considered that, getting a C or even flunking the term.

His mother would go apeshit. It would be even worse in some ways than what he had done with Sam. At least that was explainable in terms of his intelligence, but flunking history was just dumb. He had never been dumb and he sometimes thought that was the only thing which sustained him, which made him acceptable to others. Like his father, who would have preferred that he could play baseball and hockey, but had to make do with Piggy just being brilliant. And if he wasn't anymore—that was silly, because he couldn't just shut his mind down like a turbine!—but if he didn't live up to his potential, if he just refused to think, what would they do then, his mother, Dr. Mellon, his father? Abandon him? Say, "Forget it, Pig, go get lost"? He shivered, though it wasn't particularly cold in the attic, and thought he wouldn't like to find out.

"I don't want to be alone, Sam," he said softly. "I don't want them to stop loving me."

He could hear her say that nobody had ever loved her but him, so if they stopped it wouldn't be such a big blow. And him being rational and saying that you couldn't stop something that had never started in the first place. Then realizing how heart-shattering sad it was that she didn't think her mother and father loved her. *Well, you jerk, Harry certainly didn't, because he killed her! And her mom ran off and doesn't even know she's dead, which she isn't, but she doesn't know that either.*

It really was just the two of them. He said that to her. But she didn't answer, not even with her *gaaaa.*

"Maybe, you know, I could've fixed it. Somehow. About you, I mean. Like you are now." He chewed on a nail and was grateful she didn't turn around. If he had to look at that pulp which was now her face, and see the gleam of her teeth because her lips wouldn't close properly anymore, so that sometimes she reminded him of one of those actresses playing a vampire in a Christopher Lee movie, he would be stunned into silence. And he so wanted to talk!

"It would have been difficult," he continued, "explaining it. But—" He remembered how worried he had been that she'd be discovered, that they'd take her away and he'd be sent to a psychiatrist if not something worse. Because you didn't tamper with death, just with dying. Yes, he recalled that he had been worried blue before. Yet it was nothing like it was now. Because now she had killed people and everybody would say she was a monster, kind of a little girl Frankenstein.

But he understood, at least about Harry. "Emmett was an accident," he stated emphatically. "I know that. And Mrs. Williams—" He sighed, observing his nail, which he had bitten to the quick. "They can't prove you did it. I don't even know that for a fact. And besides, this is America, innocent until proven guilty. I mean, where's the evidence, Sam? Just because she's dead doesn't mean you're responsible. But people will start blaming you for every death in town. Like you're a chug-chug killing machine!" He snorted disapprovingly, having wandered away from the point, which was whether or not she actually had drowned Elvira Williams. Pig refused to ask her, even if she could say. He kept telling himself that he hadn't seen the old woman. From all he had heard, she was just found dead in the tub, and she was older than yesterday anyway. Old people did simply drop and didn't necessarily have to be pushed. Could they tell if somebody had held her head underwater? Or if it had happened naturally? He wished he knew more about forensic medicine.

"Not that Slime is going to say it's your fault, Sam. He couldn't say that because he doesn't know. Only they're going to say it, people like Charlie Volchek. If they never prove it, they'll still say it anyway. And lock us up, the both of us. You in one place, me somewhere else. Even if they argue for twenty years whether I'm guilty or not because I brought you back, they'll still see to it that I'm not running around loose. They'll think I'm dangerous, Sam. You too. Sometimes, you know, people become dangerous by accident. Like driving a car when the brakes don't hold.

"That's you, Sam. You've just made a couple of mistakes. Everybody does. Me too. At Height something happened which I never told you about. It was a mistake, because I didn't mean it." But it wasn't and he had, and he scrunched down in the rocker. The chair wheezed. Quickly he planted his sneakers firmly on the floor and listened to the silence fill up the attic once more. There was a thin webbing of sweat along his hairline and he wiped it away with his sleeve. He didn't want to remember Height or Bertram Lennard, who miraculously these last couple of days had been absent. Maybe now he was simply buried among all the dead. Pig hoped his ghostly giggle was forever choked off in his burnt-up chest.

"I could try to take you someplace else, Sam," he said, finally getting up because he had to return to bed and at least try to sleep. He led her away from the window, back to the corner, where he had improvised a lair with blankets and the extra pillow from his bed. "Like the equipment shed. Only you didn't like that because of the rats. Which I don't blame you for. Or that old house if we could get inside. But there's nowhere else I can think of. I wish," he said passionately, helping her sit down, and patting the top of her head, "that Slime wouldn't tell!"

Like a gift from the gods, Slime got a stomachache the next day and was laid up. Piggy, who dragged himself to school as though he were the one who died but hadn't been born again, was surprised when Slime didn't show up for the history midterm. He couldn't wait until it was over to rush to the pay phones outside the gym. He was so rattled he put a quarter in instead of a dime. "Big spender!" he yelled at himself when he realized how wasteful he'd been.

In a moment Slime's mother was yipping in his ear that poor Tommy was down with a sour stomach. The flu, maybe, or something he ate. But he wasn't going anywhere today or possibly tomorrow either.

Piggy's relief was so enormous he slid right down to the floor. "Please tell him I hope he feels better," Piggy said, sincerity ringing in his voice, though right then he couldn't help hoping that Slime would stay sick. Not die exactly. But laid up for a long, long time with some disease that would keep his mouth wired tightly shut. Yeah, like lockjaw, he thought, knowing there was no cure for that.

So happy he was walking on air, Piggy didn't come to his senses until he was in the middle of Main Bridge. One day . . . one day . . . What's going to happen to change things before tomorrow or the day after that, before Slime recuperates and yaps his silly head off? An act of God, as the saying went, or an unnatural event. Sure (he almost kicked himself), a tornado is going to drop on northeastern Pennsylvania and suck up Toomy's Funeral Parlor.

He had stumbled into such a foul mood that he didn't see the blue-and-white creeping along River Street, Charlie Volchek hulking behind the wheel. With his driving glasses and his brimmed hat crushed down on gray hair that sprouted like lichen from the sides, and his lips clamped tight, Charlie Volchek was a large, threatening bug. He had only to open his mouth wide and he'd swallow Piggy whole. Piggy's stomach did its ungainly flip-flop which always made him feel like throwing up.

For a moment, no more, while Piggy was frantically wondering whether Slime had spilled everything over the phone to the chief and was just playing sick because he couldn't face up to his betrayal, they stared at one another. Was it possible that Charlie Volchek had been barreling over to Mason to arrest him? In front of the whole school, Dr. Mellon, and old Waxworks, who would crow with delight . . . and worst of all, in front of his mother. He almost heard his mother scream her lungs out as the chief led him away in handcuffs.

But it was Charlie Volchek who was yelling at him. "What are you doing wandering out into the road like that? You feel okay?"

Piggy, who felt as bad as anybody could feel, without actually being sick, said, "Ah . . . I'm sorry." It was only then, of course, that he realized he had strolled right off the bridge into the middle of the street. Great, he thought, I'll get myself killed. That would really solve everything.

"Well watch where you're going," the chief snarled, and as Piggy backed off to the sidewalk, floored the police car. It bolted and screeched as it headed down to South Bridge.

He knows, he knows! Piggy thought, crazed with fear. *Even if Slime hasn't told him yet, he knows! Stupid, of course he doesn't. How would he? Who'd tell?*

By the time Pig reached his front door he had a throbbing headache. He stepped into the house, swelled to the ceiling with dead silence, and was struck by a terrible longing to hear BeeBee rolling toward him across the floor. *Oh Bee*, he wailed, *if only you hadn't died!*

If BeeBee hadn't been killed by Harry Pringle . . .

If they hadn't moved to Welling from Boston . . .

If his father hadn't fallen in love, or just "in lust," as his mother had said once nastily . . .

If, most important, Sam hadn't been battered to death by her father . . .

No—he stopped suddenly—the biggest *if* of all was: if he hadn't brought Sam back from the dead. If he hadn't done that one thing, never mind that the whole world wouldn't think it was possible, or that he wasn't exactly sure how he'd managed to pull it off, he wouldn't be standing in the middle of the living room wringing his hands. Which was what he was doing. He hadn't even gotten to the kitchen to look inside the fridge. And he was certain that there was one last chocolate doughnut in the box.

The fault was his, one one else's. He was bloated with

guilt, and as he wearily pulled himself up the stairs, steeper and harder to climb, his mind slowed down like an engine running out of power. The only thought bouncing inside his skull confirmed his responsibility and agitated his headache. Midway up the steps he briefly considered confessing, but fear for Sam and for himself too pushed that notion aside. Besides, whom could he tell?—not Charlie Volchek certainly, who'd throw him in jail and flush the key right down the toilet. His mother? She'd collapse, never mind being disappointed. His father? He reached the landing and wondered about Tony back in Boston. Tony could fix anything. Even though Piggy suspected that his father hadn't actually believed him one hundred percent about what happened to Bertram Lennard in the lab, Tony had stood beside him. Also, Piggy knew that his father wouldn't have let the police in Boston do anything serious, anything awful. He wasn't sure how he knew this, he just did. Maybe it was just the way that Tony had clamped his hand on Pig's shoulder all during the time the police had questioned him. Or maybe it was just the determined set to his jaw.

Thinking of his father crumpled Piggy to the top step, where he put his face all the way down on his knees and held his breath, trying not to give in and cry. *Oh Daddy!* he wailed, and then, before common sense could stop him, he rushed down the steps to the kitchen and dialed Boston.

"Mr. Conway, please," Piggy said to the secretary.

"Who's calling?"

"Ah . . . just say a friend from out of town."

"Your name, please," the voice, more mechanical than Bee's beep, insisted.

"Uh, well, his son," Piggy gulped.

In a second there was his father, so alive and real that he could have been in the kitchen standing by the sink. He wanted to know how Pig was, what he was doing. School . . . the town . . . had he made any friends?

"Fine, fine," he heard some stranger responding. *Tell him!* But the words were locked away in his throat. Tears were definitely now splashing against his glasses, and his nose was stuffing up. "Listen, I gotta go, Dad. See you," he said abruptly as he slammed down the receiver. A powerful wind of regret swept through him, and angrily he thumped his fist against the wall. What a dumb, baby thing to do, calling like that!

When his anger began to cool, and his heart slowed its wild, erratic thundering, he washed and dried his glasses and went back up the stairs to Sam.

Another idea was taking form in Pig's mind, one more awful and upsetting than calling his father and bawling *Help me*! like a two-year-old. Piggy tried to shrug away this new and hideous possibility, but the notion clung with sharp hooks inside his head.

Sam was in her corner, Chester tucked under one arm. She was sleeping. Piggy had never seen her asleep before, and he watched her curiously. The ruined mouth was parted like a wound and breath was hissing past her teeth. Her eyes were closed and seemed almost normal except for the thin trickle of yellow ooze seeping from under the lashes.

My fault . . . mine. . . .

Piggy quietly perched in the rocker and watched Sam sleep. The grim idea crept back in on him, and he clenched his teeth, wishing it into oblivion. But it wouldn't budge. And holding all his parts rigid, he squarely faced the notion of killing Sam. Putting her out of her misery. Making things right. No hope for her, he thought despairingly. None for me either. Sooner or later—and probably sooner if Slime blabbed—the world was going to burst in on them and then where would either of them be? Nowhere fast. But if . . . A bitter taste filled his mouth and he wondered if he were the monster instead of her.

Carefully he raised himself from the rocker, holding it steady so it wouldn't creak, and dragged over to Sam. Down on his knees, he stared into her bruised, disintegrating face and tried to believe it would be a blessing, as his grandmother always said. *A blessing*, he whispered in his head, and had to gulp air through his mouth so as not to be overcome by the stench of Sam's rotting flesh.

His hand of its own accord snaked toward the wires sticking out of Sam's skull. The hair was already beginning to grow back in a short blond stubble. For an instant he had a vivid memory of her dancing about the backyard, her long, wonderfully silky hair that he always itched to touch, swinging out around her.

His finger nudged the red wires and groped on to the blue,

when suddenly her lids popped open. Even with the pus obscuring the pupils, swallowing up the violet color of her irises, he was staring at Sam-before. As though far back somewhere in the thing she had become, the thing he had made her, was the other Sam, the one he remembered, the girl he longed to have back. And then she was gone. Blinked right out, and Sam-now was clacking her weird one word at him. Happy to see him, he supposed, feeling himself drowning in a tide of remorse. Hating himself worse than he ever had for even thinking of doing such a terrible thing, he began to cry in earnest now.

"Oh Sam," he wept, "I miss you so!"

Awkwardly she bent forward, and with a surprisingly soft touch, she patted his knee. "Gaaa," she said, with what he decided was sympathy, and he knew, no matter what, that he had to save her.

Slime's resolve to clear his conscience had, if anything, strengthened during the past two days. Piggy saw that right away.

They were walking together from the Science Building to Humans and their English exam. "There's nothing to talk about, and you can't change my mind," Slime was saying. He was being stubborn and Pig let him alone until after the exam.

The test wasn't as bad as he had expected. Some information seemed to have filtered through to his brain by osmosis during the previous weeks, and at worst he suspected he'd score an A-minus.

Then he reminded Slime, "You promised! You said we could discuss it."

He was shrill with desperation and Slime reluctantly gave in, agreeing that they could go over to River Street and make themselves lunch. Though he said, "My stomach is agitated. I think I flunked English. What did you write about *Animal Farm?*"

Piggy told him. Slime looked stricken and whimpered that if his average slipped any further he'd be asked to leave Mason and his father would kill him besides being mad.

"Some kids just don't test well. That's what Dr. Bayard told my mother. It's got nothing to do with how smart you are, you know what I mean?"

Piggy nodded his head and insisted Slime probably had done better than all right. And besides, the exam was over, why worry about it now? But Slime veered from chewing over the test to Sam, then back again, as if they were both a mush in his mind. He was so jumpy that Pig thought he was about to leave his skin. It made him mad because the worst thing that could happen to Slime was flunking out of Mason and having to go to Consolidated. Pig, on the other hand, would end up who-knew-where, and bring the world crashing down on his mother's head. He didn't think it was fair that his mother was about to get hurt as much as she was going to, and it was, he simmered, all Slime's fault. If he just wouldn't tell!

It had started to snow, finally, soft flakes like goose down drifting out of the layered sky. The dead grass and the walks and the roads were all dusted white. There was almost no wind and the world was so quiet that their footsteps as they crossed Main Bridge echoed like cannon booms.

Pig's nose was cold, and he stuck out his tongue and caught the flakes, just as he had when he was a little kid. Once he and his father had built a snowman on the patch of grass in front of their apartment building. They had even put an old straw hat that Jeannie didn't wear anymore on its head and tied a scarf around its neck. Everybody had thought it was kind of perky, like a greeting card. But then a thaw had set in and one morning they found it shriveled in half. By lunch that day it was down almost to a puddle, and the hat and scarf were missing.

A pale green Honda was coming north along River Street. Out of the corner of his eye Piggy had seen it cross South Bridge slowly, barely moving, then turn right. It passed them just as they stepped onto the sidewalk and in a blur of movement Pig noticed there were two men inside. *They're after me!* he thought wildly, then immediately told himself not to be a fool. Nobody was after him because nobody knew anything yet. Slime still hadn't told, even if he was going to.

Nerves are a curse, his grandmother used to say.

And Pig's nerves were shredded raw. He jumped two feet when Slime said, "I wouldn't mind some soup. Pea, if your mother's got a can."

"She's still at school," Piggy told him, catching his breath.

"But, yeah, I guess we got soup. She always keeps a ton of cans in the pantry."

By the time they reached the house the falling snow was thick as heavy cream. Piggy thought he'd have to shovel the walk when it stopped. He and Slime pounded their sneakers on the rubber mat outside the door before they went inside. Slime said, "Good thing your Mom locks up now. You never know. Anybody could of walked in before."

"What?" Pig said, startled.

"With all the killings, I mean." Suddenly his eyes darted sideways as he realized what he had said, and he fumbled with the zipper on his jacket. "Let's eat, huh, Pig. 'Cause I gotta get home right away. My mom will be wondering how the exams were. And there's a paper I never did for English that has to be handed in by the end of the week. I'll lose points if I don't do it."

"Sure," Piggy agreed, aware all at once that Slime didn't know that Sam was upstairs in the attic. Though how could he, since the other boy had barely been talking to him, and certainly not about Sam, whom he was desperate to forget. Or forget after he told, Pig thought, seething. It was going to be just fine for Slime. He'd have a clear conscience and everybody'd think he was a hero for telling and finding the killer, even if they wouldn't ever be able in a thousand years to get Sam to confess.

They went off into the kitchen and Piggy found a can of pea soup for Slime and one of tomato for himself. He heated them both up and got the peanut butter and jelly from the refrigerator with a large loaf of Wonder Bread. They settled on Very-Berry to drink and Pig opened a new can, pouring the bright red drink over ice cubes, since it wasn't cold.

But neither of them was really hungry. Slime was fidgety and refused to look Pig in the eye. And Piggy got a lump of sandwich stuck in his throat, making him choke. Slime had to pound him on the back and he drank a whole glassful of Very-Berry before the peanut butter, jelly, and bread sank to his stomach.

Piggy's choking made things better for a few minutes, but when he tried to tell Slime there was no reason to turn them all in, they immediately got into a fight, Slime adamant that he wasn't telling anything on himself because he hadn't done

one single thing to get into trouble. "I was only helping out," he insisted vehemently.

Piggy reminded him there was something called being an accessory. "Which is just as bad," he argued.

"Is not."

"Is too."

"Isn't."

"Is so, Slime, and you know it. If you squeal about Sam you'll be in as much hot water as I will. But that's not the point anyway. It's what will happen to *her*. They'll take her away somewhere and do awful experiments on her."

"Pig, she *is* an awful experiment!"

"She isn't! She's Sam!" But she wasn't, not really. She was something else, something that had never been born before, or invented, something that had come from the underbelly of dreams. Suddenly Pig thought of a poem that his mother liked—

She walks in beauty, like the night . . .

Only Sam walked in terror, thrashing her way through horrors—Bee's computer telling her Piggy didn't know what— not alive maybe, but not dead either. She had come out of another dimension and all her parts were askew. And her night was black, unforgiving.

But that didn't mean she should be aborted even though she had, somehow, gone terribly astray. Because still, deep down, in the marrow, she was Sam. And he had to save her!

Piggy reached out and grabbed Slime by the wrist, holding on as though they had both been tossed overboard. "If she was an old, sick dog you wouldn't put her to sleep, would you?"

"Lemme go, Pig!" Slime wailed, wrestling to free himself.

"No! You've got to see her as I do. She's Sam and I brought her to life and you just want to kill her again! Like Harry Pringle did the first time!"

"That's not true!" he cried, finally getting his arm back. "But she's bad and we shouldn't have done what we did. And she's got to be locked away!"

Piggy was so frightened that he jumped up, almost over-turning the chair, and ran around the kitchen as though he were Bee out of control. Talking, talking, words pouring confusedly out of his mouth, words cascading over one another, syllables sliding together so that sentences began and ended without making sense.

And the wanting, the longing was inside, eating him alive. Only he couldn't explain, no matter how he reached, pulling words out of memory, throwing them across the crumbs and scraps of peanut-butter-and-jelly sandwiches, the cold soup congealing in bowls. It had to do with love and with yearning, but even if he recognized that, which he did just barely, he'd never be able to make Slime comprehend what he was feeling. Because Slime was normal, a kid like all the other kids Pig had known or read about in books. And he, Piggy, was different for some reason that had to do with genes and with luck.

He was breaking away, free-falling, and it seemed impossible now that he and Slime had ever been friends, had hung out in Corney's pawing over comic books. He felt old beside the other boy, who was leaking fear like a faulty gas line.

"Slime!" he cried one last time.

And then he saw her sailing through the dining room, a ghost ship that had slipped its moorings, impossibly light on her feet, silent, the arms angled, the legs like iron bars in Jeannie's sweatpants and the face that resembled no face anymore except one of those tiny, tiny ones that Pig remembered from the museum. A face, his mother had explained, by a painter who had gone out of his mind.

Slime, so agitated already that he gripped the edge of the table tightly with both hands, must have seen something reflected in Pig's face. Or heard the wheeze of panic issuing out of his gaping mouth. Because suddenly he bolted, swung around in his chair, and cried out, a long screech of terror that went on and on until Pig thought the windows would blow out and the snow, flying in, would entomb them there.

It was impossible for Slime not to know that fate was rolling toward him across the ever shrinking kitchen floor. And Piggy could tell that he knew. Slime's face flushed the color of tomato juice, and Pig, thinking that they were like the three angles of a triangle all rushing toward one another until they collided, howled, "It's okay, Sam! It's okay!" Wired by fear, hopping from one foot to the other, tripping and hitting the sink, then pulling up, Piggy chased after Slime wanting to stop him, to make him believe that it would be all right. That somehow or other they could tumble backward through time and not be about to do something so awful there would never be any way to put it aside. Fear was making Pig stupid because it wasn't a game which was about to be played in the middle of the kitchen; it was death. No matter how loudly he shrilled, "It's okay, really! Honest!" it wasn't. Slime understood that in his marrow as he struggled with Piggy by the back door which Jeannie in her vigilance had locked.

Slime was crying now, howling for his mother, as he broke free from Pig and flung himself to the other side of the kitchen. But Sam, on whose face Piggy was certain he saw a darting flicker of sadness, from whose right, yellowy eye there seemed to be dribbling a fat, glycerine tear, was relentless. She was homing in on Slime who couldn't dodge her effectively, who was drawn toward her as if they were magnetized.

Then from somewhere, maybe from the rack on the wall above the counter, there was a knife in her hand, a long knife with a shiny blade. Piggy was mesmerized by the knife that rode up in the air in Sam's hand. That knife had a life of its own. That knife is forever, Piggy thought, and made a dive for it, for the crooked arm, and the fist that grasped the handle.

But the kitchen was suddenly too small, and there were too many of them crowding into it, as though they had multiplied. And Pig could no more stop it happening than he could have turned back time, making all this—Slime, Sam with the knife in her hand, the knife starting its downward slide—go away. He knew what powerlessness truly meant then, because though he had finally gotten a good grip on Sam's sleeve, he was just there for the ride, coming down with the arm, riding it all the way, helpless as the knife slammed home.

Slime's mouth popped open, breath whooshing out, and he sailed back, arms extended, fingers twitching, legs for a moment leaving the floor, and flew there, impaled on the knife in Sam's hand. And the three children were locked together in just that second. Sam to the knife, the knife to Slime, and Pig, his fingers almost to the bone of Sam's arm. Then they dropped away. Slime slipped to the floor, life floating out of him, as Piggy fell to his knees screaming,

pawing at Slime's body like a grieving dog. But there was
nothing he could do, not now. He had done everything, had
brought them to this moment. And it was all wrong, because
Slime, impossibly small, was dying, was dead on the kitchen
floor.

28

The long schoolday ended, came to an abrupt stop with a peal
of the final bell, and Jeannie's last class put down their
pencils, closed the little blue booklets, and rose from their
desks. The gaggle of first-formers, more subdued than normal, hurried out of the room, leaving her to straighten the
chairs, erase the examination questions from the blackboard,
and clear off her desk. She lingered in the warm, almost
stuffy classroom, reluctant to leave.

It was snowing heavily outside; she could see the steady
white curtains falling beyond the windows, the light a pearl
gray. The storm was building up muscle and would soon be a
blizzard. If she didn't go soon, Main Bridge would be
treacherous.

Her thoughts were revolving around Piggy, and she wondered how his exams had gone. She was uneasy not only
because he had done almost no studying, but, the one time
she had seen him at school that day, caught a glimpse of him
in her peripheral vision, he was crossing the campus with
Slime in tow, and he had looked so strange, so . . . she
couldn't describe it, intent maybe, that her fear—never far
below the surface—came spilling out.

She really should leave instead of dawdling, abandon the
ghosts of first-formers scraping their feet and sighing dramati-

cally, scratching their pens across the white pages. But some sixth sense told her if she stayed put, if she didn't go out into the storm which was rapidy gathering force, buffeting the building in angry clouts of wind, she would be safe. Something was there in the storm, waiting. She could feel it in her bones. Lowering herself to one of the desks, she clutched her arms across her breasts and sat thinking.

Don't move, her intuition counseled. She felt light-headed, like someone with a bad cold, and wanted to believe that if she was cautious, if she carried herself as though made of glass, all the terror would blow away. Just as the storm eventually would. She might have to wait for a very long time, forever and ever, but eventually things would be even again, placid, calm.

Only that wasn't true. People were dying in Welling, so close to them that they might have been able to reach out and touch the killer. They were awash in a sea of dead people, and they were threatened.

Hunkering down at the small desk, Jeannie felt foolish. Hadn't she, after all, stated vehemently to Charlie Volchek that they were strangers in Welling? The deaths had nothing to do with them. How could they be in danger, never mind involved?

Still, the dead were crowding in on her, on Piggy too. *They* had to be what was setting him so badly on edge, changing him. She knew she should do something and do it soon, before he was lost to her. She saw her hand extended to clutch him as he spun out into space, and she imagined herself missing him as he swept by. That image frightened her so that she was propelled into moving, ready to run now. From the desk she snatched the booklets, stuffed them into her briefcase and went toward the door. But just as she turned to snap off the long fluorescent tubes of white light, Bertram Lennard emerged from the coatroom all yellow and burning. And Jeannie whimpered, fearing that whatever she did, it wouldn't be enough or in time.

Piggy heard the front door open and close. There was no "hello" from his mother, nor the rustling sounds she made taking off her coat and hanging it up. He didn't know what to do except curl up compactly and weep, which he did, quietly pulling the door of the pantry closed after him, and folding into the dark. Behind him, next to the shelves stacked with canned goods, was Slime, or rather Slime's body.

The footsteps moved in a measured cadence through the downstairs rooms and into the kitchen, where they halted. Whoever it was was looking around, and suddenly Piggy realized it couldn't be Jeannie. Not that it mattered. He thought that if the house burned down right then and he went up in flames just as Bertram Lennard had done, he'd only be getting his just desserts.

Sam had disappeared. He didn't know where to. Maybe she was back upstairs in the attic. Piggy hadn't gone to look for her.

He knew why she had gotten so mad at Slime that she knifed him to death. But Slime had been his friend; he'd been Sam's, too. It was wrong and Pig couldn't justify it, not even to himself. She had done something so terrible she was surely beyond redemption now.

He wasn't certain why he had dragged Slime's body into the pantry, could only barely remember doing so. It wasn't as if he planned to try to hide him away, like Harry Pringle in the corner of the old coal bin.

Piggy sniffed and wiped his nose on the bottom of his vest sweater. But it didn't help. He was leaking, all his sorrow and pain running out of him, and it wasn't conceivable that he'd ever stop crying. The tears were as steady as the snow outside and as organic as his breathing.

Whoever it was in the kitchen ran water from the tap. Piggy heard the cabinet next to the sink open and the clink of a glass being taken down. Piggy brought his knees up to his chest and didn't bother listening. He wondered if he could run away, he and Sam. Not now, but when the storm quieted down. Only it seemed so overwhelming, where they'd go and how, that he put his head on his knees, his glasses cutting into the bridge of his nose.

The footsteps receded and in a moment Pig heard them climbing to the second floor. It could be Charlie Volchek coming to search the house. Or maybe one of the troopers. Eventually whoever it was, if he kept looking, would find Pig on the floor of the pantry. And though Piggy had mopped up all the blood, that someone would discover Slime too. Then, without a doubt, Sam up in the attic if that was where she had escaped to. Piggy was so scared that he began to churn, legs and arms jiggling, no matter how tightly he held on to himself.

How had this happened! he wailed silently in his head. He'd never meant to do anything wrong, only what was right. Sam shouldn't have been dead. She was meant to be living and laughing, just like any other kid.

Waxworks would have said he'd been tampering, and Pig thought now that possibly he was right. Maybe he should have determined the outcome and considered the consequences before he experimented on Sam like she was a white mouse.

All he had wanted was Sam-before, Sam to play ball again in the backyard, Sam to drink milkshakes that Jeannie made in the blender and get that funny white mustache on her upper lip, Sam's eyes to crinkle up with giggles when he told her a silly joke, Sam to sit intent over the Monopoly board, Sam to . . . He clenched his fists and heard the footsteps descend the stairs now. He expected that they would leave and go back outside, but they moved toward the kitchen once again. The glass was picked up from the sink, and for a second time the water was turned on.

Piggy saw himself being taken away in Charlie Volchek's blue-and-white. And Mr. Toomy would come and carry Slime home to the deep freeze. He couldn't bear to think about Slime dead behind him, so close that if he stretched out his hand he'd be able to touch him. He tried to pretend Slime wasn't there, but his dead friend hunkered over his left shoulder like a ghost. Somewhere Bertram Lennard was laughing and his high-pitched giggle made the cans dance on the shelves.

In another minute Pig knew he'd be howling and wished there was some empty room in his head where he could secrete himself. He could see closing all the windows, turning off all the lights, like the one now which was shining in his eyes making him blink.

"Paul?" a voice, one he should remember, asked.

Piggy, from way down where he was on the floor, raised his eyes, his glance sliding up the gray-flannel legs to the chest to the face. "Daddy?" he whispered, and started to scream.

In one unending motion Tony had him out of the pantry

and was cradling his head against his chest. "Hey, sport, it's okay. Honest."

Daddydaddydaddydaddydaddydaddy. . . .

Pig gave way, hanging on to the overcoat for dear life, his feet barely touching the ground. With some difficulty Tony maneuvered himself, with Piggy attached, to a chair, where Pig, as big as he was, climbed onto his father's lap. His arms wound around Tony's neck in a death grip, his sobs roared in his ear. Piggy could smell his father's after-shave and that made him weep even more.

"Whoa, Paul! Turn off the waterworks, will you. It's nothing to cry about."

"Oh Daddy, I didn't mean it, really I didn't. It was all a mistake!"

Piggy could feel Tony harden into stone beneath him as he asked, "What did you say?"

"It just hurt so much, Daddy, that she was taken away. Like somebody tore my heart right out of my chest. I couldn't let it happen, not again, like Bee dying." He was babbling, spraying Tony's overcoat with spittle, and he couldn't stop. It didn't matter what he was saying, just finally that it was all pouring out. Each word brought him closer to relief, the pain in his stomach easing up. A dam had burst inside and he was flooding his father with words. He was ashamed of all the tears, of not being coherent.

There was a crazy person in the kitchen. Piggy could hear him yowling and crying and talking about people dead in bathtubs and coal bins and down the stairs and right in the pantry now. Some crazy person was telling his father that his best friend except for Sam, whom he loved, loved, loved, loved—*love* echoing—was in the pantry with a knife in his tummy. That crazy person was screeching like a banshee and weeping, getting his father's collar all wet, and beating his hands on his father's chest.

"Hush, hush," Tony said, trying to quiet him like a baby.

The crazy person wondered if he'd be upended and given a spanking as though he were back in Pampers. He wished he was! A baby. Playing with blocks. Building houses and towers, not monsters. But in one swoop all the blocks went scattering across the floor as Tony stood up, dragging Pig with him. Pig felt himself shaking. His father was bouncing him, trying to get him to stand on his feet, which was hopeless because his feet didn't work; they belonged to somebody else. One of the dead people. The dead were whistling through the house on River Street and one of them had taken Piggy's feet.

Tony propped him in a chair and told him to sit still, but the crazy person wasn't listening because he couldn't hear. Someone else had taken his ears away, lobes, drums, eustachian tubes. But he read his father's lips and they were mouthing, "It's going to be all right."

His father always made everything all right. Like the time they were in Vermont for two weeks and Piggy had fallen into the pond just at the edge of the property they had rented. His mother hadn't seen him because she was in the kitchen. But Tony had, from far away. And he had gone running, flying across the grass like his feet were greased. He plucked Piggy from the water which was way, way over his head, where he knew he shouldn't have been, had been told not to go even if he was trying to catch the darting minnows below the surface. Yes, his father had pinched him right up into the air once again and thumped his back so that a spume of water sprayed out, then carried him into the house, where he finally stopped seeing neon lights exploding like Disney bursts of color in his head.

Tony would save him from drowning even if he did go into the pantry, pulling the string to flood the tiny space with light, and say softly, but not so softly that Piggy—whose ears had for some reason been returned and seemed in working order—couldn't hear, "Jesus Christ!"

He backed out of the pantry fast, and his face when he turned was chalky. "Who is that boy?" he asked, his voice a roar now.

"Slime," Pig grated, his throat as scratchy as a nail file, adding as his father looked at him stupidly, "Tommy Toomy." His glasses were all smudgy and his father tilted behind the patches of dried tears and fingerprints. "He was my friend."

"Uh huh," Tony said, not moving.

"I didn't do it, honestly I didn't. Not really. He was my friend, Daddy! It was a mistake. If he hadn't been going to tell she wouldn't have—"

The front door opened. They both heard it and Piggy stopped, mid-sentence, staring at Tony, his eyes enormous.

There was a voice, Jeannie's, calling out, "Hello," just as she was supposed to, and then, "Paul, are you home?"

It was like being on a roller coaster, where after the first terrifying swoop you were certain you wouldn't survive, would be tossed sky-high, all your bones rattling, your teeth clanging together in your jaws. But suddenly you were out of it, climbing slowly, serenely, saved, secure in the rickety car with the bar of iron to hang on to, admiring the view as you went further and further to the top, until for one endless moment you were perched between safety and oblivion, and then the car began its inexorable descent.

Piggy was starting that stomach-churning drop, roaring down the track unable to stop his mother from moving through the dining room toward him. He was glued to the kitchen chair which he grasped with both hands, to his father still in his overcoat guarding the pantry doorway, to Slime dead under the musty light with a knife like an exclamation point sticking out of his sweater, shirt, stomach. It had even pierced his tie.

It was the train in the tunnel all over again. There was no way to avoid the impact. Only the crash resounded in dead silence this time as his parents came face to face.

Piggy bit down so hard on his bottom lip he might have drawn blood. They stared at one another almost without breathing. For one picosecond, by an act of sheer will, Piggy forced himself, them, back to Boston, to that other kitchen, the one where the sun washed through the windows like melting gold. He hurtled them all into time past and almost wept hearing their laughter. He had been littler then, much, and their love had burnished him like a valuable work of art.

A howl of rage and fear battered inside his mouth, locked with clenched jaws, as that flicker of the other life, the one which they had lived and irrevocably lost, which there was now no getting back, slipped by him, vanished, and he remained stranded on the kitchen chair in the River Street house, with shivers spasming up and down his spine. *It isn't fair,* he could have screamed at them, *for us to be here and not there!*

He heard his father saying, "Hello, Jeannie," in a voice which bounced off the polished surfaces.

"What are you doing here?" She was bitter, but she couldn't stop staring at Tony. Her hand came up and stretched out, the gesture involuntary, as though the flesh and bones had no choice, as though she was being drawn to him.

His father finally stopped watching his mother and looked at him instead. *Don't tell her!* he pleaded, his eyes bulging like full moons.

Piggy couldn't tolerate his mother knowing. Not now . . . not ever. He yearned to believe that his father would fix things because he was so awfully good at that. But this time—he just knew!—his mother, who had ridden out all the terrible storms with him, would melt away.

"I was worrying," Tony said, "and I couldn't stop."

Jeannie shuddered inside her heavy coat, and wrenched her gaze to Piggy scrunched down on his chair. She asked, "Are you all right?"

Piggy couldn't answer, his tongue too heavy to form words, but his mother didn't notice. He thought that if a kangaroo were sitting at the table she wouldn't have turned a hair. Right then nothing existed for her but his father's presence, which filled up the kitchen.

"Well, that was totally unnecessary," she said stridently. "We're just fine."

A wry smile edged down the corners of his father's mouth. Only his eyes were opaque and Piggy knew his thoughts were focused on Slime in the pantry. Pig's were too. But he was also obsessed with Sam, whom he longed now to forget, or possibly just abandon at last, as his father had done to them. Only Piggy couldn't, even if he had been capable in that moment of rising off the chair. It wasn't within him to simply desert her like that, to dump her as if she were a bag of trash. She was part of him, as his father was part of them, inexorably knotted into his being.

A shiver stroked across his father's face, and he jammed his fists deeper into his pockets. But when he spoke he was quietly in control. "I think, Jeannie, that you and Paul should come back to Boston with me," he said, and Piggy's heart soared.

"What about Julia?" Jeannie cried, blotchy with anger.

"Julia's not relevant right now," he replied, unable to keep his attention from Piggy, whose head had fallen forward, his chin on his chest.

"What does that mean?" she asked, shifting back and forth in a nervous dance. "That I should just forgive and forget?"

"We should, Jeannie," he amended, not getting mad at all, though Pig, raising his head, could have screamed at his mother to stop it.

Piggy was torn in pieces, his thoughts were flying between Tony and Jeannie and poor dead Slime, and up to Sam. He hoped she was back in the attic surveying the storm as it gusted by the window.

"No, Tony. I have my own life now. Paul does too. And we don't want to be dragged along by you like extra baggage. Until, I suppose, you decide to run off with another one of your women somewhere."

He took a half-step in her direction, then drew back. "I promise you, it won't happen again. That was a once-in-a-lifetime aberration. I swear!" He was sweating, small beads of moisture inching across his forehead, as he struggled to convince her.

"You'd better leave now, Tony. We've got nothing really to say to one another."

The kitchen was electrified with tension, live wires writhing, and Piggy was afraid that the least little jarring, the smallest miscalculation, would cause an eruption of flames.

Tony still loomed in the doorway of the pantry, as though planted there. "We might have some trouble getting through the storm," he said with false equanimity, a nerve pulsing in his cheek, "but we'll manage somehow."

"Didn't you hear me!" Jeannie cried. "We're not going anyplace with you. We're staying right here."

"You can't," his father stated flatly, "you have to come."

Jeannie turned her whole body away from him, geometrically precise, and went to the sink. She wet her hands, splashing her face, which was fiery. "I have," she said, with her back still to him, "a contract with Mason. And Paul's doing quite nicely in school." She was lying and Piggy didn't have to look at his father to know that his disbelief would be obvious. They both understood that it was her pain and battered pride which were making her idiotic.

Tony's eyelids fluttered. He was losing patience with Jeannie, foolishly resistant now that her moment had come. She was just, Piggy realized, getting her own back. For Julia. For the divorce. She couldn't know that they were all way, way beyond those concerns now.

"You can't stay here, so you might as well gather together

whatever you and Paul want to take. I flew into Binghamton and rented a car, but it's a compact so there's not much room. Everything else can be sent along later."

Jeannie revolved away from the sink. As she turned, her hand found the glass on the drainboard. She threw it against the far wall. It bounced but didn't shatter as she screamed, "It's over! Aren't you listening to me!"

Tony exploded. "Go pack!"

"No!"

Piggy slid hopelessly into panic, knowing his father would have to tell, that there was no possible way to maneuver his mother out of Welling without her knowing why they had to run. And part of him so desperately wanted to escape to Boston or anywhere safe that he almost didn't care.

Yet how could he just abandon Sam, like a thing, not like a person at all. Leaving her in the attic, or out in the shed, going hungry, getting cold, colder, shreds of her toes flaking away, her computer running down.

He had such a headache he couldn't concentrate. Pain bludgeoned his skull as their voices bounced back and forth, the argument continuing, the argument which was no argument because his father was right. *If he just didn't have to tell!*

"Jeannie," Tony said one last time, "please!"

"No!" Whipping her head from side to side so that her hair swung wildly, sweeping along the tops of her shoulders.

"Then come here."

She just kept mouthing the word "No" as though it were her mantra.

"Jeannie, I don't want to do this, really I don't. But there's something you must see so you'll understand."

"Daddy!" Piggy screeched, suddenly let loose from the chair. He launched himself at his father, who held him off with his strong hands, looking over his head at Jeannie.

"Paul," his mother said, her voice sinking to a whisper, "what's wrong?" She had noticed at last what a state he was in, his hair standing straight up, his face gouged by fear.

He couldn't answer her, just hung in his father's grasp, a wide-eyed trapped animal, as she moved slowly across the kitchen, her wet boots squishing on the linoleum.

"Mommy!" he squealed, swinging his arms. But Tony held

him firmly. They swung aside together, Piggy kicking at his
father's legs, shifting just enough so that Jeannie could peer
past Tony's shoulder into the pantry.

All the blood seeped out of her face, leaving a colorless
mask that wasn't his mother anymore. Her dark eyes were
luminous with horror. She keened, her red lips trembling,
her body racked by shudders.

Tony released Piggy, who slipped to the floor and scrambled back as Jeannie bent over him, hissing, "Paul, Paul, how
could you!" He gazed up at his mother as if through a long
tunnel. In the distance was the insistent hooting of the on-
rushing train.

He longed to explain about Sam, how he had dreamed of
making her whole, of restoring life to her, that life which had
been so cruelly, so ruthlessly smashed away. But instead, he
had—somehow—created a monster. Only he was the monster. Without saying a word, he saw that in his mother's face,
and the sadness hit him like a blow, with such force that he
couldn't stay in the kitchen with them one minute longer. He
ran to the living room, for the front door and the storm,
aching to hurl himself outside into the swirling snow that
would surely cool the fever that flared inside him. He thought
he would crackle into flames as Bertram Lennard had done.

Sam was standing on the steps. She must have thumped
her way back downstairs when they were all yelling at one
another. The sight of her puce-colored face brought him up
short. She looked like a rotting prune, her stench so strong it
polluted the air.

His heart went out to her even as he wailed, "Sam, no!"
He wished her back into secrecy, but she wouldn't go, and it
was too late anyway. His mother and father had come crashing
into the living room behind him.

Time stopped with a clatter, and in the deadly silence they
could hear the power of the storm, the howling wind that
roared maniacally along River Street, assaulting the house
with thundering blows. And when the storm caught its breath,
in that ellipsis, there was Sam's "Gaaaa, gaaaa, gaaaa," like a
baby doll whose voice box had been stepped on.

Long currents of terror flowed out of Jeannie in screaming
disbelief. His father spat garbled curses. The words spilled
together in a litany.

But none of it had meaning for Sam, who angled nearer,

down the final few steps, sidling first toward one, then the other, as they—even his father, whose face was gaunt with terror—tried to scrambled out of her path.

The room exploded in confusion, as if there was a party with a hundred guests all colliding into one another, all demanding to be heard. Piggy scurried between them, grasping for Sam, still determined to keep her safe, protect her from Tony's swinging arm, the hand bunched into a fist aiming for her pulpy face. He was crying so hard he could just barely see, and there was a sharp, stiletto jabbing in his chest as he lurched in her direction. His fingers caught a wisp of sweatshirt, but she pulled free. She was going for Tony, zeroing in on him for some reason, rolling ahead, small hands snapping for his throat.

Jeannie, her own screams running loose in the room like wild animals, grabbed at the standing lamp and slammed it down on Sam's head.

"No, no, no!" Piggy shouted, and, as if it wasn't his mother at all, sailed into her, his head punching her stomach. The two of them flew backward, wound tightly together, Jeannie's fingers digging into Piggy's arms, trying to tie him to her, possibly to drag him back into her flesh. But he couldn't let her keep him. He had to save Sam. And scrambling up off his mother's body, he ran to her.

Tony, attempting to fend her off, had crashed into the coffee table and landed on his back. In an instant Sam was on top of him, tiny against his bulk, her fingers at his neck. She circled his throat, her hands made of steel, and his face went almost as purplish as her own.

"Sam, no, please, it's my dad! Sam!" Her head came around and the yellow eyes stared at him out of a hell so bottomless he felt himself being sucked inside, drawn down and sinking, the ooze rising up to his lips.

And then he had her away from Tony, who was gasping for air, breath wheezing agonizingly as his chest buckled, his lungs straining.

Piggy fell away, bumped painfully to the floor as Sam stepped over him in that crazy, tilted motion, and opening the door, went out into the storm, into the whipping snow and bellowing wind, plowing through the gathering drifts that were already a foot high.

Where was she going? What was she planning to do?

Piggy, maddened, couldn't leave her alone. He grabbed his jacket from the hall closet, struggling into the sleeves as he raced off after her.

Almost at once he was enveloped in the raging storm. He was cocooned in a white world with no dimensions, no hard edges to cling to. He swiped at his lenses, attempting to clear away the snow so he could see, but it was impossible.

When he stumbled onto River Street, he glanced behind him and saw in the distance a huge, hulking beast with bright blinding eyes. Over the howling wind, he heard the monster's roar, and for an instant before he plodded on after the weaving mirage of the little girl who was now almost buried in the whiteness, he recognized Charlie Volchek's police car. It slid from side to side on the ice-slicked pavement, the windshield wipers furiously clicking, trying to part the sheets of snow.

Piggy started to trot, pulling away from the beast that was intent on swallowing him up, and focused on the orange sweatshirt as small as a subatomic particle. He loped past cars slumbering along the curb, mounded high by snow.

As the last tinge of light dwindled away, he dragged himself through the blizzard. The streetlamps exploded, the yellow glow as translucent as dying sunlight on the snow.

The next time he looked back he thought he saw faint smudges in the gusting whiteness. His mother and father, and possibly the police chief too. But he resolutely turned from them and pushed on after Sam. Main Bridge came up on his left, the storm shrieking in the wires, yowling along the snow-piled roadway.

The wind threw up dervishes, spinning about him. His fingers were without feeling, his face whipped raw. His sneakers were sodden, his feet sculptured ice. He crawled as slowly through the storm as Sam ahead. Yet imperceptibly the distance narrowed as he was whiplashed by the stinging flakes, his eyelashes frozen into delicate lace. And the curtains of wind and snow swelled and took form, human shape, and there was Elvira Williams in a pale nightdress that hid her feet, her stringy old-woman hair flying straight back from her bony skull, and Harry Pringle with his tongue all coated flapping out of his mouth, and Emmett Sidowsky iced into a grimace of agony stumbling by his side, and Slime too, whose dark pupils were dimming, flaring out like dying stars, as he pleaded *Why, Pig, why me?* They sang and chorused, led by Bertram Lennard, now no longer burning, having tamped down into white ash. Bertram Lennard was a snowman with a straw hat and scarf, his polished bones draped in a swirling shroud.

All the ghosts of the dead cavorted beside him, and Piggy, so terrified, so frozen with pain, yearning no longer, was lost and adrift in the storm that surged inside him, freezing his heart.

River Street started its short tilt toward South Bridge as Piggy pulled closer to Sam, thinking he'd die in the storm, feeling half-dead already, not knowing anymore why he was following her, chasing her through the empty snow-filled street. All life had left Welling, and Mason, looming across the river, was nearly buried in gray oblivion. He had no sense anymore. His splendid brain clicked off as he plodded along, as vacant as Sam there in the distance. It was the roller coaster once more and he was plummeting to earth, falling so fast the breath was wrenched from him, cantilevered halfway out of his seat, with no choice except to hold tight.

On and on they trudged until Piggy was barely five feet from her, his hand groping, calling her name, which echoed back at him, heaved back into his mouth, slapping like the biting snow against his cheeks.

She turned onto South Bridge, and he forced himself ahead, ordering his legs to move, his feet to rise, as though he too now had a brain of frail wiring and microchips.

The wind was even more ferocious on the rickety old bridge that swayed above the half-frozen river, a freezing current of sluggish water studded with jagged chunks of ice. Piggy was almost whipped off his feet and had to struggle to keep his balance. Yet still the ghosts danced in the convulsing storm, pushing at him, the ghosts on the darkened bridge as the snow swooped and sailed in cruel blasts. Even Sam's orange sweatshirt, now within inches of Piggy's fingers, had gone gray, as had the magenta face which was suddenly gazing into his own.

"Sam, Sam, Sam . . ." But Sam what?

What more did he want of her?

It was over and done with. Only the ghosts remained.

He should let her die, die finally, out here in the storm, let her go back to that grave which he had cheated her of.

—I don't want to be dead in a hole in the ground. . . .

He heard her over the screaming wind, heard her cry plain as day, just as if they were still sitting on the back porch, both their eyes liquid with tears.

"Oh Sam!" he cried, and opened his arms to embrace her. Except she flung herself at him, all that weight of a rotting foul corpse. No little girl, no pretty Sam with her shiny yellow hair.

The thing in the storm came at him, shrilling her terrible sound that merged with the caterwauling of the ghosts.

South Bridge shook and trembled, swinging dangerously over the ice, the water, the river with its sharp rocks and hidden depths. And in one awful moment that would go on and on for the rest of his life, that would live forever in the darkness of dreams, Sam strained to push Piggy over the side. She was struggling to throw him down to the water and ice, to the death waiting so urgently below.

They skidded and slid together in the snow. Piggy's glasses fell off, his vision became one large blur. Sam's hands slipped from his throat and down to his shoulders as he frantically twisted and turned. He was fighting for his life with Sam there in the middle of South Bridge, beating at her not to take him to the grave with her, to the darkness and death, as the ghosts whined, pressing in on him from all sides as cold and icy as the snow and wind.

His back was against the railing and she was there jammed against his chest as he fought her without thinking, all intelligence gone, only the sheer animal instinct left to stay alive, not to sail downward on the frozen river.

He was filled with the storm and the stinking, rotting stench that settled in his marrow as he pushed and shoved until he skidded on the slick snow, and a shoulder caught her in the jaw. His knees were bent and she was above him as the shoulder came up again, and with one powerful thrust that was fueled by the screeching need to live, to go on, he lifted her right up and off her feet.

She was jettisoned over the railing. For a moment she hung there in the air as if the snow could form a net and hold her. Then she went down, down, splat against the floor of ice below, and through it. The water reached up and lapped at the splotch of orange, drawing her into the current. Her head struck one last block of ice and she sank away, out of sight as Piggy hung over the railing, crying diamond tears of ice. He was trying to see her, though without his glasses whatever was below was misted, too grainy to make out. But it pulled at his heart. And all at once the river surged, heaving her up out of the depths. Her arm rose and he knew she was calling him, reaching out to drag him down to her, to take him along on the endless journey she was just beginning to make. *Oh Sam, oh Sam,* he wept, and realized that she hadn't been trying to kill him after all. She wanted him with her when she entered the darkness. She didn't want to go alone. They were joined together as though they actually shared the same flesh. Creator and creation. How could he let her drift by herself into nothingness?

"Sam, wait!" he cried in his frenzy, darting to the other side of the bridge as she passed beneath the span. And he scrambled up the railing, the wind flailing against him, just as she came once again into view.

"Stop! Don't!" he heard behind him, and turned his head for one last look. There at the start of the bridge was his father staggering toward him, faltering in the treacherous snow. His arms were wide as he struggled to reach him, to gather him in.

"I'm sorry!" Piggy cried, knowing for certain now that he could never return. That he had a promise to keep in the freezing current below. And swerving away from his advancing father, from his mother, from Charlie Volchek too, all of whose cries he imagined he heard carried on the wind, he shouted to Sam to wait for him, that he was coming.

Then, in one soaring swoop, he flew out after her through empty space and thought with blinding clarity as he fell: So this is what love comes to.

ABOUT THE AUTHOR

DIANA HENSTELL grew up in Forest City, Pennsylvania. She has two children—Joshua and Abigail—a German shepherd, Casey, and two cats—Shadow and Rosebud. They all live in New York City. Before becoming a writer, she worked as an editor in publishing. She is the author of *The Other Side*.

THE OTHER SIDE

By Diana Henstell

A compelling tale of psychological suspense by the author of FRIEND.

For Maggie Brace, life is irrevocably altered when fire ravages the Braces' New York apartment and Maggie, alone and panicked, manages to save only one of her three small children. Now, still shaken and consumed with guilt, she is trying to resume a normal life. But her husband, David, seems distant and her son, Jebbie, now nearly six, seems so changed. Jebbie, who spends more and more time in a "secret place" under the porch . . . Jebbie, who converses with an imaginary friend he sees in the mirror . . . Jebbie, who may still be Maggie's sweet little boy—or who may now be some other child entirely.

THE OTHER SIDE